# OUTSIDE THE EDGES

DAVID IRA ROTTENBERG

A Cedar Crest Book

# Cedar Crest Books

Natick, MA USA
www.cedarcrestbooks.com

Outside the Edges
by David Ira Rottenberg

Cover Design: Wideman Illustrations
Book Design: Crystal J. Morin

First Printing – September 2017

ISBN: 978-0-910291-21-7

To Richard and Tony—
who were there.

Down in Denver, down in Denver all I did was die....

And nobody, nobody knows what's going to happen
to anybody besides
the forlorn rags of growing old....


*On the Road*
Jack Kerouac

On the Internet, I read that the average man thinks about sex fifty percent of the time. Since I am a teenager, I think about sex ninety percent of the time. And when I think about sex, I think about Melissa Worth. She sits in front of me in math. She has the most beautiful blonde hair—dirty blonde they call it—although nothing is dirty about it. She keeps her hair scrupulously clean. In class, she usually wears it in a ponytail, and the whole fifty-two minutes, the light brown and yellow strands sway in front of me like a hypnotist's gold watch and chain.

If we were in fifth grade, I could reach out and pull her hair, which would A: satisfy my desire to feel how soft it is, and B: make her turn around and glare at me which is a good way to meet girls in the fifth grade. But in the tenth, pulling Melissa's hair is not an option. Unfortunately, I have yet to work up the guts to follow through on any other plan. However, school is only a couple of weeks old, so I've got plenty of time.

I have Melissa's routine down pat. She strolls into class, gabbing a mile a minute with Katie Caulfield, her best friend, who sits next to her. When Melissa takes her seat, she removes the elastic band that holds her pony tail, tosses her head, and lets her hair spill loose. It's long enough so that some of it even grazes my desk. Then, she sweeps the strands together into another ponytail, twists the elastic band in place—twice—and shakes her head again, making the hair at the end scatter like rain. I'm always tempted to stick my hand in and let the strands shower over my skin, but even though my fingers twitch and ache, I refrain.

If you're a guy, you might suppose another advantage of sitting behind Melissa is that when she leans forward, I see lots of bare back and the elastic strap of her panties or thong or maybe even a little ass crack. But the Noyce School doesn't permit revealing clothes. We don't wear uniforms, but we have a dress code. Most of the rules apply to girls. No low-cut jeans. No bare midriffs. No short skirts. No tank tops. So, like every other girl in school, Melissa wears regular length shirts that tuck into her slacks or skirt, which doesn't hide how hot she is, but when she leans forward, I see no flesh at all.

The worst thing about sitting behind Melissa is that the class we are in is algebra. I stink in algebra. Like yesterday, Mr. Ward called on me, even though I didn't have my hand raised. Hell, I didn't even hear the question. Melissa had just leaned back, spilling her hair over my desk like a bouquet of yellow roses, and I was sitting there mesmerized when suddenly this piece of chalk hit me on the head. I glanced up to see Mr. Ward's angry red eyes, piercing into me. I knew he'd asked something, but I didn't have a clue what, and I was too stunned to say, "Could you repeat the question, sir?" which sometimes works. Instead, all I could muster was, "Huh?" Mr. Ward gave a disgusted look and moved on to Jessica Haney, who's the smartest kid in class. She answered the question perfectly. Melissa didn't turn and gaze at me pityingly. But I slunk lower in my seat and put off for another day any attempt at conversation.

Usually, my problem talking to Melissa is not as dramatic as Mr. Ward plunking me on the head with chalk. Usually, it's more like I'm hanging with Napster, my best bud, when Melissa walks by, and I'm not making any moves with Napster or any of my other friends around. Or, if Melissa happens to be in the vicinity and we're sort of alone, I immediately feel awkward and my tongue gets all panicky and confused like a car with one of its wheels stuck in snow. Same thing in math. When she parades in, she kind of knocks my breath out and I can't speak. Of course, that doesn't stop me from fantasizing. If I ever wrote down all my thoughts about Melissa, especially the x-rated ones, this book would be too embarrassing to put my name on, and no parents would let their kids read it. Only adults would read it, which would be way creepy. So, while this book is completely true, it's not everything I think and do. It's not me and my x-rated obsessions. It's me, but like the Internet without the porn sites.

# 

Since I am not very bright in math and don't lock myself in my room working on computer code or how to unlock the genome, I'm not a nerd or a geek. And since I'm not good at any of Noyce's big sports teams— soccer, baseball, basketball, or lacrosse (Noyce is too small and too politically correct to have a football team)—I'm not a jock. The only sports

I'm halfway decent at are tennis and cross-country. But Mr. Niessen, the junior varsity tennis coach, was my freshman geometry teacher and, like all my math teachers, hates my guts. The result is, I'm never going to make the varsity tennis team because I'm never going to make the junior varsity team. That leaves cross-country. I am on the junior varsity cross-country team, and next year I will make varsity, although I hate cross-country. The only reason I do it is for the letter. Noyce has these cool school jackets, the classic kind with navy blue wool bodies and white leather sleeves (blue and white being our school colors), and while anyone can buy the jacket, you only get to wear a big N if you're on a varsity team.

Four times a week in the fall, I run three miles on the cross-country course, which winds mostly through the woods. I like running through the woods, as this way I do not look like a moron to the millions of motorists driving by when I'm wearing a skimpy cross-country shirt and shorts. I try to keep my sweats on as long as I can, but even when the months get colder, Mr. Hough, the coach, yells, "Hey, Steinman, what are you? A friggin' girl? It's warm out." So I have to remove my sweats and stand around freezing because Mr. H, who is dressed in a thick sweater and coat because it's like thirty degrees always takes longer than he expects fiddling with his stop watch. At least, after I get running, I warm up. I am pretty good and at meets mostly come in third or fourth or fifth, which doesn't mean I'm ever seeing my name on a plaque in the gym, but it's enough to get me on the varsity. Next spring, if you arrive on campus and see some skinny guy about six feet tall with sort of brown hair and a smug smile on his face, wearing a blue-and-white athletic jacket with a large N, that'll be me. The smug smile will be because I know the ladies definitely like the guys with the varsity letters, which I guess in a very roundabout way brings me back to Melissa.

Last year she went to the Whitney May School for Girls, so whatever I know about Melissa I found out from Napster. (His real name is Stephen Harrison Belknap, so everyone calls him Napster after the old website.) Napster has a twin sister, Salome, who has talked to Melissa. No big deal since they're both girls.

Melissa's major into ballet, which is why she's at Noyce. Noyce loves students with special talents like ballet or the cello and lets them get out of sports and electives as long as they spend the time practicing and performing, which Melissa does, so she isn't around school much except for required classes. Of course, I can't really use that as an excuse for not meeting her as I sit right behind her in math, but it does mean she hardly knows anyone, which I like. I mean, I want her to have friends. Life sucks without friends. But if she moved in a mob of girlfriends, before too long some guy (less shy than me) who's a friend of one of her girlfriends would strike up a conversation, and just my luck, a couple of days later they'd be strolling in the hall holding hands.

#

My dad says, if you want to catch a fish, you have to think like a fish.

I don't ever want to think like a girl, but Napster's twin sister, Salome, already is a girl, so she is stuck with it. It's like Napster and I know a fish that can talk, so we get Salome to advise us. Napster says we can trust Salome because they have this special twin bond. Sure, they fight, which I suppose is normal, but when I'm over their house, even when they're just sitting on the couch watching TV, I see how comfortable they are together. I guess it's because they're used to sharing all the way back to the womb.

Speaking objectively, Salome is pretty. She's tall and slender like her mom—about five-seven—although her features resemble her dad. This might not sound promising, but due to some oddity of genetics, a girl can resemble her dad (and lots of girls do, like my bratty younger sister, Sarah) and still end up attractive. The father doesn't have to be good-looking—I mean, my dad and Mr. Belknap are no winners—but DNA or chromosomes or whatever can take a man's nose, mouth, and chin and somehow soften them and stick them on a girl and make them look good. On Salome, her dad's features—light brown hair, brown eyes, a pug nose, and a straight mouth—work. Napster has some of his dad's genes——he's short and stocky like his dad but facially he resembles his mother which means he's kind of good looking. He's got nice, regular features like his mom (roughened up a bit 'cause he's a guy) and his mother's intense violet-blue eyes. Napster has never had a girlfriend but I get the feeling girls like him, particularly as—unlike his dad—he's still got a full head of hair, although I'm sure that baldness gene is lurking. Only a matter of time.

You might wonder, as lots of kids do, if Salome and Napster are twins, why don't they look alike? The answer, of course, is they are fraternal twins, not identical. Since they are a boy and a girl, they can't be identical. Duh!

And despite my frequent proximity, maybe I am around too much because, while I appreciate Salome's looks and personality, Salome and I have this she's-the-twin-sister-of-my-best-friend thing and absolutely no sparks fly. In fact, Salome has a boyfriend—Gideon Eckstein, who everyone calls Giddy, which is ironic as Giddy is far from giddy. Salome and Giddy want to be lawyers—corporate lawyers, like their dads. Napster's dad, Harrison L. Belknap, knows Giddy's dad, so this nascent romance is looked upon favorably. However, Napster's parents don't let Salome and Giddy go out alone. The rule is, Napster and Salome have to wait until they're sixteen to date. But Giddy is over their house all the time, and at school dances, or when a bunch of kids go to the movies or to a party, they are a couple. Napster and I are very curious as to how far she and Giddy have gone, but Salome refuses to divulge, as does Giddy.

Confidence, grooming, clothes, and shoes are very high on Salome's list of how to attract girls (who would've figured shoes). However, I am more concerned about what to say, so I pump Salome for good lines. Salome claims you don't need a line. She insists all you have to say is, "Hey." If a girl likes you, she'll carry the conversation from there. If the girl doesn't, you'll get a "Hey" back, but she'll look bored, and at the earliest moment, turn away. Aloof behavior, Salome maintains, should never be mistaken for shyness. Even shy girls, if they like you, will stick around and look inter-ested. These tips are what I've gotten so far. But this weekend is Colum-bus Day, and I am sleeping over Napster's house in Winnipesaukee and expect more.

My entire weekend is dedicated to *not* thinking about school.

Unlike me, Napster never worries about school. His Uncle Harry owns the Lundgren Screw Company, and as Uncle Harry isn't married and lacks an heir, he wants Napster to take over his business (after she gets her law degree, Salome is welcome, too). I am kind of jealous that I don't have an uncle who wants to give me his business, except I don't want to go into business. Still, head of a multi-million-dollar company before he's like thirty. Boy is Napster getting laid.

#

The basements of Napster's house in Brookline and in Winnipesaukee are full of games. Pool, Ping-Pong, air hockey, and foosball rule. Every-one in the family plays. Even Napster's mom. Napster's dad is particularly good at pool. When he plays, he's got this calm, lawyerly, totally-in-control air, even when he's got a hard shot to make. He doesn't pause. He doesn't ponder. He doesn't put talc on his palms or chalk on the tip of his cue stick. He just glides around the table, shoots, and makes it. But he doesn't play much. He's always working and traveling.

In fact, I think I've seen his mom play pool more. She never plays for long, but when she does, it's memorable. She floats downstairs, watches for a minute or two, and asks, "Are you boys in a serious game?" and we say, "No," because I'm not good enough to be in a serious game. Then, she puts her drink—she usually has a drink in her hand—on the side of the table, which makes me nervous. I think somehow she's going to knock the drink over, or worse, I'm going to knock the drink over. Then, she takes a cue stick from Napster or me and knocks a few balls in. And when I say she knocks the balls in, she really zings them. It's kind of sexy the way she does it, hitting the balls hard and straight, especially since she's pretty good-looking. She's taller than Napster's dad by an inch or two and has almost a playboy kind of figure. When you throw in her violet-blue eyes (that Napster inherited), her usually non-lipsticked full lips, and natural coffee-brown hair, which she's kept long, she makes quite a package, even at forty, which is around how old she is. She's smart, too. Went to Dana Hall and Mt. Holyoke. On the surface, Mr. and Mrs. Belknap aren't an obvious couple. I mean, he's nowhere near her on the appearance scale, but Napster's dad didn't get married until he was a lawyer and pretty dynamic, confident, and successful, qualities, if you recall, high on Salome's list (his shoes are usually expensive loafers with tassels). After Mrs. Belknap sinks four or five shots in a row she laughs, and it isn't some sophisticated woman-of-the-world laugh. She laughs in this girl-like way, as if she's pleased with herself and doesn't have the self-control not to show it. It's an infectious laugh that makes Napster and me laugh, too. Then, she hands her cue to Napster or me, takes her drink, and waltzes upstairs. I think it makes Napster embarrassed, but we never talk about it.

At my house, we don't have any table games. I've pushed for them, but I always get the same answer: "We don't want you wasting your time on pool (or fill in the name of the game) when you should be studying. I thought Stephen (they never call him Napster) has those games at his house. You can play there." So I know it's a lost cause. Actually, I used to plead more when I was younger. Now, I'm not as interested in table games. They're fun to play with Napster, but it's more from habit. Now, we play mostly when we're plotting how to meet girls or, on our return, analyzing our failures.

After school today, however, Napster told me something revolutionary. He actually met a girl—a townie up in Winnipesaukee. He said she's hot and I believed him because when he mentioned her name—Darlene— his eyes glittered and he got the same sly, aren't-I-clever grin he got in cub scouts when he grabbed the last jelly doughnut out of the box.

According to Napster, Darlene's got a great butt and a well-developed chest (probably the key to her attraction, as Napster loves large knockers). However, Darlene wears a lot of make-up and has super-dyed red hair and in general looks as if she spends way too much time in beauty parlors, which is probably true as, he says, her mom owns a couple. Still, Napster got a real buzz the first time he spotted her. The problem is, the more attracted you are to a girl, the harder it is to talk, which I think is contrary to the whole spirit of procreation. It should be easy to talk to girls who turn you on and difficult to talk to girls you find unattractive. Maybe this is where Darwin and natural selection come in—the guys with the guts get the girls and therefore the most opportunity to reproduce.

Napster told me he was sitting at the counter in the Barn when Darlene came in. The Barn is this Southridge restaurant that has a jukebox and a back room filled with video games. The townie kids hang out there, and the summer kids do, too. I've never seen a fight, but in July and August when tons of summer kids are around, the local youth look at you as if you were dirt and treat the back room like their own private club. They don't like it that the local girls are interested in us and the summer girls aren't interested in them. Of course, by "us" I don't mean Napster and me. The local girls are interested in the summer guys who can drive. In the winter, the Barn is mellower. Outsiders are fewer and they're only around weekends, so there's not as much competition for girls.

Because Labor Day weekend was long since past, the restaurant was only about a quarter full, and Darlene sat at a booth with two friends. Now, Salome's "Hey" technique is all very well for school or meeting girls in ones and twos at the beach, but in a restaurant, walking over to a table with three strange girls and saying, "Hey," that's a ballsy maneuver no matter who you are. Maybe when Napster's the president of his uncle's company, or maybe if I actually get into Harvard and go to Hollywood and become a screenwriter (my career goal), we can do it. But as two sophomore high school schmucks, forget it. So, Napster's brain was whirling as to how best meet these girls.

When Archimedes' inspiration struck, he jumped out of his bath and ran around naked, yelling, "Eureka, I have found it." Napster didn't do that. He remained in his seat fully dressed. His plan was to stroll over to the jukebox located near the girls' table, punch in a few songs, and say, "Hey," as if he didn't care. If the girls responded in a positive way, he'd ask them to choose a song. The risk was if he stuttered, if he spoke too softly or too loudly, if he betrayed any sign of weakness or fear, the girls' curious glances would turn into repulsed looks as if he were a bug creeping out from under the jukebox rather than a cool guy leaning on it.

Walking to the jukebox, Napster said his mouth felt as dry as a tube of old Gorilla glue and his legs wobbled like rubber hoses. He longed for a swig of his Coke, but his drink was back at the counter miles away. Quickly, he picked three songs, all Nirvanas—C8: "Smells Like Teen Spirit"—C10: "Territorial Pissings"—C6: "Come As You Are"—selections he thought the girls might like. Popular yet edgy. But he didn't choose a last pick. He was saving that for the girls. After punching in the music, Napster surveyed his target. Furtively, the girls eyed him. When he caught the cute girl's gaze, he croaked, "Hey," just loudly enough.

"Hey," came her reply.

Billowy clouds of happiness fogged his brain but it didn't matter. He had his follow-up ready. "Gotta song?"

The cute girl furrowed her brow and glanced questioningly at her friends. They giggled. The cute girl shrugged, "You choose," which dashed Napster's spirits. He thought she was brushing him off. He punched in "Rape Me" to show her he didn't care. However, before he retreated to his seat, the cute girl piped up, "You're not from around here, are you?"

**Yes!!!**

Eagerly, Napster replied, "We have a house in Southridge. We come up summers and weekends."

"I live in Southridge, too," the girl said.

"Cool."

Boldly, one of the cute girl's friends suggested, "How about Coldplay—'Yellow'?"

"OK," Napster said. Of course, he'd already used his last pick and had to insert another dollar, but that was a small price to pay. "My sister has that CD."

"Love them. Went to one of their concerts."

"Where?"

"Onion rings!" the counter guy broke in.

Napster looked over. He'd forgotten he'd ordered onion rings. They sat on the counter far, far, far away. The cute girl didn't like that development, either. "Wanna sit here?" she asked.

**Did he??!!!!!!**

It worked just as his sister had predicted. He'd said, "Hey," and the girls had pretty much done the rest. It was like one of those Discovery Channel documentaries where you see slow motion shots of a bee descending lower and lower between the colorful petals of a blossom, and it dawns on you, even though the flower is totally passive, in its own way it's as much a hunter as the bee.

"We talked for like an hour," Napster said.

"Awesome. So you're seeing her this weekend."

"*We're* seeing her. With a couple of her friends. This is just what we need," Napster crowed. "Slutty girls."

"I thought you liked this girl."

"I do. But, dude, we're in high school. These girls are for practice."

"What if she likes you?"

"All the better. Can you believe it. She goes to vocational school."

"Vocational school!"

"Well, she's more intelligent than you think. If she wanted, she could go to college. But what with her mother owning the beauty parlors, she's studying cosmetology. After she graduates, her mother's taking her into the business."

"Wow," I said, "just like you and your uncle."

Napster's eyes widened. "I never thought of that. You see, she is like me."

"Yeah. Slutty."

"Keeping my fingers crossed. For you, too, amigo."

I grimaced. Compared to Melissa, most girls—and certainly all slutty girls—did not mean much. At my expression, Napster laughed.

"Dude, don't worry. We're not taking 'em to the prom. We'll be in New Hampshire. It's free territory."

#

The basement in Napster's Winnepausakie house is even better than in Napster's Brookline house because it's newer. It's got a humungus flat screen TV, a couple of couches, a pool table (of course), a ping pong table, and an old 32" tube TV for video games. Along one wall is a fancy bar with a refrigerator and a sink. Napster and I use the bar for making drinks, none of which contain alcohol. Napster says his mother would strangle him if she caught him drinking alcohol, which is odd since she so often has a drink in her hand. Maybe it's because she so often has a drink in her hand.

For supper, we went to Salome's favorite restaurant—Wagon Wheels—an obvious bribe to get her in a better mood. Salome was mad because she couldn't go back to Brookline early and stay at a friend's house. She wanted to go with Giddy to his cousin's eighteenth birthday party. But her parents were sticking to the sixteen-year-old rule. "It's not a date," Salome argued, "It's a family event." Still, her parents wouldn't budge even when Salome threw a fit, screaming and yelling like a five year old. It's amazing what sisters can do. I mean, my eleven-year-old sister can go into a frenzy that would make a rabid dog proud. Not that I don't get incredibly mad at my parents sometimes, but all I do is slink off to my room, slam the door, and curse. Sarah sticks around, crying, ranting, and gnashing her teeth. Salome was Sarah's slightly more mature equal. Nonetheless, the restaurant bribe worked. Wagon Wheels's specialty is lobster, and Salome loves lobster. As soon as she sat down, she tied a bib decorated with a bright red lobster around her neck and grinned, bubbling to her mother about some dress she and her best friend, Shauna, saw at the mall. Salome wanted her mom to go with her the next weekend while Salome tried it on. It was as if she'd never been mad.

Before we knew it, we were back in Napster's house in the basement, watching *On the Waterfront* on TCM. I am trying to get Napster to appreciate black-and-white movies. We were also playing Ping-Pong. "Otherwise," as Napster said, "the movie would be too boring." The score was 9-5 when Salome wandered down. "Who's ahead?" she asked.

"Napster," I said.

"You should play air hockey," Salome suggested. "Nappy is terrible at air hockey. I beat him all the time."

"Once," Napster retorted. "You beat me once like six months ago."

"That's the last time we played."

"Because you refuse to play," Napster said.

"Excuses. You always have excuses."

"Sal," I said, "that sounds like a good excuse."

"I don't want to hurt his feelings."

"Anytime, little lady, anytime. Whose serve is it?"

Napster and I got back into the game, and Salome watched the movie. After a minute or two, she asked, "Who's the hottie?"

"In the movie?"

Salome crinkled her nose, "I don't see any other hotties."

"Marlon Brando."

"I thought he was really fat."

"Not in his younger days."

"Who's the girl?"

"Eva Marie Saint."

"She's pretty."

"Yeah. But too skinny," I said, for once sounding like Napster.

"She looks all right to me."

"That's because you're a girl," I said. "Girls admire skinny. Guys like girls with more meat on their bones."

"I don't know. Melissa doesn't have much meat on her bones," Salome said.

At that remark, Napster hit a Ping-Pong ball right by me. Salome and Napster laughed, making me even more self-conscious. While Napster was supposed to pry information about Melissa from his sister, Napster was not supposed to tell his sister I liked Melissa. I tried bluffing my way out, "Why bring up Melissa?"

"I know you like Melissa."

"Who says?"

"It's obvious. You've had Nappy ask me about her like ten times, and whenever you say her name, you get this reverent look."

I blushed. "Not reverence. Just normal interest."

"As if."

"It's true."

"Double as if," Salome said.

I realized it was stupid to keep protesting, especially since Salome was our go-to source on all things female. "Do you think she knows?"

"Do you stare at her all googly-eyed in math?"

"Of course not," I protested, but too vehemently.

"Oh, my God," Salome cried, "you do."

"She sits in front of me. She doesn't know."

"Yeah. Right."

"Screwed, huh? No chance?"

"I didn't say that. Maybe she likes you."

"Well, if she knows I like her, why hasn't she done anything?"

"You're the guy...."

Here, Napster butted in. Having met one girl, he considered himself an expert. "Just say, 'Hey.'"

Salome smirked. She loved it when her brother took her advice.

I grumbled, "When? She never turns around except when Mr. Ward calls on me and I say something stupid."

Salome got this patient look. "What about when class starts and everyone walks in?"

"I'm not a total idiot. She's always talking with her buddy, Katie Caulfield."

Salome smiled knowingly. "They're probably talking about you."

"Sure."

Salome sighed as if my problem were too easy. "OK. You don't have to say, 'Hey,' in math. Is she in any of your other classes?"

"No."

"Well, she's in my history class. That's on the second floor of Merton. Where are you at eleven?"

I crossed my arms and stared at the ceiling. Ping-Pong had spontaneously ended. "I've got English on the first floor in Gardner."

"Great. Right after is lunch. Merton and Gardner are both near the fountain."

Numbly, I nodded. This was sounding very, very contrived.

"Plant yourself in front and say, 'Hey,' when she walks by. Katie Caulfield isn't in our history class."

"I don't know."

"What don't you know?"

"Well, for one thing, hanging around the fountain. It's so obvious."

"If she likes you, it won't matter."

The fountain is one of the landmarks of the Noyce campus. It's this large marble pool with a big dolphin standing on its tail in the center, squirting water out of its mouth. Supposedly, the fountain came from Europe like a hundred years ago. During breaks, kids sit on the marble rim and talk. Around exams, everyone throws coins in, wishing for good grades. The grounds crew is supposed to collect the money and give it to charity, but everyone suspects they pocket it for themselves.

I asked, "What if she nods and trots on by?"

Salome was not sympathetic. "Then you know she's not interested."

"Just my luck," I sighed. "Maybe…maybe you can find out if she likes me."

Salome shook her head. "I'm not asking. You're asking. The worst she can do is keep walking."

"There's worse."

"Like what?"

"Like this summer," I blurted bitterly, but as I spoke, I knew it was a mistake. Napster's and Salome's eyes locked on me like phasers.

"What about this summer?" Napster demanded. "A story I don't know. C'mon. Give."

I hesitated. This episode was one of my most embarrassing in a life full of embarrassing episodes. Then I thought, maybe cleansing my soul would help. Maybe if I let Salome know what a complete ass I'd made of myself, she'd show some pity and find out if Melissa liked me. I took a deep breath. "Remember when I was working at the WindStar Motel."

Napster and Salome nodded. While they go north to Winnipesaukee, my family goes south to Cape Cod. This past summer, I worked Thursdays through Sundays at the WindStar Motel in Hyannis. I mowed the lawn, cleaned the pool, and wiped off the deck chairs. When I finished, I helped the maids.

"Remember that girl I told you about?"

Napster nodded. "The foxy niece of the owner."

"That's the one."

"What happened? I thought you said she's like eighteen."

"She is. But I lied to get the job and told the owner I was sixteen, so that's what she must've thought. Anyway, we kind of became buddies. She was the slowest maid, probably on account of her being the owner's niece and she knew he wasn't going to fire her. After I finished my regular chores, Mr. Carey used to tell me, 'Go help 'Lizabeth.' She doesn't pronounce the "e" on account of she's from the south. We always cleaned her last rooms together."

"This sounds good," Napster said. "So…"

"So, one day we started talking about movies, and it turns out she's into film like I am. She wants to be an actress…."

"I can't believe you never told me this," Napster broke in.

"Shhhhh," Salome hissed.

"You'll understand," I said, "when I get to the end. She brought up Quentin Tarantino, the director, and told me how much she liked his movies, and I mentioned how much I like *True Romance*. I said it was very clever how, even though it's violent, the story follows the standard plot points of the romantic comedies of the thirties…"

"This is your come on," Napster groaned, "talking like some PBS-brained movie critic."

"She sucked it up."

"OK, Spielberg, go on."

"She loved *True Romance*. It's one of her favorites. I told her I was planning to go to Harvard and be a screenwriter…"

"And?"

"She practically jumped up and down. She told me we should exchange emails, and I thought—Wow! Opportunity!—so, I said, 'Let's catch a movie.' Huge blunder. It was like the broom in my hand had invited her to an all-night Chuck Norris Festival. Her eyes got all buggy and she kind of gurgled like she didn't know whether to laugh or to scream. — When she figured it out, she laughed. Right in my face. Not rude, cackling laughter. Hearty, belly laughing. I mean, we were standing right next to each other, and she just kept laughing. Finally, I couldn't take it anymore and walked out. We were on the second floor. All the way down, I heard her."

Salome pursed her lips, "Well, that wasn't very nice. But why would you think she'd go out? You're fifteen."

"I told you she thought I was sixteen."

"Big deal. She's not going to go out with a guy whose parents drop him off at work. And I bet she's really good-looking."

"I never said she was good-looking."

"Nappy called her a fox and you said she wants to be an actress."

"OK. She's good-looking."

"And a bitch to laugh at you like that. But talk about over reaching. For your first date ever. You're either afraid to say anything or you ask out some beautiful senior. What's up with that?"

I shrugged.

Napster wondered, "What happened the next day?"

"Wasn't a next day. It was Sunday and I didn't work again till Thursday. I was thinking of quitting, but I said, 'Up hers.' I mean, the guy paid me in cash every week."

"Even with the money," Napster interjected. "I would've quit."

"Didn't have to. The next Thursday, Mr. Carey told me she'd gotten a job as an usher at the Dennis Playhouse. He didn't mind because she was so slow and he already had a replacement. Some Brazilian girl who could barely speak English, but a fast cleaner."

"What'd she look like?" Napster asked.

"Really nice. You know soft olive skin, dark eyes and dark hair. She was only nineteen but she already had a kid."

Napster and Salome glanced at me.

I grinned mysteriously.

"Oh, my God. You didn't ask her out?" Salome said in horror.

"Nah. Just messing with you."

"Well, mess with Melissa," Salome said. "She isn't going to laugh. And don't ask her out right away. Talk to her first. See if she smiles a lot."

"'Lizabeth smiled a lot. She talked to me."

"Get 'Lizabeth out of your brain. She liked you like a kid brother."

"Yeah," Napster chimed in. "Melissa wants your bod."

Salome shook her head. "Don't pump him up too much. Otherwise he'll ask Emma out."

Emma is the headmaster's secretary. She's in her twenties and quite a knock out. Every guy in school has the hots for her.

"Michael, just say, 'Hey.' If she likes you, she'll smile and talk or walk by your side. If she looks up at you out of the corner of her eyes or if, you know, she touches you lightly on the arm, we proceed to the next stage."

"How long is the first stage?"

"Let's start by talking. Keep it casual. You can do it. I know you can. I'm such a good sister, aren't I, Nappy?"

"When you're not throwing shit fits."

Salome stuck her tongue out at her brother and said, "I really can't believe how gorgeous Marlon Brando is. What movie did you say this was?"

#

The next morning was family day, plus one. We climbed Cannon Mountain, although the biggest ascent was at 6 a.m. when Mr. Belknap yelled, "Rise and shine guys."

I mean, I don't get up that early during the week. But on a Saturday? To climb a mountain? What a waste.

The hike is an annual Belknap ritual. The avowed reason is to look at the foliage, but the deeper, unspoken reason is to bond. For the longest time, Napster and Salome looked forward to the climb, but now bonding with their parents is not much fun. In fact, one of the reasons Napster brought me along is so he won't have to bond. Napster doesn't want any buddy-buddy talks with his dad about college, law school or grades. He wants all conversation to be general. Nothing deeper than sports, and not Noyce sports—The Celtics, Red Sox, Patriots, and Bruins. But at 6 a.m. not being a member of the Belknap clan put me at a distinct disadvantage. I couldn't whine, moan, or complain. At Mr. Belknap's yell, I had to rip my raw, defenseless brain out into the cold where it lay quivering like a shucked clam. If I were at my own house, I'd've turned on my side, pulled the covers over my head and sunk back to sleep, making my dad rouse me like four more times. But as I was at Napster's house, I had to throw off the covers, get dressed, and walk downstairs with a cheezy grin and give the old, "Good morning Mr. Belknap. "Good morning, Mrs. Belknap. What a great day to climb a mountain" crap. Not that I don't appreciate how nice the Belknaps are. But that doesn't make standing around shivering in a dank, rugless room at 6 a.m. any better, especially since Napster had rolled over, pulled the blanket over his head, and fallen back to sleep. It was his dad.

In the kitchen, Salome was already making sandwiches, and Mrs. Belknap was beating a batter of pancakes. Mr. Belknap was in the basement, getting our hiking gear.

Dads are ridiculous in their preparations (and my dad is no exception), but in this department Mr. Belknap is the mother of all dads. He actually brought sixty meters of rope (I know it was sixty because the label was

22

still attached), even though we were hiking on a trail you could drive an SUV on. In addition, he handed out backpacks, flashlights, bug spray, canteens, bags of trail mix, matches, and sleeping bags—the expensive kind filled with down and very light—all for a five-hour trip, three hours up, two hours down—on a mountain so popular we'd probably see hundreds of people along the way. But Napster and Salome did not give their dad a hard time. Maybe because I was along. Maybe because it was a day where it was tradition to show family unity.

After breakfast, we stuffed the equipment into the SUV and drove to the mountain. It took about an hour. For Napster and me, it was an opportunity to fall back asleep. So, the time between leaving the driveway and the SUV jerking to a halt in the parking lot is a blank. However, the extra hour of sleep and the comforting fullness of three large pancakes made me feel better. It was still early, around 8:30, but the sun was growing stronger, tingeing the edges of the mountain air with warmth like the first whisper of heat from a camp-fire.

Not being Henry David Thoreau, I don't have a few chapters in me about our hike. We saw lots of boulders and passed a few streams. Mr. Belknap pointed out some hawks and a couple of moose. Maybe it was the altitude and the pure air, but when we reached the summit, it was kind of exalting. The sky looked bluer and the clouds seemed close enough to touch. In front of us, a whole range of tree-covered mountains danced in the wind like pagans clad in leafy garments of brilliant red, brown, and gold. As the trees weaved and swung, it was as if they were performing some ancient tribal rite. In myths, the gods always live in the mountains, and gazing across the miles and miles of valleys and peaks, I could understand why. I felt as if I were a god myself and could carve rivers with my bare hands, shoot lightning bolts from my fingertips, and dive into the sky and fly.

On the walk up the mountain, Mr. Belknap, Napster, and I talked about the Patriots. Mr. Belknap played football in high school—he was a middle line-backer—and he's a big fan. Napster is lucky Noyce doesn't have a football team. Otherwise, he'd get a lot of pressure to make the team. Not that his dad would ever come out and say, "I want you to play football." He'd just talk about it incessantly. As it is, Napster plays soccer, junior varsity, and he'll probably make varsity next year. But like me he doesn't give a fart about the team. We're both in it for the letter.

On the way down, Mr. Belknap tried a couple of times to get us started about soccer and cross-country, but Napster and I grunted monosyllabic replies. Our only real conversation was about the Celtics. When my parents quiz me about school, it's the same. Their attention is like my dad's eyeglasses—way too strong. Even if I come home thinking I have a good story to tell, as soon as my dad or mom asks, "How was school?" with that casual intensity of theirs, whatever words I have on my tongue shrivel like Saranwrap near a flame. If on some rare occasion they don't ask and I forget myself and start yakking, before too long, I realize I've said too much because suddenly I'm on the receiving end of this lecture about something or other I did wrong. It never pays to talk about school or anything. Grunts and nods are the key, except when I need something. Then, I wax loquacious.

#

On the drive back, I started thinking about the Barn. Girls. My heart thumped. I was surprised. The Barn was pretty much for Napster's benefit. My role was flying wing, so Napster's parents wouldn't know he was meeting a townie named Darlene. All I had to look forward to were Darlene's friends. Except Napster had already indicated that Darlene was the pick of the litter, and since Napster's primary concern with any girl was how well-endowed she was, this left Darlene's friends a mystery in every attribute except breast size. They were obviously smaller than Darlene.

Our departure from Napster's house was the only complication in our plan. Mrs. Belknap kept insisting she drive us the two miles to the Barn. She was all, "You boys must be exhausted from the hike today." Normally, we would've jumped at her offer, but we didn't want Napster's mom anywhere near the Barn. We kept saying, "No thanks. We'll walk." Except our protests started sounding somewhat strident, and Salome began looking suspicious. She knew how lazy we were.

We were saved by Mr. Belknap. "Oh, Leslie, I'm sure the boys don't want you dropping them off in front of the Barn. It's a beautiful night. Let them walk."

As we left the house, Mr. Belknap smiled conspiratorially as if he knew we were walking to toughen ourselves for sports. We smiled conspiratorially back, holding in our smirks until he shut the door.

As we headed toward the Barn, Napster said, "What do you think the odds are the girls show?"

"Pretty good."

"I'll be pissed if they don't. You're not going to be mad, are you?"

"Why would I be mad? This is your show."

"We can always do what we said—hang around and play video games."

"Yeah. That'll suck."

About twenty minutes later, we hit Main Street, which for a small town is a long street. The Barn is somewhere in the middle. The wooden exterior is painted rusty red and nailed to its front are life-size wooden cutouts of cows, chickens and sheep. The menu is part crunchy granola, part traditional Yankee, and part road food. You can get a veggie sandwich with sprouts, ham and eggs, clam chowder, or pizza. As Napster and I entered, our eyes scanned the room.

Almost immediately, Napster spotted the girls. He grabbed my arm and whispered, "They're here."

"Where?"

Napster hissed, "Don't look. They're in the back."

"Are they talking to some guys?"

"No. They're by themselves. Should we go right over or order something?"

"I thought you said we were supposed to meet them."

"I don't want to look too eager."

I was agreeable to anything. "Fine," I said. "Let's sit and order a Coke."

The counter guy who brought us menus fit right into the place. He had a black mustache hanging down at either side of his mouth and black hair tied into a ponytail. Even though it was almost winter, he wore a white t-shirt and jeans. I guess it was warm near the kitchen. His muscled arms were covered with tattoos. But when he brought our Cokes, he grinned and didn't look so tough. We returned to discussing the girls. I said, "Have they seen us? Do they know we're here? Because if they don't, they may never leave the back room."

"OK. Let's take our drinks and walk around."

At the front of the restaurant near the door, we examined some photographs of Lake Winnipesaukee. Under the photographs were postcards from customers with greetings from different parts of the world. Taped beneath the postcards were business cards and hand-drawn ads for guitar teachers, massage therapists, baby sitters, and yoga instructors. As I finished the postcards and started in on the ads, a girlish voice squealed, "Steve!"

"Hey," Napster replied.

I pivoted.

In front of Napster bounced Darlene.

From Napster's description, Darlene had seemed a little hard.—Not true. She was as sweet and playful as a puppy dog, doing everything except licking Napster's face and wagging her tail. She was pretty. Her hair was dyed red, but it was a dark red so, it wasn't so bad. She had wide-set blue eyes, thin eyebrows, a flat, small nose, and full lips, which were sexy even when she was smiling. Of course, she had the big boobs, which her fluffy gray sweater accentuated, and she did wear too much make-up. Lots of blue eye shadow and mascara. Her lipstick was a deep, dark red (I guess she was trying to match her hair), and she had long nails polished the same color. Yet, she was so bouncy, bubbly, and smiley, all the make-up and hair just made her look vulnerable.

If this were a nineteenth century novel like *Sense and Sensibility* (which we're reading in English) Darlene's description would make clear she was of a different social class than Napster. Those old British writers do not mince words, and everyone's social status is noted by birth, dress, income, education, and accent. America is not supposed to have class distinctions, but in reality, not much has changed. By starting something with Darlene, Napster was following instincts centuries old. He was taking advantage of someone he could easily impress. Nor was Darlene totally innocent. She liked the idea of a rich, preppy boyfriend.

"You made it," Darlene grinned to Napster. "I was wondering if you were going to show."

"I was wondering if you were. Meet Stoner."

"Hey, Stoner," Darlene said. "Come on and meet my friends."

"Why don't you guys come up here," Napster replied. "We'll get a table and something to drink."

Darlene looked at me and said mockingly, "He's so smooth." Yet despite her sarcasm, I could see she really believed it. "OK. Three diet whatevers."

Darlene went to get her friends, and Napster and I brought the drinks to a table. A few seconds later, Darlene appeared with the two girls. Darlene slid into the booth on Napster's side, and the two girls slipped into the booth with me.

The closest girl had dark black eyebrows, deep-set brown eyes, small doll-like lips (her best feature), and a short straight nose. Her black, glistening hair fell past her shoulders but looked more wiry than soft. I wouldn't have called her pretty or ugly, but something in between. Her expression certainly didn't help. She appeared irritated and bored, as if she were sitting at our table as a favor to Darlene and wanted Darlene to know it. As far as her figure went, it was almost too good. Although considering her annoyed expression, it didn't much matter. Her body was slim and firm but ripe almost—but not quite—to the point of puffy. It was as if the only thing holding her in was that she was fifteen. I figured after a few more years of good eating, entropy would set in and her body would turn as soft and squishy as a two-week-old banana and she'd spread all over.

The girl closest to the wall and farthest away was more appealing. She had an eager, inquisitive expression as if she was actually interested in meeting us. Her eyes were hazel and she had a pointed nose, sweet curvy lips, and a fresh, clear complexion. Her chestnut hair was cut just below her ears, and she wore fashionable, square glasses that made her cute face seem, as if it were backed by a brain. Unfortunately, she was chubby. While her friend filled her figure to the point of ripeness yet remained slim, this girl was—not exactly fat—but round like an overfed house cat. So really, I had no interest in her, either.

Darlene introduced us. The cute, chubby girl was Jesse, and Scarlet was her hard-faced friend.

"How do you three know each other?" I asked.

My question did not impress Scarlet. But Jesse answered with pride, "We go to the same school: Lakes Valley Technical."

That anyone could sound proud of a technical school was as astonishing to me as if a senior from Noyce had boasted of getting into Framingham State. Then I felt ashamed. I was a terrible snob. I was lucky I had parents who cared so much about my education, otherwise who knew what I'd be doing.

"What are you studying?"

"Darlene's into cosmetology," Jesse said. "Me and Scarlet do digital media. It's the best department in the school. Web design, computer graphics, video. Stuff like that. Where do you guys go?"

"The Noyce School," I said, probably with the same amount of pride as Jesse. But to the girls it was as nothing.

"Where's that? Massachusetts?" Scarlet asked, her voice full of disdain.

"Yeah," I replied.

"Napster has a house here," Darlene explained.

"Natch," Scarlet grumbled.

"What? Are we aliens?"

Scarlet shrugged. "No. My father's a plumber. He loves it when ski-birds let their pipes freeze. He says that's what's putting my brother through college."

I couldn't help myself. At the word college, I asked, "Where does he go?"

"Dartmouth," Scarlet stated impassively.

The name rocked me. "Dartmouth's a very good school."

"My brother's a brain and an athlete and everything," Scarlet said.

"In high school," Darlene added, "Scarlet's brother was an All-American in two sports and a National Merit scholar."

"Heavy dude," Napster said.

"Oh, please," Scarlet snapped, "let's not talk about my brother."

At her outburst, Darlene remarked, "Scarlet's sensitive. Her brother gets all the attention. He's like a local celeb. But we love Scarlet. She's the best designer in school."

"And Darlene's the best cosmetologist," Scarlet said with an actual touch of warmth. However, it didn't last long. She glanced at her watch. "Uh-oh. Late. Sorry, Darlene. Gotta go."

"Cut it out," Darlene said. "You haven't been here five minutes."

"Have to," Scarlet insisted. "Expecting a call." She threw a knowing look at the girls. "Jenny's meeting me outside. I'll ride home with her."

Darlene sighed. "OK. Go. Go."

Besides not being happy with my company, it seemed Scarlet was waiting for a call from a guy. I didn't care. I wasn't interested in Scarlet, and it was awkward with the five of us. Of course, I wasn't interested in Jesse, either. But at least she seemed willing to talk. In fact, after I stood to let Scarlet out, Jesse slid closer.

With Scarlet gone, Darlene commented, "Scarlet has a boyfriend who does the sound for a band. When they're on the road, he calls every night."

"What band?" Napster asked.

"Nobody you'd know," Jesse said. "A bunch of guys from Northridge. They all graduated from Lakes Valley last year with Ethan. Ethan's Scarlet's boyfriend."

"Cool," I said but inside I thought.—A sophomore going out with a guy who graduated last year. Talk about not a virgin. And if Darlene's Scarlet's friend, maybe Darlene's not a virgin, either.— I looked at Napster and could see his mind following the same path.

I turned to Jesse. Her face seemed to have virgin written all over it. Just my luck. I wondered if mine did, too. Then, something Jesse had said rang a bell:—that course in video.

"You into movies?" I asked.

A puzzled look came into her eyes.

"You said you study video."

"Oh. Oh, yeah. But it's software. Technical stuff. Darlene's into movies."

My gaze shifted to Darlene. Darlene became flustered. Her eyes darted every which way but at me. Finally, she spoke as if apologizing for a strange habit. "I love Judy Garland movies."

I couldn't believe my ears. Not many kids like old movies. OK, everyone's watched the *Wizard of Oz*, but Darlene sounded as if she'd seen Judy Garland do more than tap her heels three times and wish she were back in Kansas.

"Which ones?"

Darlene's eyes widened. "Do you-do you like Judy Garland?"

"She's OK. I've seen *Meet Me in St. Louis* and some Andy Hardy movies."

Darlene got all bouncy again. "*The Wizard of Oz* and *Meet Me in St. Louis* are my favorites. I like some Andy Hardy movies but they're not in color."

"A lot of Judy Garland movies are in black and white."

"I know," Darlene sighed. "'Cept we see in color." Then, regaining her enthusiasm, she rattled off a half dozen more Judy Garland movies she liked, a couple of which I'd seen.

Napster and Jesse gaped as if we were nerds jabbering about warp devices on black holes, or something. But Darlene couldn't help herself. She had a lot of sharing to do and very little time to do it. I was sort of concerned maybe Napster would think I was horning in on his girl, until I saw him leaning on his elbow, a bemused expression on his face, and I realized that for Napster—I was taking care of the conversation; he'd take care of the sex.

Ten minutes later, Napster caught my eye. I stopped practically in mid-sentence. "Let's pick out a few tunes," he suggested.

At the jukebox, Napster said, "Can you believe it? Darlene's as nutty as you about movies."

"You know, the films she likes are good."

Napster didn't care about Darlene's taste. "Don't you think she's hot? Underneath the table her leg kept rubbing mine."

"She was practically sitting in your lap."

"Do you mind if we take off? —Darlene and me?"

"Where is there to go?"

"I don't know. Nothing's happening here. What if I meet you at twelve?"

I looked at my watch. It was barely nine. Still, Napster seemed on the verge of something.

"OK," I said. Then, I wondered, "Is this place open 'til twelve?"

"On weekends it's open 'til one."

"You're sure?"

"Here all the time."

"Is Darlene going to ditch her friend?"

"She's not ditching her. She's leaving her with you."

"Oh.— Yeah."

Wiggling his index finger, Napster beckoned Darlene. Darlene practically leapt to her feet. Napster tilted his head toward the door. Darlene got the hint. Getting her coat, Darlene said to Jesse, "We're goin' for a walk. Wanna come?" But she gave Jesse a look that said, Take one for me. So Jesse was also playing wing. However, like me, Jesse wasn't ready to be a complete martyr. "How long're you gonna be?"

"Not long. Wait. OK."

"OK."

Holding hands like they were strolling down the Yellow Brick Road, Napster and Darlene departed. I slid into the seat opposite Jesse and hunted around in my brain for something other than movies to talk about. Luckily, I did not have to hunt long. The door to the Barn swung open and a bunch of kids entered.

"Movie's out," Jesse muttered more to herself than to me. And before I could say anything, the Barn filled. Every table was jammed. Guys lumbered into the back for the video games.

Some kids waved at Jesse or said, "Hey." One girl with a narrow face and eyes so close to her nose that she looked sort of cross-eyed stopped by.

"What're you doing here, Jess?" she said, all the time glancing at me out of the corner of her sort of crossed-eyed eyes.

"Came with Darlene. Meg, Stoner. Stoner, Meg. Meg goes to Lakes Valley."

"Hey," we both said.

I could tell Jesse enjoyed introducing me. I was a male, and I was at her table, even if we had been barely talking, which, of course, her friend wouldn't know.

Meg gripped the edge of the table with her hands and leaned over. I guess it was to see better. But as she wore this pale orange, low-cut jersey, it gave me a good view of her tits, which hung like water balloons, swaying over the table. As nice as they were, I tried not to stare. I didn't want to play any eye games with Jesse—she notices my gaze and follows it smack into Meg's tits. Naturally, our eyes swivel back and meet. What then? Do I blush? Do I shrug as if to say, nice knockers on your friend?

I suppose the trick was not to meet Jesse's eyes on the way back. I couldn't prevent myself from looking at her friend's tits. I thought that if I looked and then looked somewhere else for a beat, maybe it wouldn't be so embarrassing. I mean, excuse me, but her friend was leaning over the table. It wasn't as if I was staring up her skirt.

Anyway, Meg must've realized what she was doing or felt she had put on a good enough show because she straightened up still talking a mile a minute. "The movie was terrible. All this gore. Some of it was funny you know, but they always have to throw in lots of blood. I mean, I fully realize the title's *Dawn of the Dead*, so duh, it's not like I didn't know, but still, you know."

"Sure," Jesse said.

"Everyone was up for it, so I wasn't gonna be like a retard and go, 'Eeeewww, not me.'"

"Who was there?"

"Everyone 'cept you, Darlene, and Scarlet. Where is Darlene, anyway?"

"Off with Stoner's friend." Jesse rolled her eyes.

Meg grinned, knowingly. "Do you wanna ride home?" she asked. "Who knows when Darlene'll remember you're even here."

That sounded promising for Napster.

"When're you leaving?" Jesse asked.

"Soon. I've got my mother's car. I have to drive Nicole and Annie home."

"Where are they?"

"Still in the theater talking to Gloria. Do you wanna come or do you wanna stay?" As Meg said this, her glance fell on me. Since Jesse had floated the impression, however faintly, we were involved, it seemed for a moment Jesse would maintain the pretense and stay. But in the end, the quick, comfy ride home tipped the scale, although Jesse said to her friend as if we had some boy/girl matters to finish, "Give us a couple of minutes," and Jesse shot me a sweet smile Meg couldn't miss.

"We've got some drinks and fries," Meg said. "We didn't eat, like, anything at the movie. Three bucks for a small soda when you can buy one here for half. What kind of idiots do they think we are? Don't be long. We'll be in the car."

"OK."

Jesse said to me, "Darlene's mother was gonna drive me, but Meg lives practically next door. It's silly to make Darlene's mom drive miles out of her way. Do you mind?"

It meant sitting in the Barn alone for another couple of hours, but Jesse and I weren't interested in each other. And even though Jesse had seemed willing to talk—if we ever did find something to talk about—it wouldn't change how I felt about that chubby belly of hers.

I said, "Nah. I don't mind."

"Sure?" Jesse asked.

"Sure. I come up here pretty often with Napster. We'll see each other again."

Jesse smiled and put on her coat. Her parka was decorated like a Christmas tree with lift passes, and I realized we could've talked about skiing. This was New Hampshire, after all. Crap. With a last good-by, Jesse headed for the door. It shut behind her with a bang.

I thought maybe I should order again. I felt kind of odd. On the one hand I was sort of glad Jesse was gone; on the other hand, Jesse leaving was kind of a downer. Eating would give me something to do, and I couldn't just take up a booth.

I took my jacket from its hook, laid it across my seat to save the table, and walked to the counter. I am one of these thin types who can eat as much as I want and never get fat. That is the good part. The bad part is, I am always hungry and constantly scavenging for food like a wild dog. I debated whether to go straight for the pie and ice-cream or lead up to it with a couple of slices of pizza. It's funny how deeply you can get into decisions like these. The money's in your pocket. Your stomach's scream-ing to be fed. But you still can't figure exactly what you want. What's odder is how often I get it wrong. I mean, how can I be hungry and not know what I want? But more times than not I order, only to discover what my sister or my mother has is ten times better than what I have. Of course, the good thing about mothers is all you have to do is stare at their plate and they'll say, "Do you want some of mine?" or "Do you want to trade?" or "Do you want half?" Sisters are an entirely different story. I could as easily take food from my sister's plate as I could from a leopard's. But as I was now alone, the onus of choosing was completely on me, and I wanted to choose right.

Down, down, down I dove, trying to listen to the thin, quavering voice of my taste buds. But after wandering around the depths of my stomach, trying to let the force be with me, trying to be the hunger, I realized my eating Zen had no clue. I'd have to guess, and just at that moment when I'd given up, the revelation came—miraculous, mysterious, and exhilarat-ing,—like a snowstorm on a math quizz day—pizza, then apple pie.

After this epiphany, I was ready to order, and my attention shifted outward. As it did, I suddenly became aware of a pair of eyes a few feet from mine—eyes so pure and sparkling, they were like staring into a bright tropical lagoon. For a moment, it was like all I could see was turquoise. My gaze ratcheted back. The whole picture fell into place. The eyes belonged to a girl. A really pretty girl. She must've walked up to the counter while I was lost in my mind/stomach meld. I hadn't been remotely aware of her presence. But now I certainly was and, in a rare moment of spontaneity, I uttered, "Hey."

"Hey," she replied.

That I had unwittingly used Salome's "hey" technique flickered through my brain just as the counter guy asked, "Ready to order?" That he addressed us both helped.

"You go first," the girl said to me.

"You were here before," I responded, even though I really wasn't sure. "That's OK. You go."

The counter guy glanced from one of us to the other. "Should I choose?"

Embarrassed, we both laughed.

"You go," I said to the girl.

The girl peered up at me from out of the corner of her astonishing blue green eyes and I thought (but more distinctly) a Salome sign. She turned to the counter guy. "Two slices of pizza, please."

"Just sold the last slice," the counter guy said. "If you want pizza, you have to order a whole pie."

"Oh," the girl said. "I don't want a whole one. Can't I get two slices?" She put on an adorable pout, which melted me but didn't budge the counter guy. "After ten, you have to order a pie."

The girl sighed, "Well, what else've you got?" She glanced at the menu but the counter guy said, "The only thing hot is pizza. Everything else is put away."

"Damn," the girl uttered, more in frustration than anger. But it emboldened me. "Let's split one."

Suddenly shy, the girl glimpsed down. "Noooo, that's OK. Thanks." But the counter guy heard my offer. "Tell you what. If you both want slices, I'll stick in another pie. Anything on it?"

"Two plain is good for me," I said by way of encouragement.

The girl considered. "OK. Same for me."

"Ten minutes," the counter guy said, which couldn't have been more perfect. The girl and I moved away from the counter to make room for the next person, even though there wasn't a next person. As casually as possible, I stayed within talking distance.

The girl was tall—about five seven with straight blonde hair that ended just passed her shoulders. Her figure was nice:—long legs ending in a firm, round butt and breasts that were a perfect pair of cupcakes. When she walked, she put it all together, moving fluidly like a woman, not a girl. She had one of these classic faces that stare out at you from magazine covers— the large, turquoise eyes (that seemed to get lighter or darker every time you-looked at her), the straight nose, the perfectly shaped full lips, and straight white teeth that, when she smiled, dazzled enough to make you blink. I don't know what it is about a smile but some girls can really zap you. The only sour note was that she was obviously a junior or senior. Still, as I'm six feet, lots of people think I'm older—except, of course, that damn 'Lizabeth,—which wasn't a good memory to dwell on if I wanted a chance with this girl. We'd already had sort of a conversation, and we were both waiting for the pizza. This was my chance. THINK!

I noticed lift passes stapled to her jacket. I didn't have to be a moron twice. Most of the passes said, Stowe.

"You ski Vermont."

"Whooops," she said, looking down at her jacket. "I do. That's where I'm from."

"I've skied Stowe. It's great."

I pushed the right button. She became enthusiastic. "It's fantastic." She flushed. "I mean, it's fantastic here, too."

I laughed. "I'm not from New Hampshire. Just visiting. I think Vermont is pretty." I leaned nearer and whispered, "Prettier than New Hampshire."

She grinned, "It is, isn't it?"

"What brought you here? I assume not the foliage?"

"I'm with my mom. She sells prefab homes. She's meeting some guy who's putting one up on Lake Winnipesauke."

"That's where I'm staying. My friend's family has a place."

"Awesome lake," she said, standing on tiptoes and glancing toward the ovens. Happily, our pizza was still cooking. I didn't care how long we waited. The girl had my complete attention. I just hoped her mother wasn't outside in the car. A long delay might bring her in. It would also mean she was getting her slices to go.

As she peered, I said, "It's worth the wait."

"What?"

"The pizza. They make the thin crust."

"I love thin crust. The thinner the better. New York pizza is the best. I always have lots of pizza in New York." She unzipped her parka as if to stay.

Joy. Joy.

"My mom went to sleep at nine," the girl continued. "I got bored and hungry at the same time, and the hotel restaurant closes at ten, and they wouldn't let me in the bar, not even to get food."

Only one place could be called a hotel in Southridge. "You're at the Crispin Inn?"

"Yeah. They said, to get food at the bar, I had to come with my mother. As if. So I said, 'What if I order from the room?' They said, 'The bar doesn't take orders from the room,' so I walked down here. What jerks."

"Yeah," I agreed but thankful they were.

"Pizza," the counter guy yelled.

#

On the counter, our pizza steamed and bubbled, its pools of melted cheese and tomato sauce shimmering. The counter guy cut his master-piece, his hands moving quickly as if this were his millionth pie. As he cut, he asked, "To go?"

I held my breath.

"Here," the girl said.

"Me, too."

The girl fished around for her wallet in a large leather pocketbook and placed seven singles on the counter. I set a five dollar bill and two singles on top of hers. The counter guy grabbed a pair of aluminum trays and slid our slices onto them.

We lifted our trays and faced the restaurant. Another marvel. The only table available was mine. I saw her eyes drift toward the counter where three guys slouched, wearing motorcycle jackets with a skull and cross-bones on the back.

"The empty table's mine," I mentioned. "Do you want to share?"

The girl hesitated. She took another glance around the restaurant. No one seemed ready to leave. The three guys at the counter were talking loudly. I suppose some guys look cool in motorcycle jackets with skulls and cross-bones on the back. These guys did not. They looked like they took being bad seriously. The girl said, "Well, we're sharing the pizza…"

It was as if some spell had transported me into this magic meet-the-girl-of-your-dream zone.

We set our trays down on my table, and I hung my parka back on the hook. A minute ago, I was sitting tongue-tied with Jesse. Now, sliding into my booth was this slender, blonde, fairy-tale princess, and somehow I was saying all the right things. How long would the enchantment last? Maybe not long. The girl was totally into her pizza, and I seemed forgotten. She was separating her slices, making happy purring noises as if she were five years old. But she wasn't. She was seventeen or eighteen, and the purring noises were cute and sexy at the same time.

"Something liquid to wash the food down?" I asked.

She looked up. "Whooops. Good idea. When I get hungry, I forget everything."

I stood, trying to be in control. "I'll get it. What do you want?"

"Diet Pepsi." She fished around again for her wallet.

"Don't bother."

"No. No. No. Not OK," she said, handing me a couple of dollars.

In a minute, I returned with our drinks and her change. Her pizza was still uneaten.

"You're so hungry," I said. "You didn't have to wait."

"It was too hot anyway. I hate burning my tongue on the first slice."

"Me too."

We each took a cautious nibble. The temperature was just right.

I couldn't stop watching her. She took a couple more bites, purring to herself as she ate. "You're right. This is good." She took a few more bites, then, grudgingly, placed her slice back on her plate, wiping her fingers with a napkin and thrusting her slender hand toward me. "Danielle."

"Michael."

We shook.

Once the edge was off Danielle's appetite, we talked. Her mother was French and came from a town called Vittel, which is in the foothills of the French Alps. Her father was American and served in the army in Germany. Her parents met skiing. The whole family was big into skiing. Her parents got divorced when Danielle was ten. She didn't have any brothers or sisters. Her mother stayed in Stowe where Danielle was born. Her father moved to Colorado and remarried. She had a half-brother and half-sister. Every summer, she went to Colorado for a month and didn't get along too well with her stepmother but it was OK. She went to Stowe High and was...a senior. My ears burned with the sound of 'Lizabeth's laughter. Maybe Danielle sensed it, or maybe it was the obvious thing to say, but she asked, "What year are you?"

Somehow, I couldn't lie and say, "Senior." Instead, the biggest fabrication I could force out of my mouth was, "Junior." I don't know why. I mean what's the diff? A lie is a lie. Even worse, I added, "I'll be seventeen February 8th," adopting Napster's birthday which was closer than mine.

What was wrong with me? Why say sixteen when I could say seventeen, and why use Napster's birthday? I could've made up any date. Danielle would probably meet Napster. Maybe even tonight. His birthday wasn't likely to come up but, damn, way to ruin this.

"I'm one of the youngest kids in my class," Danielle said. "I just turned seventeen in September." Great. She was making us closer rather than farther apart. Danielle went on and asked, "Where do you go?"

Danielle hadn't heard of Noyce, but when I told her the senior class only has eighty kids and last year nineteen went to Ivy League schools, she was impressed.

The best thing, however, was when I asked her what subjects she liked, she replied, "English and French. English because I love to read, and French because I'm good at it. My mother and I go to France every summer to visit my grandmother."

Wow. The next half hour we spent talking about Paris, books, and writers. She had even read Jack Kerouac, though only his poetry, not his books. She said, "My mom went to the Sorbonne and is a big Beat fan. She has this old vinyl of Kerouac reading his poetry. My mom says she wants to take me to San Francisco, but every time we travel, it's France. Not that I expect much sympathy," Danielle giggled.

I loved Danielle's giggle. It made me think of snow, hot chocolate, and sleigh bells.

Glancing down at Danielle's plate, I saw only two curls of pizza crust left…

"How about some dessert?" I asked. If we ordered more food, Danielle would stay.

Danielle patted her stomach. "I'm pretty full," but I could see doubt in her eyes.

"They have great apple pie," I encouraged. "It's home-made. They heat it up and add ice cream for free."

Her eyes kind of half shut. "Hmm," she purred, "that does sound good." Then, her resolve stiffened. "Honest, I've had enough."

"How about if we split one? We split the pizza. Let's split dessert." I felt as if I were still in the zone.

Darlene's resolve melted like the ice cream around our hot apple pie.

Carefully, Danielle divided the pie in half. (Well, sort of half. I got the bigger piece.) As soon as we both had our slices, she scooped up some ice cream and pie on her fork, making more *hmming* noises.

As I watched, I wondered where Napster and Darlene had slunk off to. It was too cold to walk around for hours. Napster must be scoring big. But I wasn't jealous. Danielle was one of the prettiest girls I'd ever seen. Better-looking even than Melissa. God, what if I had two girlfriends? I mean, Danielle was in Stowe. Melissa was in Brookline. I could see them both. They would never know. I'd be the coolest guy in school. It would drive Napster crazy.

Taking another slice of her pie and ice cream, Danielle leaned back dreamily. "My uncle works for Ben & Jerry's, but the ice cream here's almost as good. He's my father's brother. Before the divorce, whenever he visited, he always brought a couple of pints. Now, I hardly see him. Are your parents still married?"

"Yeah."

"Lucky."

"Fifteen minutes till closing," the counter guy shouted.

I looked at my watch. It was eleven forty-five. I got up and went to the counter.

"I thought you stay open till one on weekends."

The counter guy shook his head. "That's only in the summer."

Just like Napster to get it wrong.

I went back to my seat.

Danielle said, "I guess we should finish up."

"Guess we have to. Except my friend's off with some girl, and I'm supposed to meet him here."

Danielle shrugged. "Text him and come back to the inn with me. The inn stays open all night."

Wow. She wanted me to wait with her. One of Napster's escapades was finally paying off.

I grabbed my cell and typed—: *Barn closed. Meet at Crispin.*

Walking to the inn was surreal. We strolled together on the deserted street under a big yellow moon glowing in a mist of silver stars. Beside me, Danielle's sneakers crunched on the pavement, and every once in a while, her shoulder brushed mine.

It was the Saturday of a long weekend, and Danielle and her mother were likely staying until Monday. I could ask Danielle to the movie for Sunday night. It was *Dawn of the Dead*, but in Southridge, what else could we do? Hang in the Barn? We'd just done that. With no license and no car, I couldn't drive anywhere. And despite Meg's review, I had heard *Dawn of the Dead* was good. Maybe Danielle liked horror movies or we could go as a goof. Only, what if Napster wanted to go with Darlene? Could I get them to lie and say they were juniors? Napster would. Would Darlene? She was bound to be alone with Danielle in the bathroom. Girls always went to the bathroom together. Would she give me away? Would that be part of some female code? Or would she keep my secret to stay on Napster's good side? Girls don't care about other girls, not when a guy's involved.

My thoughts spun with angles while every nerve in my body absorbed the sensation of Danielle. She had this wonderful smell—like wild mountain flowers and pine trees—and every time I took a breath, I felt as if I were breathing her in.

When we entered the lobby, Danielle touched the sleeve of my coat and said, "Let's go into the room with the fire."

A touch! A definite touch! Salome knew what she was talking about. Maybe something could happen tonight.

#

The lounge in the Crispin Inn sprawls in a corner between the bar, the main dining room, and the lobby. An old burgundy leather couch and a couple of matching burgundy leather chairs laze around the stone fireplace, warming themselves. A thick, oak mantelpiece stretches over the fireplace, and above the mantelpiece broods this large, smoky photograph of the inn taken about a hundred years ago. Except for the new wing and lots of paint, the inn doesn't appear much different.

We plopped down on the couch, and Danielle sat tantalizingly close. It was just the two of us, but it wasn't like we were alone. The bar was full, and every once in a while, one of the bartenders drifted down to the end of the bar and scoped us out. It wasn't so much that the bartenders were nosy. It was more from boredom and we were in plain sight. Equally annoying were the customers wandering in and out who gave us the once over when they passed.

Sometimes we stared at the fire. Sometimes we talked animatedly.

When we switched from favorite books to favorite movies, I felt good because we shared so many, although, unlike Darlene, the only black-and-white movie Danielle had seen was *It's a Wonderful Life*. But at least she liked it. She said we shared so many favorite films, she thought she'd enjoy the black-and-white ones, too.

I hoped her faith in my taste extended to when I brought up *Dawn of the Dead*. I didn't want her suggesting movies in Laconia. I mean, even if we went in her mother's car, what if she wanted me to drive? It was an issue I had to confront soon because in the midst of our discussion of the best teen movie ever— *Clueless, Fast Times at Ridgemont High, American Pie* or *Heathers*, Danielle reached up, covered her mouth, and yawned.

We'd been in the inn for almost an hour. Any moment, she was going to say, "Time for bed." I had to ask. I couldn't weasel out.

I sat up straighter on the couch, paused like a diver on a cliff and... leaped. "Are you...uh-uh...around Monday?"

"What?"

I thought I'd spoken loudly but I had to repeat myself.

On my second try, she responded, "Y-y-yes." But her voice had so much "why" in it, I could almost see the question mark.

"Tomorrow...uh...Sunday night...would...would you like to do something?"

Her green eyes filled with wonder as if, Harry Potterlike, I had waved my wizard's wand and conjured up a dozen hot apple pies all topped with ice cream.

"What would you want to do?"

I tried to answer as if it were an obvious choice. "We could go see *Dawn of the Dead*."

For a moment, her face maintained its expectant look. Then her eyes squinched, her mouth opened, and laughter jangled through the room, only this time it didn't sound so pleasant.

I thought, how could I ever ask out a girl again? I imagined a doctor holding a stethoscope to my heart and pronouncing, "He died from mortification." But unlike 'Lizabeth's laughter, Danielle's subsided. Catching her breath, she said, "Not a big horror fan but I don't know, it could be fun. I almost thought of suggesting it to my mom, but no-way would she get it."

Blood roared back through my veins. Trying not to show too much excitement, I said, "So you'll go?"

"Sure." An impish gleam flickered in her eyes. "If I get scared, you won't mind me clutching your arm?"

"No. Clutch away."

The transition from depression to euphoria made me dizzy and somewhat out of control. I almost chortled geekishly. With the date set, I was actually glad when Danielle turned her face slightly and gave another yawn. I didn't need Salome to tell me: —get while the getting was good.

"If you're tired, you don't have to wait here with me," I said.

"Oh, my God, sorry. We started out real early today."

"Go to bed. I'll wait in the lobby." I stood. "I'll call you tomorrow." I even remembered to ask, "What's your last name?"

"Donahue. Danielle Donahue."

"Your cell?"

She reached into her bag and scribbled her number on a scrap of paper. I had her name and her number.

"I hope you find your friend," she said.

"Since I'm staying at his house, I'm sure I will."

We walked around the couch, and on the way out of the lounge, Danielle ducked behind a pillar. Like a dog on a leash, I followed. Danielle stopped, turned, and before I knew what she was doing, she leaned up and kissed me. And not on my cheek. She kissed me on my lips. I mean, it wasn't like it was a passionate tongue kiss, but her lips conveyed definite pressure; pressure after a startled second I returned. Then, she pulled away, smiled, and sashayed out of the room.

I remained rooted to the spot. Her lips tasted sweet and promised a lot more than sweet. For a minute, I stood there savoring the sensation. As Danielle had cleverly situated us where we were hidden from the bar or lobby, I didn't have to move. At last, I shook myself—half consciously, half in reflex—the way a collie shakes himself coming out of the water. It was like I was putting my body and brain back together. It was twelve fifty-five and I'd been kissed by a girl. An amazing-looking girl. A senior. Wow. I couldn't wait to tell Napster.

\#

I didn't have to wait long.

At one-fifteen, Napster slouched into the lobby.

Darlene, it turns out, has a key to the Beauty and Beyond Salon her mother owns. When Napster and Darlene passed it, Darlene asked Napster if he wanted to peek inside. Naturally, Napster said, "Yes," and ten seconds later, the two were entwined like snakes on the waiting room couch where they remained, writhing, until Darlene had to go home.

I told Napster about Danielle, but I changed my mind about telling him how she'd kissed me. A: because it didn't amount to much compared to Napster's making out with Darlene for like the whole night, and B: because Napster is very crude when it comes to girls, and Danielle seemed so much finer than just a girl, if you know what I mean.

In *The Princess Diaries*—my sister's favorite book on CD (she loves listening to books on CD)—Mia Thermopolis and her buddies talk incessantly about kissing—French kissing—but my friends and I don't. I know how much Mia talks about kissing because, once down the Cape when my mother and sister were out shopping (of course) and my father was at a neighbor's, working on the neighbor's boat (what else), I was bored, and my sister's Walkman lay on the couch. I stuck on the earphones and there was Anne Hathaway herself reading *The Princess Diaries*. I recognized who it was right away.

I didn't have to listen long to learn all Mia Thermopolis thinks about is tongues. I don't know if this is generally true when it comes to fourteen-year-old girls—. I don't think it is, because I know a lot of girls cruise the internet looking at porn. Well, a lot of guys tell stories about girls cruising porn sites. They say they caught their sister or they know someone who caught his sister or they know someone who knows someone who cruised porn sites with a girl, but I have never caught my sister who is only eleven cruising porn sites, and Napster has never caught his sister, although the two sometimes joke about it. But I can't believe that girls don't. I mean they have to be thinking about more than boys' tongues, and the Internet's how to find out about something bigger than a tongue.

#

When we awoke the next day around noon, Mrs. Belknap was heading out to join Mr. Belknap, who was already in the car. All Napster and I got was a slightly sarcastic, "Since you boys missed breakfast, I made sandwiches. If you want anything else, look in the fridge. We'll be back around four." We didn't even have to relate our carefully prepared parent-friendly version of the night's adventures.

In the kitchen, Salome sat at the table, reading, half a sandwich on her plate. She sulked at us for a moment before saying, "Look who's up. When did you guys roll in?"

Salome gets annoyed because even though her parents say they raise her and her brother equally, she knows they don't. They're more lenient with Napster. She was irritated her mother didn't grill us about our evening.

Napster ignored her question and examined our sandwiches. He lifted the bread and shook his head, muttering, "Tuna fish, tuna fish, tuna fish."

He turned to Salome. "What've you got?"

"Tuna fish."

"Man," Napster said, bringing the plates over to the table, "Mom, must've been in a rush."

"They're going antiquing."

"So we're lucky we got this." Napster looked at me. "Grab a tuna and a chair."

I did. Napster asked Salome, "What's to drink?"

"What am I? Your waitress? Go look."

Napster did. He asked if I wanted some cider.

"Sure. Thanks."

Napster brought over a couple of glasses and inquired of his sister, "Why didn't you go?"

"Oh, I just love antiquing. —Not." Salome took a bite of her sandwich. However, never one to lose her train of thought, she resumed, "When did you two blow in?" With narrowed eyes, she gazed from Napster to me. "You both look very smug. Something fishy's going on, and it's not in the sandwiches."

Napster chewed, pretending he didn't have a clue what she was talking about.

"What were you guys up to?"

"Nothing," Napster said.

"Don't 'nothing' me. You can 'nothing' Mom and Dad, but I sense something."

Napster turned to me. "Salome thinks twins are like mutants. She's sure she's Jean Grey, X-Woman."

Salome was not deterred. "I'm right, aren't I? I don't know which of you has the cheesier grin. I want it now. Spill."

"OK, OK. But it doesn't leave this room. You tell no one. No parents. No one at school. Not Shauna. Not Giddy—"

"What? What?" Salome was all eager. "Did you guys rob the Barn?"

"Promise," Napster insisted.

"Cross my heart. This'd better be good."

Napster paused to build the suspense—as if it needed building. "I met a girl."

Salome's mouth fell open, "No way."

"Way."

"Who?"

"Someone from town."

"A townie," Salome whooped. "You met a townie. What's her name?"

"Darlene."

"Daaarleeeene. How?"

"In the Barn."

"Wow, I should start charging. Details."

"She's a sophomore at Lakes Valley."

Salome's eyes opened wider. "You mean the vocational school."

"Yep."

"No wonder you want it secret. Mom and Dad would be so proud. —A vocational school girlfriend."

"She's not my girlfriend. We just met."

"That look on your face says you kissed her."

Napster didn't say anything, and immediately Salome squealed. "You did! I can't believe it. My big brother finally made out."

"I'm not your big brother."

"You elbowed your way into the world a minute and a half ahead of me."

Probably to divert attention from himself, Napster said, "Stoner met a girl, too."

Salome held her hand over her heart. "Oh, my God, now, I really am going to charge. Who'd you meet?"

I didn't want to talk about it, but Salome repeated, "Who?"

"Danielle."

"Oooooh, Danielle. Does Danielle go to Lakes Valley like Darlene?"

"No."

"Where does Danielle go?"

"She lives in Stowe. She goes to school there," I said.

"She's a senior," Napster threw in. "Like the maid in the motel."

Salome's jaw nearly hit the floor. I wished I had a camera. "A senior. You really have a thing for older women, don't you? And you haven't even kissed a girl!"

"I think he has now," Napster said.

"Oh, my God," Salome said. "You kissed a senior. With your tongue? Did you stick your tongue in a senior girl's mouth! Oh, my God, tell me about it. Look how red he is, Nappy."

Naturally, my face got red. Salome and Napster were having a wonderful time at my expense, and all this talk about Danielle was making me edgy. I looked at my watch. It was already a few minutes past one. The thought thundered in my brain. Call! Don't mess this up. As quickly as I could, I told Salome the story. By the end, I was as twitchy to get going as I am near the end of math class. It was twenty passed one. "Gotta make a call," I said.

"To Danielle?" Salome teased.

I figured agreeing was the easiest way out.

"Yes."

"Well, go call." Salome saw the agonized look on my face. She wasn't interested in gumming up the romance. "Give her my best."

I tried to leave the kitchen casually, as if it didn't really matter, but it was like when you have to go to the bathroom badly but don't want anyone to know it. You move nonchalantly as fast as you can. That's how I headed for the bedroom.

My cell was on the night table. I dug in my wallet for the scrap of paper with Danielle's number and punched it in. After four rings, Danielle's voice said, "Hey, talk to me."

I didn't.

It was a recording. I was stunned. This wasn't the plan. Maybe Danielle had switched her cell off last night and forgot to turn it on. Maybe she was talking to someone or still asleep. Maybe she was out and had left her phone in her room. Maybe she had changed her mind and was just not answering. I sat on the bed nervous as hell. I waited five minutes and called again. Same message. I couldn't sit in Napster's room all afternoon calling. I thought of texting, but a text was too easy to ignore. I wanted to speak to her. Maybe I could try her room in the inn.— Why hadn't I called earlier? Why had I slept so late? In my stomach, an oily regret churned. I found the hotel number in a phone book, but I was so panicked it took three attempts to dial. When the hotel operator came on, I croaked, "The Donahue's please."

"Room number?"

"I don't know."

A long pause ensued. When the operator returned, in her snotty operator tone, she said, "The Donahues checked out."

"Checked out?" I almost collapsed on the bed. The oily waves in my stomach heaved like deep ocean swells. "How can that be?"

"I don't know, sir. But they're no longer here."

"You're sure?"

In the same snotty tone, the operator said, "Yes, sir. I'm sure."

"I thought they were supposed to stay 'til Monday."

"I wouldn't know, sir."

"Did they move to another room?"

The operator sighed. This conversation bored her. She had much more important things to do. "I'll check."

Another few seconds ticked by.

The operator's voice came back. "There are no Donahues staying at the hotel. Is there anyone else you wish to speak to, sir?"

"No."

"Thank you for calling the Crispin Inn." The phone clicked and she was gone.

Checked out. How could that be? It must be some mistake. In my mind, I saw Danielle saying it would be fun to go to the movie. Asking me to call. How could she agree and leave? Was she deliberately making a fool of me? But why? She asked me to sit with her in the Inn? We talked for hours. She kissed me. Damn. I tried her cell again and got an out-of-range message. Fuck. Up around Lake Winnipesaukee this happens a lot. With all the mountains, reception is iffy. But not when you are in the same town. Only, we weren't in the same town. The Donahues had checked out. It seemed impossible yet true. I wasn't going to watch *Dawn of the Dead* with Danielle. We weren't going to sit in the back row, holding hands. How was I going to tell this to Napster and Salome? Just a minute ago, they were so impressed. Now, it was back to poor Stoner.

I slumped into the kitchen. When I entered, I was saved from reporting the news. Napster and Salome took one look at my face and knew.

"Oh, my God," Salome exclaimed. "What happened? She discovered you're a sophomore?"

"No. She left."

"Left?" Napster and Salome twinned.

"Checked out. Gone. Vanished. Vamoosed."

Napster shrugged. "So, she left. What's the big deal?"

I swallowed nervously. "We were supposed to see *Dawn of the Dead* tonight."

Napster started in surprise. I hadn't told him. I had hoped he would take off with Darlene and I could go with Danielle to the movie.

"Holding out on me, huh? Was it a date or just your plan?"

"I think it was a date."

"You think," Salome said. "Either it was or it wasn't."

"Well, I asked and she said yes. We just hadn't set a time or anything. I was supposed to call today."

Salome eyed me carefully, "And you kissed her?"

"She kissed me."

"Hmm. Well, maybe something happened and she had to leave."

"She could've called."

"Does she have your cell?" Salome demanded.

I shook my head. I had remembered to get hers, but I hadn't given her mine. It didn't seem necessary at the time. After that kiss, I wasn't thinking too clearly.

"Does she know where you are?" Salome continued.

I hadn't thought of that, either. "No. But she could've left a message at the Inn."

Salome scoffed. "Does Danielle even know your name?"

"Of course." I snapped.

Salome bore in. "Your last name?"

I'd made a point of getting her last name but couldn't recall if I'd told her mine. I looked at Salome and she looked at me. I had to admit, "I don't know."

Salome shook her head. "So she doesn't know your last name and you expect her to leave a message. What is she supposed to say, "If a guy named

Stoner calls, give him this?"

"Michael. She calls me Michael."

"OK. Michael."

I didn't say anything. I just looked more depressed.

Salome took pity, "Really, I guess it's possible. I was just kidding about the message."

Napster cut in, "Forget the message. She's not going to leave a message. You've got her cell. Wait a couple of days and call."

That made sense. I did have her cell. A ray of hope pierced the darkness.

"Call but be realistic," Salome said. "The girl's a senior. She lives in Vermont. Even if you get a hold of her, how are you going to see her? You don't have a driver's license. You don't even have a learner's permit. You're fifteen."

Napster smiled confidently. "The girl wants Stoner. We'll think of something."

"Yeah," Salome said. "The bus."

#

Napster and I decided to see *Dawn of the Dead* anyway. Napster figured he'd invite Darlene, and even though Salome shares Danielle's dislike of horror flicks, she came along. Salome couldn't pass on an opportunity to check out her brother's girl.

Unlike me, Napster had no trouble reaching Darlene. Although it's not a fair comparison. Napster had already spent hours making out with Darlene, and she lives in the same town. Still I felt my failure, particularly when Darlene insisted Jesse come with us. Jesse was Darlene's best friend, and she didn't want her staying home alone.

Mr. and Mrs. Belknap were thrilled that the three of us—that is, Napster, Salome, and I—were going to the movies. They didn't know Darlene and Jesse were waiting at the theater. They liked that Salome and Napster were doing something together, and I'm sure they liked even more we'd be off their hands.

Outside the theater, Darlene and Jesse already had their tickets. That *Dawn of the Dead* was R-rated didn't matter. The kids at the ticket booth never ID'd you. All the townies know each other, and the theater plays pretty tame movies, anyway. Even the R-rated ones.

When the three girls met, they squealed and cooed, although you could tell they were checking each other out like crazy—make-up, hair and clothes. Darlene wore less make-up, and it helped. Jesse looked the same: same pretty face, same chubby body. Salome was in full LL Bean mode: walking boots, tan corduroy pants, and a faded blue denim shirt.

After Salome, Napster, and I bought tickets, we loaded up at the refreshment stand and sat in an empty row in the back of the theater. Napster settled in beside Darlene, and I squeezed between Jesse and Salome.

*Dawn of the Dead* turned out to be good:—Zombies go wild in Milwaukee, and a bunch of people end up hiding in a mall where most of the action takes place. The movie is surprisingly funny, scary, bloody, —and only occasionally stupid. Even Salome enjoyed the flick. When the lights went back on, we were jittery, excited, and relieved to be back in the real world where no one was biting anyone's arms or legs, although some of the guys in the audience were biting their girlfriend's shoulders and necks, and their girlfriends were pretending to be annoyed, squealing, "Stop it," and pushing them away.

What I like about zombie movies (and horror movies in general) is the "wait before the first attack." You know it's coming. The screenwriter and the director know you know, and it's kind of a game how clever they can be surprising you. Most of the time, the attack takes place after a couple, usually a teen couple, has sex. Whatever bad is going to happen, happens then. This fact is to me somehow reassuring. It makes me feel that, while I might be a virgin, at least I do not have to worry about zombies or other supernatural embodiments of evil ripping my head off. This feeling is similar to, but the opposite of, the comfort I get watching Hercules/Xena-type movies. In these Roman/Greek/Egyptian style epics, it's standard that at some point a virgin is sacrificed. However, I am again safe as those ancient (or future) civilizations rely exclusively on *female* virgins. Frustrated teen male virgins, while leading lonely, tortured lives on whatever planet (or in whatever century) they're raised, have one saving grace: they are an unsavory, gristly lot unfit for any angry god or demented manifestation of evil who needs appeasing.

After *Dawn of the Dead*, we shifted in accordance with Southridge tradition to the Barn and grabbed a booth. Almost immediately, the girls departed to take a pee. Napster and I felt they wouldn't be too long, because how much plotting could Darlene and Jesse do in front of Napster's sister. Or was Salome plotting as well? Unfortunately, Salome would never tell. The Free Masons, the Illuminati, the Priory of Scion, the Rosicrucians, and the Knights Templar guard no secret more zealously than women guard the Mysteries of the Ladies Room. As if to prove the point, when thirteen minutes later the girls reappeared, they chattered happily until they neared our table. Then, they clammed up tight. Whatever confidences had passed between them were sealed forever from our ears.

In my role as Wingtainer, I suggested a super jumbo hot fudge sundae with five spoons. Napster, growing ever more confident and comfortable, didn't bother to join the discussion of what toppings to put on. He placed his hand around Darlene's shoulder and said simply, "We're gonna take a walk by the bridge." A narrow river twists through Southridge, storming down a twenty-foot drop. At one time, a mill was located beside the waterfall, which was probably the reason for the town, but the mill is long gone. At night, the falls are lit.

No one asked to go along, but as Napster and Darlene slid out of the booth, Jesse gave her usual warning to Darlene: "Don't forget. Your mom said twelve."

"Yeah, yeah," Darlene replied.

Then, the two disappeared.

By way of explaining her insistence on Darlene's prompt return, Jesse mentioned, "I'm sleeping over Darlene's tonight. Her mom's nice, but she's a Born Again."

"Strict, huh?" Salome said.

"Oh, she's all right," Jesse said, "but she goes totally bizarro if we're late."

I thought, maybe Napster wasn't going to get as much off Darlene as he figured. Or maybe Darlene's into one of those rebellion things and he'd get more.

"Is Darlene Born Again, too?" Salome wondered.

"Just her mom," Jesse said. "Darlene can really quote Bible, though. When she was little, her mother made her memorize all these psalms. But it was worthwhile, I guess. Darlene's got this super memory. Once when she was sleeping over my house, we drank like three beers and took two shots of Bacardi, and Darlene stood up and quoted six psalms by heart. Long ones! Then, she threw up and started to cry. I had to hold her head over the toilet for like half an hour and reassure her she wasn't going to hell."

"Cool," I said.

"Yeah," Salome agreed.

I could tell Salome enjoyed the story as much as I did. The cultural gap was closing.

Salome asked Jesse, "What groups do you like?"

As they talked, "Oh, my Gods," "Totallys" and "Awesomes" sprinkled their conversation like glitter. But for me, the moment with the brightest sparkle was at eleven fifty-six when Napster and Darlene appeared, four-whole minutes before the Barn closed, slightly disheveled but grinning from the after-effects of an hour and a half of teen love.

Salome, Jesse, and I huddled outside while Napster and Darlene said good-bye. As we were leaving for Boston the next day, this was Napster and Darlene's last night for a while. The three of us glanced sheepishly at each other, wondering how long we were prepared to wait while the two chewed each other's lips off. Once more, the first to break ranks was Jesse. She yelled over her shoulder, "C'mon, Darlene, it's cold."

We all turned, and Darlene and Napster pushed their bodies apart. It was like tearing one of those black rubber cups off a window. You could almost hear the suction pop. Darlene hurried over to Jesse and Napster swaggered up to Salome and me and we headed home.

#

At Noyce, sports start at two-thirty and last until three forty-five unless you're on a team in which case they go until four-thirty or five unless it's a Friday, in which case there's a game, and those who are not on a team are supposed to stick around and root for a team, which hardly anyone does, except when one of the teams goes on a winning streak and a buzz starts. Sometimes, when a team does well, an article comes out in the *Boston Globe* that generates a crowd. But I was on the cross-country team that never does well, never causes a buzz, and which no one ever watches except sometimes Mr. Hough grabs a few kids at the soccer game to cheer us on because the finish line is right behind the soccer fields. This is nice of Mr. Hough and great for Phil Rosenbloom, who is the fastest runner on the team and who wins a lot of meets. However, once Phil wins or comes in second, every-one goes back to watching the soccer game. I mean even parents don't watch cross-country. Not that I care. Last fall, my parents showed up on home coming day, and my dad took a picture of me crossing the finish line in fifth place, which was considered good because I was a freshman. The cool thing about the picture is no one is ahead of me. Everyone is behind, so it looks as if I'm winning (which is a big family joke), and my dad blew up the picture and has it hanging in his office.

Cross-country does have the virtue of short practices. You do your warm-ups, run the course, and leave, which meant on D-Day—the day determined by Napster and Salome for me to call Danielle—I was out of the shower and ready by three-thirty. By four, I was in my room at home, phone in hand.

I took a couple of deep breaths, mentally prayed for my Vermont goddess to answer, and dialed. After two rings, she did.

"Hey," Danielle said.

"Hey," I said.

So far so good.

Her voice sounded friendly and eager to talk. Did she know who I was? Had she checked her caller ID? At least, she didn't sound as if she were in the middle of another conversation.

I charged right in. "Danielle, it's me, Michael."

During the pause, I sensed her sifting through her list of all possible Michaels. It wasn't a long list. "From Southridge?"

"Not from Southridge but, yeah, that's me."

"Wow, I'm *so* glad you called," she cried. "My mom and I had to leave early. My mom's clients changed like their kitchen cabinets or something, and my mom didn't trust anyone else to get it right, so we hauled ass back to Stowe, but I couldn't call. You didn't give me your cell."

OK. She could've checked her missed calls, but I let that pass. I said, "I figured it was something like that."

"I felt real bad."

"No biggie. How are you?"

"Good. You?"

"Fine," I said and stalled. All the mental rehearsing I'd done, forgotten.

I grasped at a familiar straw. "Any snow?"

"It snowed in the mountains last night, but not much."

"Yeah." God. How feeble. But like my downhill skiing, once started, it was difficult to stop. "Got your outfits ready?"

"Just bought an awesome pair of ski pants. Red with blue and gold stripes. Can't wait to wear 'em."

"You're not shy on the slopes."

"I can ski. One of the good things about living in Stowe. Where are you? Way down in Boston?"

I didn't like how she made Boston sound so far.

"Not way down. Only a few hours."

"Six hours by bus. And I hate the bus."

It didn't sound like Danielle would be visiting any time soon.

"There's lots of things to do."

"I suppose. Lots of clubs, if you're old enough."

"Well, we had fun in Southridge, and there's nothing to do there."

"True."

"Do you hike?" I asked, since she seemed to like the outdoors.

"All the time," Danielle said.

OK, this was good. I said, "My buddy and I hiked Cannon Mountain." I left out the rest of the Belknaps to make it sound as if Napster and I really dug hiking. "Napster— you know, the guy I was waiting for—every year in the fall we hike a mountain," I said, borrowing Napster's family routine. It went nowhere.

"Once a year!" Danielle exclaimed. "In the summer, we hike a mountain every week."

My mind spun. On Cape Cod where we live in the summer, I walk a lot. On the beach. Around the neighborhood. Could I call that hiking? No. It sounded stupid. Maybe out near Truro and Provincetown where there's lots of open land and dunes you could call a long walk a hike, but I wasn't sure. I played it safe and stuck with what I knew. I said, "We go to the Cape every summer."

Danielle accepted that. "Cape Cod's pretty. I have an aunt who lives in Yarmouth."

"Only a couple of towns away," I said.

"She's my aunt on my dad's side. Now I hardly see her."

Damn that divorce. "Miss her?"

"A little. But it's OK."

"Sorry."

"I'm used to it. Listen, Michael," Danielle said, "you're a nice guy. A really nice guy but…"

Uh-oh.

"…We've got to straighten something out. I don't want to give you the wrong impression."

"What?"

"When we met, when I went to the Barn, it was because I was hungry and my mother was asleep and I wasn't expecting anything to happen—not that anything happened—but…our…ah…meeting…It was — it was just kind of an accident."

Talk about going downhill. God. How could I rescue this? The familiar queasy dread in my stomach was sure I couldn't, but nonetheless I replied, "Not just an accident. Serendipitous."

"*Serendipitous.* Good SAT word. What's it mean?"

"It's when you discover something in an unintentional or unexpected way, like Newton discovering gravity when the apple fell on his head. Or Christopher Columbus looking for India but finding America."

"Got it."

"There's a movie, *Serendipitous.*"

"Really. Who's in it?"

"Mmm…uhh…Don't remember…" Why am I such a dork? Here I am hanging onto this call by my fingertips and suddenly I'm talking movies—movies where like a broken pump, I can't even dredge up the stars' names. Still I rambled on. "It's not that good a movie anyway. It's about two people who meet in this serendipitous way. Then, they separate for some nonsensical reason—even though everyone knows they're made for each other—but just before the movie ends, they get back together in another serendipitous but typical Hollywood way."

Danielle laughed. "Michael, you really are a nice person. Very bright. Very funny. But…"

Another "but." The ball of uneasiness in the pit of my stomach grew, "What?" I said. "Is it the hiking?"

Danielle couldn't help herself. She laughed again. This time pretty hard. I guess she really did think I was funny. "No, Michael, it's not the hiking." However, quickly her voice lost its humor. "It's just that I have…It's only fair you know. I—I have a boyfriend." When she said, *boyfriend,* her tone got sickeningly sweet like a candy heart filled with caramel and marshmallow. "A boy I like very much. In the restaurant when we met, it all seemed so innocent. Well, it was innocent. I was bored and we started talking and you were funny only….my boyfriend…Jared [SNAP]….We've been dating for nearly a year [CRACKLE] and we…well, I can't do anything behind Jared's back [POP]."

Just like that. Those cupcake breasts. Those long legs. That firm ass. Gone. And a few days earlier, she had kissed me. OK. The kiss wasn't a mad embrace and, OK, we hadn't actually dated, but now it's "I can't do anything behind my boyfriend's back." You bitch, *you kissed me*. I thought again of those breasts, those legs, that ass and even though I knew, nothing I could say or do would alter Danielle's mind, somehow I couldn't just hang up. The end was too quick, too abrupt, too final. If I were cool, if I were a bad boy, I could say, "Fuck you," and forget her. But being me I still clung to some hope, however faint,—if not for the present, for the future. She was a bitch, but such a good-looking bitch. I said, "You have friends. You talk to other guys. What's wrong with talking?"

"As friends. Sure," Danielle said. "You know what I told you about my mom was true. When we left, it was completely unplanned. But when it happened, I was glad. I didn't want to leave without saying goodbye, but even if we'd stayed, I couldn't have gone to the movie. I wasn't thinking. It wouldn't have been right. I…I love Jared."

There's that bastard Jared again. "You love him, huh?"

"Yes. It's like it was meant."

How can girls say such stupid things? She's a senior. Next year she'll be in college. How long will high-school Jared last? How many more Jareds will there be?

"Since that's clear," I said, "why make such a big deal about us hanging out?"

"What's the sense?"

"You said I was interesting and funny."

"You are, but you're in Boston. I'm in Stowe."

"Which makes even less of a reason not to talk."

"I don't think it's right."

"It's on the phone. We're on the phone. Unless…maybe…maybe you think something could come of it."

"Don't flatter yourself…I like you. But not like I like Jared."

"Sounds like he's a jealous guy."

"He is not. I talk to boys all the time."

"Except for the ones you like."

"Look. You don't know Jared, and you don't know me. We split a pizza. Once. That's it. I think it's better to just say good-bye."

Danielle had complete control. She had Jared. I had no one. I could irritate her. I could make her angry. I could manipulate her words. But I couldn't say anything to get her back, and the pathetic thing was, I wanted her back.

"I know I'm being mean," she bore on. "But it's better to make the break clean."

Now it was like I was some clingy pest, chasing her when she was the one who had led me on. It was as if by her nastiness, she was even taking back her kiss. It would forever be associated with this call.

"Michael. I have to go. I have a lot of homework to do."

"Yeah. Homework." It was almost funny. She wanted me to be the one to hang up, but I promised myself no matter what she said, no matter how disagreeably she said it, she would have to end the conversation.

I said, "You don't want to be unprepared for school."

"I know. Grades are important to me."

"Yeah. See you at Harvard."

"Very funny, Michael."

"It wasn't a joke."

"Just because I don't go to a fancy prep school like you where practically everyone gets into an Ivy League school doesn't mean I don't have to study." Whoa. Good one Danielle. She added, "I have a big paper due."

"Well, don't let me stop you." Then, after another long pause where no one spoke but I heard her breathing so I knew she was there, she said, "Bye," and the phone clicked and went dead like it does when a bitch has hung up on you forever.

Unless we met at Harvard.

#

At supper, I must've looked as bummed as I felt. My mother asked, "What's wrong? Are you OK?"

"I'm fine," I said, annoyed my depression showed. I tried looking happier but five minutes later my mother asked, "Are you sure you're OK?"

"Yes."

"Well, you're so quiet."

"I'm always quiet."

"No you're not," my mother said. "You haven't said a word all night."

"Well, I don't have anything to say. OK?"

My father interjected, "Don't be rude to your mother. She's just asking if you're all right."

"Sorry for living," I said.

My father sighed and my mother asked, "Do you want some dessert?"

"What is it?"

"Chocolate cream pie."

"Did you make it?" I asked, probably sounding like a spoiled brat but, I guess I am a spoiled brat.

"No. I didn't have time today."

"It's from Rebecca's," my sister said. "We bought it on the way home from school, stupid."

"You're the one who's stupid."

"Not as stupid as you, stupid."

My mother said, "Must you two constantly bicker? I'd hoped by now you'd be old enough to stop calling each other names."

My sister and I glared at my mother. She ignored our looks and said to me, "Now that you know the pedigree of the pie, do you want a piece?"

Normally, it amuses me when my mother tosses out phrases like "the pedigree of the pie," but as I was still in a bad mood, I didn't smile. However, Rebecca's is one of the best bakeries around—as good or better than home-made—so I said, "I'll have a piece."

My father corrected, "I'll have a piece, please. Whatever happened to please and thank you?"

"Dad, I'm fifteen. You're talking like I'm a baby."

"When you act like an adult, I'll talk to you like an adult."

Now, I sighed. I mean, it was enough with the age thing. But I said, "I'll have a piece, pleeeease," with just the right amount of sarcasm to tick my dad off. He remarked to my mother, "Why does he have to act like that?" I love it when he talks about me as if I'm not there.

"Let's just everyone eat," my mom said. "Who else wants pie?"

#

After supper, I listened to my iPod, flipped on my computer, and immediately got an IM from Napster.

> AstonMartinNow: (I think he wanted to use Lamborghini, except it's harder to spell.) How'd it go with Lady D?
>
> DownInDenver: Over. She left me on the highway like road kill.
>
> AstonMartinNow: Harsh. I thought she kissed you.
>
> DownInDenver: She did. She has a boyfriend.
>
> AstonMartinNow: And she kissed you. What a ho!!!!
>
> DownInDenver: Yeah
>
> AstonMartinNow: So, fuck her.
>
> Down In Denver: I wish.
>
> AstonMartinNow: Long distance relationships suck. At least, you kissed a senior. On to Melissa. She's the one. Stick it to her.
>
> DownInDenver: I wish.

#

Mr. Moorland is your classic English teacher—short and thin with not much black hair covering his head. He wears horn-rimmed glasses and has a pasty white face as if he spends most of his time indoors reading books and correcting English papers. In class, he never raises his voice or gets angry, but he does have this surprisingly dry sense of humor. Only not many kids get his jokes. They are so caught up in his mild manner and nerdy appearance they think he is always serious.

For instance, last week when we started *Sense and Sensibility*, Mr. Moorland said, "I want everyone to understand the social and historical context in which Jane Austen wrote this book. Who wants to research how much a pound (that's English money) was worth in 1811?" A couple of hands rose.

"Who wants to research the political conditions?" A couple more arms floated up.

"Who wants to tell us what the fashions were?" Naturally, some girls lifted their hands.

"OK," Mr. Moorland asked without skipping a beat, "Who wants to find out what songs were popular on the radio?" Honest-to-God, a couple of guys stuck their hands in the air. Then Mr. Moorland, completely straight-faced, said to the guys—I think it was Spence O'Neal and Conrad Stephenson—"Well, we can't have you both research the radio. Who wants TV?" At the mention of TV, their hands hesitated and Dana Foster, who considers himself a brain, shouted, "They didn't have TV!" Duh. What a genius.

Mr. Moorland's expression didn't change. "That's right. No cars. No malls. No TV. No radio. No CDs. No movies. No computers. No cell phones. No iPods. Oh, my God, how did people live?"

Well, everyone did laugh at that. But Mr. Moorland just went on in his dry manner, holding up a feather, which he said was actually a quill pen. He took out a bottle of ink and a piece of paper and made us come to his desk one by one, dip the pen in the ink, and write our names. We only have eleven kids in the class, so it didn't take long. But writing with a quill pen is tricky. You can't use too much ink or too little or push very hard or the ink splotches.

Mr. Moorland said we should appreciate every word Jane Austen wrote because at that time everyone wrote with a quill pen, and when Jane Austen wrote at night, she had to use candlelight. So her writing didn't just take intelligence, it took painstaking labor.

As Jane Austen is a woman and her two heroines are obsessed by marriage, I thought reading the book might help me gain some insight into the female mind. However, the only thing I discovered was that, in many ways, the female mind is similar to the male mind. I mean, all the Dashwood sisters think about is men. All I think about is women. But this perception did not provide me with a clue as to how best meet Melissa.

Thus, what with Danielle dumping me and me feeling more desperate than ever, post English, despite my reservations, I followed Salome's instructions and positioned myself on the rim of the Dolphin fountain, pretending I was leafing through one of my notebooks but mostly glancing at the main entrance to Merton Hall.

Kids poured out of class, and after a few minutes, just as Salome predicted, I spotted Melissa. Alone. She was half-way down the steps, partially hidden behind three tall senior basketball jocks. Katie Caulfield was nowhere in sight. Immediately, I launched myself toward the Merton sidewalk, pacing myself to arrive just as Melissa did. I kept my eyes down, not wanting our glances to meet too soon.

However, closing in, I suddenly sensed danger, as you do sometimes, and looked up, straight into the chest of the tallest of the three basketball jocks—Danny Dospenski. Before we collided, Danny grabbed me by the shoulders and shoved me out of his way.

"Watch where you're going, douche-bag," he growled and marched on.

In the life of a sophomore, it was no big deal. It wasn't as if Dospenski had shouted the words or stood around taunting me or that I didn't kind of deserve it, or that it was unusual for seniors, especially jock seniors, to call sophomores douche-bags. He might even have said the same thing to one of his friends. But in this case, as Melissa was close behind, and he said it right when I was about to greet her, it shook Salome's plan right out of me.

I stood on the sidewalk, or more precisely just off the sidewalk, where Danny Dospenski had pushed me, dazed and depressed. Kids still poured by, talking and laughing, but I only vaguely saw or heard them. I kept telling myself, tomorrow I could say "Hey" to Melissa. Tomorrow I wouldn't mess up. When it came to meeting Melissa, tomorrow was like my best friend. In the meantime, since I was standing motionless on the grass while the whole school walked by, I realized I was making more of an ass of myself than I already had. I needed to get a grip and head on over to Grosvenor.

I shifted my legs into gear and stepped back onto the sidewalk. And I guess there is a god of serendipity—that and Danny Dospenski—because just as I reached the pavement, I bumped, blam, and I do mean BLAAAAAM-MMMMM, right into Melissa.

She must've stopped to talk to someone as our meeting—uh—collision was timed perfectly.

As Melissa is a ballet dancer and in very good shape, our collision neither knocked her down nor inflicted injury. Actually, it felt kind of good. I could feel the soft mounds of her breasts as we hit. OK, I would have preferred a "Hey," to the "Ooof," we both emitted, but "ooof" got the job done. Melissa teetered about a foot from me, looking a bit tousled and startled but otherwise fine. Once she recovered, she exclaimed, "Oh, my God, are you all right?"

"Me?" I was astonished she could think our bump could've hurt me. "I'm good. You?"

"Fine."

As she was smiling, I added, "It was kinda fun. I'm ready to bump again."

Melissa blushed. A charming blush. The center of each cheek burst light pink in the shape of a star.

"What if we walk instead," she said. "We're late. Come on." Then, she reddened again. "Err...umm, you're not waiting for anyone, are you?"

I pulled in beside her. "Nahhh. Just trying to remember," I lied, "if I left my sweats in my gym locker or book locker."

Melissa nodded. "That happens to me. I've got ballet stuff everywhere."

"It's easy to forget," I said.

"For sure. Did you remember?"

"What? Oh. Oh, Nope. Doesn't matter. Plenty of time to find them. I don't run 'til three."

"Running? Like track?"

"Track's in the spring. I do cross-country."

"Oh. Fun?"

Well, I didn't want to tell her I hated it and was doing it just for the varsity letter, particularly since she was into ballet and must like athletics. Instead I replied, "It's OK. I'm pretty good at it." (True). "I don't really do it so much to win." (Also true, especially since I never win). "When I'm running, I just kind of zonk out and get into this mental state where everything slips away and it's just me and the road and the trees." (Also true but if varsity letters weren't cool, I'd drop cross-country as fast as Algebra II—that is, if I could drop Algebra II.) However, I definitely said the right thing.

"Know the feeling," Melissa gushed. "I'm that way with ballet. When it's right, when everything's together, the music just flows out of my head and my whole body feels like one big whoop of joy—incredibly light and free and natural. I just love it."

From her words, I could see Melissa's dancing was on a whole different level. My runner's high was more or less feeling numb. I said, "Ballet sounds a lot better than cross-country."

"And ballet is co-ed," Melissa giggled. "We have boys in our class."

"In tights?"

Melissa nodded.

"Are you sure they're boys?"

Melissa did not smile.

"Kidding." I said. "Just kidding."

Melissa said, "I know. Ballet scares boys. It's silly, though."

"I'm not scared."

Melissa's eyes lifted hopefully. "Have you—have you ever been to a ballet?"

"Well, my mother took me once..."

"...to *The Nutcracker*," Melissa finished, and we both laughed.

At Grosvenor, we waited in line for the doors to open, not that it was exactly a line—more like a herd of hungry kids. However, it's kind of a democratic herd given that where your spot is doesn't matter. Once the doors open you still have to wait at your table until Birdsong, the head-master, says grace.

"I guess lots of kids go to *The Nutcracker*," I said.

"Uh-huh. When did you see it?"

"A couple of years ago. My sister wanted to go, and my mother took me along."

"Was it the Boston Ballet?"

"It was at the Wang," I said.

"Then it was the Boston Ballet. I must've been in it." Although her tone tried for matter-of-fact, I could tell she was proud. I would've been proud, too. The Wang is huge. It seats like three thousand people. It must take a lot of guts, never mind talent, to be on a stage in front of that many people.

"Wow. I must've seen you. Who were you? A cute little mouse?"

Melissa shrugged, "I've been dancing since I was five. I've had lots of parts."

"I remember there were lots of mice."

"A mouse is not as fun as it looks. The costumes are hot, and they're hard to see out of."

"I wish I knew you then. That would've been cool."

"You know, I read something you wrote," Melissa said, changing the subject from her to me.

"That thing for *The Looking Glass*."

Melissa nodded. "I liked it."

"Most people thought it was weird."

"It was. But good weird," Melissa said.

The doors to the dining room opened and the pack started to move. As we were swept along, Melissa lifted her hand above the mass of bodies and waved.

#

Walking to math the next day, I felt anticipation and dread. How to greet Melissa? I did not want to act too chummy, but I didn't want to act too stand-offish. In a way, I wished I could just bump into her again. It made acting natural easy (and I loved the feeling of her breasts against my chest) but I couldn't bump into her every time we met.

Still the dread of greeting Melissa was as nothing compared to the dread of Mr. Ward making a fool of me again. It seemed much worse to appear like a dolt in front of a girl you knew than a girl you didn't. The previous night, I even spent an extra hour on my math just to give myself a fighting chance.

At the door to 483 Hampton Hall, I stopped. My eyes riveted on Melissa's seat. Empty. A relief. No pressure. No need to nod or speak. I grabbed my chair, opened my math book, and tried to look interested. What a joke.

The classroom is long and rectangular with four large windows in the back. Mr. Ward insists on keeping the windows open, even when it's freezing. He says, "Fresh air keeps students alert." He doesn't accept any objections. Even when the girls whine, he admonishes, "Wear a sweater or put on your coat."

Most classes don't have assigned seats, but Mr. Ward is one of those teachers who likes everything his way and his way is precise, organized and annoying. The first day of class, he took out a seating chart and said, "I don't care where you sit, but once you choose a seat, you sit there for the rest of the year."

Everyone looked around at everyone else. We were already seated. It was the first day, so a few kids were like Melissa. They were new and didn't know anyone. A few others were already sitting next to their friends. I was happy in the last row behind Melissa, and since there were twelve kids and twelve chairs, it would have been awkward for anyone to move. Whoever moved would have to switch with someone else, and maybe that other person didn't want to switch, so naturally, as Mr. Ward knew before he said anything, no one stirred. Then he drew up his chart and that's where we sit.

About a minute later, Melissa came in with Katie.

Katie wears glasses and is tall and somewhat frumpy and speaks mostly to other girls. She is not ugly, and if you look at her for a while, she grows on you. Maybe if she dressed better and wore cooler glasses or got contacts and was a lot less shy, she'd be hot. She seems to have a nice figure, although with all the loose clothes she wears, it's hard to tell.

As the two girls rushed in and sat down, Melissa seemed to look in every direction but mine.

What did that mean?

Melissa threw her backpack down and, as usual, I gazed at her hair which hung free. In preparation for tying it into a pony tail, she shook her head and slid her hands down her hair's length, gathering the golden strands into a bunch. Then she slipped an elastic band off her wrist and snapped it around her hair close to her head. Her fingers moved like a ballet—graceful, dexterous, and delicate. Sitting behind her, it seemed as if I'd seen her do these movements a thousand times, but I never tire of watching. After she twisted the elastic on, she reached down into her backpack and pulled out a couple of colored pencils. As she leaned over, she turned her head and glanced at me. Of course, I was staring, but instead of giving me a cold stop-staring-at-me-you-perv look, she winked. It was so unexpected, I almost laughed, a sure death warrant from Mr. Ward. I actually clamped my hand over my mouth. Melissa understood the gesture, and as she sat back upright, her shoulders shook.

Class began.

#

"Talk about money!"

That's what Tony Anderson exclaimed in English.

He'd researched the economics of *Sense and Sensibility*.

When Jane Austen wrote Mr. So-and-So or Miss Such-and-Such has a modest income of 1000 pounds, Tony calculated it was the equivalent today of $500,000! Even the Dashwoods, the main characters in the book who are supposed to be poor, live in a four-bedroom "cottage" with three servants. If the Dashwoods are poor, Tony asked, how poor are their servants?

This question propelled the class into a political discussion—aristocracies versus democracies—and we enjoyed wasting a bunch of time before Mr. Moorland brought us back to the main subject: the love life of the Dashwood sisters. Marianne is the emotional sister who has this intense, obsessive crush on this not-very-good guy, Willoughby. Elinor is the intellectual, rational sister who "admires" a guy named Edward Ferrars. She's too logical for love or passion. The girls tore into Elinor until the bell rang. Then I sped off by the fountain to wait for Melissa, my heart beating so loudly, I could dance to it.

When Melissa appeared at the top of the Merton Hall stairs, her face was not exactly blank.—I guess it was what I would call self-absorbed. She was thinking about ballet or school or whatever. Most of the classroom buildings at Noyce were built in the 1920's and the stairs were designed more for looks than for walking. The steps are too low to take one at a time and too high to take two at a time, so you kind of shuffle as you climb up or down. It's not uncommon to see kids, particularly new kids, trip, and as I watched Melissa, she forgot one step and stumbled. She recovered quickly, but for a moment she looked more like a crippled duck than a swanlike ballerina. As she caught herself, she saw me walking toward her.

"Didn't trip," were her first words.

"Didn't say you did."

"You have this mocking look."

"Whoa. No mock in these eyes. These eyes are a one hundred percent mock-free zone."

"Well," Melissa said, her two pink stars shining, "sometimes I can be a little clumsy."

"A clumsy dancer?"

"I know. I know. On stage I'm not, but in real life I drop things, bump into things..." Melissa's eyes apologized guiltily.

"Our collision was definitely my fault."

Melissa shrugged. "...And trip."

Well, here my eyebrows rose.

Melissa insisted. "This time I didn't..."

"I believe you. The stairs reached up and grabbed your ankle. They're rascally that way. And you escaped their clutches very gracefully."

"Exactly," she grinned.

"Focus," I said. "On stage you focus. At school, I guess you're more spaced. I could see it on your face when you were walking down the stairs."

"You were watching me."

Crap. Had my attempt at witty banter got me into trouble? I stammered, "I...I was sort of waiting for you when you uh–uh..."

"Tripped and nearly broke my neck," Melissa laughed.

Whew, it was OK.

"You looked very good on the recovery," I said. "I'd only deduct half a point."

"Thank God Carmen Silva didn't see me."

"Your ballet teacher?"

Melissa shook her head. "Student in ballet class."

66

However, I detected a hint of antipathy.

"You don't like her?"

"She's OK. We're the two best dancers in class," Melissa said. But behind her baby-blue eyes and sweet smile, I sensed a determination to be undisputed number one.

"Your rival?" I asked.

"Nope. We're friends."

I didn't believe her. "But deep down you hate her."

Melissa smirked. "She can be a bitch."

However, just as Melissa's ballet class was getting interesting, she held her stomach and wailed, "Ohhh, I am sooo hungry. Why do the doors take sooo long to open? I didn't eat anything this morning."

We'd reached Grovesnor and were once again waiting outside.

"I guess anorexia is not a problem."

"No. Over-sleeping is. What is that called?"

"Not going to bed early enough."

"Hmm. Needs improving in math, but I predict an 800 on your verbals."

"English is my strength. What time do you get through homework?" I asked.

"Eleven. Eleven-thirty."

"Me, too. When do you go to bed?"

"Eleven-thirty. Twelve."

"Me, too. When does the alarm ring?"

"Six-thirty," Melissa groaned. "But I always hit the snooze button."

"Twice?"

"Twice is good. Three times is awesome, but it means no breakfast."

"So now you're wide awake but hungry."

"Exactly. Which makes it worse."

Melissa whimpered a few more times, "Open the doors. Open the doors," before the pack of kids in front of us stumbled forward. As the herd surged, some of the guys started mooing.

This time as we parted, Melissa spared one of her hands from her belly and patted my shoulder.

#

In Napster's Brookline house four of us played foosball. I would have preferred if it were just Napster and Salome, so we could talk about Melissa, but Crusty Weinstein and Giddy were over. Giddy was visiting Salome—afternoons are permitted if a parent is around—but he was taking a Salome break and playing foosball with us. I don't think this made Salome happy, but that's what happens when you have a male twin. You meet a lot of your brother's friends, but they also like to hang with your brother. Salome was finishing a paper in her room, pretending not to care.

Crusty goes to Noyce—he's in my English class—and kind of a pain. I don't know how he got his nickname—I suppose I could ask him—but it fits. He never tries to get along, and by getting along, I'm not talking being some toady ass-licker. I mean, if a few guys are shooting the bull and someone says, "Curt Schilling's fastball averaged ninety-six miles per hour in his prime. "And everyone says, "No one could hit that," or "He could really burn 'em," or "Fucking Yankees still can't hit him," Crusty will say, "Not true. Schilling's fastball averaged ninety-four. Go ahead. Look it up."

I mean, give me a break. Who cares? We're just bullshitting, but Crusty loves arguments, and he annoys by more than what he says.

Crusty wears a yarmulke. All the time. He has a little gray wool one stuck to his hair with a bobby pin. He's not even religious. I mean, he tells dirty jokes, swears and chases girls. As if they're going to like him. And it's not like it's his yarmulke that drives the girls away. Noyce emphasizes tolerance and diversity. It's just that he's so irritating. To me, his yarmulke is the symbol of all the ways he aggravates. If someone else wore a yarmulke because he was like from Israel or Orthodox or something, I wouldn't mind.

You might think by these comments that in some way I'm not living up to the Noyce Tolerance and Diversity Code. Not true. I'm actually half-Jewish or maybe completely Jewish because I was bar mitzvahed. My mother's Unitarian and my dad's Jewish; however, my sister and I originally were brought up as neither. My parents did the neither thing because they're both atheists. Personally, I don't know how anyone can be an atheist. To me, that's as crazy as being a Bible-thumping Jesus freak. I mean, how can you be positive there is or isn't a God? It's much more logical to be an agnostic and accept the possibility of either.

My grandparents on my father's side are Jewish, and they were pretty upset that we weren't brought up Jewish. They might even have settled for us being brought up Unitarian. As long as we were something. But my grandparents on my mother's side didn't care. They just believed everyone should be nice, and since I am most of the time and so is my sister, they're happy. But my grandparents on my father's side—Poppy and Ticky (Don't ask me why we call my grandmother Ticky. I think it was something I said when I was like four and it stuck.) always said to my parents, "You're not Jewish. You're not Unitarian. What are you? I'll tell you what you are. You're nothings. The kids are nothings. They don't know what they are. They don't know what to believe. It's shameful." But my parents did not care because they never made us go to church or temple. Since my last name is Steinman anyone who knew it probably thought I was Jewish (if they thought about it), but it never came up in conversation. Wait. Sorry. Jewish kids occasionally asked me what Hebrew school I went to, and when I told them I didn't go to any, they'd say, "How'd you get out of that?" And I'd say, "My parents don't care." And they'd say, "Wow, are you lucky." But kids who weren't Jewish never talked about it one way or the other. They never asked me how come I didn't go to church. Maybe it wasn't important. Maybe they figured I was Jewish.

But when I was eleven and a half my grandmother, Ticky, got sick. Serious sick. When she complained about me and my sister being nothings, it was much more difficult for my parents to ignore, particularly when my grandmother was in and out of the hospital and said that it would mean so much to her if they would let me get bar mitzvahed.

This went on for a while and my grandmother, Ticky, didn't get any better. She just got worse and, finally, my parents gave in and promised they'd ask me, and if I said it was OK, they'd have me bar mitzvahed. Well, what was I going to say? My grandmother who was pretty small when she was healthy was getting smaller and smaller and tireder and tireder and spending more and more time in the hospital and at home in bed, and it was really sad looking at her with her little head lying on this big pillow and her hair all white and practically disappearing and her arms bony and thin and splotchy and purple from intravenous needles. But whenever my sister and I entered her room, she'd break into this smile so radiant you could almost believe in heaven. She'd lift her head from the pillow and offer us a piece of candy from this big glass bowl she kept by her bed. She hardly ate any herself, but when she saw us, she'd stick a shaky hand in the bowl and scoop around for a good piece and hold it out for us to take, which, of course, we did because even if we said, "No thanks," she wouldn't believe us. She'd hold out the candy until we took it and then she'd laugh and say the exact same thing she always said:—"Sweets for my sweets." So, just like with the candy, I had no choice but to get bar mitzvahed.

Getting bar mitzvahed meant taking Hebrew lessons every Sunday morning with Rabbi Wiseman, which is not as bad as it sounds. The class didn't start 'till eleven and it only went an hour and a half, and Rabbi Wiseman is a lot less obnoxious about being Jewish than Crusty Weinstein. The idea is when you turn thirteen, you are considered an "adult" member of the temple, and you read the section of the Torah—the first five books of the Bible—that is traditionally read on the Saturday nearest your birthday. So, that's what I did. The hard part is you have to read it in Hebrew, which is why the lessons.

The sad part was that my grandmother, Ticky, died a few weeks before my bar mitzvah. She never got to see it. But she did know I was studying with the rabbi, which made her happy, and my sister took some Hebrew lessons, too. On the day of my bar mitzvah, everybody felt pretty good about it, especially my grandfather, Poppy, who cried a lot. He kept wiping his tears with this big white handkerchief, which he kept in his back pant's pocket and apologizing to everyone for crying, although no one minded. We all knew how happy it would have made my grandmother. So I do not consider myself intolerant, but Crusty Weinstein still irritates the hell out of me.

While Giddy, Napster, Crusty, and I played foosball, naturally we started talking about girls. Because it was the end of September, and we had already analyzed every decent Noyce girl a dozen times, we talked about movie and TV stars, and Crusty was his old cantankerous self. I mean, right in the middle of our analysis—face, personality, intelligence, body—OK, mostly body—Crusty'd break in and pronounce in his loud, sneering voice, "Scag."

Giddy: Have you guys seen Piper Perabo? She's hot.
Napster: Piperwho?
Giddy: Piper Perabo. I saw her in *Cheaper by the Dozen*.
Napster (in disgust): Why'd you see that?
Giddy: I had to take my sister.
Giddy has a sister, Megan, a year younger than Sarah.
Giddy: Perabo is a fox. She was in that lesbo prep school movie.

Napster: Oh, yeah. I think I saw that. Who'd she kiss?

Giddy: I forget.

Napster: Doesn't matter. Girls kissing is always good.

Giddy: I bet she's intelligent, too.

Napster: Intelligent enough to be in a lesbo movie. But no tits. Stoner would like her.

Me: I saw her in *Coyote Ugly*. She is hot. She kinda reminds me of Ashley Mitchell.

Ashley Mitchell is one of Noyce's better-looking seniors.

Napster: Get off it. Ashley Mitchell looks like a partridge.

Me (thinking about it): Sort of. A cute partridge.

Crusty: Scag. Scag.

Napster (ignoring Crusty): What about Mischa Barton? She's got great tits. And she's always kissing other chicks.

Me: You mean on *O.C.*?

Napster: Yeah. They've got a lot of great chicks on that show. Rachel Bilson is on it.

Crusty: Rachel Bilson is half Jewish.

Giddy: How do you know that?

Crusty (with his usual obnoxious air): Just know.

No one challenged Crusty. Everyone figured if ol' yarmulke-head knew anything, he'd know that. (Occasionally, Crusty is called yarmulke-head, especially by me. I invented the nickname. He doesn't seem to mind. It's hard to insult Crusty.)

Napster to Crusty: So if she's half Jewish does that mean you'd fuck half of her?

Crusty: Maybe.

Napster: Which half? Top or bottom?

Crusty: The front half. You can fuck the back.

We all laughed. It was a good one, especially for Crusty.

Napster to Crusty: I'll take that offer. Just not at the same time.

Everyone laughed again, but not quite as loudly as for Crusty.

Napster went on: How about Jennifer Garner on *Alias*? She's got great tits and she kicks ass all the time.

Giddy to Napster: Why don't you just watch *Baywatch* reruns. That's the best tit show ever.

Napster: I do watch *Baywatch* reruns but *O.C.* and *Alias* are much cooler.

Crusty: Mischa Barton, scag. Jennifer Garner scag. Rachel Bilson, half scag.

Giddy to Crusty: You are out of your fucking mind. (Giddy to Napster and me.) What about Kiera Knightly? She's pretty and I bet she's intelligent.

Napster (making a gagging sound): That girl has no knockers at all. Who cares about her mind?

Me: You don't...Have any of you guys seen Brittany Snow?

Giddy: What show is she on?

Me: *American Dreams*. She's pretty.

Napster: Brittany is blonde and sort of pretty but way skinny. Stoner likes any girl who hasn't outgrown her training bra. He even likes that chick on the *Gilmore Girls*.

Giddy (to me): You watch the *Gilmore Girls*.

Me: Sarah watches the *Gilmore Girls*. I see it sometimes when she's got it on.

Giddy: Sometimes? I bet you sit there drooling.

Me: Alexis Bledel is hot.

Napster: Christ, he knows her name. Next thing, you're going to say Julia Stiles is hot.

Giddy: Julia Stiles goes to Columbia. She's smart and pretty.

Napster: Deirdre Flynn and Sandy Belcher go to Columbia. Would you sleep with them?

Deirdre Flynn and Sandy Belcher were co-editors of *The Looking Glass* and got into Columbia last year. They are both nice girls and loved my stories but no one would call them hot.

Giddy: Come on. You can't compare Julia Stiles to those two. (He thought for a moment.) You know them, don't you?

Me: (nodding).

Giddy: Text 'em and see if they know Julia Stiles.

Me: (snorting).

Giddy: They could be in the same dorm.

Me (snorting again): Yeah. And they're gonna fix you up.

Giddy: Heh, I have a girlfriend. I don't need fixing up.

Me: (Silent. I had no retort to that).

Crusty: Keira Knightly, scag. Alexis Bledel, scag. Julia Stiles, scag.

Me (angrily to Crusty): Who do you like? Who isn't a scag?

Crusty (smiling): Natalie Portman.

Giddy: Natalie Portman is hot. And she's smart. She goes to Harvard.

Napster: No tits.

Me (to Crusty): The only reason you like Natalie Portman is because she's Jewish.

Giddy: Is she?

Crusty (proudly): She was born in Israel. But I'd like her even if she weren't Jewish.

Me: You're such a yarmulke head. I bet you only beat off to Jewish girls.

Crusty (ignoring the loud laughter): I like Jewish girls.

Napster: What difference does it make if a girl's Jewish or not? Their holes are in the same places.

More laughter.

Me (to Napster): You should write an essay on that for Mr. Morgan.

Mr. Morgan teaches the Tolerance and Diversity class. This got a few snickers.

Crusty: Except Napster discriminates against girls with small tits.

Napster: You got that right.

Me: What about Elisha Cuthbert? Who can-not like Elisha Cuthbert?

Napster (agreeing): Elisha Cuthbert is the whipped cream. I could lick her all day.

Giddy: Any day. Any where.

I turned to Crusty.

Crusty: Ah, she's OK.

Me: OK? You are seriously brain damaged. Now, if her name was Elisha Cuthberg...

Even Crusty laughed.

Me: What about Margo Harshman. She's definitely growing fine. She kinda looks Jewish.

Crusty (shrugging): I know Natalie Portman. That's enough.

Giddy: Who's Margo Harshman?

Napster: Ah, you know Harshman. She was on the Disney Channel. *Even Stevens*. She was the class tease. Stoner had the hots for her when he was, like, eight.

Me (shrugging): I just saw her in this stupid movie my sister rented. She has filled out fine.

Napster looked at me skeptically.

Me: I'm telling you, you would have no trouble with her. Her body's almost as good as Elisha Cuthbert's.

Napster (looking interested): Nature does do wonderful things to little girls.

We all amened to that.

Me (trying to make everyone happy, even Crusty): How about Rachel Weisz? She's hot and I know she's Jewish.

Napster: She's got great tits. She's definitely hot.

Giddy: Is she intelligent? I can't stand dumb girls.

Me: She's English, anyway.

Giddy: So she sounds intelligent. That's almost as good.

Crusty: I don't like her as much as Natalie Portman but she is hot.

At this point, Salome entered the room: Who's hot?

Napster: Rachel Weisz.

Salome: *The Mummy* girl? You guys wish. C'mon Giddy, I've finished my report. Let's go for a walk.

Giddy (protesting): Not the Mall. Not the Mall. I'm not going to the Mall.

But he stood and followed. Salome has nice breasts, and as she led Giddy out of the room, a nice ass. And she's intelligent.

#

An hour later, Crusty headed home. I didn't. I was eager to fill Napster in on the latest news.

When I told him, Napster grew excited. "Ask her out."

"Check with Salome."

"That's what she'll say."

"Check."

"You are stubborn."

"I want it from the fish's mouth."

"Salome is good," Napster conceded.

"I wonder if her '"hey"' technique would work on Kristen St. Claire."

Napster sniggered. Kirsten St. Claire is a junior, and is generally considered the prettiest girl in school. She looks like her name implies. A tall blonde blue blood. If you've ever seen *High Noon* with Grace Kelly, that's Kristen St. Claire. She's got these perfect Anglo-Saxon features—: the clear blue eyes, the straight nose, the perfectly shaped lips that don't exactly curve up at the end or curve down but just kind of linger in the middle, projecting this cool, elusive, self-possessed equanimity. If you are lucky enough to see her smile, her teeth are naturally straight and white. No dentist would dare put braces on them. A rumor floated around school some talent agent saw her this summer and wanted her to go to Hollywood but her mother wouldn't let her. I would love to have that rumor verified, but I don't know anyone who talks to Kristen St. Claire. I don't even know if she belongs to any clubs. I just see glimpses of her walking to class. A glimpse is enough. It fills your beauty quota for the day. But the funny thing about Kristen St. Claire—even though she's so beautiful—she's hard to imagine naked. It's like trying to imagine Napster's mom naked, but for different reasons. I mean, with Napster's mom, it's hard to imagine her naked because she's Napster's mom, and while good-looking, she's old. Whenever I try to imagine her naked, which happens sometimes (sorry, my mind does it, not me), it creeps me out so much, the picture goes all blurry. I see her face, but her body's out of focus.

Kristen, of course, is seventeen, and there's nothing creepy about imagining her naked except she's just so damned perfect in this regal, I'm-way-out-of-your-league way, her picture goes equally blurry. It's like when I'm in some fancy store, I'm afraid to touch anything because it might come crashing down. That's how I feel visualizing Kristen naked. It's as if I'm afraid to touch her even with my thoughts. As if in some way I might damage her perfection. Sometimes when she's around I pump myself up and say, "—You can do it. Go ahead. Imagine." But the most I get is this glow. No details. Maybe if I got into Harvard, I could picture her naked. Maybe I could even ask her out. I mean, I'd be a Harvard guy. But for now all I want to do is break through the glow.

Napster said, "Forget Kristen. Melissa is real. She likes you. She'll go out. We can double."

"Double?"

Napster nodded. "Darlene's coming to Boston. She's staying with an aunt in Medford to check out some cosmetology school."

"What're you doing?"

"A concert in Davis Square. Darlene's aunt owns an electrolysis center there. Between Darlene's aunt and mother, they cut, wash, pluck, and die every hair on a woman's body."

However, I wasn't interested in the professional pursuits of Darlene's family. I stuck to the main topic. "Who's playing?"

"Nelly Furtado."

"Isn't she kind of out?"

"Girls like her. Darlene said it sounded fun."

"How much is it?"

"Thirty bucks."

"For two?"

"No, dummy. For one."

"Wow. Sixty bucks. That's a lot of money."

Napster shrugged. "Sometimes you gotta pay to play. My dad says that. I bet Melissa likes Nelly Furtado. Her stuff's good to dance to. She's not going to refuse. Then I can tell my parents I'm going with you."

What Napster said was true, but I was still thinking about the money. Napster could see I was hung up on the sixty bucks and coaxed me in that convincing way of his. "You've got the dough. Why else did you work all summer? Think of that lovely face, that great ass."

"I'm thinking. I'm thinking. What about keeping Darlene secret? Salome knows. Now Melissa will."

Napster hadn't considered that. He paused for a second. "Hell, I don't care. Melissa doesn't know anyone, and even if she tells the whole school, so what? It's not getting back to my parents. Besides, I'm doing this for you."

"Yeah. Right."

#

"Mr. Steinman."

I jumped. Mr. Ward was standing in the front of the classroom, glaring down at me. "Please answer the question."

Caught again.

He knew I didn't have a clue. I'd been minding my own business, admiring Melissa's pony tail, psyching myself up to ask her out on the way to lunch. Salome had texted, "Go for it," except this would be my third "accidental" fountain rendezvous in a row, and I didn't want Melissa to think I was obsessing. I was, of course, but I didn't want her to think it. I'd expected, once you met a girl, you could relax. But the closer we got, the more I worried. I guess because there was more to worry about. Only now I had to worry about Ward.

"Sir," I said. (Notice how I threw in the "Sir." As long as I had the remotest chance for a B- it was "Sir.") "Uh. Could you repeat the question?" This time I remembered.

I was hoping Ward was in a good mood because maybe his wife, who is skinny and freckled like he is and who teaches history—I got a straight A from her in the ninth grade—had blown him the night before. Except Mr. Ward was not feeling generous from the gratification of hot lips or even a hot breakfast. In fact, his beady, pink eyes had spotted something. Exposing his long, sharp teeth up to his gums like one of the evil sharks in *Finding Nemo*, he raised the ante. "If you paid more attention to me rather than Ms. Worth's hair, you would've heard the question."

At this witty remark, everyone roared. Even though I was sitting behind Melissa, I could see her cheeks flame. From the heat of my own skin, I knew my face was equally red. Ward loved it. Proud of his handiwork, he tossed his ever-present chalk high in the air and caught it. It's his classroom trick, and he's very good at it, I'll give him that. When the hilarity quieted, he pointed to Stacy Fong, one of his favorites, and asked her the question—whatever it was—I was too freaked to hear. It was all I could do to pretend to pay attention for the rest of the class. Luckily only ten minutes remained. Staring at Mr. Ward on a normal day is bad enough. After what he'd done, I thought I'd puke.

However, Mr. Ward had settled one thing. I wasn't going in for my third meeting in a row with Melissa. I wasn't asking her to the concert by the fountain or on the walk to Grovesnor or while waiting in line. I doubted whether I would talk to her that day. I needed a night to recover. I hoped one night was enough for Melissa as well. We had to buy the tickets. Napster had checked, and they were going fast.

Almost as fast as Melissa.

When the bell rang, she grabbed her backpack and accelerated out the door like a Porsche 911 GT, except without the roar and puff of smoke.

I sat in my chair as long as I could to ensure Melissa was far away. I had embarrassed her enough for one day.

As I stood, Joe Stassio came by. "Ward's an asshole, isn't he?"

Since Mr. Ward had left, it was safe to agree. "Hell, yes."

"Are you seeing Melissa?" Joe Stassio asked.

Oh, no, I groaned to myself. He said it as if he were interested in Melissa himself. Joe Stassio was not that good-looking and kind of a nerd, so I wasn't too worried. But it portended no good. Melissa was getting noticed.

"I barely know her," I said.

"Oh. I've seen you two walking together to lunch. You look like a couple."

"She's nice but—"

"OK," Joe Stassio said. "Just thought I'd ask."

#

In English class, the girls got their panties tied in a knot again. Phil Kohl observed how formal the manners were in Austen's day, which seemed an innocent enough remark except the girls thought the formality of Georgian society made it crueler. They hated how girls had to wait at home for men to call on them, practically sell themselves at dances, and then have the deal sealed with dowries.

Naturally, the guys didn't think those customs were so bad, particularly the part about the dowries.

The highlight of the discussion was a dustup between Michelle Waterson and Zip Cody, whose real name is William Cody. He claims he's a descendant of Buffalo Bill Cody, but instead of Will or Cody (nicknames he would've liked), everyone calls him Zip for—think postal—reasons. Zip is a tall, big-bellied guy, and when Michelle loudly announced, "Willoughby's a jerk," Zip labored to his feet.

"Willoughby ends up with a rich wife, a huge mansion, and a stable of horses," he sneered. "Compared to either of the Dashwood sisters, just the horses are much the better deal." At this witticism, all the guys laughed and Zip beamed. He should've quit while he was ahead, except he tried for extra suck-up points and rattled on about how important it was to own horses before there were cars and how his great-great-great uncle, Buffalo Bill, owned dozens of horses and how he, Zip, was planning on owning horses, too.

What Zip didn't realize was that Michelle Waterson was patiently waiting in ambush. When Zip bragged about all the horses he intended on buying, she sprang. "And we know what you'll name them: "Big Mac, Double Burger and Whopper." At this, everyone broke up, girls and guys. In fact, so much laughter rocked the room, even if Zip had a retort—which he didn't—no one would've heard. Like a McFlurry left in the sun too long, Zip sagged slowly back into his seat.

However, I felt much better. On the ladder of despair, it's always comforting observing someone on a lower rung.

Then it was my turn to give my report on the scientific advances in the early nineteenth century. No matter what, I'm confident in English, although my report was boring. "England was in the middle of the Industrial Revolution, yadayada. Inventions like the cotton gin and the steam engine increased production, yadayada…" Much more interesting was my Google search the night before. What with it fresh in my mind that Willoughby had knocked up a girl (thank heaven, not Marianne), it was only natural (for me, anyway) to wonder what birth control devices existed in eighteenth century England. Obviously, not very good ones, as Willoughby's little "blunder" proves.

However, googling condoms did turn up their existence. They even used condoms in ancient Egypt. Whatever you look up, it seems ancient Egyptians invented them or practiced a form of them or buried their Pharohs with them. Clearly, Egyptians were a clever bunch. When a local tribesman wanted to make the beast with two backs (we're not talking camel here), he simply wrapped the ol' wonderwanger in a bit of papyrus and pounded away. In 5000 B.C., papyrus had lots of applications:—scrolls, clothes, blowing your nose, wiping your ass, stuucking your honey. However, along with the Pharohs, the secret of the papyrus condom vanished thousands of years ago, which is probably why the birth rate in Egypt is so high. The next breakthrough—er—here I guess we should say the next advance in birth control did not occur until the 1640s in England when someone who had the eponymous (second SAT word) name of Dr. Condom created a "balloon-like shield" out of sheep guts for Charles the II. It seems Charles combined an enormous sexual appetite with an equally prodigious fear of syphilis. However, with Dr. Condom's invention, the Royal Rake could indulge his predilection for young ladies without anxiety. What Bill Clinton did for the blow job, Charles the II did for the condom. The British became regular users from the 1600s on—except, of course, for Willoughby.

It wasn't until 1839, when Charles Goodyear invented the vulcanization process, that prophylactic science bounded into the modern era. In addition to tires, gloves, washers, and inflatable boats, rubbers (but in this case, not for the feet) were mass-produced, which pretty much takes us to the present era, except for those exotic and erotic refinements of lubricated, textured and flavored condoms hanging in every CVS, supermarket and 7/11 (although it still takes balls to buy them).

Thus, sated with all things prophylactic, my deviant teen brain like Zip Cody's should have rested. However, another thought surfaced: What did girls use before Tampax? As I say, I do not try to have these thoughts. They bubble up unbidden. Unfortunately, due to my great success googling "condoms," I had no qualms investigating menstruation, and at the push of the Enter key, about a gazillion listings appeared. Many more than for condoms.

Although teachers stress the value of curiosity, let me now aver questions sometimes pop into your head to which you are better off not knowing the answers.

This was one of those times.

Probably everyone has heard the expression "on the rag," and I guess I suspected at some time in the history of mankind—well, here we definitely want to say womankind—females did use rags. And it's true. I found this site called the Museum of Menstruation (really, it's there!), which has everything I did not want to know about The Curse.

As with condoms, ancient Egyptian women—who else?—developed a form of feminine hygiene made of papyrus—what else?—but as with papyrus condoms, this secret, too, is lost, entombed, perhaps, with Nefertiti, Cleopatra, and Hatshepsut in the lower left hand corner drawer of their pyramid powder rooms. Thus, in medieval times, women did use rags, and at discovering this amusing revelation, I should have congratulated myself and hit the EXIT button. But oblivious to what lay ahead, I thought I could uncover more humorous oddities to amuse Napster and the guys, only the oddity I discovered wasn't so amusing. I scrolled down the page and read— in Germany in the eighteenth century, women didn't use rags. They didn't even wear underwear. They dripped blood on the floor!

Aaaaarrrrrggghhhhhh!

That's what it says. They dripped blood on the floor!

The barfometer in my brain went off and I pictured women of various ages and sizes, strolling around Berlin, trailing blood in streets, sidewalks, stores, classrooms, kitchens, dining rooms, living rooms and bedrooms.

If this picture makes you gag as well, sorry. But this is what happens in a stream of consciousness novel. You never know where your consciousness is going to stream.

Thankfully my menses research did not lessen my desire to ask Melissa to the concert. Teen hormones saw me through, as well as the knowledge, accumulated from way too many TV ads of pretty, smiling, young women playing tennis, swimming, and horseback riding, that today we have three levels of absorbencies for those light and heavy days, plus a complete array of outdoor fresh aromas.

#

Crossing the campus to lunch, I couldn't help but notice it was one of those perfect fall afternoons:—the sun blazed and blustered, a proud, solitary figure, while under a cloud-wispy blue sky, the wind gusted with just enough briskness to make you breathe deeply but not enough to make you shiver. The skirts of the girls (the few girls who were wearing skirts) fluttered and flapped as they headed toward Grosvenor. And despite my travails with math, I couldn't help but admire how beautiful the school was. The large and imposing brick and stone buildings set among the green manicured lawns bespoke of wealth, tradition, privilege, and power. Maybe, I thought, when I was older, I would look back at the school with something akin to fondness. But just at that moment, Zip Cody appeared, head bent, shoulders stooped, arms hanging slackly by his sides, lurching morosely toward lunch.

I matched my pace to stay behind him. He was so large, even all slumped in on himself, he made for good cover. Ahead of Cody, Melissa and Katie strolled toward Govesnor, but as long as I stayed behind Zip, I was out of sight. Only I forgot—on Wednesdays Emma posts next week's lunch seating arrangements, so students mob around Grosvenor's bulletin board like fans around a Red Sox scalper with play off tickets. The teachers don't have to look. They stay at the same table. Naturally, this makes some tables better to eat at than others, and as kids find their table assignments, groans of dismay and yips of glee cut through the air with as much intensity as if it were final grades.

I had completely forgotten this weekly ritual, and when I entered the hall, off to one side stood Melissa and Katie, waiting for the throng to thin, a good strategy, if you can endure the suspense. But what it meant was that as soon as I entered the hall, our eyes did a quick tango and the red stars in Melissa's cheeks lit. Still, I got a raise of her hand and had no choice but to walk over.

As I approached, my own cheeks burned, but Melissa's had already returned to normal color which I hoped meant she was mostly over Ward's joke.

"I forgot new tables are today," I said.

"I hate new tables. As soon as you get used to one, you have to switch."

"Well, you get to meet a lot of new kids."

Melissa shook her head in exasperation. "My table this week is practically all freshmen."

"Well, maybe next week it'll be better," I said, hoping it wouldn't. I would've hated her sitting at a table of all seniors. Mentally, I wished, maybe it'll be a table of all girls.

After a pause, Melissa said, "Mr. Ward is such a creep."

I was glad she brought the subject up since it was floating between us like some kind of embarrassing body odor.

"Creep doesn't begin to cover it." I said, the color deepening on my face.

I mean, Melissa was clearly with me on this, but her sympathy made me feel once more like the class buffoon, which hurt even more since I *was* the class buffoon. I glanced over at the bulletin board. A good-sized crowd pressed around it. Maybe I wasn't a brain with the x's and y's, but I could do the chivalrous thing and get Melissa and Katie their table assignments.

"I'm going in for my table." I eyed Melissa and Katie. "I can look for yours." Quickly, the girls nodded. It was all the encouragement I needed. Like a knight on a white charger, I wheeled off. For some reason, although

Emma posts four lists, the crowd is always thickest around the two in the middle. My strategy is simple—attack from the flank and edge in, keeping as close to the wall as possible. As usual, my strategy worked. With a minimum of pushing, squeezing, and elbowing, I established a forward position near the right-side list, and using my height to full advantage, I peered over the heads of three freshmen and two junior girls.

Spying the crucial info, I beat a hasty retreat.

"Kind of a mixed bag," I announced.

"Uh-oh." I didn't want to keep Melissa and Katie dangling. That wouldn't earn me any maidenly tokens of appreciation, so I said right off, "Melissa, you've got Miss Nye's table." Miss Nye teaches French and Spanish. She is a recent Wellesley graduate and everyone likes her. I sat at her table at the beginning of the year, and she told lots of funny stories about college. She's into the same music we are, and best of all, she doesn't make anyone talk French or Spanish at lunch. Some of the language teachers do that, particularly if you are in their class. It is a tremendous pain. At lunch, you want to relax. But with Miss Nye, there's no "Me podrias pasar la sal, por favor" crap.

Katie's table was the bad news. I couldn't help grinning as I told her, "You're at Birdsong's."

"Oh my God, no!"

At her friend's disaster, Melissa hooted loudly. It was hard not to. It isn't as if Birdsong is a bad guy but he is the headmaster and way old, and the school often has guests—ancient grads or local politicians or wealthy donors—for lunch. This means, if you are one of the ill-fated four at Birdsong's table, you have to be polite and up on Noyce dining etiquette, which consists of one hundred and eight rules written down by Helen T. Pritchard, the headmaster's wife about six headmasters ago. The cover of the rule book is blue, so it's called the Blue Book. It's given to every new student and includes sentences like Rule 28: "After stirring his tea, the well-mannered Noyce student places his spoon on the saucer directly behind his tea cup. He never places his spoon on the table." Or Rule 52: "The proper Noyce student cuts his toast into four quarters and then applies butter and jam to each quarter as the quarter is eaten." Even though the book was written by a woman, all the examples are "he." In 1898, grammar had not succumbed to political correctness, and the school was all male, anyway.

Mrs. McDonough, the head of the English Department, is modernizing the book, and the "sexist" language is being changed. However, the new edition has yet to come out.

When you sit at Birdsong's table, you have to obey the rules, and if you fail to pass the salt with the pepper or forget to slice, and then butter and jam your toast, Mr. Birdsong clears his throat like a baby lamb and gently admonishes, "Chip or Mopsy or Avery"—or whatever your name is—Mr. Birdsong knows everyone's first name. It's one of his headmaster tricks—"perhaps it would be best if you reread your Blue Book. It includes a clear explanation of (whatever you did wrong). I know these rules may seem archaic, but a superior education is not just Chaucer and Euclid. At Noyce, we prepare our students how to behave as ladies and gentlemen in whatever situation that may arise. Civility is not the foundation of society, but it is the framework which upholds it." It is the very earnestness with which Birdsong delivers lectures like these that makes them so unbearable. I mean, you have to reread the damn Blue Book just so you won't disappoint him. That was what was so funny. Except Katie didn't appreciate the humor.

I had meant to do her a favor. Instead, I was the bearer of bad news. I've found we all have these pools of associations in our minds. Since I was horning in on Katie's relationship with Melissa, her best friend, I was already in the pool of things Katie didn't like, and now I'd added another negative—a week at Birdsong's. It wasn't my fault, but it didn't matter. This was Katie's pool, and I was up to my neck in it.

Somewhat tensely Katie asked, "Whose table are you at?"

"Mr. Parker's." Parker was a science teacher, a bland sort of guy in his sixties. He had taught at the school for, like, forever and was placidly waiting for retirement. Sitting at his table was neither good nor bad.

Melissa didn't help much. She grabbed Katie's arm on the way into the dining room and grinned at me over her shoulder. "Don't worry, Katie," she said. "If you've lost your Blue Book, I'll lend you mine."

#

Around seven, Napster called.

"Whazzup?" he asked. "I saw you huddled with Melissa before lunch."

"Yeah," I sighed.

"Don't sound so happy. It makes me nervous. Does this mean you didn't ask?"

"I had a setback in math."

"You always have setbacks in math."

I hadn't told Napster what happened. I explained what Mr. Ward did. I described how everyone in the class laughed and how red Melissa's face turned. It didn't faze Napster. It didn't happen to him. He said, "The two of you looked pretty cozy in Grosvenor."

"I don't know."

"Believe me. Moonlight was shining in Melissa's eyes every time she looked at you."

"Ward's joke made me out like some kind of perv."

"You are a perv."

"But not a perv perv. A normal perv."

"I couldn't have said it better. Ward is a jerk-off. Just go for it. I got the tickets."

"You what?"

"I bought the tickets. I had to. They were nearly sold out."

"What if Melissa doesn't want to go."

"No problemo. Darlene's got a cousin in Boston you can go with."

"Another fix-up! I don't want to spend sixty bucks on a fix-up. You haven't seen her, have you?"

"No. If you don't want to go, I'll get Crusty."

"Crusty!" I exclaimed. "He's not going to go with a cousin of Darlene's. She's not Jewish. Everyone's a scag to him except Natalie Portman and Rachel Weisz. Oh, and the front half of Rachel Bilson."

"Except they're fantasies. Darlene's cousin is real."

"Crusty will never spend sixty bucks on a cousin of Darlene's."

"He's loaded."

"Even if he does, which I doubt, what is Darlene's cousin going to make of Crusty's yarmulke?"

"She's seen yarmulkes before."

"Sure. On the Pope. Does the Pope hold his on with a bobby pin?"

Napster groaned in aggravation. "If Crusty doesn't want to go, Salome and Giddy will. I can tell my parents Salome and I are going to the concert."

"Like they'll believe that."

"It doesn't matter. You're going to go. Melissa'll come through. Just say the words. Make me proud."

#

The next day in math, Melissa's hair shimmered in front of me like a waterfall. Whenever she moved her head, my usual obsession of sticking my hand in and feeling the golden strands splash over my fingers gripped me. But I knew better. If Ward caught me fixating on Melissa's hair and made another wisecrack, I would never have the guts to ask Melissa anywhere. Ever.

I needed something to occupy my mind. Gazing around, I noticed Dory Binkley, whose seat is technically to the left of mine. I say "technically" because Dory keeps his chair off in the corner behind Billy O'Connor, who's on the J.V. soccer team. Billy is another big guy, and Dory situates his chair behind Billy to remain as much out of Mr. Ward's sight as he can. Every day when Dory arrives, he shifts his chair directly behind Billy, an initiative I admire. Mr. Ward not only lets him get away with this, Ward has yet to call on him. Dory must either get incredibly good or incredibly bad grades. Since he never says anything in class, I can't be sure. However, Dory goes to Noyce, so he must have some brains.

Still, today Dory was up to something.

I mentioned earlier how Mr. Ward keeps the windows open because he thinks it'll keep us awake and maybe we'll pay more attention. (Well, it's cold and I am awake, but I am not paying attention.) Since it's October, it's not unusual for one or two big, black summer flies to come looping into the room, particularly because the screens have plenty of holes. You know how the cold affects summer flies. The longer they last into the fall, the slower and lazier they become.

As I observed Dory, one of those big, stupid summer flies meandered in. Now, Dory is kind of a slow guy himself. Not a fat guy, but a guy who looks likes finding a comfortable place to sit is a high priority. He always has a stolid expression on his face like a slab of meat. Even when he laughs, which is rare, not much animation enters. But as the large, lazy fly loafed toward him, Dory's hand shot out like the paw of a bear, fishing for salmon. In one motion, Dory caught the fly, shook it a couple of times, and threw it down on his desk. The fly bounced like an eraser and lay on its back, its legs in the air as if dead. Employing the point of his pen, Dory tested the fly, pushing it around on his desk and flipping the fly over on its legs.

Then, like a master surgeon, Dory operated. Grabbing the fly's wings with the thumb and index finger of each hand, he yanked. No agonized, shrill fly scream reached my ears. Its body did not even twitch. None the less at the amputation, I flinched. But like driving by an accident, I couldn't prevent myself from staring.

The fly wasn't dead. After a few moments, it recovered its tiny fly consciousness and wandered around Dory's desk like an ant. Dory seemed pleased. As he played with the fly, he didn't hurt it anymore. He just nudged it here and there to prevent it from crawling off his desk. Maybe if Dory had gotten distracted, the fly could have snuck down the side of the chair and escaped, but one thing was for sure, the fly was not flying anywhere.

I sort of hoped Mr. Ward would call on Dory. Normally, I wouldn't wish this on anyone—even a bitch like Danielle—but Dory, I felt, deserved it. It would give the fly a chance to get away, and I was rooting for the fly. True, the fly wasn't going to last much longer. This was October, and the first frost would kill it, but if I were a fly I would prefer to die in the cold with my wings attached than wingless on Dory's desk. And Arab terrorists complain about their treatment at Guantanamo. I'd like Dory to do some guard duty and see who complains.

The bell rang.

I avoided a last look at Dory's desk.

But I did hear the slam of his math book.

#

After English, I waited at my usual post by the fountain until Melissa strolled by in the lemony sweater and tan slacks she had on that day.

I strolled over. "How was History?"

"Good. English?"

"Fine. Hungry?"

"Famished."

I knew I had to ask right away before we hit Grosvenor and got bunched up in the herd and kids could overhear or maybe Katie came by or (more likely) I totally lost my nerve.

As my insides lightninged and thundered, I uttered, "Doing anything exciting this weekend?"

"Nah. The usual. Ballet, homework; homework, ballet. Pretty dull."

Exactly what I'd hoped. The perfect lead in. "I've got an idea."

It took a second for my words to register, but when they did, Melissa's eyes widened. "What?"

Now that I was committed, the invitation flowed. "Want to go to a concert?"

Melissa stopped and turned toward me. "A concert?"

"Yep."

"When?"

"Saturday."

"Who's playing?"

"Nelly Furtado."

"Really?"

"Yes."

"Where?"

"Davis Square."

"Really?"

"Uh-huh."

"Where's Davis Square?"

"Two T-stops after Harvard Square."

"Really?"

"You're saying 'really?' an awful lot."

Expertly, Melissa kicked a pebble with her toe. It skipped across the green Noyce quad. "I say 'really' a lot when I'm...when I'm...well, it's a bad habit I get into sometimes."

"Doesn't matter. So, Napster's got these tickets...."

"Who's he going with?"

"No one you know. Not from around here." I felt I had to pin her down. "Want to?"

"Um. Sure. Yeah. Cool. But I'll have to see if it's OK."

My heart turned gold. "When will you know?"

"Um-uh... tomorrow? Is that OK?"

"Sure."

"What time does it start?"

"Eight."

"Really? Ooops, sorry."

It suddenly seemed very quiet.

We both gazed around and saw we were standing in the middle of the quad, far from Grosvenor. Everyone else was gone.

We glanced at each other and dashed for the door.

#

Wednesday I walked to math fast enough to get there first. That's how eager I was—except coming early is for kids who know all the answers, or who want to suck up. When I reached the doorway and observed Mr. Ward standing with his back to an empty classroom, erasing the blackboard, I realized my mistake. Only before I could slink away, Mr. Ward's sixth sense for torturing kids kicked in and he noticed me. For a moment, his mouth opened in surprise more like a goldfish than a shark, and his tongue flicked back and forth like a tail fin as he groped for what to say.

Recovering quickly, he began, "Mr. Steinman, what an unexpected pleasure to see you early. Is this a sign you're taking math more seriously?"

What could I say? If I said, "Yes," he'd know it was a lie and give him an excuse to prove it by calling on me more. If I said, "no," it was a straight out insult and reason for him never to give me a break on anything—a test or my grades—so I did my own open-mouthed imitation of a goldfish and stood gasping and gurgling. Ward's thin lips morphed into his usual evil, shark-toothed grin, and he said, "Why don't you grab that eraser and finish up the blackboard."

"No, no, no," I wanted to protest. "I have to be in my seat when Melissa comes in so she can tell me her answer, not standing up front like a brown-nosing asshole." But out loud I said, "Yes sir," and grabbed an eraser.

By the time I finished, everyone was in class, including Melissa. As I walked past her, she gazed at me with her beautiful golden-brown eyebrows arched quizzically. I tried shooting her a meaningful glance, but can you really say, "I got here early to see you and was roped into cleaning the blackboard," with your eyes. The worst part was as I took my seat, I had no idea whether the concert was on or off, and I had to wait until class ended to find out. Mr. Ward is not the kind of teacher you pass notes on or whisper when you think he's not looking. Mr. Ward is the kind of teacher who grabs the note and reads it out loud or makes you stand up and say what you were whispering. And since Mr. Ward had already made that wise-ass comment when I was minding my own business, admiring Melissa's hair, I wasn't about to give him a real reason to say or do anything. I waited, feigning attention until, after about a billion years, the bell rang.

At the first clang, Melissa swiveled around. "I can go."

Now, it was my turn. "Really?" I squeaked.

"Yes," Melissa laughed. "Really."

More calmly and I hope more deeply, I replied, "Sweet."

#

Melissa lives at One Eighty-Eight Beacon Street in Boston. An easy subway ride (who would've thought my love life and the MBTA would be so inextricably combined?).

Except one catch marred the prospect of our otherwise perfect evening. Although Melissa tried to be blasé about it, Cinderella had to be home thirty minutes before the clock struck midnight, or as far as any future dates were concerned, I had as much chance as a pumpkin. But I could live with that. I am not a rebel. I am not a bad boy. I just wanted to have a good time and as much sex as possible, which, considering that I was taking Melissa to and from the concert by subway, would not be much, which I'm sure was exactly what Melissa's parents had in mind. But it was our first date and nice guys (which I am) respect girls.

The question is—do girls respect nice guys?

On TV, even Miss Sweetness incarnate, Rory on the *Gilmore Girls*, dumps Dean, her nice guy boyfriend, for Jess, this total bad-boy loser. Jess is completely messed up, treats her like crap, and is destined to spend his life as a garage mechanic or in jail.

Or Wynona Ryder in *Reality Bites*. She has a choice between Ben Stiller, a nice guy who's making tons of dough and is totally in love with her or Ethan Hawke, who can't make a dime, is a musician in a loser rock band and who drops out of college a month before graduation, a sure sign of self-destructive, loser behavior. So, who does Wynona choose? Ethan Hawke, of course.

In *Ten Things I Hate About You*, Julia Stiles falls for Heath Ledger, who looks about thirty and acts about twelve. Another total loser, yet what else—Julia loves him.

Or consider Jane Austen, that Most Esteemed and Supreme Lady of English Literature. She knows what turns girls on. It's Willoughby, the cad, not Colonel Brandon, the nice guy. OK. Marianne eventually marries Colonel Brandon, but, if in 1811 they printed posters, whose portrait would every proper English girl order her maid to affix to her bedroom wall? Willoughby's, of course. He hangs in the hall of fame of literary "bad boys" right beside Heathcliff, Rochester, and Darcy.

What goes on in girls' brains that makes them like bad boys? OK. If you're a girl, you're screaming, it's not my brain, stupid. I get that. But nice guys can be hot. I mean, guys like girls who are hot, but guys don't like total loser bitches. OK, guys do like total loser bitches, if they're hot enough, but they prefer sweet girls. So why do girls prefer guys who bully them, want to have lots of unsafe sex, and then disappear? What is it about the female psyche that finds this kind of relationship alluring?

You'd think whatever it is, I could be bad just to tap into it. You'd think I could make a date with Melissa and not show up or bring her home late or act moody and distant the whole evening. Then, she'd fall all over me. But I can't, even if it helps getting laid, which it does because loser bad guys get laid a lot more than anyone else. Only the idea of dropping out of Noyce a month before I receive my diploma is just too far beyond even my most mutinous thinking (besides which my parents would kill me). Yet last year, Doug Harrison, a total loser senior, stole a final exam out of Mr. Walcott's desk. I mean, he didn't just look at the questions. He actually stole the exam, so Mr. Walcott would know it was gone. And rather than throwing the exam away, he kept it in his locker where a teacher could find it. I mean, talk about asking to get expelled. (He didn't even wait until a month before school ended; he stole the exam right before Christmas.) He ended up getting a GED degree, and I hear he's going to some obscure college in Iowa. But why? Why did he do this? He was parading around school with some scary hot babes, and I remember thinking, he's going to miss out on all those girls. But I guess he doesn't care. He gets babes wherever.

In *Heathers*, Wynona Ryder goes around the school "caf" with a clip-board asking The Question of the Day: "You win five million dollars from Publishers Clearing House, but on the day Ed McMahon gives you the check, aliens land on earth and say they're blowing up the world in two days. What do you do?"

It's a funny scene. One I've always liked. So I decided to investigate the female psyche and ask my own Question of the Day. I made it simple and straight to the point. "Why do girls like bad boys?" But I didn't ask during lunch A: because teachers sit at all the tables and you can't go around with a clipboard asking stupid questions, and B: if I ended up making an ass of myself, I didn't want to do it at school. Like a dog, I had enough sense not to crap in my own yard.

I went to the mall, and whenever I observed girls I didn't know but thought I could speak to without getting scorned, scoffed, ridiculed, humiliated, arrested, or otherwise shat upon, I asked. Although I found it hard to say hello to Melissa at school, I had no trouble talking to strange mall girls. I think the clipboard helped, and that I wasn't trying to meet them. I'd approach a bunch of girls—they were always in bunches, like grapes—and as I walked up, they'd stare suspiciously. When I stopped, they'd cross their arms and look me up and down as if to say, "This'd better be good." But when I asked my question, mostly they giggled. Of course, giggling is not an explanation. I'd have to urge, "Does anyone have an answer?" and almost always at that point, one of the girl's cell phones would ring, and she'd drop out of the circle. Another girl would want to know why I was asking, and I'd tell them I was writing a book. Another girl would ask, "What's the name of the book?" I'd say, *Outside the Edges*. (I have the title already.) The girls would consider. One girl would say, "I like it," or "That's not bad," which made me think maybe the book has a chance. And finally, one of the bolder girls would answer while her friends listened and nodded. Sometimes I'd get two answers from one group. Usually one. Of course, I only asked groups with at least one pretty girl, and sometimes I'd get a good conversation going, particularly if the girls went to private school or if they knew someone at Noyce or if one of the girls had seen *Heathers* and got the connection. Then I'd say to myself, you fool, find out their IMs, get their cell phone numbers. But at that, I froze.

As long as I was doing the survey, I was loosey goosey, but as soon as a hint of ulterior motive entered my brain, my throat locked. What if they refused? What if they got snobby and said, "We'd rather not." What if they laughed? One girl laughing at you is bad enough. But three or four? And the mall has such long, straight corridors (way, way longer than the stairs at the WindStar).

So I stuck to my Question of the Day, and what made it easier was knowing that Saturday night I was going to the concert with Melissa. A girlfriend. Sort of. Almost.

**Why do girls like "bad boys?"**

Alison, junior at Wellesley High: Bad boys are more fun. Good boys are boring.

Megan, sophomore at Newton High: Bad boys are dark and moody and seem more sensitive.

Ashley, junior at Dana Hall: A lot of girls have this attitude like they can save the bad boy. They think their love can change the guy. As if. But, hey, it's fun trying.

Katrina, freshman at B.U.: It's an emotional obsession. Girls get addicted to the swings, depending on how they think the guy feels about them.

Julie, senior at Weston High: Bad boys are a challenge. They're like a status symbol. Nice boys are too easy.

Marissa, senior at Wayland High School: Nice boys are too possessive. When you're with a bad boy, you can be bad, too.

Emily, freshman at Wellesley: Bad boys are arrogant, which translates into confidence, and that's attractive to girls.

Lisa, junior at Buckingham Browne and Nichols: Bad boys are exciting. Which is prettier: a wild stallion or a tame horse?

I asked a lot more girls, but it didn't take long before the answers got repetitive. The girls kept saying the same things in slightly different ways. But what became clear was that girls don't look for anything they say they look for in a guy. They don't look for intelligence or a sense of humor. They don't look for a good listener or someone who'll like them for themselves. Bad boys are not known for any of these qualities. Still, I did get to talk to a lot of cute girls, and even if I didn't get any of their last names, in some hazy, vague way, I left the mall with a sense of having glimpsed deep into the female psyche, which was kind of like peering through a thick tropical jungle tangled with sinuous green vines sprouting heart-shaped leaves with pungent pastel petalled flowers until off in the distance like a dream drifted this vast languorous river with seemingly no boundaries, nothing to hold onto and no sense of where it turned or where it was going; yet somehow, it flowed through this lush, primordial world. It was maddening how foreign, shadowy, and capricious the river was, particularly when I felt how fiercely girls attracted and how profoundly its dark, undulant mystery lay at the core of their allure.

#

Simple.

Take the streetcar to Melissa's. Meet Melissa's parents. Say as little as possible, as politely as possible. Exit with Melissa. Watch the concert. No need to talk much as the music will be loud. Head back to Melissa's apartment and—if I am going to be a wild stallion—kiss Melissa no matter what. Who cares if she turns her head. Who cares if she pushes me away. Well, I did care. I guess it's all my mother's fault. She raised me to be a nice, polite, trail horse, and girls want wild stallions. And my mother is a girl. At least, she was a girl once. What was she thinking?

I told myself, don't gnaw on this. Our date was still a week away, but how could I not, particularly in math with Melissa sitting in front of me.

The current fly population in the class didn't provide any distraction, either. It was really cold, and no flies buzzed in. Dory sat in his chair, leaning back, staring off into space. So little of interest was going on in class, sometimes, I listened to Mr. Ward. That's how bad it was.

Talking to Napster, I didn't mention any kissing concerns. It was too *Princess Diaries*. When we discussed the concert, we went over logistics. Napster wanted to meet at the electrolysis center.

"Which just happens to be near the Somerville Theater."

"It's the other way around. The Somerville Theater just happens to be near the electrolysis center. If the Somerville Theater weren't in Davis Square, we'd do something else."

I got the idea. "So it's all about four walls and a couch."

"Any port in a storm."

"But kind of creepy. Are you and Darlene making out midst the plucked chin and mustache hair?"

"Don't forget the pubes."

"Gross."

"Not as gross as girls who have hair sticking out of their bikinis. I hate that."

I agreed. "Are any of Darlene's aunts gynecologists?"

"She hasn't mentioned it." Napster sounded disappointed. But he rallied. "You know Crusty's mother is a gynecologist. Her office is on the side of his house."

"Have you seen it?"

"Once. When I stayed over."

"You stayed over Crusty's?"

"Crusty's not so bad."

"If you like arguing. What was it like?"

"His house?"

"Duh. The office."

"Cool. The examination table had stirrups and everything. Crusty is so lucky."

"I don't think Crusty gets to look. Anyway, I bet Crusty's mom only sees orthodox women. They probably wear yarmulkes on their muffs."

"You have a fixation with Crusty's yarmulke. Get over it."

"I would but it's always there."

"Just you and Melissa meet us at the electrolysis center. Darlene says it doesn't smell as bad as a beauty parlor. Boy, do they stink. Darlene says the waiting room's like a doctor's office. You and Melissa can join us if you want. That's why I want you to meet us there. It'll give Melissa the idea."

"She has to be back by eleven-thirty. By the time the concert's over, we'll just make it to her house."

"Leave early. That's what Darlene and I are doing. She's supposed to be at her cousin's by twelve."

"You know Darlene. You've already made out with her."

"Leave early," Napster repeated. "That's what a bad boy would do."

I had told Napster about my Question of the Day. He liked it. He thought of himself as a bad boy, and I guess, in his own way, he was.

#

At home all I mentioned was that Napster and I were going to a concert, but immediately my mother's ears perked up. "Where is it?"

"Somerville."

"At the Somerville Theater?"

"I think. Yeah."

"They still have concerts?"

"I guess. We're going."

"In college your father and I saw some good groups there."

I know my parents were young once, but do they have to remind me? Thinking of them going on a date to the same theater was freaky. It was like once when I was looking for the remote for my parent's bedroom TV, I checked my dad's night table drawer and saw an open box of lambskin condoms. Yuck! Of course, I thought about stealing one, as it would be a lot easier than buying one, except what if my dad noticed and asked me about it? Aaaaargh!!!??? So, I left them all in the box. —I hoped, at least, my mother's familiarity with the Somerville Theater would make her less likely to raise objections. And she didn't. After her brief detour down memory lane, she reverted back to normal mother mode and asked, "When are you planning to be back?"

"Twelve-thirty." My usual time.

"Don't be late. The last streetcars leave Boston at twelve."

Actually, on Saturdays, they run until twelve-thirty, but no sense in prolonging the discussion. "OK," I said.

"What kind of concert is it?" my mother asked.

"A folk-pop kind."

"I didn't know you liked folk."

At this point, my sister, who was eavesdropping from the couch in the den, piped up. "He doesn't. Who are you going to see?"

"Nelly Furtado," I shouted, but as soon as the name left my lips, I knew I should've kept my mouth shut because my sister exclaimed, "You and Napster are going to see Nelly Furtado. Since when?"

"Since now."

My mother's antenna immediately shot higher. She turned to me. "You and Stephen are going to see Nelly Furtado?"

I sneered, "You don't even know who Nelly Furtado is."

As Sarah skulked into the kitchen, she blurted, "Girls like Nelly Furtado. Michael doesn't have a single Nelly Furtado CD."

Now, I figured the direction my mother's cross examination would take was whether Napster and I were really going to the concert. Instead my mother surprised me. She stayed outwardly calm, but just below the surface her voiced trilled with excitement. "Are you and Stephen taking girls?"

I was stunned. I didn't say anything, but my face betrayed me with a blush as bright as a clown's nose.

"You are, aren't you," my mother burbled. "That's so sweet. Who are you taking?"

My mother had guessed too much to lie my way out, so I tried revealing as little as possible. For myself as well as Napster. I knew he wanted to keep Darlene secret, and I didn't want my mother telling Mrs. Belknap anything. They don't talk much but one has to be careful.

"It's not a date. We're going with a bunch of kids."

However, once roused, my mother wouldn't stop. She seemed to love the idea of me going with a girl. She said, "But some of the kids will be girls."

"Yes."

My mother inquired, "And is one of those girls a special girl?" The way my mother said, "special girl" made me almost sick. Her voice got sappy and motherly and proud all at the same time.

My face changed to red again. Mentally, I noted I must proceed cautiously with anything relating to Melissa. I obviously was very sensitive about her, making it even harder to lie.

"Well, who is this special girl?" my mother went on, taking my blush for confirmation.

"Mom, will you quit this 'special' business. There is no 'special girl.'"

My mother sailed right on. "Oh, I think there is."

"Cut it out, Mom."

At my pained growl, my mother eased up. Sort of. "OK. Let's forget the 'special.' Is there one girl you're more interested in than the others?"

"Mom, that's the exact same thing."

"No, it isn't."

"Yes, it is. Just forget it, will you?"

My mother's tone got hurt. "You mean you don't think enough of me to tell me who it is."

"God," I said, writhing on the rack of her inquisition. "Why are you making such a big deal?"

"All right," my mother said, "I won't make a big deal. I understand it's just a bunch of kids." Still, she wouldn't let it go. "Just tell me—who do you like a little more than the other girls? I'm curious." Curious! Yeah, the way the CIA is "curious" about Al Queda. "You can tell your mother."

God, she was a pain. It was probably a mistake. I mean, I really hated confirming or saying anything. But she wasn't giving up, and I guess I was so proud, not just that I was going out, but that I was going out with Melissa, her name finally burst from me, "It's Melissa Worth. Satisfied?"

"Melissa Worth." My mother pronounced her name as if it were a movie star's. "And she goes to Noyce?"

"Yes."

"A sophomore?"

"Mom, you're making this into a big deal again."

"Just tell me where you're going to meet her."

This was a trick question. I had said a bunch of kids were going, which implied I wasn't picking her up, but my mother again got the better of me. Without thinking, I said, "She lives on Beacon Street in Boston between Exeter and Dartmouth." I mentioned it because I knew she wouldn't mind my going to that address. But it also revealed that if I were meeting Melissa at her house, she was more "special" than I'd admitted. Indeed as soon as I conceded I was meeting Melissa, she responded, "So, you're picking her up."

"God, Mom, someone has to get her. It's at night."

"Good. So you volunteered. I'm glad you're being such a gentleman."

"That's me. The gentleman."

"Well, that's a very nice area," my mother said, concluding her examination. "It sounds like it'll be a fun place to see." Like Mrs. Belknap, my mother's into antiques and houses and how they're decorated.

But Sarah didn't stop. She chirped, "Mikey's going on a date. Mikey's going on a date. I can't believe it. My brother's taking a girl to a Nelly Furtado concert. You must *reeeally* like her."

However, having extracted the information she wanted, my mother took my side. She said sharply, "Sarah, leave your brother alone." And for the rest of the week, Sarah pretty much did. My whole family left me alone. Except occasionally Sarah would stare at me and giggle.

On Saturday, I once more became the center of attention. When I went to the kitchen to eat an early supper, my sister got very quiet and watched the proceedings with this awed expression.—I mean, I am her older brother, and despite her mocking and pestering, I know deep down she kind of worships me. Even funnier, she came into my room later and acted as if she was a woman of the world who could give me advice. She said stuff like, "I looked up Nelly Furtado on the Internet. If you need something to talk about, you can say she's from Victoria, Canada, and played the ukulele and trombone in high school." Or, "If you kiss her, don't stick your tongue in her mouth right away. You might gross her out."

I shooed her away like a fly. Where was Dory when you needed him?

When I went downstairs to leave, I could feel my mom's appraising gaze. I knew she wanted me to turn around like I was trying on a suit at Louis, not that I was wearing anything close to a suit. I was just wearing a sweater and a pair of pants. OK, the sweater and pants were nicer than what I normally wear to school, but not by much. However, even without seeing the clothes from the back, my mother nodded approvingly and said, "Very sharp." I wanted to go back to my room and put on an old pair of jeans.

My father wandered by and actually asked me in this man-to-man tone, "Do you need any extra cash?" I mean it wasn't as if we were going to the prom. It was really embarrassing.

Eventually, I escaped the house. My sister, my father, and my mother saw me off at the door, waving like I was an explorer going to the North Pole. I left without looking back. The sight was so damned mortifying.

#

The Back Bay of Boston where Melissa lives was developed in the late 1800s and most of the apartment buildings rise four or five stories with an air of genteel elegance. The sidewalks are lined with ornate black wrought-iron fences, small gardens, and red brick facades with intricate gray stone carvings that trim the antique doors and windows. In a way, the area reminds me of the Noyce School in that it was built with old money and looks it.

One Eighty-Eight Beacon Street where Melissa lives is easy to spot. It's newer—it was built in the 1960s—and is much taller:—fourteen stories. But if the building lacks the quiet, dignified air of old money, the people in it enjoy the benefits new money brings, which I suppose is just as good.

As I neared the building (and the prospect of meeting Melissa's parents), my internal organs tried to escape down the street screaming, but they were stuck like I was. It wasn't as if I could call Melissa and ask her to meet me in the lobby. Resolutely, I turned into her front walk and entered the brick and glass foyer. I searched the directory for Melissa's last name. It wasn't a long list. Even though the building is fourteen stories high, each unit is on its own floor. Fourteen stories, fourteen names. Melissa's unit occupied the ninth floor. I rang the buzzer. After a few seconds, a woman's voice asked, "Who is it?"

It didn't sound like a maid. Immediately, I assumed my model young-man tone. "Michael Steinman."

"Michael," the voice said, "come right up."

The door buzzed and I entered. I marched past a pair of large abstract paintings dappled with different-size drops of crimson, gold, and azure. A third, larger painting displayed two green, gold, and brown chains criss-crossing a shiny black background. I didn't pause to admire the art. I was only interested in Melissa. I jumped straight into the elevator, which wasn't very big. Eight people would rub shoulders. But the elevator didn't have to be big. Just very select. I mean, when I got to Melissa's floor, the elevator opened right into her front door. I could reach out and ring the bell. Before I did, a woman's face peered through a small window in the door. It was a forty-year-old woman's face with light brown hair perfectly coifed as if she were ready to go out. It was the face of a woman who in high school was really good-looking—blue-blooded good-looking like Kristen St. Claire. If she were at Noyce, I don't think we ever would've been friends. Her forehead was high, her nose, la-di-da elegant, and her eyes, which were pretty, quick, and gray, were very good at sizing you up. Wherever she went, I'm sure she hung out with the school royalty, vacationing summers in Newport or Martha's Vineyard or the Hamptons where she played tennis, rode, and sailed. Her face was the face of a woman who went to Vassar, Sarah Lawrence, or Wellesley and who interned at *The New Yorker* or the Guggenheim. Maybe she no longer painted or wrote poetry, but she definitely belonged to a few museum boards. Body-wise, she had a decent rack—too blue blooded to have an enormous rack. That would be in poor taste. As she let me in, her quick, gray eyes gave me the once over. I felt like a starving artist, applying for a grant. Even though her voice was polite and gracious, her gaze did not reveal whether my application was viewed favorably.

"Your coat," she said, taking it and hanging it up in the hall closet. "Come into the living room. Melissa is almost ready. Would you like a Coke or anything?"

Mrs. Worth wore a simple black dress with the obligatory string of pearls. In Mrs. Worth's case, they were real pearls as were the matching earrings. I was once in the car when my mother clued my sister in on how to tell. I guess it's something every girl needs to know. What my mother said was real pearls have this deep ivory sheen and aren't quite round, just like the ones Mrs. Worth had on.

To the offer of a Coke, naturally I said, "No, thank you, Mrs. Worth."

"Well, have a seat." She escorted me into the living room. "Mr. Worth is just finishing up a call."

As I couldn't think of what to say in response to that, I didn't say anything. I sat down gingerly in a stiff armchair. Then, I had an idea. "This is a great apartment."

"Thank you. We've been here a while, but we still consider it a work in progress."

When my mother drags my sister and me to the Museum of Fine Arts, my mom oohs and aahs over the antique furniture collection. She would have been quite happy in Mrs. Worth's living room. Although the building was from the 60s, Mrs. Worth's furniture looked like it had been made during the revolution. The armchairs were stern and straight and constructed of dark, highly polished maple with flat green embroidered seats. The couch matched the armchairs and looked equally hard and austere. No one could have gotten comfortable in this furniture since it was made, like, two hundred years ago.

In the middle of the wall across from me stood a colonial-style fireplace framed by slabs of black marble and grooved white wooden columns. Mrs. Worth had too much taste to have fake logs and a gas flame, but I don't think a real fire had ever burned in it. Across the top was a white wooden mantle on which rested a simple silver-framed picture of Melissa wearing a pink ballet costume. Hanging over the mantelpiece was a very detailed painting—a landscape of the Charles River as it must've looked a hundred years ago. But if you wanted, you could see the river in its present state by glimpsing out the large picture window. On either side of the window were two more green armchairs. Next to the living room was a formal dining room with a long polished mahogany dinner table surrounded by six mahogany chairs. Over the table hung a very simple silver chandelier, which might have once held a dozen candles but which now was wired with small flame-shaped lights.

Sucking up, I said, "Everything is really beautiful."

Mrs. Worth laughed a pleased, throaty laugh. "Thank you. If you had come a few weeks ago you might not have thought so. We had this rug put in"— her eyes tilted downward—"and the place was a mess. But we're slowly getting back to order."

I looked at the thick, gold, wool rug. Unlike everything else in the apartment, it actually appeared cozy. It made me want to take my shoes off and slide my feet back and forth or lie down and roll around on it naked with Melissa. I hoped the sudden gleam in my eyes didn't reveal what I was thinking.

"The rug is great," I said. "The color is perfect." I was trying to mimic things my mother might've said. I thought I was doing well as Mrs. Worth simpered.

After we discussed the rug, Mrs. Worth began a new tack. "So you're a friend from Melissa's school."

"Yes." I was about to add we were in the same math class, but I didn't want to plant anything about math in Melissa's mom's mind, so I said kind of lamely, "We know each other from lunch mostly."

Mrs. Worth said, "Melissa tells me you're a very good writer. She liked a story you wrote for the school magazine."

I perked up. Maybe I would get that grant after all. Although usually I never mention it, I said, "I'm an associate editor of *The Looking Glass.*"

"That's the name of the school magazine?"

I nodded.

Mrs. Worth said, "I'd love to get a copy."

"The school mails out a copy of each issue to all the parents."

"I must have missed it."

So much for my grant.

Suddenly, Mr. Worth entered. His hand stuck out toward me. He was wearing navy blue suit pants with red pinstripes and a white oxford shirt. His wing-tip shoes were dark brown, as was his belt, which had a thin gold buckle. His socks were navy blue. The only indication he wasn't still in the office was that he didn't have on a tie. If you were going to make an ad for a guy to trust your money with, Mr. Worth was the guy. He was tall with sandy, gray-flecked hair and a gaze of calm intelligence. If I had to guess I would've said Yale and Harvard B-school, or maybe in modest undertones, New Haven and Cambridge.

For a moment, hope flashed that Mr. and Mrs. Worth were not only going out but staying out late and we could ignore Melissa's eleven-thirty curfew. However, Mr. Worth crushed that. He sat on the antique couch as if he didn't really want to and said to his wife. "We need to leave right away if we're going to be back by ten-thirty." Despite his hurry, he turned to me. "I understand you go to Noyce."

Ignoring that I had already answered the question for his wife, I said, "Yes, sir."

"I noticed on the school's donor list there's a Dr. Leonard Steinman. Is that your dad?"

I flushed. "Yeah. But my dad's not a doctor doctor. It's an engineering degree. He's a software engineer." My dad was really aggravated when I showed him the brochure and he saw that Noyce had added a Dr. before his name. Whoever put the donor list together must have added it to make his name look more prestigious or something. My dad grumbled that people would think he told them to put his name in that way. You know, really phony. But my mother said, "Oh, honey, just forget about it. The school's an academic institution. Naturally, they're going to put in everyone's academic degrees."

"Well," my dad growled, "they should have put Ph.D.," but he stopped complaining. My mother's very good at keeping everyone calm, particularly at the dinner table. Maybe it's because everyone's hungry and wondering what she's got for dessert. Anyway, once I affirmed Dr. Leonard Steinman was my dad, Mr. Worth seemed to relax. He smiled as if welcoming a junior member into the firm. "Your father has a very good reputation in Boston." Again, not knowing what to reply, I didn't say anything. After a pause, Mr. Worth added. "I understand you and Melissa are going to a concert."

"Yes."

Thank God, I heard a door open, and Mr. Worth turned his head. Loudly, he announced, "Well, look who's ready."

From the hall, Melissa cried indignantly, "Daaad," and like a fairy-tale princess swept into the room, only she wasn't wearing a gown and glass slippers. Melissa was dressed in a soft lilac sweater that stopped just above her low rise, stretch denim jeans. Between the sweater and her jeans, a thin crescent-like curve of flat pink belly peeked out. Because of the school dress code, I had never seen even an inch of her stomach, but the inch I saw now took my breath away. Melissa walked over to her father, and he put his arm around her. After a second, Melissa glided out of his grasp and grinned—at me.

"Hey."

"Hey."

My heart did a few cartwheels at how pretty she looked. Her hair was straighter and silkier than I'd ever seen it, her eyes seemed brighter, and on her lips she had this pink glossy lipstick that made them appear as if they existed for two purposes: smiling and kissing. I had seen them smile.

I wanted to feel them kiss. Then, I caught myself. Her parents were still in the room while I was drooling over their daughter. Could they read my mind? Would they really let me walk out the door with her?

They did.

Mr. and Mrs. Worth got up from their chairs, and Mrs. Worth said, "The two of you better get on your way. You don't want to be late for the concert."

"No, sir," I said. "I mean, no Mrs. Worth."

Melissa snickered, but Mr. Worth forged straight ahead. "You know how to get there?"

"Yes sir. The Red Line goes straight to Davis Square."

Mr. Worth nodded. "And you're walking to Park Street?"

"Yes sir."

"Well, don't walk through the park. Stick to Beacon."

"Yes sir."

Mr. Worth added, "And you know Melissa has to be back by eleven-thirty?"

"Dad, enough," Melissa groaned. "We've got to go," and her eyes swiveled to her mom for help.

Mrs. Worth got the message. "I'm sure the two of you will do just fine. Melissa, you've got your cell?"

Melissa nodded, and Mrs. Worth ushered us to the elevator door. She pushed the button and the elevator rose. Mrs. Worth gave me my jacket and handed Melissa her coat. I opened the elevator door, and Melissa and I stepped in. Mrs. Worth gave us a quick, "Have fun," before waving as the elevator door swung shut. Melissa did not wave back. Instead, she pressed the button for the first floor.

As we descended, Melissa breathed a sigh of relief. "My parents didn't act ridiculous, did they?"

"No. But your dad volunteered to drive us."

"Oh, my God," Melissa said. "I'll kill him."

"Only kidding," I laughed. "They were OK."

Melissa looked up at me, her eyes full of concern. "I was afraid my dad might give you a hard time. You know the first job he had was teaching math. He told me he loved calling on kids who didn't raise their hands."

I felt my jaw drop.

Melissa giggled. As the elevator stopped in the lobby, she said, "Got you back. My dad's always worked in banks."

I exclaimed, "Why you…" and reached out to grab her but she dodged, exiting the elevator, giggling.

#

What with the historic brick and brownstone apartments on one side and the pond and the gardens on the other, the walk from Melissa's building to Park Street is very scenic. A crowd was out and everyone seemed caught in the weekend buzz. It sweetened the air like spring. Most Saturday nights, I've spent with Napster and maybe a few other guys. It's fun, but you can't enjoy a Saturday night to its fullest with guys. But this Saturday night, I was with Melissa. I was one of the lucky ones. We were part of the scene.

"So what's with you and ballet?" I asked.

"What do you mean?"

"The story. Everything. Right from the beginning. When did you start?"

"I was five, I had lots of energy and I was driving my mother crazy. We lived in a house, and I used to make obstacle courses with boxes and furniture. I'd run up and down the halls, jumping over them. When I saw the Olympics on TV, I told my mom I wanted to be a gymnast, but she couldn't stand the idea of me in a gym, so she hauled me to the ballet and that was it. I loved it."

"What about now? You're there every afternoon, aren't you?"

"Yep. I'm in Level 5i." Melissa said.

"Which means?"

"Well, 7i is the highest. It kind of goes by age. Level 7i is for the seventeen and eighteen year olds who are graduating high school. The 'i' is for intensity. It's for those who are really serious about ballet and want to join a company."

"Right after high school."

"That's when most kids get in, if they're lucky."

"You don't want to go to college?"

"It's not that I don't want to go to college. I'm going to apply and all. It's just that if I get into a company, I'm going to dance and do college later."

"Doesn't anybody go to college and then join a company?"

"A few. But ballet careers aren't very long. If I can dance with a company when I graduate, I want to dance."

The determination in Melissa's voice was unmistakable.

At Park Station, we descended the stairs to the Red Line. It's a level below the Green Line and you just keep on walking down. The Red Line runs under the Charles River and connects Boston to Cambridge.

"You're at the ballet every day after school for hours," I said.

"It's *Nutcracker* time."

"Who are you this year?"

"A bon-bon."

"Sounds delicious," I grinned, but Melissa replied, "A bon-bon is a good role. I know it sounds stupid."

"Not stupid. Cute."

Melissa grimaced. "Whatever. Most kid's roles have very little dancing. The bon-bons dance. I mean, I love to dance, even in class, but in front of three thousand people, it's such a rush."

"I hate standing up in front of a class with ten kids," I said, thinking Melissa is definitely not your ordinary high school girl.

"I hate standing up in class, too," Melissa replied. "But on stage it's different. With the lights, you don't see anyone. The audience is all dark. It's like walking on the beach on a foggy night. You hear the waves. You know they're there, but you don't really see them. On stage it's like that. You sense the audience. Feel them. But you're in your own world. Separate."

With all the Worth's money, I wondered where Melissa did her beach walking. I knew it must be somewhere good. I was hoping it wasn't too far. "Where do you go summers?" I asked.

"What?"

"The beach. Summers. Where? What beach?"

"Oh right. We go to Nantucket. Where do you go?" she asked, as if everyone goes somewhere.

"Centerville."

"On the Cape?"

"Yeah."

"Nice. We're only a ferry ride apart."

"A long ferry ride. Four hours," I said, thinking of the last time I'd been to Nantucket.

"Take the High Speed," Melissa said. "That's what we do. It's only an hour."

"True," I said, musing that the high speed cost seventy bucks. The ferry's only twenty. Girlfriends are not only worrisome—they're expensive. But as I thought about seeing Melissa on the beach in a tiny bikini, I figured maybe I could ask for a raise at the Windstar. However, Melissa was already back to ballet. She said, "Would you…would you come to a performance?"

"To see you dance. When?"

"*Nutcracker* starts right before Thanksgiving."

"Cool. I'm in."

Melissa got excited. "You mean you'll really come? You're not just saying that?"

"Why wouldn't I? I told you I went once with my sister. But that was before I knew you."

"How old's your sister?"

"Eleven."

"My brother's nineteen. He's at Brown."

"What's he studying?"

Melissa made a face. "Sanskrit."

"Sanskrit!"

"You know, from ancient India."

"I know what Sanskrit is," I said. "I just can't believe anyone would study it. I mean, studying Sanskrit makes Latin seem practical."

"I know," Melissa said. "It drives my dad crazy. My brother's heavy into Eastern religion."

"But I bet daddy loves his ballerina princess."

Melissa nodded. "My dad thinks I'm going to dance for a few years and then go to college and be a banker."

"I wonder who gave him that idea."

Melissa smirked. "Nothing's wrong with banking."

"Yeah. You can sit around a boardroom with a bunch of bankers—in a tutu."

Melissa retorted, "Soooo not funny. I'll wear a business suit…"

"With a tiara."

Melissa's lips fought to maintain a firm line but lost the battle and crumpled into a grin. "Don't we just looooove the comedy."

"Next time my dad wants to discuss my future, I'll invite you."

Everyone in the subway was staring. People in subways are usually pretty grim, which somehow made our talking and laughing more special. It was as if we were in our own romantic comedy and had reached the "Falling in Love" sequence. You know the one—there's no dialogue but lots of syrupy music and shots of the happy couple playing in the park, riding a Ferris wheel, feeding the ducks, laughing in the subway... Until reality intruded itself.—I'd been so engrossed in talking to Melissa, I'd forgotten to keep track of the stops. Had we passed Harvard Square? Was Davis Square next? Or had we gone by both, in which case we'd have to get out, wait for another train, and go back, turning our rom/com into a Three Stooges short with me as Larry, Curley, *and* Moe.

I peered through the train window. Steel girders flashed by. A light glowed ahead. It grew larger and brighter. With a whoosh, the train rocked into the station. As the airbrakes hissed and the wheels squealed, signs rolled by—Davis Square—Davis Square—Davis Square. Whew. I'd snapped to just in time. Melissa had no clue how close to calamity we'd come.

I stood as if I knew what I was doing and grabbed Melissa's hand. "Our stop."

The train doors opened and Melissa jumped up and let me lead her off.

When the train doors closed, I realized we were still holding hands. What was I supposed to do? I didn't want to drop her hand like a bag of beans or hold on like I was too clingy. Between the two, I preferred holding on, so I did. Melissa didn't let go, either.

We followed the crowd to an escalator. The upward angle of the escalator was steep, as if we were rising out of a mineshaft, and instinctively we both grabbed for the railing. It broke our hands apart, but it was natural.

At street level, we walked the two blocks to the electrolysis center. It was in a small brick building with a glass door, which led to the center on the second floor. Darlene had explained to Napster they locate the centers in out-of-the-way spots like second floors, so the hairy women clients won't feel embarrassed.

I pressed the buzzer, and after a pause (just long enough for Napster and Darlene to uncouple), Napster's voice wobbled out of the speaker. "Hey, Stoner. Hey Meliss. C'mon up."

"Why don't you guys come down," I shouted. "It's almost time for the concert."

"You gotta see this place," Napster's voice urged.

"We'll be late."

"Concerts never start on time."

I turned to Melissa. She shrugged.

At the top of the stairs, Napster opened the door to the Yes, You Can Electrolysis Center. He and Darlene stood next to each other like a married couple. Napster's introduction went, "Darlene, Melissa. Melissa, Darlene."

The girls smiled and nodded. I wondered what Melissa thought of Darlene. I didn't care what Darlene thought of Melissa.

Napster's hand swept around. "This place is so bad."

My eyes followed his gesture. The first thing I noticed were two imitation black leather couches. Both the couches seemed new and clean except that the padding didn't spring back instantly. One of the couches still had indents from Napster's and Darlene's bodies. Besides the couches, the room included a couple of imitation black leather armchairs, a coffee table piled with lady's magazines, and a thin, industrial-strength, dark-brown rug. On the walls were "before" and "after" pictures, but I did not examine them because I did not want to see pictures of hairy women "before" or "after."

Napster loved the place. He spoke as if he were conducting a tour. "Wanna see where the clipping and shearing takes place?"

"It's not a pet shop," Darlene said. "The hair is removed with needles."

Napster gazed from me to Melissa. We both shook our heads no.

"Squeamish, eh?"

"C'mon, Stephen," Darlene said. "Your friends don't want to see the back room. We're gonna be late."

I wanted to high-five Darlene and shout, "Right on," but I just said, "Yeah, let's go."

"OK. OK," Napster agreed. "But this place is ripe. Look at that."

On the wall, printed in large, red serif letters, was the company slogan: "Hair today—Gone tomorrow." Beneath was a table covered with brochures and a small stack of business cards.

On our way out, Napster commented, "I grabbed a card to give to Ellen Spanini."

I spluttered. Ellen Spanini is a junior with black hair and a very noticeable moustache. Every time you see her, you think, why doesn't her best friend or her mother tell her? But as long as I've been at school, she's had it. I mean most of the freshmen guys don't have moustaches as heavy as hers. Melissa's only been at Noyce two months, but when our eyes met, she spluttered, too. Obviously, she knew Ellen. We couldn't help glancing at Napster, and when we did, the three of us broke up. Darlene, who couldn't have known Ellen Spanini but who nonetheless got the joke, broke up with us.

Napster is a guilty pleasure. I hate to encourage him but he always makes me laugh.

#

The Somerville Theater looked like Grosvenor Hall before the dining room doors opened—a lot of kids milling about and no one too concerned about missing anything. I couldn't believe how many kids had tattoos, dreadlocks, and pierced facial and body parts. A few girls at school have tattoos on their backs right above their butts—you get to see those mostly during sports—or small tattoos on their upper arms or ankles, but they're to look cool, not freaky. And no one's allowed to have "exotic" hair styles or facial piercings.

Birdsong drove the school piercing policy home my freshman year. During morning assembly, he stepped to the podium wearing this tan floppy fishing hat with the brim pulled down and covered with fish hooks shaped like flies. Birdsong wore it without mentioning it or acting as if anything were unusual. But just before dismissing us, he took the hat off and pointed to one of the hooks. "This is a Black Gnat. I caught a wiley brown with it in the Black River in Wyoming." Pointing to another hook, he said, "This is a Royal Wolf. It caught a five-pound rainbow trout in '78' in Colorado. Now this one here," he said, aiming a gnarled finger at a strange black-and-yellow thingie," is a zug bug. I love the name zug bug, don't you? In '85' in the Florida Keys, this darn zugbug hooked a seven-pound tarpon. I am very proud of that fish." During this speech, I thought along with the other new kids that Birdsong had lost it and by the end of the day we'd have a new headmaster. But then Birdsong's eyes snapped into focus and he stared at everyone seemingly one by one. "These hooks look great on this hat," he said, holding it high, "but I never want to see anyone's face looking like this hat." It drew a big laugh, and I realized Birdsong wasn't the headmaster for twenty years for nothing.

However, at the beginning of winter term, a small puncture penetrated the previously impervious Noyce piercing policy. Puja Narayana turned up on campus, wearing a diamond in her nose. Puja had visited India with her family and returned with the diamond and you could tell it caused a stir, particularly among the girls because, like I said, Birdsong was adamant about facial piercings. Rings were in your ears or on your fingers or you were out. But here was Puja, as American as Abigail Adams—I mean, she was born in Boston—waltzing around campus with this diamond in her nose and no one, not even Birdsong, had the balls to say anything about it. As she is Hindu and diamonds in the nose are religious or something, the school was caught in this dilemma: cultural and religious tolerance vs. no facial piercings. The administration couldn't decide which way to go, so they didn't go anywhere. They kept their mouths shut. But all the girls kept eyeing that diamond in Puja's nose, and while on the one hand, they didn't like that she was getting away with something they weren't, on the other hand, they loved that Puja was putting one over on the school.

After about three days—that was all the time it took—two more Indian girls, Uma Kumar and Amika Amaruddha, got their noses pierced. Then Brooke Kaiser broke the cultural and religious barrier and showed up with a diamond in her nose. Brooke is very pretty, although in an arty kind of way, and she has at least one tattoo on her ankle and probably others in places I can't see but would like to. When she got her own nose diamond and no one said anything,—well, I wouldn't say the dam burst, —but three more girls got their noses pierced, so I guess unofficially, it's now accepted.

Puja got a real social boost out of it. She's running for class secretary, which normally she never would have because she is a quiet sort of kid. And the odds are she's going to win, which is no big deal, but it came about because her brother, who is a freshman at MIT, dared her, which shows you how fickle Fate is—since it always occurs in the future, it doesn't give a damn what happens in the present.

However, compared to the theater crowd around us, Puja's nose diamond was as nothing. People's faces looked as if they'd been targets in a dart game, and their bodies reminded me of my wildest paisley ties. And this is describing the visible. I shuddered to think what existed beneath their clothes. This was the funkiest, punkiest, krunkiest group of people I'd ever seen. The Disneyland of skin. I mean, like the anti-Donald, Mickey, Goofy and Tinkerbelle parading down Main Street, only their costumes didn't come off.

Napster, Darlene, Melissa, and I stood around, trying to act blasé, but we were gawking like five years olds. Even Napster was intimidated. I could tell because he wasn't making wisecracks.

In the lobby, an usher, albeit a bearded one in a torn jersey and jeans, took our tickets. He nodded toward the orchestra for Napster and Darlene, while Melissa and I got thumbed toward the balcony. Due to our buying the tickets late, we couldn't get four seats in a row. I let Napster take the orchestra to make it easier for him to sneak out with Darlene. I was happy with Melissa in the balcony.

As the theater was small, even the balcony was close to the stage, which was littered with mikes, amps, wires, guitars, and drum kits.

When we sat down, Melissa snapped open her program as if she were in a new class. The opening act was eastmountainsouth, a group with a guy and a girl singer and a few backup musicians.

Melissa leaned toward me. "Ever heard of these guys?"

"Nope. You?"

She shook her head. "They look seriously folk."

"I can do folk," I said. "My father listens to Dylan."

"My mom listens to classical. My dad doesn't listen to music at all. Can you imagine? In the car, no radio. No CDs. Nothing. Once when my dad drove me to the Berkshires to this ballet performance at Jacob's Pillow, I forgot my iPod and I had to sit for, like, the whole trip in silence. Out and back! Ninety minutes each way! We didn't talk or anything. My dad said he likes to listen to the silence. He's soooo bizarre."

"Maybe that's where your brother inherited his Buddhist tendencies— your dad's silence bit."

"Oh, my God!!! You are soooo right. Mystery solved. I can't wait to tell my mom. My dad always blames her."

At this point, a pudgy, middle-aged guy wandered onstage and started tapping a mike.

"Is this on? Is this on?" he repeated until the sound guy upped the AMP and the pudgy guy's voice boomed so loudly accompanied by various electronic squeaks and whistles, a few girls in the audience screeched and covered their ears. The sound guy turned down the mike and the pudgy announcer guy started counting "One, two, three, one, two, three," until the volume reached the correct level. Since it was the Somerville Theatre, which seems to pride itself on the abnorm, the announcer guy wasn't a slick DJ from MAGIC, WBCN or KISS. He was this dorky guy with a weak chin and thinning brown hair who grew it long enough on one side to comb it over to the other. What do these guys say when they go to a barber? "Give me the dumb comb over that everyone will mock me for when I'm not around."

Once the volume was set, the announcer guy started in on his patter. "Thank you all for coming. I know you're eager to hear Nelly Furtado. She's gonna treat us to some wonderful new tunes and some favorites you all know. Nelly told me how much she loves Boston and how excited she is to be in this beautiful, historic theater" (I thought of my parents), "but before she's out, we've got this great new group—eastmountainsouth. I listened to them rehearse, and I can tell you, they're the real deal. Tight harmonies and a whiskey-smooth, blue-grass sound. So let's give it up for eastmountainsouth."

The announcer guy switched the mike to his left hand and put his right hand to his ear, waiting for the roar that never materialized. "C'mon. Show me how much noise you can make."

Nothing.

I felt embarrassed for the guy, but the lack of audience reaction didn't faze him. Maybe he'd been president of the audio-visual club in middle school and was used to being ignored. Gathering himself up, in his best announcer voice, he enthused, "Hey, Boston. Put your hands together and let them hear you back stage. Straight from the Blue Ridge Mountains to you—EAST—MOUNTAIN—SOUTH."

Out of pity for the guy and politeness to the group, the audience roused up some applause from somewhere. I guess the lesson is, as an adult it doesn't matter how much of a dweeb you are. You can still get a good job.

Eastmountainsouth consisted of four backup instrumentalists and the guy and girl singers who both played guitar. Everyone wore jeans and t-shirts except for the girl who wore jeans and a fancy loose-fitting blouse decorated with brown, blue, and pink swirls. Some of the guys had beards; some didn't.

The guy singer didn't have a beard, but his hair was long—long enough to tie into a pony tail and he was good-looking. Better looking than the girl, which was a disappointment to me, but maybe more girls than guys buy CDs and the band had thought this through.

The band picked up their instruments, and without any preliminaries—no tuning or talking—began. The girl, who did most of the singing, had one of those pretty, nasally twangs that, even if you don't like folk or country, is hard to resist. Her voice floated and wheeled like a bird over a meadow. You never knew exactly where it was going to swoop or turn, but listening, you couldn't help but soar along. At the end of the first song, Melissa turned to me and mouthed, "She's good!" I nodded.

You could almost hear the click as we connected. I mean, if Melissa had hated the group or if I had, it definitely would have caused the first glitch in our relationship. We would've sat next to each other like two computer parts that didn't fit. Once in a while, it might be fun to not agree and it's definitely fun to like someone who introduces you to new things, like Melissa with her dancing, but I was glad on our first date our eyes matched messages.

#

Forty-five minutes later, eastmountainsouth ended, bowing off to pretty strong applause. Our chubby emcee returned and yammered on about all the fabulous music the evening held in store after intermission when Nelly Furtado would appear, but before he was finished most of the audience, including Melissa and I, were on our way to the lobby.

Napster and Darlene stood in the snack line, holding hands. However, as soon as we met, Darlene ducked off with Melissa to the bathroom. The ballerina and the cosmetologist. I wondered what secrets they'd share. For a moment, the hope arose maybe Darlene would tell Melissa about the big make out session planned in the electrolysis center. Maybe, as in a stupid teen movie, Darlene'd dare her to join. Except it seems to happen a lot more in movies than in real life. At least in my life.

I mean, where is the sexual revolution when you want it? I keep reading articles about all these fourteen-year-old girls who give guys blow jobs at parties. All you have to do is jump in a closet, and before you can say, "Please," a girl has her mouth clamped over your dick. Uh-huh. Right. At my friends' houses, their closets only contain clothes.

I mean, if some girls in the ninth grade were giving oral sex, I'd hear about it. Hell, I hear about it if some girl lets a guy squeeze her tits. OK. Occasionally, a rumor appears about some girl who's supposed to have done it with some guy at a party, and maybe it's true and maybe it isn't, but it's not a revolution. It's not a wave. It's not even a ripple. For sure, it isn't closets full of girls with their mouths open. If only those closet stores my mother frequents stocked that option. "Yes, Mrs. Steinman, you can get the sweater bins, the cube organizer, and the stack baskets. And for your son's room, we have a new closet enhancer just in: the multi-function fourteen-year-old girl with glossy peach-flavored lips and optimal head motion in any position. Reversible, adjustable, and available in two models—with or without braces—free standing or wall-mounted. She's the storage accessory every boy needs."

By this time, Napster and I had arrived at the front of the line, and we both ordered popcorn. I asked if he liked eastmountainsouth. He said, "Darlene liked them. That's all that counts." Napster had his own revolution, and it wasn't about the music.

Around the corner, I observed the girls coming up the stairs. They were smiling and chatting, and I tried to see from Melissa's expression if Darlene had clued her in about leaving early. However, Melissa's face looked as fresh and innocent as it always did. Maybe fresher and more innocent since she'd obviously just done something to it. But whatever she and Darlene were talking about, they were talking about it fast and furious. It seemed like all it took for girls to become friends was one pee.

It was an unfortunate thought for me to greet them on. As the girls approached, the first thing Melissa did was reach out for some popcorn. Automatically, I tilted the container toward her. She grabbed a few kernels, and I couldn't help thinking, I hope she washed her hands.

Why is my mind like this, Lord? Why?

#

"Three minutes," the bearded usher yelled.

The four of us headed to our seats. As Melissa and I started up the stairs, my glance caught Napster and Darlene disappearing into the orchestra. My buddy put his arm around Darlene's waist, and for a second his left hand dropped lower and he actually squeezed (or maybe patted) Darlene's ass.

I must admit, from a cosmic perspective, considering the life span of the entire universe, my buddy squeezing (or patting) his girlfriend's ass is no big deal. Guys have been squeezing (or patting) their girlfriends' asses for thousands and thousands of years. But seeing the guy I've played Cowboys and Indians with, Battleships with, joined Little League with, and fought numerous Grand Theft Auto battles with reach out and squeeze (or pat) his girlfriend's ass, it kind of shook me. We had attained a new level, or, at least, Napster had, and what impressed me most was that he did it with such aplomb, as if he did it every day. Darlene seemed to take it the same way. She just tucked herself in beside Napster and let him pat (or squeeze) her ass some more.

As the theater lights darkened, the chubby emcee trotted back onto the stage. He was breathless in anticipation. He was introducing the star of the night. He gripped the mike and began, "It's a great pleasure." but during intermission, the sound guy had turned off the mike. The emcee started tapping it again and, suddenly, it blared on and the emcee jumped. Everyone in the theater laughed, but even the laughter didn't bother the guy. He'd been a nerd longer than I'd been alive. I forget all the adulation he packed into his introduction, but when it was over, he stayed around long enough to clasp the lovely, gracious, and talented Nelly Furtado's hand before leaving her with her band—all nine members.

Nelly Furtado paced center stage in a white jersey with gold spangles and white jeans, and just from the nervous electric energy pulsing from her, you knew she was going to be good. When she turned and smiled, she scattered sunshine all the way to the balcony. Before she was a few bars into her first song, everyone loved her.

She sang "Turn off the Light" from her first album, and even though you probably know the song, unless you've heard Nelly Furtado do it live, you haven't really heard it.

She pranced from side to side, singing and showing off her moves. Melissa focused on her as intently as if she were leading ballet class. But in the middle of her fourth song, a strange thing happened. A few people in the orchestra stood and shuffled their way to the aisles. Next thing you know, they're dancing. A few more rose. Soon it was a whole bunch. Then, it's people in the balcony. Just as I realized where this was going, Melissa turned to me and cried, "Let's."

When you're drowning, your whole life is supposed to flash in front of you. At Melissa's cry, my entire life didn't whiz by, but my dance life did. From dance class in gym in the third grade to the moment last year at the Spring Fling Bring Your Own Bling when I finally got the courage to ask Lucinda Lowery to dance. Unbeknownst to me, Lucinda considers herself this super fabulous dancer, so when we got on the floor, she took one look at my flailing limbs and actually backed off a couple of steps and danced as if she were alone. If that weren't enough, when a girlfriend of hers, Candy Berg, walked by, she grabbed Candy's hand and danced with her. Suddenly, it was as if I were dancing by myself. Lucinda didn't even glance my way. After a few seconds, I slunk off the dance floor. I mean, at Noyce some people do dance by themselves, but I'm not one of them.

I don't blame Candy Berg. She's a nice kid and attended the same Hebrew classes I did with Rabbi Wiseman. She probably didn't even realize I was dancing with Lucinda. But as I walked off the floor, I remember thinking, "Wow, have I been shot down. Lucinda would rather dance with another *girl* than me." And I'm not insinuating any lesbian thing.

Now, I was supposed to dance with a ballerina! A girl who's practically a professional. I knew I couldn't tell Melissa I didn't like to dance. Dancing was her friggin' life. I was screwed if I stood and screwed if I didn't. But I was determined I wasn't going down in flames in my seat.

Thankfully, the next song was "I Am Like A Bird," which has a strong beat. To my relief, as we started to dance, Melissa didn't stare in horror. In fact, even though she was looking right at me, she smiled. It wasn't some phony, encourage-the-spaz smile, either. She didn't seem to give a damn I was wobbling, writhing and wriggling like a worm on one of Birdsong's hooks. As she danced every day with great dancers, I guess she didn't care how I danced as long as I danced.

Melissa didn't show off. She didn't make a spectacle of herself. She didn't flaunt fancy, complicated dance moves. I mean, she was good, but no one who looked at her would have thought—, this is a girl who's taken ballet for ten years. She danced like any girl at school who was a good dancer.

After Nelly Furtado did five more dance numbers, she announced she would sing a few songs from her latest album. These songs were slower and folksier, and everyone in the orchestra and the balcony sat down. To keep her balance on her way back to our seats, Melissa put her hand on my shoulder. She didn't need my shoulder to keep her balance, but she held onto me—her man.

When we reached our seats, her hand fell away, but I couldn't forget the sensation or its implications. I thought, maybe we could join Napster and Darlene at the electrolysis center.

I checked out the time but it was much later than I thought.

Melissa caught me looking and asked, "Is it late? Do we have to go? Furtado's awesome."

"If you want to be on time," I said. "Another twenty minutes..."

Melissa sighed. "That sucks but probably it's best."

Except we stayed like forty.

When we rose to leave, Nelly Furtado was still doing encores. We felt guilty and embarrassed, particularly when we had to crawl over four people's legs to get to the aisle. At their dirty looks, I wanted to point at Melissa and say, "It's not me. It's her. She's the one who has to be home early."

#

On the subway ride, Melissa was subdued and a little tense. We were going to be late, but not by much. When we pulled into Park Street, we were still a few minutes on the good side of eleven-thirty, so as we climbed the stairs to the street, Melissa called her mom. Her conversation went, "Hi... Heading to Beacon...Lots of people are out...Yes. We're sticking to the sidewalk...It was great...Can't talk...Love you...Bye."

"You really are something," I said.

"Pourquoi?"

I looked at her.

Melissa grinned impishly. "You mean now that I called my mom and told her we're on Beacon, it's like I got home on time."

"Parents," I said. "Can't live with 'em. Can't live without 'em."

"Ahh, they're OK."

We didn't even have to walk fast.

It was cozier and sweeter than walking beside Danielle in Southridge, only in Boston you don't see the sky as much.

"Who knew Nelly Furtado would be so good?" Melissa said.

"Do you think anyone at school'll believe us? We can show 'em our ticket stubs and make 'em jealous."

"The first person I heard talking about Nelly Furtado in, like, a year was you."

"Did you think I was out of my mind?"

"A little."

"But you came anyway."

"I thought it had possibilities."

"And?"

"It did."

We walked on for another few minutes in silence but not an awkward silence. A cozy, comfortable silence. Until abruptly Melissa stopped and grabbed my arm. Like Wily Coyote in a *Road Runner* cartoon, I slammed on my brakes. "What?"

Melissa pointed behind us. "My building. We passed it."

"Oh."

We turned around, and at the sight of the shiny aluminum One Eighty-Eight, my heart thumped. This was it. We proceeded down the flower-lined entranceway, although since it was October, most of the flowers were dead. I opened the door. As we walked into the foyer, Melissa reached into her pocket and pulled out her key. She turned and faced me. "Thanks for such a nice evening. I really enjoyed the concert." Melissa gazed up, still holding the key. Our eyes met. The silence roared. I had to do something. I extended my hand, hesitated, and then grasped her wrist. It was enough. Melissa swept close, her head tilted upward. Her lips sought mine. My arms held her against me and we kissed for a long time...until gently but firmly she pulled away.

"Gotta go," she murmured.

Melissa opened the interior door and strolled through. As the door shut, she glanced back, giving me one of her flirty, crooked smiles. It was sweet, tender, and sexy all at the same time, and best of all, meant just for me.

#

Lying in bed in the darkness, I felt like I was still kissing Melissa. The memory was that strong. It wasn't as if the earth shook or the sky opened up, but Melissa's lips were soft, warm, and enthusiastic. I was kind of tired and dazed, but content. Any time I wanted, I could push the repeat button in my brain and play the scene over again.

Eventually, I must've fallen asleep because before I knew it (although it was really nine hours later!) I awoke with sunlight flooding my room and my head throbbing with that go-away-day-you're-way-too-early ache.

As it was Sunday, I stayed in bed for another hour, dozing on and off until my brain felt better. Finally, I dragged myself to the bathroom but returned to my room, knowing as soon as I went downstairs I'd get quizzed. However, as much as I didn't want to talk about the concert, hunger eventually drove me out. About half past noon, I stole into the kitchen. Unfortunately, my mother was there. It didn't take long for her to start in. Pretty much the first thing after, "What do you want to eat?" was "How'd your date go?"

"I told you it wasn't a date."

"Well, how'd whatever you want to call it go—what do you want to call it?"

"I don't want to call it anything. I want everyone to forget it."

"After we've had something approximating a conversation. Well?"

"It went fine."

"Fine. That's all you've got to say."

"Yes."

"Did Melissa enjoy herself?"

Now, my mother rarely remembers the names of any of my friends except Napster, who she's known since we were, like, in first grade. But Melissa who she's never met and whose name she's only heard once, *her* name she remembered.

"It was a good concert," I said. "I think everything went well."

The ends of my mother's lips twitched as if they wanted to smile but they didn't. She knew how much it would annoy me. "And this singer— what was her name?"

"Nelly Furtado."

"Was she good?"

"Yes."

"And the theater. How did that look?"

"It was a good place to hear the concert, but it looked kind of ratty. Like a hippy way down on his luck."

My mother grinned. "That's how it looked when your father and I went there. I guess it hasn't changed much."

I hated comparing notes about the theater, but it was better than talking about Melissa.

"I'm glad you both had fun," my mother continued. I could tell she was dying to ask more questions, but she didn't press me, and I didn't give her any encouragement. I said, "Can we get back to food? I'm starving."

At this statement, my mother eyed me inquisitively. She almost asked another question, thought better of it, and slid into normal mother mode. "Do you want an extra sandwich or some soup? I've still got some left over vegetable soup."

I took the sandwich.

#

My father cornered me in the den. I was watching the pre-game show. The Patriots were playing Buffalo. I like Drew Bledsoe, the former Pats' quarterback and now the Buffalo quarterback. I hoped the Patriots would win but Bledsoe had a good game.

"Your mother and I have to leave," my dad said. "I'll try to get back for the second half. Save a seat."

"Sure."

"What do you think?" he asked. "Give me a score."

"Patriots 27, Bills 21."

"You think the Bills will get that much?"

"I hope so."

"You still have a soft spot for Drew, don't you?" my father said. "It's business, you know. The Patriots have to stick with Brady. He's a winner."

"I know."

Having softened me up with sports talk and given me my life lesson for the day, my father inquired, "How'd the date go?"

I groaned, "Dad, I already went through this with Mom."

"I don't have to get information second hand from your mother."

He looked like he would feel hurt if I didn't tell him something.

"The Somerville Theatre's a cool place. We both liked the concert. Melissa's father said he'd heard of you," I added because it had nothing to do with Melissa and I thought it would make my dad feel good. "He said you have a good reputation in Boston."

My father beamed. I guess four sentences from me is pretty effusive, and he liked what Melissa's dad said. "What's Melissa's father's name?"

"Worth."

"What does he do?"

"Something to do with banks."

My father laughed. "Something to do with banks. I bet he's Frank Worth. Frank Worth is part owner of the Wentworth Bank and Trust. It's one of the biggest private banks in Boston. They must have quite a place."

Without moving my gaze from the tube, I said, "Yeah. It's at One Eighty-Eight Beacon. It's like a whole floor."

Shaking his head as he walked out of the room, my father said, "You don't have a clue how lucky you are."

But I do have a clue. I appreciate The Noyce School, even though I hate it. And I really like Melissa. And I love that her building is near the subway. At least until I get my license.

#

My sister bothered me next. She wandered into the den, acting as if she wanted to know what was on TV, even though she knew I was watching the Patriots and she hates football. She says it's because when Napster and I and some of the other guys played in the backyard, we made her stand still and hike the ball for both teams. "What fun is that," she said which was true but we didn't force her. She wanted to play.

However, over the years, I have felt the sting of her revenge as in now, when at the start of the game, she stood in front of the TV and asked, "Did you kiss her, Mikey? Did you lock tongues? You can tell me. I won't tell anyone."

"First of all," I said, "It's none of your business. Second of all, get out of the damn way. You're blocking the TV."

"If you tell me, I'll get out of the way."

"If you want to keep your head, you'll get out of the way NOW!"

Sarah moved just enough for me to see if I leaned to the right.

"Tell me. Really, I won't tell anyone."

"God, you are annoying. Go back to your room and call your friends."

"If you tell me, I'll have something to talk about."

I laughed. "You just promised not to tell anyone."

Sarah blushed. "My friends aren't anyone."

"You're not kidding. And neither are you. Scram. Beat it. Go away."

"I think you kissed her."

"Why?" I asked, curious because she sounded so sure of herself.

"Helloooo. If you didn't, you'd make something up."

"You are such a numskull."

"I can't believe it. My brother kissed a girl. That is sooo cool."

I threw a pillow at her which she caught and threw back.

I grabbed it as it flew by almost crashing into a lamp. I stood as if I was going to knock her head off, and she backed away. At the door, she said sarcastically but still with a hint of admiration in her voice, "You are soooo cool." Then, she ran off probably to tell her friends.

If only fifteen year old girls were as easy to impress as eleven year old sisters.

#

My father did not make it in time for the start of the second half, but in the middle of the third quarter when the Patriots were up by three touchdowns and my interest in the game had waned, Napster called.

"Hey," he said. "How'd it go?"

"Fine. How 'bout you?"

"Fun and games. We missed you though. "

"I doubt it. I'm sure you were busy."

"We were. But it would've been more fun with you and Melissa breathing heavy on the other couch."

"We had a good time."

"Watching the concert."

"It was good."

"Whatever gets you off."

"It was our first damn date."

"Don't be so sensitive. Hey," Napster said, changing the subject (sort of), "did you catch the news?"

"What?"

"It's all over the Internet."

"What?"

"Another kid got laid by his teacher."

"You mean the fourteen year old."

"I knew you'd know. I was talking to Crusty, and he was like, 'Huh?'"

"That's because she's not Jewish," I said.

"Can you imagine? He's in the ninth grade. What a lucky stiff."

"Stiff is right."

"Why can't we get teachers like that?" Napster moaned. "You'd think for what our parents are paying, Birdsong would hire a few bootylicious babes who'd have a thing for high school guys. That kid gets laid in public school for free, and we get teachers like Mrs. Driscoll. She's so flat you could turn her sideways and use her for an LCD. And they say private school kids are spoiled. Listen. Why don't you start a campaign in *The Looking Glass?*"

"For what?"

"To get Birdsong to hire hotter teachers."

"*The Looking Glass* doesn't print editorials. It's a literary magazine. *The Scrivener* is the school newspaper."

"You're such a wuss."

"'Cause I write for the literary magazine?"

"'Cause you won't write the editorial."

"Why don't you write it? *The Scrivener* accepts stuff from anyone."

"You're the writer. Maybe the hottie teacher would lust after you. Older women like you."

I was not taken in by Napster and refused to be distracted. "I saw this Fox News babe talking about how the kid's mother got him to confess. Now, there's a wuss."

Napster agreed. "My mother could've pulled out my fingernails and I wouldn't've have said a word. I mean, the asshole has this incredible thing going, and he tells his mommy."

"What I can't believe is how the Fox News babe said the kid's psychologically damaged for life."

"Yeah," Napster sneered, "Please, teacher, damage me. How can adults spout such crap? I saw the same news babe."

At this point, my dad, who'd returned, came into the room, so I hung up. Napster hadn't even asked if I'd kissed Melissa. I guess (like my sister) he assumed it.

#

On Wednesday, I asked Melissa to the movies. It wasn't much of a get. Melissa had already mentioned on Friday nights she goes to bed early because Saturday mornings she has ballet practice. Her stated free evening is Saturday. But when I asked Melissa, she still went through the whole what-a-surprise routine, as if my suggestion were some new idea she'd never thought of. It was kind of like watching my sister open a present when she knows exactly what it is because she requested it. Sarah shakes the box and ooohs and ahhhs as if she doesn't have a clue. I guess it's a girl thing. The formalities, the protocols, the pretenses, the modesties are so important. I was just pleased we were going on a second date and my first kiss jitters were over.

For the subway ride to Melissa's house, I took *Sense and Sensibility*. We've got a paper to write on how each of the main characters exhibit obsession. It was a sign of how comfortable I'd already grown with Melissa that

I could sit on the streetcar and actually comprehend what was on the page. I never could have read the book on the way to our first date. This week I'm practically James Bond.

#

Cut to shot of Bond sitting in the penthouse suite at Claridge's in a silk reading jacket and ascot. In one hand, he holds a martini—shaken not stirred—in the other, a book. (I've seen them all on AMC and, yes, it's Sean Connery. Who else?)

Cut to Fanny Action riding in a BMW 645 convertible, looking all busty and beautiful.

Cut to BMW pulling up and the doorman opening the door.

Cut to Fanny Action entering Bond's hotel room.

Fanny Action (all innocent): James, what are you reading?

James Bond (matter-of-fact with his slight Scottish burr): *Great Expectations*.

Fanny Action (flirtatiously): For you or for me?

James Bond (straight-faced): That depends on whether you're a big Dickens fan.

Dissolve to: naked back of James Bond lying in bed beside Fanny Action.

Fanny Action (softly nuzzling Bond's ear): Oh, James.

Cut to close-up of Fanny Action, glancing down and squealing in surprise: Oh, James!

Fade to reality: me in the streetcar, reading Jane Austen.

#

When the elevator stopped at Melissa's floor, this time the face peering out the window was Melissa's.

I stepped into the hall, hoping I could avoid the whole parent thing. Maybe Melissa would just put on her coat and we could go. But as soon as I entered, Melissa's mother shouted, "Is that Michael? Meliss, bring him into the den."

Melissa grimaced but nonetheless led me down the hall. As we walked, Melissa whispered, "My dad's watching his favorite show. It's all about stocks." She rolled her eyes. "My mother tapes it for my dad every Friday and they watch it together today. It's like you can't breathe too loud when it's on."

I whispered back, "I think my dad watches the same show."

She smiled sympathetically. "Then you know."

I nodded.

Another bond.

In the den, the furniture was contemporary and designed for the living. Mr. and Mrs. Worth sat in two beige cloth armchairs, watching TV. As they weren't dressed to go out, they looked like your regular Boston Brahmin couple, relaxing for the evening. Mrs. Worth was wearing black slacks and a white woolen sweater. Mr. Worth was wearing chinos and a brown-and-red checked flannel shirt.

Mrs. Worth said, "Nice to see you again, Michael. You're going to the movies?"

"Yes, ma'am." I don't know if I've ever said "Yes, ma'am" to anyone, but it was better than the first time when I said, "Yes, sir." I don't know what it is about Mrs. Worth, but when I talk to her, words like "ma'am" just pop out.

"What are you going to see?"

"I don't know. I guess we'll decide when we get there."

"The Copley has eight screens," Mrs. Worth replied. "I'm sure you'll find something. Have fun."

"Thanks." I thought we were going to escape without a word from Mr. Worth, but at the last second, he addressed Melissa and me. Without turning his head toward us, he said, "Same time?", using the inflection of a question yet somehow making it clear it was an order.

"Yes, dad," Melissa said in a tone of half sarcasm, half obedience. Mr. Worth did not reply. His eyes remained glued to the TV.

#

As the elevator door shut and we headed down, Melissa and I kind of glanced at each other. Then we burst out laughing, partly because her parents were so funny watching the TV and partly because we were so glad to get out of her house. As we walked into the lobby, Melissa said between giggles, "I can't believe you called my mother 'ma'am.'"

"Well, it's better than last week."

"When you called her, 'sir.'"

"Your mom doesn't hate me, does she?"

"No. She told me you were a polite young man."

"What did you say?"

"Oh, I agreed, but I was thinking it's lucky she didn't see you grab and kiss me."

"Didn't grab."

"Yes, you did," Melissa said. "I thought you were going to chicken out, but you didn't. It was nice."

Melissa's comment kind of astonished me. I mean, I did not grab her. I was too scared to grab her. Maybe I clutched her wrist, but I was barely holding it when she flung herself into my arms. "What if I'd chickened out?"

"What if?"

"Would you have gone out with me again?"

Melissa shrugged. "I was wondering how much I liked you and then you kissed me and I decided I liked you."

Wow. I had no clue our relationship hung on a kiss. I thought we'd had fun at the concert. Napster was right. I guess Melissa wanted to make out as much as me.

#

Our choices were *Kill Bill: Vol. 1* (on two screens), *Intolerable Cruelty, Under the Tuscan Sun, Lost in Translation, School of Rock, Good Boy!* and *Out of Time*. For me, that meant no choice—*School of Rock* was it. But I was a gentleman. A polite young man. I asked, "What do you want to see?"

Melissa gazed at the marque. "What do you want to see?"

"I asked you first."

Melissa didn't rush. She considered carefully. I suppose she was trying to pick a movie I would like, too. Finally, she said, "*School of Rock?*"

Yes!

#

It was good. Jack Black was funny, and when the movie was over, it was still early—9:45. We had plenty of time to get something to eat, go back to Melissa's house, and if her parents had dutifully retreated to their bedroom, make out on the long, comfortable couch in the den.

The Copley Cinema is in the middle of this giant mall that twists and turns through three hotels and an office complex. Nonetheless, Melissa seemed as comfortable as if she lived there. You could say this was her home away from home, although I'm sure Melissa would object that the ballet was her second home. However, when I asked where we should eat, she said, "Marche," and grabbed my hand as if we were heading to her kitchen for a snack. "My mom and I go there all the time."

Marche is set up like a county fair. You circulate through a maze of booths. At each booth, someone serves a different type of food: pizza, pasta, sushi, stir-fry, chicken, smoothies, crepes. The idea is, you check out each booth, pick the food you want, and as you leave, you pay. I liked the place right away, although when you get the bill at the end, all those dishes add up.

Melissa chose a strawberry crepe and a smoothie. As usual, I was starving and selected pizza, French fries, a smoothie, and a blueberry crepe.

As we ate, I wondered, "Jack Black at fifteen. Nerdy or cool?"

"I dunno."

"Well, would you have gone out with him?"

Melissa shrugged.

"Think about it.

Melissa pondered. "Depends."

"On?"

"How fat he was and how funny. If he wasn't fatter than he is now and just as funny, I probably would."

"So, we don't like fat and we like funny."

"And confident. Jack Black has lots of confidence."

Salome was so right. "That's because he's a movie star. It's easy to be confident when you're a movie star. I'm confident about writing. And I'm not fat. And," I added after a beat, "I can be funny."

"You are funny."

"I bet when he was fifteen, Jack Black wasn't so confidant."

"Probably he worried about blimping up," Melissa said.

"Why? You think he wanted to be a ballet dancer?"

"Nooo. But fat kids get picked on. I bet he gains weight easy. He has that kind of physiology." From Melissa's dance background, I figured "fat and physiology" were subjects she knew. She went on, "Maybe he's always wished he was thin. Maybe that's one of his secret thoughts."

"Secret thought?"

"You know, like who you have a crush on or what you want to do when you finish school or things you worry about. At sleepovers, me and my friends sometimes share ours. Don't you?"

"What?"

"Share secret thoughts?"

"With who?"

"Stephen, I guess. He's like your best friend, isn't he?

"Yeah."

"Well?"

"I guess we talk about stuff but we don't trade secrets. Baseball cards. Comics. No secrets."

"Michael, you don't trade secrets. You share them."

"What's the diff? You tell your friend a secret. She tells you one. Isn't that trading?"

"Trading is a negotiation," Melissa said in exasperation. "It's about winning and losing. Sharing is friendship. Sharing makes you closer. You've never done it?"

"Nope. If Napster and I are going to play video games, we tell our parents we're going to a movie, so they won't give us a hard time. We have plenty of those kind of secrets."

"Michael, those aren't secrets. Those are lies."

"Whatever. They work. We never sit around trading secrets. But if you want," I grinned, "I'll trade secrets with you."

Melissa didn't like my grin nor my sticking with the word "trading".

"No way," she said.

"I have some good ones."

In spite of herself, I could see Melissa become intrigued. A good secret is hard to resist. "What?"

"You tell me yours first."

"Nope. You tell me yours."

"No. You tell me yours."

Obviously, we could go on like this for hours but that wouldn't get me anywhere, particularly near Melissa's couch. So, I caved, "OK. OK. Here's a secret I'll share." Shamelessly, I threw in the word "share" and hoped my secret was personal enough and revealing enough for Melissa to think I was taking her little trading game (it is trading) seriously. "In seventh grade, I was as tall as I am now. It really bothered me because my dad is tall and I didn't want to grow to be like seven feet or something."

"How tall is your dad?"

"Six-five."

"That is tall. How tall are you?"

"Six feet. In seventh grade, I was one of the tallest kids. Talk about being weird."

"You could've played basketball and been real popular."

"That's the thing. I'm not good at basketball. I mean as tall as I was, I didn't even make the team."

"Poor baby."

"Hey, are you mocking my secret?"

"That was sympathy."

"I heard mock."

"No, no, no. No mock. This is a 100% mock-free zone," Melissa said, mimicking (some might say mocking) me.

I gazed at her amused. "Let's hope so. Hey. I've thought of another secret." It had just popped up and I knew it was good, although I now realized trading secrets was trickier than I thought. After telling your secret, you had to be careful the person you told still liked you.

"Go for it."

"I worry…about death. Death totally freaks me out."

Melissa gasped. Not a gasp of disgust. A gasp of recognition. "Death freaks me out, too."

"What bothers you?"

"I worry about ending. I'd like to believe in something. Angels and wings work in ballet but in real life…."

"Yeah," I said. "Nonexistence is scary. Sometimes, at night waiting to fall asleep, I think—floating around wouldn't be so bad like some kind of—what's the word?—not a spirit or an angel or a ghost…"

"…an ethereal body."

"Yeah. An ethereal body. You have thought about this."

"*Sixth Sense* is one of my favorite movies," Melissa said.

"Too creepy. Have you ever seen *Topper*? It's black and white…. I'm into old movies."

"How not surprising. Writes stories. Editor on the literary magazine…."

"Wait. Have I shared another secret? Is liking old movies another secret?"

"Liking old movies isn't a secret. You could tell that to anyone. I could watch an old movie, if it's good."

"*Topper*'s good. Super funny. Though not very *Sixth Sense*. The dead people look exactly like they do when they're alive except they walk through walls and stuff. No bullet holes. No broken heads. No gashes. No blood."

"If only…"

"Yeah," I said. "Ethereal bodies work for a movie. But what's the science? What is an ethereal body anyway? What's it made of?"

"Ether," Melissa said.

"Yeah. Ether. Whatever that is? I've always tried to figure what's the least I could deal with death-wise—not like I have a choice—but my body and my senses I can give up. I don't need to float around. To me, the least I need—the absolute minimum—is to think. I don't know how thinking would work without a brain, but that's what I want."

"Oh, my God," Melissa said. "Me, too. Though I'm kind of partial to ethereal bodies. It would be trés cool. I'd be so light and flexible, just imagine the incredible turns and leaps I could do."

"Can't get away from ballet, can we?"

"I live for ze dance or in zis case—die for eeet. Though I'm like you. I'd be happy just to think."

"Thinking is enough."

"Ohh, to be a disembodied, sentient, eternal entity," Melissa intoned.

"Exactly."

"Though you know what?" Melissa said.

"What?"

"Sometimes I wonder if thinking for eternity would get boring."

"Like a bad black-and-white movie."

"Like a very, very long, bad, black-and-white movie."

"Or no shopping."

"Michael."

"Or maybe, like in *The Matrix*, life's just a dream, and you can dream shop whenever you want."

"So now we're into the life-is-a-dream gag, huh." Melissa tapped my arm. "Well, let's be clear about one thing, mon cher. You are definitely in my dream."

"Nothing could be more wrong," I said. "You are obviously in mine."

"Au contraire. —I'm *totally* sure you're in mine."

"Well, how about this. What if we pinch each other really, really hard and see who wakes up and who disappears."

"Not necessary," Melissa said. "I had ballet practice this morning and you know nothing about ballet. Like what's the difference between a relevé and a sauté?"

I wasn't going to let Melissa one-up me with her ballet crap. "Well, do you know anything about *Grand Theft Auto*? I beat Napster at it all the time, and he's very good at games."

"Which means?"

"The whole life-is-a-dream-thing is bullshit."

"Damn. I knew it," Melissa said. "So, I still have to practice. Dreaming I'm a principal at the NYCB means nothing. Ms. Levatova *always* says, 'The only way to do it is to do it.'... Hey that reminds me. Just thought of a secret."

"A ballet secret?"

"Kind of." She leaned over confidentially. "Just remember you cannot tell anyone. Especially anyone at school. Especially Stephen."

"I won't. I get it. It's a secret." I was pleased. If she was telling me a secret—a ballet secret, no less—my secret must've passed muster. We were sharing. I promised again. "Seriously, I won't tell." I know I'm putting Melissa's secret in this book, but all the names are changed, and by the time anyone reads this, she'll be in some ballet company and I'll be in college and it won't matter.

"Just remember, OK?"

"OK. Shoot."

So, I worry..." and here her voice got thin and whispery. "I worry about my boobs."

I crumpled my napkin and threw it on my plate. I was not impressed. "All girls worry about their boobs." I mean on TV, movies, and in books that's all you hear—girls worrying about their boobs. As evidence, I nearly mentioned Mia Thermopolis in *The Princess Diaries*. But I caught myself. Listening to *The Princess Diaries* was a secret I was not yet ready to share.

"I know," Melissa said. "But all the other girls in the world want big boobs. I'm just the opposite. I worry my boobs will get too big. You can't be a ballet dancer with big boobs."

"Why not?" I said. "You dance with your feet."

Melissa crossed her arms and gave me a stern stage stare.

"OK. OK," I apologized. "My bad."

Melissa waited while I tried to rid my face of my grin. It was a struggle but I managed. Then she asked, "Have you ever seen a ballet dancer with big boobs?"

"No. But I haven't seen many ballet dancers."

"Well, I have, and I can tell you, there aren't any. Ballet is all about the line."

"Straight lines, I gather."

Under the table, Melissa kicked. She missed. Cross-country is good for leg speed.

Melissa continued, "Ballet is all about ideal form, proportion. Big, bouncing boobs don't fit in. Last year, this beautiful girl, Regan Vardi, who's this wonderful dancer, well, over the summer she filled out..."

"And they tossed her?"

Melissa shook her head, "They don't toss girls out of ballet school because they have big boobs. But she didn't make it into a professional company. They told her if she wanted to go on dancing, she should think of modern dance or Broadway or pole dancing or something."

"Pole dancing. Mint. What did she do?"

"She went to college."

"Where?"

"Princeton."

"Hey," I said. "That's not so bad."

"I know. But I want to join a company. I don't want to be flat—. I don't want guys to hate me, but..."

"You're not flat," I said. "Not all guys want girls with big boobs."

"C'mon."

"Girls with big boobs look—you said it—out of proportion."

"You seriously think that?"

"Is it so difficult to believe?"

Melissa shrugged, "I don't know. All guys are supposed to think about is big boobs."

"Plenty of guys like girls with big boobs, but plenty of guys like girls with small boobs." I wanted to tell Melissa entire porn sites were devoted to girls with small boobs, but this was another secret I was not ready yet to share. It's odd in a way. All guys—certainly all high school guys—cruise porn sites, but if you talk about it to a girl, you're a perv. Even discussing porn sites with other guys in the wrong situation can make you a perv, even if they cruise more porn sites than you. So I didn't mention my porn proof. I just added, and I think I phrased it aptly, "You have a very nice figure. I wouldn't change an inch of you."

Melissa looked pleased but still worried that on a full moon night some mosquito, tick, or other cursed member of the Arthropod undead might bite Pamela Anderson or Carmen Elektra or Dolly Parton and then bite her and she'd wake up with huge jugs and be stuck in the chorus on Broadway or pole dancing (I'd definitely pay to see that), rather than starring in *Swan Lake* at Lincoln Center. However, the reality is she just isn't built that way.

"Big boobs are not in your future," I said, "unless you get implants."

"My mother told me girls stop growing when they're seventeen."

"You're nearly sixteen now."

"I know. One more year."

"You've got it knocked. Sorry. Pun. Unintended."

"Whatever." Melissa didn't care as long as her tits remained the perfect size for ballet. She looked at my empty plate and then the exit. "Shall we?"

#

Creeping down the hall of Melissa's condo, I prayed to the gods who watch over sex-starved teens, *Please let Mr. and Mrs. Worth be in their bedroom.*

They were.

The place was as silent as Nefertiti's (or Cleopatra's or Hatshepsut's) tomb.

From the hall, we ducked into the kitchen where Melissa shut the door. "Soda? Juice?"

"No thanks." I just wanted her.

For a minute or two, we stared at each other. Melissa leaned against the refrigerator, and I leaned against the island in the middle of the kitchen. I wasn't feeling awkward. As a matter of fact, I was feeling confident. I mean, I'd already kissed Melissa, and from what she'd said about her wanting me to kiss her, I knew she wouldn't object if I kissed her now.

I appraised the territory. Her face was tilted down. Her eyes glanced up. Her lips were slightly parted and, as we faced each other, it seemed as if her chest was rising and falling in rhythm with mine. It was as if an electric charge was building between our bodies that at any moment would spark out and connect. When I couldn't resist anymore, I stepped forward, and this time I did grab her. For a few minutes, we savored the bond of our lips and bodies. Then, as if by silent but mutual consent, we held onto each other all the way to the couch in Melissa's den. It was kind of weird. We'd started our date in the very same room. Melissa's parents had sat in the two beige armchairs glued to the openings and closings, ups and downs, and ins and outs of the world's stocks, bonds, and mutual funds. Now the armchairs were empty and Melissa and I were stuck together on the couch, lost in the opening and closings, ups and downs, and ins and outs of our own stocks, bonds, and mutual fun.

#

Cynthia Swansey stood in the entranceway of *The Looking Glass* office. She was waiting to see me.

I wondered if she put out. Cynthia Swansey is one of these Goth types who walks around school with an angry look on her face and a cloud of doom floating over her head, which was why I was wondering. I mean she is a total rebel. An outlaw. An artist. Does virgin fit into that list? I think not. But she is fifteen and a sophomore, as I am, so I would not give any odds on the state of her hymen.

While dark and moody is not really for me, if you talk to her for a while and she forgets she's supposed to be angry, you can coax a smile onto her face that would make a girl scout proud. I think she's into Goth because her parents are divorced and her dad lives in Europe and never sees her. Her mother has remarried twice, both times to younger guys, but she is single now. Her dad's really rich, and Cyndi lives in this big mansion near school. The rumor is her dad stays in Europe because he's got some legal problems and can't come to the US. I guess that kind of crap can mess you up. Cyndi could have expressed her messed-up-ness in a lot of ways, but since her mother probably hates her Goth getup, she expresses it that way.

The first day of school, she came to class with her hair dyed purple and green, and Mr. Birdsong sent her home to think about it. The next day she returned with her hair dyed plain black. Not exactly plain black. It's that super black—like Darlene's super red—but Mr. Birdsong didn't send her home, so she keeps her hair that color. She wears the same outfit every day—black shirt, black chinos, and black boots. On occasion, she adds something red, like a scarf. Still, she must like Noyce because, let's face it, she's here. I don't think she gets the grades she should, but as my parents constantly remind me, neither do I. She's into art and writing poetry, which is why she was outside *The Looking Glass* offices. Cyndi's contributing three drawings and a poem to the fall issue.

The poem is called "Wish List":

tinsel sparkles on the floor
like the crumpled glitter of life.
stars shed tears on the moon as pious
as pubic hair, adorning
the tree where bing crosby croons—
christ is born.


daddy sent a card.


he doesn't care
every afternoon
mother fucks a guy from the health club,
while I stare in the mirror
at the Snow White
heart tattooed on my lower back.
I love it as much as the guys in school
love staring at my ass.

(reprinted with permission of *The Looking Glass*)

Naturally, the poem created a stir among the editors, particularly about the line "mother fucks a guy from the health club." I mean *fuck* appearing in the literary magazine is controversial enough, never mind it referring to Cyndi's mother. Noyce is very progressive and no one believes in censorship, but the magazine does go out to all the parents and alumni (including Cyndi's mom), so we had this huge fuss. I was pushing for the poem, but I am only an associate editor. Karen Wechsler, one of the co-editors-in-chief, hated it, a couple of the other senior editors loved it, and in the end, everyone was too afraid to take responsibility for printing it and threw it in the lap of Mr. Moorland, the faculty advisor.

After a couple of days, the verdict came down we could use the poem as long as we printed *fuck* like *f**k*. Everyone thought Mr. Moorland was cool for allowing us to use the poem, even Karen Wecksler, although Cyndi grumbled a bit. In the end she said, "OK," but I wondered what Cyndi's mom was going to say when and if she ever read the poem. I even went so far as to ask Mr. Moorland because he is my favorite teacher and I didn't want him fired. What he said surprised me. He actually called Cyndi's mother and emailed her the poem. After she read it, he said she laughed. So that was it. The issue'll be out by Thanksgiving.

Cyndi's drawings are these weird pen-and-ink figures—really detailed and beautiful—but her subjects are always vampires or other strange, supernatural, blood-sucking creatures. Mr. Phillips, her art teacher, puts them in every school show and told her to submit her stuff to *The Looking Glass*. Cyndi wants to go to Hampshire College, which would be perfect for her because it's a rebellious, arty place, light years from Noyce. But I love seeing her here, sticking out from all the preppy kids. Of course, other strange kids go here, but they're mostly just strange.

I kind of got into Cyndi last year when we were in history together and I made the biggest fool of myself ever. We were studying Louis XIV, learning how lavish and flamboyant his court life was and how Louis wasted tons of money on extravagant galas and balls. The next week when Mrs. Redmond, the history teacher, asked me to describe what Louis XIV was famous for, without much thinking I answered, "Louis the XIV was known for his great balls."

Everyone in class cracked up, including Mrs. Redmond. In the midst of the hilarity, I glanced at Cyndi, who sat a couple of seats away in the last row like me, and who leaned her chair back like me, so I could see her clearly. At my remark, her usual dark expression vanished, and she laughed with her head thrown back, totally animated and into it. Despite my embarrassment, I felt kind of proud at having done something, however stupid and temporary, to shake the gloom out of Cyndi all the way down to her Goth soul.

However, in *The Looking Glass* office, Cyndi was not smiling. After handing me her three drawings, she said, "Whatever you do, please do not put anything of mine next to Gloria Shimer's poetry."

Gloria writes poetry in rhymed couplets about love, friendship, and—no lie—kittens.

I shrugged. "I have nothing to do with the layout."

"Why are her poems even in *The Looking Glass*? Shimer is hopelessly Bambi-brained."

Even though I felt the same, I defended Shimer. Not because I felt obliged to stick up for *The Looking Glass* or Gloria or anything, but Cyndi's disdainful tone automatically made me take the opposite tack. I said, "Some of her rhymes are kind of clever."

Cyndi made a sour face, and in perfect valley-girl speak, said, "She makes me barf lemon drops and lollipops."

Although Cyndi was making fun, I couldn't believe she could do such a great valley-girl accent. Along with her smile and her laughter, it was another chink in her Goth armor. It emboldened me to ask, "Why do you always draw vampires?"

"My mother asks the same thing."

"And the answer is?"

Cyndi paused thoughtfully, curling a strand of super black hair around a super red, nailed finger. "I don't know. Maybe because they suck blood and live forever."

"Like they actually exist."

"They're real in my head."

"Do you watch *Buffy*?" I asked.

"Please don't get me started—vampires for twelve year olds."

Napster and I kind of like *Buffy*—at least we like Alyson Hannigan ever since she was in *American Pie*. But I didn't tell Cyndi that. I said, "Buffy vampires suck blood and live forever."

"They have no personality. They act like retards. Oh, excuse me. That's how all TV characters act. If you want vampires, read this book called *Vamped*. It's got vampires."

"Never heard of it."

"It's about this cool futuristic world. Very few humans are left, so the vampires drink synthetic blood from cartons, you know, like the way you buy milk. Real blood is too expensive. Only the vampires don't like this artificial, processed, factory-made blood so..."

"Wait. Wait. Wait," I interrupted. Sometimes I get these intuitive flashes—I hope it's my writer's instinct. "I am picking up this vibe."

"What?"

"Are you a vegan?"

Cyndi look startled. "Why do you ask?"

"The way you talked about vampires not liking synthetic, processed blood. Are you?"

"What?"

"A vegan?"

"Trying."

"Isn't that kind of contradictory? You don't eat meat but you love vampires."

"Vampires don't eat meat."

"They suck human blood…."

"So?"

"So, no pig's blood. No cow's blood. No lamb's blood."

"Stop! You're making me sick."

"Animal blood you can't talk about, but human blood, no prob."

"When a vampire sucks human blood, it's dark and mysterious and beautiful, and the person gets to live forever. Killing animals is just cruel."

"Fish?"

Cyndi confessed, "I still eat stuff like tuna."

"Tunas bleed."

"And once in a while I eat like a cheeseburger."

"Hmm. Well done I assume."

"Very well done, but just once in awhile," Cyndi protested. "I haven't had a cheeseburger all this year."

"Have you switched to vegan meals at lunch?"

This question I knew was the true test. Mrs. McCutchen, the head of Culinary Services, has this rule. You can switch to a special diet at the beginning of every semester, but once you switch, you have to keep that diet the whole semester. McCutchen's experienced enough to know if you don't give kids the chance to switch, they'll bitch and moan. But if you make them stick to their decision, the number of kids switching will be really low.

"Not yet," Cyndi said. "But I will."

"Ahhh," I said. "You will. Some-day waaaay down the road."

"Not waaaay down the road," Cyndi said, annoyed I'd gotten her. "I don't have to make an official proclamation to be a vegan. Just talk to Wechsler. Make sure my stuff is nowhere near Shimer's. You can do it. I know you can." Then, she stopped being annoyed long enough to bribe me with one of her rare but dazzling smiles. The glow from that smile was like the halo around a twenty-dollar bill dangling in front of a derelict.

"OK. I'll try," I said, surprised I actually meant it.

#

The reason I bring up Cyndi is that Mrs. Moorland, Mr. Moorland's wife, is the faculty advisor in charge of the Halloween dance. Mrs. Moorland teaches Spanish, and she picked Cyndi to head the decorating committee. I think she has the same wry sense of humor Mr. Moorland has. The dance is coming up soon, and Melissa has informed me she wants to go. It's on a Friday night and, even though Melissa doesn't go out Friday nights because of her Saturday morning ballet class, the Halloween dance is big enough to warrant an exemption.

What Melissa failed to mention is that Katie is staying over Melissa's house Halloween night, so Katie is coming with us. Since Melissa doesn't want Katie to go without a guy, Napster has been recruited. Melissa said Napster and Katie will be good together. Her reasons are they're in the same French class and their book lockers are across from each other, which Melissa told me she considers an omen. After I told Napster of Melissa's plans, he considered it a bad omen. I don't know what Katie thought, but Napster has no choice. I've flown wing for him; he's flying wing for me.

Once the Katie/Napster business was settled, Melissa asked what costume I was wearing. She actually assumed I had considered it. Melissa is clueless about guys sometimes. I think it's because most of the guys she meets are in her ballet classes. Now, I'm not going to be stupid and say all ballet guys are gay. I mean, I know who Mikhail Baryshnikov is, and that he's nailed a lot of movie stars—female movie stars. But ballet guys wear tights, and even a straight ballet guy would think nothing of wearing a Halloween costume. So Melissa was surprised when I told her, "I'll probably stick with what I wore last year—my Henry Higgins outfit."

Melissa, being into theater, knew who Henry Higgins was. "The guy in *My Fair Lady.*"

"Yeah. My mother loves that movie. I get to wear my normal clothes, only I add this tweed hat she bought for my dad and this umbrella." However, regular clothes, a tweed hat, and an umbrella were not acceptable Halloween attire in Melissa's eyes. "You can't wear the same thing two years in a row."

"Hey, in elementary school, I wore the same Spider-Man costume every Halloween for three years. I just stopped because my mother said it wouldn't fit and threw it away."

"But this is high school. Besides," Melissa said, groaning at my stupidity, "Cyndi Swansey is doing the gym. It's going to be Goth. I heard she actually got a coffin. How can you go as Henry Higgins?"

"Changed. I can wear one of those...uh...uh...English hats with a visor at both ends, switch the umbrella for a curvy pipe, and go as Sherlock Holmes. Sherlock Holmes is Goth. He's moody. He plays the violin. And he takes drugs."

Melissa shook her head. This was going to be far more difficult than she thought. "A hat and a pipe aren't a costume. I just told you, it's going to be major, major Goth. Don't you know Cyndi Swansey?"

"Sure."

"She could be really pretty if she didn't dress like she does and use that strange make-up. But you know she's gonna cover the gym with tons of black crepe and stick vampires, werewolves, and warlocks everywhere."

"So..."

"So, how can you stroll into the gym in chinos and an Oxford shirt with a stupid deerstalker hat and one of those...those Meerschaum pipes?"

"C'mon," I said. "How do you know all that?"

"All what?"

"That it's a *deerstalker* hat and a *Meerschaum* pipe."

"It's-it's Sherlock Holmes."

"Yeah. But you know what they call that stupid pipe and hat."

Melissa shrugged. "I don't know how I know. I just do."

Melissa was not only pretty and talented but really, really smart. I knew she was going to get an A in math and probably everything else. She could get into any college she wanted, and instead she's going to dance. It was so aggravating. But sort of wonderful. And I guess I should be thankful. It meant one more opening at Harvard.

Meanwhile, Melissa refused to let me distract her from her main theme. "Since we're going together to the dance I want you to look..." She eyed me up and down, as if calculating how much costume she could goad me into. "...um...at least, halfway decent." We'd only gone out twice, and already she knew me.

It was then my writer's intuition struck once more. "You actually want to win, don't you?"

As it is a costume dance, prizes are awarded.

"My mom says, it only takes a little more effort to come in first than second, so make the effort and win."

"Wow, my mom never says anything like that."

"Mikey, please. Be serious. We've got to decide what we should wear." I caught the shift from "you" to "we" and figured since Henry Higgins and Sherlock Holmes had been, for me, eliminated, we were now talking about her.

"So, who are you going as?" I asked.

"That's just it. I don't know. Ideas?"

As it was her costume, I was happy to throw out suggestions.

"How 'bout *Bride of Frankenstein?*"

"Frankenstein got married?"

"Sort of. There's a bride anyway."

"This is an actual movie?"

"Yes."

"Black and white?"

"Yeah."

"A comedy?"

"No."

"Not a comedy."

"Does it matter?"

"No. I'm not going as Frankenstein's bride. Who'd have a clue?"

'OK. How about a gypsy?"

"Please."

"Witch?"

She wrinkled her nose.

"What about a vampire victim? You could wear a white nightgown and have bloody teeth marks on your neck."

"Better. My mother has just the nightgown, too. It's all lacey and see-through and sexy…" At the words *lacey, see through* and *sexy*, I tried looking positive and encouraging but Melissa added, "…'Cept she'd never let me wear it."

I pondered a minute. "What about a character from one of those Goth comic books? You could go as one of those…uh…like a fairy, only more Goth than fairy."

"You mean a sylph."

"Yeah." I stared at her amazed again. "A sylph."

Melissa shrugged. "Two whole ballets are about sylphs."

"Sylphs are Goth."

"True. They're sad and romantic and a little dark. But no one is going to get that either."

"I don't know," I said. "You'd look cute with wings."

Melissa smiled. She couldn't resist a compliment. "For Halloween, I want to wear black."

"Black, huh?" Who would've thought color was important. I gazed up in the air mentally sifting through a few of the Goth comics I'd flipped through. An image came to mind.

"How about one of those warrior women? They wear black."

"A warrior. That's not bad."

"A warrior *princess*," I added, hoping the word princess," sealed the deal. It did.

"A warrior princess," Melissa mused. "Mmm. Like Xena. She's kind of Goth. Only futuristic. That would be sooo cool."

For a moment, I thought of mentioning Goth warrior princesses have huge jugs, but why stomp on the fantasy, especially since I suggested it? I said the obvious. "Go for it."

Melissa jumped to her feet and strode back and forth. "I bet I can put together something really sick. You know, long black boots. Tight black daisy dukes with a black cut off jersey. And you know one of those…um… you know…laser guns." Her description started a stream of very pleasant images almost as good as the lacey, see-through nightgown.

"Sounds hot, except rethink the gun."

Melissa nodded. "Good catch. A more politically sensitive weapon is needed. I'll buy a couple of those creepy comics for ideas." Then Melissa's eyes lasered onto me. I felt like a Ken doll she'd taken down from the shelf. "Now, about you…"

#

After a string of really bad ideas topped by Melissa proposing I go as an archer wizard, which sounded OK until she described him as Robin Hood only in black tights, I refused any more suggestions. Politely. But firmly. I was prepared to give up the dance. I was prepared to give up making out Halloween night. I was even prepared, if it came down to it, to give up

Melissa, but I was not wearing tights.

When Melissa realized she was up against steel, she relented. "OK. Do what you want. But no hats. No pipes. No umbrellas. Make it Goth. Make it really, really Goth."

"Worry not. Goth, it is."

Then because I had a couple of weeks before Halloween I forgot about costumes or, at least, tried to, except I didn't reckon on Melissa. Persistence was part of her personality. She was a ballet dancer, after all. Finally, four days before the dance, I ended all deliberations, agitations, speculations, and negotiations and went to one of those costume places that pop up around October.

The store was on Beacon Street in Brookline, tucked between a J.P. Licks and a Chinese restaurant. The place wasn't very big, although the proprietor was enormous. She was a woman in her fifties with frizzy brown hair, glasses, and a body that was a combination of weight lifter and fat lady in the circus. Muscles bulged from her muscles. Her butt protruded from her slacks in lumps like a tarp covering an overloaded pickup truck, and her stomach simultaneously swelled and drooped like a beach ball three-quarter's inflated. As for her breasts, I hate to remember her breasts. Picture a pair of massive mammaries like a cow's udder only (I assume) without the extra nipples. Around her face and neck, her skin sagged like melted cheese. As she stood on what I imagined were two very tired feet, I had no worry about her stirring from behind the cash register. I wandered around the store happily unharassed. From the empty boxes and hangers, I could tell lots of costumes were gone but plenty remained. I knew Melissa hated store-bought, but I hoped I could find a couple of stray pieces I could combine into something unique.

Sticking out of a pile on a table, I caught sight of a pointy ear that was part of a mask—a black cat's head—maybe a jaguar—that pulled down over your face.

Black was Goth. And Melissa was into black, at least, for Halloween.

Hanging from a rack in another part of the store, I found a pair of wings—not white, fairy, sylphlike wings, but black leathery, bat wings and I thought—a match—with the cathead this could work. I didn't exactly know who or what I would be, but whatever it was, it was Goth, and if I were going to wear this much costume, a mask that fit completely over my head was a bonus.

To accompany the wings and the cathead, I could wear a black turtle neck jersey, black jeans, black boots, and black gloves. I had all that. The question remained: what would I be? Melissa would want to know. I mean, the essence of a costume is that you are something. I needed to have a name, a phylum, a genus, a species, something—anything—just as long as I could tell Melissa and she would think, "OK, he is whatever-it-is. It's not great, but it's Goth and I can appear in public by his side." And while the most important person to please was Melissa, I knew if I didn't come up with an appropriate appellation, I would be in for a long night of explanations, puzzled looks, and wiseass remarks from everyone I knew.

When I got home, I assembled the entire costume and tried it on. I examined myself in the mirror. I liked it. It was bizarre and, OK, sort of stupid, but I hoped it was cool stupid. Best of all, staring at my cathead and wings in the mirror, I got an idea of what I was, and it was Goth. Very Goth. Caught in the enthusiasm of the moment, I went off to show my parents and sister.

After a long moment of silence, my mother said, "Very interesting, Michael. But what in the world are you?"

I now knew.

I said, "That's your mistake. I'm not from this world. I'm from a supernatural Goth world. I'm a griffin."

I knew what griffins were from having read *Harry Potter* and lots of King Arthur stories in my youth. They're mythical, catlike, winged creatures.

My sister got this puzzled look and said, "Don't you mean Hippogriff?" Sarah, of course, had read *Harry Potter* as well.

"Nah," I said. "Hippogriffs are horsey. Griffins have cat heads and bird wings."

Doubt squirreled around in Sarah's eyes, and she ran to the computer. When she returned, she shouted gleefully, "Wikipedia says griffins have the body of a lion and the head of an eagle." (OK. So, I wasn't exactly right about the griffin. But I was close. Except close does not count in Sarah's eyes.) "You're not a griffin," she screeched, bending over in hysterical laughter. "Wikipedia says" —more screeches and laughter— "you're a *gaaaargooooyle*." My sister's laughing was not a good sign. But it is always hard to tell whether she is laughing because she is eleven and wants to make fun of me, or she is having a reaction normal people will share.

"Gargoyle, griffin or hippogriff," I said, trying not to let my sisters' antics bother me. "No diff." I turned to my parents. "It's Goth, don't you think?'

My dad said, "We don't know what Goth is. Do you mean gothic? Gargoyles are certainly on gothic churches."

My mother nodded.

"Well, there you go," I said. "How do you like it? Be honest."

"Honestly," my mother said. "Hmm. Well, it's nice. It's certainly unique um…and…and very nice." Parents are not the best people to ask for honest answers. In parent-speak, "very nice" meant my mother thought it was awful but didn't want to hurt my feelings. But I didn't care. It was a costume. It was Goth, and the strange bat wings fit perfectly over the turtleneck. They didn't extend far and get in the way when I walked. Best of all, when I pulled the cat mask over my head, no one at the dance would know it was me.

#

Friday evening. October 31. All Hallows Eve.

My father drove me to Napster's house, and from there Napster and I took a bus to school. Katie and Melissa were meeting us at the gym. Melissa said her father insisted on dropping them off because it's Halloween and all sorts of crazy people were out. She said when her father picked them up, he could drive Napster and me home—Napster's staying over at my house—but I declined. Being driven by Melissa's father would make it too much like junior high. Ugh.

Nine more months until I get my learner's permit.

When I arrived at Napster's house all griffined up, Napster laughed quite a lot, but I think that was because the last time he saw me in this much costume I was wearing my Spider-Man getup.

Napster was dressed as Jack the Ripper. At least that's the title he gave his outfit. It consisted of one of his father's old tuxes (they were practically the same size), a bow tie, a cape, and a top hat (his mom rented the cape and the top hat). He said he was inspired by my Henry Higgins outfit. Salome tried to convince him to wear a ruffled tuxedo shirt, but he refused. Instead, he wore a regular white dress shirt, but the bow tie was one you tie yourself. His father taught him how. We both felt stupid, but since I had the cat head on, I was stupid anonymously, which is much the better kind of stupid.

The gym is about a five-minute walk from the main school entrance. By the time Napster and I arrived, it was eight-thirty. Music blared from the open doors, and the dance was filling up. A red strobe light flickered inside, which was supposed to look eerie but made the place look more like a strip joint.

A big banner hung over the gym doors with Sunnydale High printed on it. A nice touch. It's the name of Buffy, the Vampire Slayer's, school. Knowing Cyndi's attitude toward the show as well as our student body, it set off ripples of ironies in my head. We handed our tickets to a freshman who was managing the door. Napster said to me, "I hear Cyndi bought a bunch of mice she's going to let go during the dance."

"I heard that, too. But I don't believe it. How would they ever catch them? We'd have mice all over the school."

"We already have rats. I see 'em around the dumpsters. What difference is a few mice?"

"The difference is, no one brings the rats. They come on their own."

"Yeah. They get into the dance for free. We pay ten bucks."

After our hands were stamped, we entered the gym. Emerging from between the grand stands, we both sort of went, "Whoa."

It was our reaction to the decorations. Cyndi had outdone herself. As Melissa had predicted, black (and red) crepe streamers hung from the rafters. In the stands, various giant toads, frogs, lizards, owls, vampires, and werewolves perched as if observing the proceedings. Dozens of plastic bats and crows swayed from fishing lines. Some drooped pretty low. Kids hit them as they walked by, making them look like they were flying. Paper murals draped the walls covered with large versions of Cyndi's drawings. They were her strange, ghoulish female creatures all with long, sharp, teeth biting men. However, the best decoration was the coffin. It really was there. It was this creepy pine box filled with slimy rubber spiders, roaches and beetles, and a skeleton, sitting upright. A rubber snake curled out of one of the skeleton's eyes, and a couple of rubber roaches poked between the skeleton's teeth. Next to the coffin was a miniature graveyard about ten-feet square with a tombstone and a skeleton hand sticking out of the dirt. Written on the tombstone was Josiah T. Birdsong. I don't know how Cyndi got away with that. Behind the graveyard was the refreshment table with two big punch bowls. In one, the liquid was black; in the other, orange. Floating in each was a plastic head with blood painted around the neck and an apple stuffed in its mouth. But no pumpkins. We were in a pumpkin-free Halloween zone.

As absent as the pumpkins were Melissa and Katie.

They were supposed to have arrived already. Melissa's father seemed like one of those prompt types.

"Let's go find the girls," I said.

Even though it was eight-thirty, in dance time it was still early. Most kids lurked around the periphery of the gym floor, and except for some well-known couples, the crowd was separated into clumps of guys and girls. The time wasn't right to dance, nor was the song. Everyone needed to warm up and a really good song, like maybe "Ignition" or "Satisfaction" blast on.

Napster and I prowled the gym, checking out people's costumes and looking for Melissa and Katie. Everyone recognized Napster since his face wasn't disguised, and since everyone knew I hung with Napster, all the guys asked as we walked by, "Is that you, Stoner? Hey, Stoner, are you in there?" Then they leaned close, peering into the cat's eyes, which were just holes, and up into the cat's mouth, which was wide open. To get them out of my face, I quickly confessed, "Yeah. It's me." So much for anonymity.

Of course, the next question was, "What are you supposed to be?"

"A griffin," I answered.

"Don't you mean hippogriff?" Every cursed kid has read *Harry Potter* (or at least seen the movies).

"Nah. I'm a griffin," I insisted. It sounds much better than a gargoyle, and I knew no one was going to run to a computer like my sister and look it up. I didn't want any questions or debates on the anatomical differences between hippogriffs and griffins, and I definitely didn't want to bring up gargoyles.

Actually, I felt pretty good about the costume. While no one guessed what I was or seemed overly impressed when I told them, no one laughed hysterically, either.

After we circled the floor twice, I spotted Melissa.

"Wow!"

Now, I understood why her father had insisted on driving her to the dance. She looked hot. Way hot. I wouldn't let her out like that on public transportation, either. As planned, Melissa wore thigh-high black boots, tight black short-shorts and a black cut-off jersey. Her hands and arms were covered with long black gloves and a long black wig hid her blonde hair. But the kicker was her weapon of choice—a whip—and while it was definitely politically correct (how many mass murders have been committed with a whip), it added more than a touch of the erotic. She held the whip casually but imperially in her left hand, doing the whole warrior princess thing, and, I must admit, my insides quivered. (Am I a fetishist and not know it?) But I can definitely affirm, describing the outfit is nothing like seeing it. Being this ballet dancer, Melissa didn't have an ounce of fat on her. Even Napster was impressed. He elbowed me and gave me a go-get-her grin. When Melissa saw us, she dropped her aristocratic attitude and waved with her non-whip hand.

"Well?" she asked as we approached, gracefully indicating her outfit. "You like?"

"Not bad," I said.

I gestured, but not as gracefully, to my own outfit. "What do you think?"

Melissa held her whip hand in front of her mouth, giving me a slow once over, up and down, front and back. As she scoped out the bat wings, she giggled. "Oh, my God, what are you?"

Inside my cat's head, I smiled confidently—not that Melissa could see it. "I'm a griffin."

"I don't know," Melissa said, resting her chin on her whip handle and appraising me doubtfully. "I think griffins and hippogriffs have birds' heads. I would say you're more of a…a gargoyle."

I was glad I was wearing the mask. It hid how surprised, stupid, and annoyed I looked. I mean, here was Melissa—Miss Ballerina and Miss Brain—at it again—, blithely discussing the physiognomy of griffins, hippogriffs, *and* gargoyles, and as always she was right.

"C'mon," I said. "Have you read every *Harry Potter* book twice?"

"Actually, yes" Melissa shrugged. "And last summer I went to Paris for two weeks. My mom and dad were uber-seriously into museums and churches—Muisee du Louvre, Musee de L'orangerie des Tuileries, La Cathedral Notre Dame, La Basilique du Sacre Coeur—I was soooo mad. Like, how many hours a day can you spend in musty old churches and museums, even if they are pretty? We could've been shopping in these totally awesome boutiques but noooo, my parents were insanely, deliriously culture nuts. My dad loved to keep saying, "Churches are soaring monuments to the human spirit."

"I told him, 'shopping makes my soul soar.' But he wouldn't listen."

"He really has this Buddhist thing going, doesn't he?"

"Oh, why couldn't I have known you then? One mention of this and my dad would've been so freaked, we could've spent the whole trip shopping."

"You must've gotten in some stores."

"Some," Melissa admitted. "Not enough. But I did see more than my share of griffins and gargoyles, and you, mon coeur," she said, pointing her whip at me, "are a gargoyle."

"Well, then, fine," I said, trying to maintain a sense of dignity, "I'm a gargoyle." Except it's hard to maintain a sense of dignity when you use the word, *gargoyle*, especially about yourself. Some words are inherently funny, and unfortunately, *gargoyle*, is one of them.

Melissa stroked my fierce cathead's nose and appeased me by saying, "I like it. It's Goth and it's cute. Particularly the wings. You could fit right on top of Notre Dame." She glanced at Napster and leaned close to me and feigned whispering, "Who's the guy in the tuxedo, cape, and top hat? Henry Higgins at the Hookers Halloween Cotillion?"

"Good guess," Napster said. "But not good enough. I'm Jack, the Ripper."

"Jack, the Ripper," Melissa nodded. "I knew hookers were involved. I hope you left your knife home with your mom."

"Look who's talking—Donna, the Dominatrix."

"You mean Melissandra, the Warrior Princess of Melissandria, the fifth planet of the Melassandrian star system." My warrior princess grabbed my hand, "Let's go find Katie....C'mon, Jack."

#

As Melissa and I walked, Napster fell in behind. No sooner had he, than he let out a whistle. "Dude, wait. Stop. Hold it. Treat your eyes to this."

I turned my head.

Napster pointed. I'd been so busy enjoying Melissa from the front, I hadn't noticed her back. From the top of her butt to the bottom of her jersey glowered a giant, round tattoo. A pentagram was drawn on the inside, and in each of the five triangles a mystic symbol glimmered—a half moon, a falcon, a heart, a key, and a serpent. In the center shone a large ruby.

"Wicked tattoo," Napster said.

"It's a talisman. It's supposed to bring good luck in relationships." Melissa eyed me when she said this.

I gulped nervously. "Awesome."

"Isn't it? Makes the whole costume."

Napster shook his head. "I don't know. I like the whip."

"You would," Melissa replied,

Meanwhile, I examined the tattoo. My sister and her friends put on fake tattoos that wash off all the time, but this one was big, and it looked kind of permanent.

Melissa gazed at me, a curl on the side of her mouth accenting her amusement like a spice. "Look at Mikey. He's wondering if the tattoo's real."

"No, I'm not."

Melissa teased. "You've never seen my back, have you? You're wondering how long I've had this big monster tattoo. Maybe I really like tattoos. Maybe I have them everywhere."

I looked at her skimpy costume. "There's not too many places left."

"Oh, there's a few."

"Let's see," I said, advancing toward her.

"You wish," Melissa said, pushing me away.

"Maybe I like tattoos," I said. "You've never seen my back. Maybe I have a tattoo."

Melissa grabbed the back of my jersey and pulled.

"No tattoo."

I took the glove off my hand, stuck my index finger in the mouth of my cat's head and licked. "Let's see if your tattoo smudges."

Melissa dodged away. "Don't you dare."

I gloated. "Who put it on?"

"My mother," Melissa confessed. "I had to kneel in the bathroom with my head between my knees for like an hour."

I imagined Mrs. Worth applying the tattoo. I guess she still has the soul of an artist. "Good job."

"I know," Melissa said. "I'm thinking of getting the same thing for real only smaller."

"Where would you put it?"

"Ankle maybe."

Napster suggested, "Put it on your ass."

With her whip hand, Melissa gave Napster the finger.

#

Katie finally showed. She'd been chatting with some friends in the lobby. Katie was dressed as a vampire—a glamorous, romance-novel vampire;—at least that's what she said—but I think Katie was getting away with a better costume scam than Napster or I ever had. I mean, it was just a dress. OK, it was a dress with a vampirish quality. It was long and black and velvety, but that was it. Since Katie's hair is long and dark, and it flows in waves down to the middle of her back, it fit right in with her so-called costume. Katie didn't even wear false, pointy vampire teeth or put on weird, vampirish make-up. I wondered if she got any crap at the door. Probably not because her dress was strapless and pretty bare in front, and it turns out Katie has quite a pair of rockets, which I'm sure was all the freshman at the door saw. Probably, Katie didn't even have to show her ticket.

This new exposure of Katie's firm teen breasts had a stimulating effect on Napster. He beamed. As I've said, Katie is not what you would call good-looking the way Scarlett Johanson, Kristen Bell, or Rachel Bilson are good-looking. None of her features are what a prospective cheerleader would wish for, but that doesn't mean they don't fit. For whatever reason, her full lips, prominent nose, large brown eyes, and high cheek bones give her face this exotic elegance. Katie is beautiful the way Uma Thurman is beautiful. I suppose it's like the way kids love food that's doused in sugar but adults appreciate caviar. Katie is caviar.

Katie's biggest problems are the black rimmed glasses she always wears (even in her vampire costume), her baggy school outfits, and her shy personality. However, with her newly revealed Playboy figure, she could keep her baggy outfits, her glasses, and her shy personality and still get dates.

Katie certainly had Napster's attention. She stood in front of him with those glasses, which I guess she justified because they were black and she needed them to see, and said, "Hey."

Tearing his gaze away from her breasts, Napster said, "Hey."

I said, "Hey," and Katie turned to me with a nice smile. With Napster, I guess I had, at last, tossed something positive into her pool. The problem was Katie didn't seem to know what else to say. Or maybe she knew but was too nervous. After "Hey," she stood in an awkward silence biting her lip and fidgeting with her dress. At least in this sense, Napster as a date is a blessing—he is loud and funny, even though he can be somewhat crude. He started things off in fine form. He said, "Let's sit. My rule is —never be one of the first hundred on the dance floor."

I chuckled at that one, what with Miss Ballerina standing there.

"I'll get some punch," Napster added, turning to Katie. "Do vampires prefer black or orange?"

Although obviously still nervous, Katie had no trouble with a direct question. "Orange sounds good."

Melissa chimed in. "Orange for me, too."

#

The lobby was filled with tables and chairs, and I took off my cathead and we sat. The punch tasted like a mix of Seven-up, Orangeade, and Kool-Aid. Even five years old, I would've hated it. Katie probably would have preferred to occupy herself drinking the punch but it was so sickeningly sweet, she couldn't. After a few sips, she glanced at Napster and me. I could see her thinking hard. "Do either of you play an instrument?"

We shook our heads.

Katie sighed.

"We like music, though," I said, helpfully.

"Classical?"

"Hip hop, rock, rap," Napster said.

"Sometimes I like Mozart," I added, hoping to score points with Melissa for aiding her shy friend.

"Ohhhh," Katie gushed. "Mozart is my favorite. He composed a lot of music for—I guess you guys know I play the flute." Napster and I nodded. "You know what's funny?" she chirruped. "Mozart wrote the most beautiful music for the flute, even though they say he hated it. But how can you write such beautiful compositions for an instrument you hate? Especially the flute?"

"I don't hate the flute," Napster said.

"Neither do I," I said.

"Who could?" Katie agreed. "The sound is so pure. That is if you play it well. When my teacher plays, she makes a tone…it's like crystal. I love to listen to her. I hope someday I can play as well. She plays in the Pops. She knows Keith Lockhart."

Since everyone's expression remained blank, Katie added, "Keith Lockhart is the conductor of the Pops."

A gleam suddenly appeared in Napster's eyes. I knew it meant trouble. With a straight-face, he said to Katie, "Have you ever been to band camp?"

This line was a reference to *American Pie*. In the movie, Alyson Hannigan plays a nerdy but horny girl who talks endlessly about band camp. She ends up sleeping with the sex-starved virgin, Jason Biggs. Napster has the DVD, and we've seen the movie like ten times and the topless scene with Shannon Elizabeth about a thousand. When Napster asked Katie the question, I bit the inside of my cheek. I didn't want to laugh, which would lose me all the points with Melissa I'd just gained. Napster mocking Katie was one thing—he was like that. Melissa knew what Napster was like when she fixed them up. But if I piled on, I'd be in trouble. However, I needn't have worried. Katie was not as vulnerable as she looked. After all, she was Melissa's friend, and when served up a gopher ball, she had no trouble hitting it out of the park. Without skipping a beat, she responded, "Band camp. I love band camp. You learn so much—like all the different things you can do with a flute."

I don't know if you know what a spit take is. I do because I love movies. A spit take is when two people are talking and one person says something so surprising and outrageous, the other person who's just taken a big gulp of a drink spits it out, usually in this big spray. That's where the humor is. Well, when Katie said, "like all the different things you can do with a flute," Napster, who'd just taken a gulp of his orange punch, was so surprised, astonished, and amused, he did his own version of a spit take. Because he isn't an actor, and we weren't in a comedy sketch, he didn't spray the punch all over the table and us. Instead, he tried holding his laughter in, couldn't, and ended up coughing, spitting, and drooling all over himself, which was even funnier. Melissa and I roared. Napster wasn't upset—except for nearly choking to death and dripping orange streaks over his white shirt—but he couldn't stop laughing. He liked to mock and tease but he didn't mind if someone got him back. "Alyson Hannigan is my favorite actress," Katie wryly remarked.

"*Buffy* or *American Pie?*" I asked

"No doubt. *Buffy.*"

"Who is Alyson Hannigan?" Melissa asked.

Katie turned to Melissa. "Alyson Hannigan plays Willow Rosenberg on *Buffy*."

"Oh, I don't watch TV," Melissa said.

Napster was aghast. "Never?"

"I've seen *Buffy* a couple of times. Is she the one with the red hair?"

"That's her."

"I didn't know she was your favorite actress," Melissa said to Katie.

Katie nodded. "She's married to Alexis Denisof, who plays Wesley."

Napster gazed at Katie with more interest.

Katie continued, "They broke my heart when they took *Buffy* off the air."

"There's still reruns," I said.

"It's not the same."

"Heh, classical music is all reruns," Napster said.

Katie paused. "I never thought of it that way." She smiled admiringly at Napster.

Just then, the DJ played the Red Hot Chilli Peppers' "Higher Ground."

"Finally," Melissa said, "a good song."

I got the hint. "Dance?"

Melissa nodded. "Just don't smudge my back til…"

"…after the contest."

As we stood, I glanced at Napster. He didn't glance back. He was too busy talking to Katie.

#

One of the best things about the summer is that girls wear as little as possible. It's like they compete to see who can wear the least and not actually be naked. It doesn't matter where the girls are. The mall, the street, the shore, they always show a lot of flesh. But here it was nearly winter at the Halloween Dance, and Melissa was almost as bare as at the beach. Even better, we were close dancing—well, Melissa was dancing—I was bumping hips and rubbing bellies as much as possible.

After an hour, it dawned on me that my time to take full advantage of this costume was not unlimited. When the dance ended, my warrior princess was going home. The next time I'd see Melissa was on Monday, fully covered in school clothes. Crap. I had to think of something. Fast.

Or Napster did.

Napster doesn't dance much. He's better than I am (that doesn't mean much), but mostly he stands around. Tonight, however, he was dancing. Katie's strapless dress and her joke about the flute had obviously persuaded his one thinking organ (not his brain) of her desirability.

Glancing around at the two from inside my cathead (you have to wear your costume on the dance floor until the prizes are awarded), I thought, what if Napster got to fool around with Darlene in New Hampshire and Katie down here? Once, long ago in a distant galaxy, I had dreamed of having two girlfriends. Now, Napster was doing it. And as soon as he graduates from Babson, his uncle pops him into the corporate microwave and in two minutes he's running the company.

As I mulled over Napster's good fortune, I saw Salome. She was drifting toward her brother. They almost never go near each other at school. It's like they don't want anyone to know they're twins or even related. But suddenly Salome, dressed totally in this whole black get up—black eye make-up, black lipstick, black slinky dress, and black stockings—was beside Napster, checking out Katie. Giddy, I'm sure, was around, but Salome kept up the conversation with Napster and Katie, acting very casual but every once in a while hugging Napster or messing with his hair. What did this mean? Was it some kind of deep twin thing? Could it be that Salome was jealous? I don't think I've ever seen Napster and Salome hug except at birthdays or something. It convinced me more than ever that something between Napster and Katie was clicking. What was even more interesting, Salome hadn't acted that way with Darlene. But like a dog who's pissed on a tree to mark her territory, after two songs she was gone. I took that moment to wander over with Melissa.

As soon as the four of us met, Melissa and Katie rushed together, chattering like birds. Napster and I stepped aside.

"What are we going to do?" I asked. "Melissa's dad's coming at twelve."

Reading my mind, Napster said, "Now, you want the electrolysis center." I knew there was a reason we were friends. "Don't worry," he said. "After the awards…."

Napster was never without a plan.

At ten-fifteen, right at the end of "I Like the Way You Move," when everybody's energy was high and the momentum—even mine—was to keep dancing, Gabby Hanes, the senior in charge of the Awards Committee, signaled the DJ, Joel Dworkin, to stop the music. Someone flipped on the overhead lights, and we all shielded our eyes and groaned. The dance was just beginning to feel like a scene. But once the lights were on, despite the decorations and the costumes, we were back in the school gym. However, Gabby didn't care. She had a speech to make and awards to give, so she stood on the stage, saying, "Test, Test, Test," just like the dork at the Somerville Theater. She was dressed as a platinum blonde, blue-eyed Marilyn Monroe, which I appreciated for the old movie reference and the Goth connection.—Marilyn Monroe took drugs and committed suicide. And once the volume on the mike was right, Gabby started spouting.

Listening to Gabby—real name Gabrielle Cardona—introduce teachers' wives and students was a pain. However, I did enjoy when Cyndi Swansey appeared not dressed in a costume, unless you consider how she dresses every day a costume, and everyone on the floor went wild, whistling, stamping, and clapping because Cyndi had done such a great job. Gabby didn't even try to introduce Cyndi over the tumult. Gabby just handed Cyndi the mike. Cyndi seemed shocked and confused that so many people were cheering her.

Once Cyndi held the mike, the crowd settled into this expectant silence. For most, it would be the first time they'd ever heard Cyndi speak. People were incredibly curious. Cyndi took a deep breath, and even though she was the weird Goth on campus, her words were surprisingly mundane. "Thank you all for coming to the dance. I hope everyone likes the decorations." Loud clapping and whistling. "We tried hard to get it right. Eddie Poole, Mary Foster, Jimmy Edwards, and Deirdre Flaherty worked late last night and most of today getting the gym ready, so we owe them a big thanks." More applause and whistling. "Also, I'd like to thank Mrs. Moorland for giving us a tremendous amount of advice—but only when we asked." A few laughs and applause. "And finally I'd like to say it's nice to be at a Noyce event where I look like the normal one." After setting us up with the ordinary, Cyndi slipped the collective student body a jab in the ribs and everyone loved it. The crowd broke into loud laughter and even louder clapping, stomping, and whistling.

Cyndi gave Gabby back the mike and retreated to the rear of the stage.

As Gabby took the microphone, I knew Cyndi's decorations were so good and her speech had ended on such a funny, self-deprecating note, if Cyndi wanted to, she could ride this success to the top. Cyndi could actually be popular. Well, have some popular friends, which is sort of the same thing. But unlike Puja who took her fifteen minutes and ran with it, on Monday I knew Cyndi would creep around the peripheries of the school, speaking to practically no one, although a lot would want to chat her up. But even if they managed to corner her, I was sure Cyndi would respond with some bizarre and inexplicable crack like "After school, come over to my house for some milk and cookies and tarot readings." I know this because Cyndi has said stuff like that to me at *The Looking Glass*. But I have never taken her up on her invitations, although Napster keeps insisting I should. Napster figures Cyndi is both wild and horny and maybe I could get some black lipstick rings around my dick. But I am not Napster. Cyndi's clothes, makeup and hair do not put her on the short list of girls with whom I want to share my first sexual experiences. It's odd, in a way, because I find Melissa's Goth warrior princess outfit very erotic.

With the mike once more secure in her hand, Gabby got down to her most important task: the costume prizes. Guys first to build suspense toward the girls because the girls were the only ones who cared.

Tony Androtti: third prize for the Skull Cowboy.

His costume was a character from the classic Goth comic book: *The Crow*. I thought the skeleton suit, the raincoat, and the black cowboy hat was OK. But, Melissa was not impressed. She hissed, "Store bought," just loudly enough for Napster, Katie, and me to hear. With her whip, she kind of half prodded, half tickled me in the ribs and said, "Your costume is better than that."

Corey Adams: second prize for Captain Barbossa.

Captain Barbossa is a pirate in *Pirates of the Caribbean*. Not Johnny Depp. The other guy, Geoffrey Rush. Corey Adams is one of these super hairy guys, and I don't mean on his head. He keeps his hair in a buzz cut. Although only a junior, he has to use a razor twice a day to look clean-shaven, and in school you can see his chest hairs sticking over his t-shirt. I had the misfortune of dressing beside him once in gym, and his entire body was covered with thick black hair. Gross. When you see a guy like that, you have to wonder what girls see in men. I mean, it's true girls are not falling all over Corey Adams. But you've got to figure someday he will be married and some unfortunate woman will pass his hairy genes on to future generations. But maybe she won't think of herself as unfortunate. Maybe she will love Corey Adams and his hairy arms, legs, back, and chest. How is it possible that women who are pretty, delicate, neat, and clean fall in love with guys like Corey Adams? With Napster? With me? With Dory? I guess that's part of nature's mystery. Anyway, Corey kind of looks like Geoffrey Rush, plus he had a real live monkey on his shoulder, just like in the movie. His costume wasn't anything special: a three-cornered hat, a fancy white tuxedo shirt with ruffles, and a red cummerbund tied around his waist, but he did have the monkey. Katie commented, "I heard his father's a vet and he's had the monkey for years."

"Two stars for the costume," Melissa pronounced, "but ten for the monkey. It's sooo cute. You've got to give the guy credit, even if his dad is a vet."

Gary Williams: first prize for Zombie With Ax In Head.

Gary is a senior, no surprise. The Noyce School has a tradition of favoring seniors. However, his outfit wasn't store bought and he obviously put some effort into it. Of course, he's applying to four art schools, so it was easy for him to put in the time. He probably got credit for it. Art teachers are suckers for stuff like that, particularly Noyce art teachers who are into the "art is whatever you think it is" crap, such as a couple of hubcaps nailed to a board or a hair brush with a comb stuck in it, both of which I've seen at student art shows.

Gary wore a zombie mask, which he made out of special plastic modeling goo. The mask featured one missing eye and an ax stuck in the back with blood splatters. His clothes were in shreds, and he was carrying another head by the hair. Crusty, I think, told me that Gary wants to go to Hollywood and be an F/X guy, and now he has his first credit: first prize at The Noyce Halloween School Dance. "I've always been partial to zombies," Katie sighed. "Between a werewolf, a vampire, and a zombie, I will choose a zombie every time. They're kind of like pets. I think they have more soul."

I said, "Isn't a zombie a dead person without a soul?"

"I think zombies are the walking dead," Napster replied. "Just because you claw your way out of a coffin doesn't mean you don't have a soul."

"Ssshhhhh!"

The "ssshhhhh" came from a bunch of senior girls standing behind us who thought the award ceremony more important than our metaphysical discussion on the nature of the zombie soul. What morons. However, we shhhed and Gabby moved on to the girls' prizes.

Melissa Worth: third prize for Warrior Princess.

It ruins the suspense. But what can I say? That's how it happened. Melissa won third prize right off. At the announcement, Melissa's cheeks burst into stars. She squeezed my hand and started toward the stage as if she belonged. Napster and I cheered loudly, and Katie gave one of those shrill whistles people do by putting a couple of fingers in their mouth. I guess she was skilled at this due to her nine years of playing the flute.

Melissa had no trouble attracting the crowd's attention. She didn't climb onto the stage by the stairs. She leaped as effortlessly as Xena or any other warrior princess. The stage was about three-and-a-half feet high, so anyone could jump it, except Melissa didn't take a running start. She advanced toe first in some sort of ballerina lope, and when she was still pretty far from the stage, seemingly without effort, she soared upward, landing gently a few steps from Gabby. The casualness of her movement combined with its grace and athleticism like a gazelle bounding over the Serengeti, drew an appreciative murmur from the crowd. Not breathing hard, she took the trophy from Gabby, and managed to look pleased, proud, and modest all at the same time.

The trophy was a small plastic statuette of a vampire that Cyndi must have picked up for a couple of bucks at some Halloween store. Upon receiving it, Melissa curtsied. I mean, how many girls even know how to curtsy? But again, she was so natural and graceful and it was so in keeping with her warrior princess attire, she got away with it. When she stepped back, she received more applause and a few scattered whistles from the guys, which wasn't for the bow or the leap but for how hot she looked. Hearing the whistles didn't make me feel proud. Melissa was definitely making herself known, and it wasn't for academic achievement. I didn't like the idea of the guys who were whistling, chasing after her on Monday.

Fran O'Brien: second prize for Punk Rocker Costume.

This award made Katie furious. "The costume's totally store bought," she hissed. "I saw the exact the same thing online. No way she's better than Melissa. If she weren't a senior, she wouldn't rate a booby prize." I liked the way she stuck up for her friend, but what did it matter? The statues were exactly the same, only Gabby bestowed printed certificates that said first, second, or third prize. Except for Gary Williams, it wasn't as if it was going on anyone's college apps.

Selma Melyeux: first prize for Queen of the Night.

Selma was a junior, and not even Katie could object to her winning. She was costumed to the max and beyond. She had spent most of the evening being carried on a palanquin. (You know what a palanquin is. It's one of those chairs or thrones like in the movie *Aladdin* surrounded by curtains and attached to two long poles that slaves carry. I didn't know what it was called, either, until I researched it). In Selma Melyeux's case, she had four guys wearing gold basketball shorts and covered in gold body glitter carrying her. She sat inside the curtains dressed like an Arabian princess in loose-fitting silk pajama pants and a tight silk blouse with a bare belly and a gold plastic crown. Selma's on the heavy side, so she didn't set off sparks for me, but she's such a character, all night a throng surrounded her. She only emerged from her palanquin when somebody asked her to dance, and afterwards she retreated back. It was a long way to go for first prize, but no part of her getup was store bought. When Gabby announced her name, Selma's four slaves carried her up the stage and lugged her passed Gabby. On her way by, Selma simply stuck her hand out through the curtains and grabbed the statue. Her slaves then carried her down the other side. At this bit of showmanship, the crowd cheered and laughed so loudly for so long, Gabby's concluding speech was cut short. Someone dimmed the overhead lights, and the DJ put on White Zombie's, "I Am the Boogieman," and we all went back to dancing.

# 

After a few more songs, the four of us revisited the lobby for soda. The orange punch was undrinkable, and we did not dare try the black, so we used the vending machine in the hall. I took off my cathead and gloves and deposited them near my coat. Melissa set her trophy (and third-place certificate) beside the cathead. Napster left his top hat, but he kept on his cape (which I think he was beginning to like) and we found an empty table. As we downed our Cokes—Katie and Melissa drank diet Sprites—Napster went into his sensitive rebel act. It's hard to imagine Napster as sensitive or rebellious, but he's started doing it a lot around girls. He thinks they suck it up. I think they do, too. He's too intelligent to be self-destructive, which is requisite for a full-on bad boy; so, instead he's settled for sensitive rebel. It'd be great if I could put on the same act. But like I said, I have difficulty putting on acts. Napster complained about homework and grades and then moved on to how we'd be better off if we only had to study subjects we wanted, stuff that would help us in our careers. This part went over big with Melissa and Katie.

"There's so much more about music I could be learning," Katie moaned.

"English is OK," Melissa agreed. "But I can't believe next year I have to take chemistry. Like I want to be a doctor. I'm a dancer."

"Yeah," Napster said. "They don't have a clue. This school is the pits. The teachers. The classes. The phony preps." Somehow Napster got away with this line, even though he never wears anything that doesn't have a Brooks Brothers, Lacoste, or L.L. Bean label. Let's blow the dance and go outside."

"OK," Katie said. Everything Napster said was OK with Katie.

I turned to Melissa, hoping she would go along. Exiting the dance was obviously part of The Plan.

"Sure."

It was ten forty-five, and the freshman ticket-taker had long ago abandoned his post. All the doors were wide open. Even though it was the end of October, the heat from a couple of hundred dancing teenage bodies kept the gym warm.

When we walked outside, a yellow moon was crawling up the sky and bare trees flung tortured, twisted shadows on the ground. Maybe it was because it was Halloween, but even the familiar brick and stone buildings frowned down at us. Dark corners and peaks made the staid old architecture seem menacing, as if something evil lurked behind the walls (even more malevolent than Mr. Ward.) The whole school had turned spooky and forbidding. From the small, abandoned cemetery tucked behind a row of trees next to the soccer fields, you could almost hear the skeletons rattling out of their graves. As we walked through the main quad, we passed the creepiest, most sinister part of the campus—the old stone library with its castle-like appearance. Battlements encircled the roof and its lone turret stretched ominously into the sky. Even though the turret has its own entrance and small windows at the top as if for a room, no one is allowed in. A ton of rumors swirl around why.

Rumor One: in the fifties, a senior girl got pregnant and jumped out of a window and killed herself. Rumor Two: the original headmaster, Alistair C. Moore, had a crazy daughter locked in the tower for thirty years and her ghost haunts the place. Rumor Three: Noyce has an exclusive secret society (like Skull and Bones at Yale), and every year Birdsong initiates six seniors in a ceremonial chamber at the top of the tower. Rumor Four: my favorite—Ms. Mitchell, the librarian, (who's not that bad looking) is a lesbian and uses the tower for trysts with other female faculty members. When searching through the library's dreary Dewey-decimaled aisles, this rumor injects an erotic change into my otherwise boring book hunt. I can fantasize which female faculty members Ms. Mitchell cavorts with, and exactly what she does to them. An even hotter variant—Rumor Four-A: Ms. Mitchell lures unsuspecting female students into the tower. Imagining Ms. Mitchell stripping Pamela Peters, who is in my history class, is far more exciting than imagining Ms. Mitchell stripping Ms. Nichols, who is my history teacher.

As Melissa and I walked, perhaps stirred by the spooky surroundings or the equally jittery thought of Ms. Mitchell, Melissa snuggled closer.

"Let's head to the tennis courts," Napster said.

The tennis courts are in the old part of the campus near where the original gym was before it was torn down. Wooden stands form a U around three sides of the main courts, creating lots of hiding places underneath. I figured Napster was steering us toward a couple of semi-secluded corners, so we could make out there, as Noyce couples often do.

If Napster had said, "Let's go sneak into the shadows and make out," the girls would have squealed "ewww" and run back into the gym. But as Napster said, "Let's head to the tennis courts," even though it meant exactly same thing and everyone knew it, it was OK. I guess that's the poetry of romance. The best parts are left unsaid.

The faculty house Mr. Moorland lives in is on the way to the tennis courts. It is a white farmhouse that has one of those historical plaques on the side proclaiming it was built in 1782. I've never been inside, but it is built on a knoll, and beneath it, kind of like a basement, is a barn. Mr. Moorland uses the barn as his garage. It holds three cars: Mr. Moorland's, Mrs. Moorland's, and this antique from 1925 that belonged to the original Harold T. Noyce's son, Harold T. Noyce II. It is a Pierce-Arrow convertible with a black canvas top and a long, maroon hood with headlights that stick out like frog's eyes. Between the headlights is a large chrome radiator with a silver archer on top, which is the Pierce-Arrow symbol. The chrome radiator with the silver archer is the coolest part of the car, but I also like the froggy lights and the whitewall tires that are almost as narrow as bicycle wheels. They have spokes rather than hubcaps, and two spare tires are mounted on the running boards on either side of the car.

The school owns the Pierce-Arrow, but Mr. Moorland is responsible for it, although you wouldn't think of him as a car guy. Maybe the Pierce-Arrow reminds Mr. Moorland of the Jazz Age (we're studying *The Great Gatsby* next semester). The school maintenance guys take care of the car, and only three people are allowed to drive it: the head maintenance guy, Mr. Moorland, and Mr. Birdsong. Every year, it is a tradition that, on Senior Day in the spring, Birdsong drives it around campus and takes the seniors with him. Not all at once, of course. But it is a big car, and Birdsong drives it with the top down. Ten kids cram in, and since there are only about eighty seniors, it's pretty easy in one afternoon to give the whole class a ride.

As we neared Moorland's house, Napster said, "Let's peek in the barn at the Pierce-Arrow."

Immediately, I got what was on Napster's mind. He wasn't interested in the Pierce-Arrow. He was interested in somewhere warm. And with my scantily clad warrior princess under my arm, I had to agree. Except the barn was directly under Mr. Moorland's house, his wife was currently chaperoning the gym and Mr. Moorland was home babysitting his two kids and probably up waiting for his wife to return. However, details like these never bother Napster. All that was on his mind was the partially open door and all the nooks and crannies the barn held for two couples to get lost in.

Melissa didn't help any, either. She piped up rather naively, "What's a Pierce Arrow?" As this was her first year at Noyce, she had not yet observed the spring ritual.

Napster eagerly informed her, "It's a car that belonged to old Noyce. It's totally rad. Do you want to see it?"

Melissa's eyes met Katie's. "Sure," Melissa said.

I didn't say anything, but I was wondering how much trouble we could get into if Mr. or Mrs. Moorland caught us making out in their barn. I figured if everybody had their clothes on and we hopped up quickly like we really were looking at the car, not much. Mr. Moorland's always gives me straight A's, and he and his wife were good guys and it was a dance night. Kids are always found in crazy places making out on dance nights. Mr. or Mrs. Moorland would probably just say in this sad, disappointed tone, "You should know better than to do something like this," and I would think, "Yes, I do know better. It's Napster's fault. He doesn't care about getting into Harvard. All he cares about getting into is some girl's pants." That's what I'd think, but of course I wouldn't say anything. I'd just hang my head down with everyone else as if I were ashamed and slink out of the barn with Napster and the girls and run back to the gym, thanking my lucky stars that nothing worse had happened and that Mr. and Mrs. Moorland hadn't threatened to notify our parents or Birdsong or the student disciplinary committee.

In the meantime, Napster needed no more encouragement than Melissa's "sure" to start for the barn.

When we got to the door, even Napster had the sense to stick his head in first. We waited while his eyes adjusted to the gloom. When he turned back, he whispered, "It's safe. The car's in the back. C'mon."

Napster slid through.

Katie…

Melissa…

Me.

At first, all was darkness. Gradually, Moorland's two cars—a Honda Civic and an Accord—formed. Deeper in the shadows, resting regally on wooden blocks like a king reclining on a divan, lay the Pierce-Arrow. I knew from having seen it last spring that it was maroon, but in the dimness you couldn't recognize the color. All you could see was its size and shape, which was large and sleek enough to draw a whispered, "Awesome," from Melissa.

As we crept forward, Melissa held my hand. We moved cautiously. No one wanted to make any noise. When we reached the car, Melissa placed her whip hand on the hood. "It belongs in a movie."

"Let's sit inside," Katie said.

It was like a fish volunteering to leap into the net. Even in the darkness, I could see Napster's grin.

Opening the driver-side door, he grabbed his cape, gave it a devilish twirl, and slipped in behind the wheel. Katie opened the passenger door and Melissa and I tumbled in the back. I was happy in the back. Old Noyce rode in the back. It was intended for millionaires. We had tons of room. The seats were cream-colored and made of soft leather. The interior walls were mahogany. Everything was spotlessly clean and smelled almost new. For the last eighty years, crews of dedicated Noyce maintenance men had meticulously waxed, polished and oiled the car. Sinking into the seats was like sinking into a warm tub.

Immediately, Melissa giggled to Napster behind the wheel. "Saks, Jeeves." Shopping was never far from her mind.

Napster laughed, "Whatever you say, Paris," but instead of grabbing the wheel, he grabbed Katie and they disappeared in another flap of cape.

Melissa and I did not need further encouragement. In a second, we were horizontal, our arms wrapped around each other. The back seat was almost as roomy as her couch at home, except instead of Mr. and Mrs. Worth in their bedroom down the hall, Mr. Moorland was (hopefully) in his bedroom upstairs.

#

I've read that some people like dangerous places to have sex. I'm not one of them. Danger does not enhance my libido. Lying in the back of the Pierce-Arrow, it wasn't that I didn't enjoy kissing Melissa. I did. It hadn't taken us long to reach the point where kissing was a pas de deux of tongues, circling, sliding, probing in ever changing choreography. But no matter how much I enjoyed kissing Melissa, in the back of my mind, I couldn't forget Mr. Moorland above, and that at any moment Mrs. Moorland might leave the dance and stroll home by the barn.

If she saw the door open, although it was open when we found it, would she think it odd and look inside? Like hearing your parents clattering around the house when you're in your room trying to watch porn, these worries diverted my attention from the task at hand. As did my costume. You've probably never been lying in the back seat of a 1925 Pierce-Arrow dressed as a gargoyle, but I have and I can say position is everything. It took lots of shifting, twisting, and bending before Melissa and I sandwiched ourselves together tightly enough so that nothing could come between us except perhaps a little mayonnaise. Sliding my hands over her body, I had never felt so much smooth, bare skin. It was as if sparks were shooting up through my fingers all the way to my wings. Thoughts of the Moorlands gradually receded the way the awareness of your parents fades when you shut off the lights and the good part begins. Everything was sensuous, sweet, and silent, except for a lot of heavy breathing, the smacking of lips, and the occasional creak of the seats. Long minutes passed. I was content and hoping I could really get somewhere, what with there not being much cloth between my hands and the ripest, tenderest parts of Melissa. I was even thinking Napster deserved congratulations as the evil genius behind this operation when suddenly this ferocious **AAUUUOOONNNKKK**— like the squawk of an angry goose—only magnified like a gazillion times— blasted into my brain— followed, but less loudly by an "Oooops! Oh my God!" from Katie.

In her maneuverings to get more comfortable or perhaps just closer to Napster, Katie had hit the damn horn.

Since Melissa and I were linked as intricately as two ballet dancers, we leaped as one from the seat. I don't know what muscle groups we used, but if Baryshnikov had ever jumped higher with a partner, it was because the two weren't in a Pierce-Arrow.

Disentangling ourselves in mid-air, Melissa and I scrambled out the back as Napster and Katie slid out the front. The four of us stood in the blackness trembling, our nerve endings as taut as the elastics on my old braces.

For a minute, no one talked or moved. The surge of adrenalin running through my body kept my mind acutely aware. Spider-Man's spidey senses couldn't have been more alert. But after the stupendously loud honk, the barn descended back into silence.

Napster whispered, "I don't hear anything."

Our ears strained up, up, up through the kitchen, the dining room, the living room, the bedrooms. No children cried. No lips muttered curses. No slippered feet stomped down stairs. As more and more we felt safe, we glanced at each other in our frozen postures, trying to hold back relieved titters.

"Closing time," I whispered.

No one argued. Not even Napster. Like burglars in a cartoon, we tiptoed toward the garage door. Again, Napster reached it first and turtle-like stuck his head out. We waited motionless. Napster waved for us to follow and, one behind the other as we had entered, we squeezed through.

When the four of us stood outside in the night air, we nearly broke into fits of laughter. But we needed to get farther away. We grabbed each other's hands and ran as fast as we could. It wasn't until we were beyond the tennis courts almost halfway to the gym that we stopped, looked at each other, and could no longer contain ourselves. Howls of mirth exploded like soda fizzing out of a shaken can. We roared, wailed, and shrieked, bent and gasping, no longer caring who saw or head us. We were safe, far from the barn. Except as our hysterics subsided, I gazed at Melissa holding her sides and realized she was using all five fingers from both hands.

Instantly sober, I pointed, "Where's your...?" and made a snapping motion.

Melissa stared aghast at her empty gloved hands. "My whip!"

"Didn't you leave it in the gym?" Katie said.

"No, no, no," I said, flashing on Melissa's whip hand stroking the hood of the Pierce-Arrow. "She had it in the barn."

Frantically, Melissa's eyes held mine as she thought back. "You're right. I had it in the car."

I would have laughed if it weren't so appalling. If Melissa's whip were still in the Pierce-Arrow, someone was going to have to get it and, unfortunately, I knew who that someone was. Me. I mean, this is what guy's do. This is what guys are for. It didn't matter that it was Melissa's whip, that she forgot it, that she was the damn ballerina, and if she got kicked out of Noyce, it wouldn't hurt her career a whit. I was the man, and if I was ever going to get my hands on Melissa's body again, I would have to do the manly thing and retrieve the cursed weapon. This was where feminism ended and letting the big dope do it began. All these thoughts flitted through my mind in an instant, along with images of Birdsong's frowning face and me, explaining to my parents why I chose to make out in, of all places, the school's Pierce-Arrow. Still, none of it prevented me from saying, albeit grimly, "I'll get it."

"I'll go," Melissa volunteered. But even though she said it sincerely, everyone knew I was going to say, "No," which I did. "It's safer just me. I'll meet you back at the gym." Before Melissa or anyone could object, I took off. The sooner I went and the faster I ran, the better off I was.

\#

Not waiting for my eyes to adjust was my mistake.

I was over-confident. Having been inside the barn just a few minutes before, I slid through the doors quickly, and once in, couldn't see a thing.

My hands waved in front of me like an ant's antenna but not as effectively. BLAAAMMMMMM. I walked straight into a post. My head hit the post so hard, I actually saw stars. It definitely was not as pleasant as bumping into Melissa. You know those cartoons where a character gets hit with a frying pan and stars circle around his head. That's what it was like. Literally. Blue, red, and green stars twinkled in front of my eyes. For a moment, I even thought how cool they looked, but that was before the pain throbbed. My only solace was that, while hitting my head on a post hurt, it didn't make much noise.

As I stepped away from the post, my heel landed on a rake. THWUNK-KKKK! The wooden handle slammed into my back. In reflex, I lifted my foot, and the rake clattered to the ground. I froze. The clang was nowhere near as loud as the horn, but it was loud enough to make me quake. I stood with my head throbbing, my back aching, my mouth silently cursing, and my hands weaving antenna-like in front of me, groping in the darkness for dangerous objects. I was going to ruin my life, and as I was now by myself, I wouldn't have the satisfaction of getting kicked out with Napster. But hearing no sounds from above of Moorland or his children steadied my nerves. The old farmer knew how to build barns.

Dealing with the post and the rake had one good effect—it gave my eyes time to adjust. Glancing down, I saw the rake slanted between my feet. If I'd taken another step I would have tripped and landed on a box of toys. If that hadn't roused Moorland, a shotgun wouldn't. I picked up the rake and set it against the post. I didn't care if it was in the exact same spot. Once I got out of the garage with the whip, I was in the clear.

Creeping over to the Pierce-Arrow, I set my feet slowly and carefully. At the door, I grabbed the handle. The door opened noiselessly. In 1925, America manufactured quality. I bent down. Greedily, my eyes scanned the floor and the seat. For a moment, everything swam. No whip. Shit. If Melissa dropped the whip on the dirt floor in this darkness I'd never find it, and with Mrs. Moorland heading this way, there was no time to look.

I folded my wings and bent deeper into the car. Like talons, my fingers scrabbled along the back of the seat. Maybe the whip was lost somewhere under the cushion, but my hands were already halfway. Then, suddenly, the side of my little finger brushed something. The rest of my fingers scurried up. The object was long, round, and plasticy. The whip! Our wriggling bodies had shoved it completely behind the cushion. I couldn't blame Melissa for forgetting it. My hand probed deeper and I grasped the handle and extracted it carefully kind of like pulling my cellphone out of the bottom of my duffel bag. With the (politically correct) weapon firmly in my possession, I bent my wings again and scrambled out of the car. I told myself, "Don't hurry. You're almost home free." Standing on the barn floor, I pressed the car door shut. I turned and tiptoed toward the barn entrance, making sure to avoid the box of toys, the post, and the rake. As I edged through the narrow opening, I saw Melissa on the hill framed in the moonlight. She'd waited. I held the whip high. Melissa waved her arms triumphantly, jumping up and down. I ran. If Mr. Hough had had his stopwatch, he would've been impressed. He always complains I don't have much of a sprint. He never provides sufficient incentive.

\#

In the gym lobby, Napster and Katie sat at a table. As soon as Napster saw us, he stood. Melissa brandished her whip over her head. Napster cupped his hands around his mouth, "Way to go, Stoner." Katie gave the V sign with both hands. A second later we joined them at the table. Napster had a Coke and diet Sprite lined up ready. In the light, Melissa stared at my forehead, "Oh, my God, look at you."

Melissa's tone became all motherly. "You've got a nasty bruise." She reached out, gently touching the bump.

I winced.

"It's a little swollen," Melissa said. "But mostly it's just red. What happened?"

"Did you hit yourself with the whip?" Napster snickered.

"No," I said. "I walked into a post."

For some reason, everyone thought this was hysterical. In the midst of their hilarity, I said. "I'm the guy who notices the whip's missing. I'm the guy who gets it, and you three think it's a joke."

Melissa said, "No we don't." Except she couldn't stop giggling.

"Cut it out, guys."

"Sure," Napster said, chortling.

I glared at them.

"It's nice to see some color back in your face," Napster said. "When you saw Melissa's whip was gone, you could've won the contest as a ghost."

"With that bruise on your forehead," Katie added, "You could win as a zombie."

Melissa stopped giggling and stroked my arm. "Don't listen. You're my hero. I'm proud of you." She leaned over and gave me a kiss on the cheek, whispering, "You're the reason I forgot the whip."

"What's this? Secrets?" Katie inquired.

"Oh, it's the 'ooops' girl," Melissa said. "It's you we have to thank for that awful 'auooonnnk.'"

"We saw a rabbit in the road," Napster said.

I said, "It sounded more like Mother Goose."

"Sorry," Katie apologized. "I was shifting around."

"At least, you didn't put the car in reverse. From now on, no more shifting."

"I'll give her parking lessons," Napster volunteered.

"Yeah. In about four months when you get your learner's permit."

"Hey, I said parking, not driving. We've got two cars and a long drive-way." Napster raised his Coke. "To Stoner—The Most Illustrious and Noble Retriever of the Whip."

The girls raised their drinks. "To Stoner."

I raised my Coke and added, "To the Pierce-Arrow Company and the engineers who designed a horn loud enough to frighten the dead but not loud enough to wake an English teacher and his two kids."

We clicked our cans and drank. It tasted fine. We were still students in good standing at the Noyce School. However, my standing with the Worth family was in jeopardy. From where she sat, Katie tilted her head and peered closer at Melissa's back. "Lean forward."

Melissa did. As she leaned, we saw what Katie had observed—long streaks smeared Melissa's tattoo. Seeing the concern on our faces, Melissa muttered, "What? What?"

"Your tattoo looks like one of my kindergarten finger paintings," Katie said.

Melissa glanced over her shoulder, trying to see.

Napster grabbed my arm and turned my hand over. It was stained with green. I turned my other hand over. The same. Napster and Katie burst into peals of laughter.

Napster said between gasps, "Looks like Stoner's been doing some finger painting of his own."

"Wait till Mr. Worth sees your hands," Katie said.

Talk about a ghost. Melissa quickly ordered, "Go in the bathroom and wash it off. Go. Go. Go."

I went.

With soap and water, most of the color washed off. When I returned, I held up my hands. Faint traces of the greenish color remained. Melissa said, "Put on your gloves."

"Your dad's not going to see me, never mind my hands."

"Please, Michael."

I put on my gloves.

#

At twelve precisely, the gym lights flooded the dance floor, transforming our Goth world back into our real nightmare: school. Melissa found her coat and fished out her cell. In an instant, she was talking to her dad.

"You're here.......Where?........OK.......Third prize.......Yeah. Second prize was a senior. First was good.......See you in a sec."

Melissa shut the phone, put her coat on and shoved her cell in her pocket. She leaned toward me and we kissed. When we broke apart, Melissa turned to find Katie. She and Napster were locked in their own embrace. Melissa beamed. Cupid could not have looked prouder.

#

"I can't believe it," I said to Napster as we waited for the bus. "You actually like Katie."

"Katie's OK."

"Don't give me any 'OK' crap. You like her."

"Sure. I like her," Napster said. "Didn't you see those breasts?"

"How about the way Katie got you with that *American Pie* stuff," I said.

"I liked the way she jumped into the car."

"What are you going to do when she wants you to listen to classical music?"

Napster pretended to be offended, "I'm not a total troglydyte."

"Troglodyte. Where did you come up with that?" (Third SAT word, but I guess I can't take too much credit as Napster said it.)

"I got it from Sal." (Change credit to Salome.)

"You mean your sister called you that?"

Napster nodded.

"She knows what kind of guy you are."

"Look who's talking. In the back seat, you and Melissa weren't discussing Jane Austen."

"I'm not saying I don't like Melissa's body."

"You better not, dude. With that whip and firm ass."

"Yeah."

"The way she leaped on stage, she must have some leg muscles. If you ever stuck your head between her thighs," Napster said, "she could crack your skull like an eggshell."

"What a way to go."

"You won't have to worry about going to heaven. You'll already be there."

"Amen to that, bro. But enough about me and Melissa. The subject is you and Katie."

"Not a big deal."

"You're going to see her again?"

Napster didn't respond. I figured that meant yes.

"I feel a disturbance in the Force," I said. "You're going to date a girl you actually have to talk to."

"You're such a snob. Just because Darlene goes to vocational school…"

"Hey. I've talked to Darlene. We both like old movies. I've never seen you talking to her. And speaking of talking, what are you going to do when Melissa tells Katie all about Darlene?"

"Nothing. Girls are very competitive. They love it when you've got a girlfriend. It makes you more desirable. Someone else wanting you makes them want you more."

"So you're going to go out with both of them."

Napster grinned.

#

Sunday at noon, Napster took off for home. Monday was a school day, and even though his parents knew Napster wouldn't start studying till eight, they insisted he be home early. My parents are the same way. I guess it's a parent thing.

At twelve-forty-five, I did my Patriots prep alone. I fixed myself two peanut butter and jelly sandwiches and a Coke and stashed a quart of Haagen-Dazs ice-cream behind a bag of frozen vegetables in the freezer. Most importantly, I banished my sister from the den. The only cloud hanging over an otherwise perfect afternoon was that my parents were home. With them lurking, who knew when some bizarre "grade improving" or "character building" project might waft through their brains. How and why parents get these ideas—that I need to clean out the garage or get an early start on my math—is beyond me. The problem is, when someone like Napster gets a stupid idea, I can say, "Shove it." When my parents get a stupid idea, squashing it requires a lot more tact. Just having to deal can take half the game.

However, for the moment, the 36-inch TV was mine.

The phone rang.

Since Napster had just left, I ignored it. I did not expect a call from him or Crusty or any of my other friends. It was almost 1 p.m. and everyone was undoubtably home watching the game.

A moment later, my mother walked into the den with this self-satisfied grin, glittering like it was radioactive. "Pick up the phone. It's your friend, Melissa."

My mother could have yelled that from downstairs. Instead she walked all the way up to the den just to see me blush. Now, I was confronted with a terrible choice. Did I talk out in the open or abandon my primo spot in front of the TV? I sighed. It was really no choice. "I'll call her back in my room."

As I stomped off, something unusual struck me. My heart wasn't beating fast. It's true I was startled when my mother said it was Melissa, and I did blush. It's also true Melissa had never called before, so this was new. But what surprised me most was that I was annoyed. I mean, Melissa was calling right before the game.

I shut the door to my room, grabbed my cell, and dialed. Melissa answered after one ring. "Hey," I said.

"Hey.......I just talked to your mom."

"I know. She didn't ask any embarrassing questions, did she?"

"Nope."

"You didn't tell her anything?"

"Like what?"

"I don't know. Anything? She's kind of nosy."

"She sounded nice."

"She is. But nosy."

"All mothers are nosy," Melissa said. "Part of the job description. I just said, 'Hi, Mrs. Steinman. This is Melissa. Is Michael there?' and she said, 'Hi, Melissa, Michael's in the den. I'll go get him.'"

"Did your parents say anything about your tattoo?"

"My dad noticed as soon as I took off my jacket."

"Uh-oh."

"He said, 'How did your tattoo get so smudged?'"

"I bet he was thinking of me," I gulped.

"I know," Melissa said.

"He's gonna ban me from your house."

"Noooo. I told him it got messed up dancing."

"Yeah," I said. "Horizontal dancing."

Melissa giggled.

"Your dad bought it?"

"Like a suit at J. Press."

I could see in Melissa's life dancing covered a lot of sins.

"What about your mom?"

"She was in bed."

"I bet she doesn't buy things so easily."

"She is tough." Then Melissa's probing began. "How about you and Steve? Did you guys like the dance?"

Since I knew where this was heading, I cut right to the chase, "You mean, did Napster like Katie?"

Melissa tittered, and in the background I heard some accompanying tee-hees.

"Is Katie there?"

"She is."

"How come she's not home practicing."

"The flute?"

"Yeah."

"Oh, she will. She's going to play for me when we hang up."

"Sure."

More titters and tee-hees.

Talking with Melissa was fun. At any other time I'd have been happy to while away the minutes in mindless chatter. But checking my watch, I saw it was ten past one. I'd already missed the start of the game.

"Seriously," Melissa began. Then she and Katie had another fit of giggles. "What did Stephen say?"

"Napster is very closed-mouthed about girls."

"He wasn't very closed-mouthed last night," Melissa said, launching herself and Katie into more tee-hees.

When she paused to breathe, I mentioned, "Melissa, the game is on."

"What game?"

"The Patriots game."

Melissa's voice knotted in disdain. "Football?"

"It's a big game."

"You mean," Melissa pouted, "you'd rather watch football than talk to me."

Yeah, I thought, I would rather watch football than talk to you. Right now, I wouldn't want to talk to Evan Rachel Wood. I wouldn't want to talk to Alexis Bledel. I wouldn't want to talk to Elisha Cuthbert. (OK. I'm lying. I would want to talk to Evan Rachel Wood, Alexis Bledel, and Elisha Cuthbert. Fuck the Patriots. But Melissa I could talk to any time.) However, out loud, I said, "I'm talking."

"Why don't you turn on the TV?" Melissa suggested.

"In my room?"

"You don't have a TV in your room?"

"You do?"

"Sure."

"I thought you don't like TV."

"I don't. I hardly ever watch it."

I groaned. "You don't like TV. Your parents give you one for your room. I love TV. My parents won't let me have a TV, even if I buy one with my own money."

"We can put the game on and tell you what's happening." Melissa said to Katie, "Turn on the TV…. What channel?"

"CBS," I said. "Just flip through."

"We've got like hundreds of channels."

"It's CBS. It'll be a low number."

"OK."

While Melissa and Katie hunted for the Patriots game, their dialogue went like this:

Melissa (to Katie): Keep switching.

Katie (to Melissa): There's a football game.

Melissa (sounding very knowledgeable): What teams are they? On Sunday there are lots of games.

Katie (to Melissa): I don't know. One team has red uniforms.

Me (shouting in the phone): The Patriots have white and blue uniforms. The Jets have green. It's blue and white and white and green. Melissa, blue and white and white and green. Melissa...Melissa....

Unfortunately, Melissa was not listening.

Melissa (authoritatively to Katie): I'm sure that's wrong. Keep switching. Hold it. Wait. Look in the corner. What does that score say?

Me (yelling into the phone): Score. There's a score. What's the score? Find out the score.

Katie (triumphantly to Melissa): It says Patriots and Jets.

Me (yelling): What's the score? The score?

Melissa (calmly to Katie): He wants to know the score.

Katie (calmly to Melissa): Patrots 3. Jets 3.

Me (frantically to myself): Two scores. I've missed two scores.

Melissa (coming back on the phone and announcing proudly): Did you hear. It's 3 to 3. We've got the right game.

Me (aggravated): Yeah. Thanks.

Melissa (annoyed): It's a tie. What's the problem? You haven't missed anything.

Me (trying to get back to the game): Look. I think Napster likes Katie. I think he's going to ask her out or something. That's all I know. Guys don't effervesce about this stuff.

Melissa: Oh, I see. We girls effervesce.

Me: Yeah. You do. I bet Katie has told you exactly what she thinks of Napster. What does she think of Napster?

Suddenly, I was greeted by silence. Another clash of codes.

Me (teasing): Ahhh. When it comes to spilling the beans about how Katie feels, we're not so eager.

Melissa: She likes him…a little.

Me: Well, Napster likes Katie….a little.

Melissa (sarcastically): As much as he likes *Darleeene*.

I guess Napster was right. It didn't seem as if Darlene was a problem. Melissa sounded derisive and combative. As if Katie was in a battle for

Napster's affection and Melissa sounded confident Katie would win. I guess Melissa and Darlene hadn't bonded as well as I'd thought. Melissa had already thrown Darlene to the dogs. But this was a fight I definitely did not want to get in the middle of. I said as firmly as I could, "I don't know."

"No?"

'No."

Melissa sighed as if this were a project she would have to work on and sailed the conversation in a new direction. "It's November. *Nutcracker* starts just before Thanksgiving. Seeing you is going to be harder." Happily, her voice sounded sad. "Will you come to one of my rehearsals?"

"Sure. Let's talk about it at school."

"You just want to watch your stupid football game, don't you?"

This was a difficult question to answer, since I did just want to watch the stupid football game. I was thinking what to say when Melissa jumped into the pause. "OK. Go ahead. I don't care."

"See you tomorrow before lunch."

"OK. Katie's going soon, anyway." I guess the girls had as much information as they figured they could get and wanted to chew it over.

"Say good-bye to Katie for me," I said.

"You say good-bye."

"Good-bye, Katie," I shouted.

Katie yelled, "Good-bye."

Then Melissa came back on the phone and said "Bye," so softly and sweetly I would have not watched the football game for another half hour. But I said to myself, Don't crawl. Just say, "Bye," and hang up and hope the score's still tied.

#

The next day in math, even though I was ducked way down in my seat (or maybe because of it), Mr. Ward called on me. First question. First person. Me.

Since I'd wasted half the night reading a Raymond Chandler mystery from a box of discarded books I'd found on the sidewalk on my way home from school and never even started my math homework (how does he know that?), I hemmed and hawed. For his part, Mr. Ward tried a new form of torture. He taunted, "Guess."

And waited.

Waited.

And waited.

The whole class sat in suspense.

I felt like Phillip Marlowe tied to a chair in a seedy hotel room.

Grinning like a blood-thirsty gunsel, holding a blackjack, Ward had my exit blocked. His red, unmoving eyes bore into me. I couldn't get away. Finally, I guessed.

As everyone in class cracked up, including Melissa and Katie, it was clear I was way off. Katie I didn't care about. Sooner or later, Napster was going to break her heart. But Melissa!

On our walk to lunch, she tried making up for it. "Ward is such a jerk. When he told you to guess and stood there staring, I thought I was going to die."

"I did die about ten times, only I must've caught your brother's Buddhist bit because every time I reincarnated and was back in math."

"An etheral body would have worked sooo much better."

"True," I agreed. "I could've floated out the door or disappeared."

"I would've liked to have seen Ward's face for that. What an asshole. Worse than an asshole. A wart on an asshole."

"That's good," I said. "'A wart on an asshole'. How'd you come up with that?"

"Ballet class. Carmen Silva. I told you about her."

"The friend you hate?"

Melissa nodded. "It's a girl thing. Don't try to figure it out. Carmen speaks fluent Spanish on account of she's, like, from Argentina, and she's always yakking about this ranch her father owns. She says the hands there call each other lots of weird swears in Spanish, like 'You son of a dog's pubic hair.' So, after class, we make up the same kind of swears in English."

"Amusing?"

"Trés."

Having Melissa call Mr. Ward "a wart on an asshole," and hearing her say "son of a dog's pubic hair," got me over my down mood. It was actually kind of exciting. I mean, how many times do you hear a girl (especially a cute girl) say, "pubic hair," even if it's only a dog's?

We reached Grovesnor and hung around outside. There was still room in the lobby, but it was nicer outside. Melissa glanced at me sideways and said, "Want to come to my ballet class Saturday?" The pink stars on her cheeks reappeared. Calling Mr. Ward "a wart on an asshole" and talking about a dog's pubic hair didn't bother her— inviting me to her ballet class, she blushed.

"To help you guys with swears?"

"To see me dance. We can spend the rest of the day together. Have supper. Go to a movie."

"Sure." I wanted to see Melissa dance. I wanted to see the girls in her class. I definitely wanted to meet Carmen.

"You know this has to be our last Saturday for a while. We've got sooo many rehearsals. And November performances start, and final exams are coming, and my parents..."

I held up my hands. "I got that memo."

"What about Steve?"

"What about Steve?"

"Would he...um...would he...uh...want to come along?"

"To your class?"

"No. To the movie."

"Did Katie get you to ask? She must really..."

"Not a chance," Melissa interrupted, full of indignation at the very idea. "It's just, Katie wants to see me dance, and then I thought we could meet Steve, go to a movie, and all come to my house after."

"If this is our last Saturday for a while," I objected, "maybe we could go to a movie by ourselves." I didn't really care if Napster and Katie came along to the movie. What bothered me was the "after." With Melissa and me occupying the couch in the den, I suspected my bud and his new squeeze—no matter how much I warned him—would end up on the green couch in Melissa's living room, which looked like something the appraisers on *Antiques Roadshow* would "conservatively value at auction" for what it costs to go to Noyce for a year, and I didn't think a Napster/Katie make-out session would help its provenance. I for one preferred Mrs. Moorland finding us in the Pierce-Arrow than Mrs. Worth finding Napster and Katie groping each other on her revolutionary war couch.

"We'll still see each other every day at school," Melissa suggested.

"Math and five minutes before lunch..."

"Well, what can I do? You know I have ballet...."

"I know," I said.

"Sooo…"

"Wait. Wait. I've got an idea."

Melissa arched a skeptical eyebrow.

I tried countering by raising my own eyebrow, but I can never do one. Both of my eyebrows go up at the same time, which ruins the effect. Melissa has great eyebrow control. Could it be that damn ballet?

I said, "I'll come to your class myself. Let Napster and Katie go out on their own. When *The Nutcracker* starts, we'll all go see you dance. That'll give us another time, and I'll get to see you dance twice," which was true but anything that delayed Napster and Katie using the Worth's apartment as the set for their own personal porn movie was the real plus for me.

Melissa mulled this over. For a moment, she liked the idea and the sun shone. Then gray clouds formed. "*The Nutcracker's* a two-hour ballet. It's not just mice. There's tights. Lots of men in tights."

"So?"

"So, Steve'll never agree."

"Yes, he will," I said. "This way Napster gets to have like a real "date" with Katie. His parents won't object. I mean, think of it. Napster at the ballet! Who could ever stand in the way of that?"

Melissa smirked. "Who could?"

"So we're on?"

"On."

The sun burst through.

The doors opened for lunch.

#

Katie looked different. Sitting in math, I was wondering what it was when it hit. She wasn't wearing glasses. All through class, I thought she would put them on, but for the entire fifty-two minutes, no glasses. She just gazed upward with that alert I'm-eager-to-learn-look that sometimes forms on your face in school like a zit. I know because it's formed on mine, so I didn't blame her for it. Three days after hooking up with Napster, she was wearing contacts. Had she already planned on switching? Was it a coincidence? Or should I put it down to the Napster effect? Had my buddy awoken the teen temptress smoldering within her?

When Katie strolled into class two days later, all such questions were resolved. Her beautiful dark brown tresses were tinted with blonde high-lights, and at every step, they bounced and glistened like a Clairol commercial. As for her clothes, rather than her usual frumpy outfits, she had on a skirt that showed off her long legs and this low cut blouse that showed off her breasts. I believe I've mentioned that Katie has nice breasts, but other than on Halloween, she never did much with them. Now they were working for her hard. Double hard. Looking at them, I almost got hard myself, and this was in math.

Even Ward's pink eyes bulged when his gaze caught sight of those tits. For a moment, I almost bonded with him. I knew how he felt. I mean, suddenly seeing Katie's sensational knockers where before had swelled this well-covered chest was, I am sure, a jolt. Fifteen-year-old girls with breasts like that are why they have statutory rape laws. Maybe, if I were lucky, Katie would wear a push-up bra every day, and that would make one (two) less reason(s) for Mr. Ward to glance my way.

#

This afternoon, we drove to Beaver Country Day for a cross-country meet.

Beaver Country Day really is the name, and it used to be an all-girl's school. I am not making this up. What were they thinking? However, it is now co-ed. I mean, when they cheer, they actually yell, "Go Beavers!" I heard this with my own ears. And no one laughs. The guys don't laugh. The teachers don't laugh. The parents on the sidelines don't laugh. The girls certainly don't laugh. And we don't laugh, although on the bus back to Noyce, Sandy Connors yelled, "Go Beavers!" and we did laugh. Even Mr. Hough. Anyway, we won. I came in fourth, as usual. After I crossed the finish line, Mr. Hough grabbed me and grunted, "Steinman, next year if you want that varsity letter, these fourth-place finishes better be third." Phil Rosenbloom is graduating, and Mr. Hough is anxious. Everybody wants something from you. I don't know how he knows how much I want that varsity letter, but he does.

When I got home, Napster called. Napster loves making attention-grabbing headlines, and this one was in 72-point type. Not only were he and Katie getting together for Saturday, but she was sleeping over! I mean, they've only gone out once to the Halloween Dance, and everything with Katie—and Darlene—is on the sly.

"You're shitting me," I said.

"Believe it, dude."

Then, it hit me. "Salome invited her."

"Bing. Did you think I told my mother I was having a sleepover with a girl?"

Immediately, I was envious. I could see if you have to have a sister—and I suppose in order to have women in the world, a lot of guys like Napster and I have to have sisters—the only sister to have is a twin sister.

"Salome barely even knows Katie," I said.

"I know. You should've seen Salome checking out Katie at the dance."

"I saw. It was this total head-to-toe chick checkout."

"You're right there," Napster said. "Any second, I was expecting Salome to bend over and sniff Katie's ass."

"Well, the scent must've passed."

"Yeah," Napster said. "They're kind of similar. Brainy. And Salome likes classical music. She once even took flute lessons."

In awe, I said, "It's like God is helping you get laid."

"It amazes me sometimes."

"When I see you with a yarmulke like Crusty, it'll be a sign you wore your first rubber in combat."

"That's *your* sign. You're the one who's obsessed with yarmulkes."

"Just Crusty's. So how did you convince Salome to do this?"

"It was Salome's idea," Napster said, full of familial pride. "At the bus stop, she said, 'The symphony's gonna be on Channel 2 Saturday night. On our surround sound, it'll be awesome. If you want, I'll ask Katie if she'd like to sleep over.'"

"Wow," I said. "Tough decision. You're gonna have Katie in her night-gown."

"Probably a thick woollie covered with pictures of Mozart and Beethoven."

"That's the old Katie," I said. "The new Katie is out at Victoria's Secrets, buying lace Teddies."

"If only."

"What does Salome get for this? A sleepover for Giddy?"

"My parents would never fall for that. They know Giddy. That's why Salome thinks it's such a good idea to have Katie over now."

"Salome's got to have some angle."

"Katie's local. My parents love the whole culture bit. Salome told 'em Katie is in the Boston Youth Orchestra. They sucked that up. So Giddy's coming over for the symphony. Do you want to bring Melissa?"

"I told you, we're going to a movie."

"If you change your mind, plenty of basement corners are still available and, I promise, no car horns."

#

The Boston Ballet studio is located in the South End. At one time, the South End was one of the seedier sections of Boston. Now it's trendy. Hip restaurants, bars, stores, and condos swank up the place. The ballet being cool, arty, and stylish fits right in.

Inside, the squarish brick, granite, and glass building, a pretty college-type girl sat at a reception desk. Beside her loafed a guard. Both glanced at me briefly. The guard went back to reading the sports section of the *Herald* and the girl went back to answering the phones. I guess I looked like I belonged, which kind of made me feel insulted. Then I thought, lots of regular guys must pass through the doors—brothers and boyfriends of the dancers. That was me. A boyfriend.

Melissa had told me to go to Studio 3 on the second floor.

Other than the guard and the receptionist, I didn't see anyone, but as I climbed the stairs, I heard a piano playing. The tune seemed familiar. Then like a moron, I realized it was from *The Nutcracker*.

The atmosphere in the building reminded me of the mall. You just sensed girls. Hot looking girls. Everywhere. But other than the receptionist, I didn't see any. Then I reached the studios on the first floor and spotted some. But the girls were my sister's age. Ten or eleven. They were dressed in black leotards and sprinkled about in a large alcove like jimmies on an ice-cream. They sat or leaned against the walls, reading schoolbooks and listening to iPods. A few were stretching and bending. A couple glanced up. Most didn't.

I rounded the corner and climbed to the second floor. As I went up the stairs, a bunch of dancers descended. These girls were older, old enough to be dancers in the company. Like seniors at Noyce, they talked and laughed as if they owned the place. As they flowed down the stairs, I couldn't help comparing them to Melissa. There were four. All lovely. Radiant really. Their faces glowed like blossoms just opened to the sun. Their bodies reminded me of flower stems—narrow but strong—easily maintaining a straight, upright structure without an ounce to spare.

Well, Melissa has the same slimness, and the same strength and posture, and she is certainly equally pretty. But there was something extra about these girls—something intimidating. Melissa didn't have their swagger, their confidence. But I guess that was natural. Melissa is a student. Nonetheless, I felt a flutter of concern. Melissa is so focused on this goal, I'd hate for her to be disappointed.

I reached the third floor, turned to the left, and found myself in a scene the duplicate of the eleven year olds downstairs. Except these girls were my age. I glanced around to see whether Melissa was among them. She wasn't. But for the moment I didn't care. What four years had done was amazing. Puberty rocks. It was an ever-changing kaleidoscope of curves—convex and concave—and wherever my eyes slid was equally enticing: blondes, brunettes, and redheads, all in burgundy tights, lolled about the place. Some of the girls were putting on street clothes, getting ready to leave. Even though these girls were dressing, they were the sexiest. Each time one of them stuck her legs in her jeans and lifted them up, wriggling her beautiful ballet butt, it jolted me. Tights make even slender girls look somewhat pearish. Jeans gave the girls' hips, legs, and ass the perfect shape.

While I was enjoying the scenery, the girls occasionally eyed me. Mostly they studied, listened to their iPods or finished dressing. Some had cell phones and talked.

After I figured I had gawked as much as I could without getting thrown out, I went over to the glass door of the studio and peered in. Melissa was one of twelve girls in the room. Even though she was in the front row, she didn't notice me. She was listening to the teacher. When the teacher knelt and pushed the button of a boom box, the girls started dancing. They glided into a circle and began spinning on their toes to what Melissa had told me was "The Dance of the Sugar Plum Fairies." As they moved, I could see this was not gym. This was not an exercise group. This was not a hobby. These girls twirled in unison, their legs as straight and sharp as scissors. Gone was spaced-out Melissa.— When I run cross-country, I try not to think how tired I am, how much farther I have to go, how cold it is, how skimpy my stupid cross-country outfit is, and that I am doing it just so I can stick a varsity letter on my high school jacket. —But these girls were into it. These girls were serious. They were aware of what they were doing. What the girls on either side of them were doing. Where every arm, hand, leg, and foot was. How it should move. How it should look. And most importantly, who and what the teacher was observing.

Naturally, I paid most attention to Melissa. Now that I saw her dancing, I thought maybe my doubts of a moment ago were unnecessary. I couldn't believe her astonishing flexibility and control, —particularly when the girls suddenly stopped, shifted their weight, and, as one, pointed their left foot straight out and, without a pause, swung their left legs high above their waist as effortlessly as if they were raising their arms. The movement was incredibly smooth, light, graceful and erotic, all at the same time.

Another pang swept through me.

The teacher clapped her hands, and the class halted as if on a dime. One minute the girls were twirling, the next they were standing loose with their hands on their hips. Baby ducks couldn't obey their mother faster. I could just make out the teacher's voice as she rattled off instructions in this technical dance-speak that included a lot of French words. She pointed at a few of the girls, gesturing with her hands what she wanted them to do.

With a nod, the teacher dismissed the class, and the girls broke ranks like an army platoon. In ones, twos, and threes, they scattered, chatting with their friends and picking up their equipment: —towels, tape, Band-Aids, combs, water bottles, notebooks, socks, ballet shoes, cell phones, iPods, and granola bars. They stuffed their supplies into large tote bags and slung them over their shoulders. The teacher opened the studio door, and each girl slipped out, politely bidding the teacher goodbye.

Melissa was third out. Our eyes met and instantly, she morphed from super ballerina to girlfriend. "You came!" she squealed, running over and hugging me.

"Did you think I wouldn't?"

Melissa shrugged. "Oh, you know. Guys and ballet."

"No prob here. Your class is all girls."

"Come on, Michael. Grow up."

Melissa dragged me to where a clump of girls were talking. "I want you to meet my friends."

As we neared, the girls, pulling sweaters and jeans out of their tote bags, glanced our way.

"Hey, Meliss," one of the girls said.

"Hey." Melissa tugged me forward by the hand. "This is Michael. Michael—Ariel, Lindsey, Tasha, Heather, Carmen."

I nodded. The girls eyed me back. Melissa had pretty friends.

"I enjoyed watching," I said. "It was great."

"We were kinda ragged," Melissa complained.

"For a moment, you were perfect," I said.

Melissa replied, "It's not supposed to be for a moment."

One of the girls, I think it was Carmen, undid her bun and shook her hair. The change was dramatic. This big rush of golden red hair poured down like sunshine after a storm. "Melissa is a perfectionist," she said, peeking out at me from behind a silken ray. Her eyes were large, tawny, and luminous.

Lindsey, I think it was Lindsey, said, "We can't be anything but perfect." Lindsey bent over to put on her dungarees. As she bent, I caught a glimpse of her breasts. She was wearing the same burgundy leotard as everyone else, and when you looked at her straight on, she didn't seem much different; but when she stooped, I could see even Napster would like this girl. She was a couple of inches taller than Melissa and statuesque. If she continued growing, her destiny was definitely Broadway or Vegas. Anywhere else, her figure would make her the queen. Here, she was pitied.

As if they were so used to dancing together, they did everything in unison: —Ariel, Tasha, Heather, and Carmen grabbed their jeans and stuck their feet in the legs. None of them were as endowed as Lindsey, but watching them wriggle into their tight jeans was another jolt. I hoped the girls didn't notice my knees buckle.

Heather, I think it was Heather, said, "I heard next week we're getting fitted for costumes." She smiled at me as she said this, even though the information was meant for the other girls. Heather lifted her hands over her head and pulled on a sweater. I kept thinking to myself, how could I not have known about this place? I mean, here I was, surrounded by five practically perfect girls, and even I could see, dense as I am, how much they were flirting.

I would've thought, as Melissa's boyfriend, they would've left me alone. Then I remembered what Napster had said. It was Melissa's liking me that brought it on. Girls were competitive, and they were vying for my attention. If I had entered this place unattached, it would have been hard to meet one of these girls, never mind the five. It was another of life's many conundrums. (Fourth SAT word. Well, three for me; one for Salome.) When you're attached and unavailable, it's easy to meet girls. When you're alone and desperate, girls are difficult as hell to meet. Still, in the back of my mind, I was musing, perhaps I could interest Sarah in ballet lessons.

The girls prattled on for a few minutes about costumes. As they talked, I noticed the girls' eyes shift (still in unison) from me to my right. I turned my head.

I didn't like what I saw. It was a guy wearing black tights and a loose black sweater, bearing our way. He was a cool-looking guy. You might wonder how a guy in tights can look cool, but this guy did. He had black hair, very dark eyes, and a narrow, serious face. His body was muscular, and he didn't seem at all self-conscious about his stupid tights. He seemed confident and natural. His walk was smooth. I wish I could say it was gay smooth, but it wasn't. It was athletic smooth. Animal smooth. He eased forward, silent and dangerous like a panther, gliding through the jungle. Even worse, he was only a couple of years older than me. If he were at Noyce, he'd probably be a senior. I looked down at the girls. Their eyes were fixed on him. Even Melissa's. From being the center of attention, I didn't exist.

"Chey," he said in a throaty Russian accent.

As one, the girls chirruped, "Hey, Yuri."

"Chas anyvone seen Yoel?"

"No, Yuri," the girls said.

"If chyou see chim, ask chim stop at Studio Four."

Boldly, Carmen began, "I hear you're doing 'The Russian Dance'."

Yuri's face lost his intense expression. He appeared almost puckish, like a boy caught with his hand in the cookie jar but who was confident he could grin his way out. It was a very charming grin. It had probably gotten him in and out of trouble with a lot of cookie jars of various sizes, shapes, and ages. "I cham lucky," he said. "In Russia, even when young, ve do zis dance."

"I can't wait to see you," Carmen oozed.

"It vill be fun. First *Nutcracker* in States. Chard but fun."

Ariel, I think it was Ariel, said, "I saw the Kirov in London last year."

"Ahh, Mariinski dancers are good. That's where I study before parents move chere. Don't forget. Tell Yoel I am Studio Four."

The girls chirped together, "We will," and watched Yuri slink away, his ass muscles bobbing in his tights. The girls stared openly. Talk about eyes popping and mouths drooling. I couldn't have stared harder if it were Jessica Alba. After Yuri disappeared, the girls glanced at each other and burst into giggles. When their laughter ended, the girls gazed sadly down at their things. They picked up their dance bags, books, scarves, and cells phones. "Bye, Meliss," they said. "Bye Michael."

Sweetly, they smiled, Yuri's bobbing ass momentarily forgotten. In a group, they headed out of the room. As they rounded the corner, I heard another burst of giggles. Gradually, the sound faded.

Melissa turned to me. As if Yuri's appearance had never occurred, she said, "I'll change. Won't take long. Then, let's walk."

#

At this time, I didn't know when a city girl suggests, "Let's walk," it actually means "shop."

It was a lesson I learned.

I thought we were just sort of wandering around, but the route Melissa led me on traversed the shortest distance between 19 Clarendon Street and the Copley Mall. As we crossed Columbus Ave, Melissa asked, "How'd you like my friends?"

"Fine."

Somewhat edgily, Melissa said, "When Lindsey bent over to put on her jeans, I thought your chin was going to scrape the floor."

I almost retorted, "What about you drooling over Yuri's ass," but I didn't want to mention anything about Yuri, especially his ass. It bothered me less to defend myself. "She was leaning over right in front of me."

Melissa said, "They all flirted with you like mad."

"I guess."

"Did you like Carmen?"

As I knew Melissa and Carmen were rivals, I feigned ignorance, "Which one was Carmen?"

Melissa did not seem taken in. Nonetheless, she replied, "The one with the gorgeous auburn hair."

"Oh, yeah. She's OK."

"OK? She's beautiful. And her technique is soooo good. Did you see the way she made up to Yuri?" Suddenly, Melissa broke into an exaggerated imitation, "'Yurrrriiiiii, I can't waaaaiiit to see you dance.' How obvious can you be?"

"What's the diff?"

"No diff," Melissa said. "But soooo annoying. Carmen speaks perfect English. But when anyone compliments her on her dancing, she goes all cutesy and says, 'Ohhh, I was born in Argentina. —My mind's American, but my feet are Spanish.' What bull. It's not her feet that's Spanish. It's her butt."

"Whoa-whoa-whoa," I laughed. "Cat fight."

Ignoring my laughter, Melissa muttered, "Carmen makes me soooo mad sometimes. Like this afternoon in class, the teacher put her first so, of course, Carmen throws me this smarmy grin like it's such a big deal."

"Is it?"

"What?"

"A big deal."

Melissa shrugged. "Usually it's me or Carmen that's put first. Sometimes it's Lindsey or Ariel. But whenever it's Carmen, she puffs up like she's just won Miss America and I'm her runner-up."

"We could put the two of you in a ring in tutus and toe shoes and let you battle it out. It could solve the whole guys-don't-like-ballet thing."

Melissa shot me one of her I-am-not-amused looks. "You're not crushing on Carmen, are you?"

I was stunned. Where did that come from? I didn't even want to talk about Carmen. I mean Carmen was cute—more than cute—Carmen was totally love worthy, but one ballerina was enough for me. Even though I'd told myself not to mention the guy, I found myself replying, "Didn't you say Carmen only has eyes for Yuri?"

Melissa said, "All the girls like Yuri. He's the best dancer in school. His family left St. Petersburg because his father was afraid of the Russian mafia or something. But it must've been serious because Yuri was at the Vaganova Academy, which is like the best in the world."

"He's not in your class, is he?" I asked, hoping I had guessed right.

"He's eighteen," Melissa said. "In 7i. Next year, he'll dance with a company."

By this time, we had reached the mall, although, as I said, I hadn't known the mall was our destination. But for Melissa, from walking by to suggesting "a quick peek" was merely a matter of a moment. And once inside, Melissa's mind became completely absorbed by clothes. As I followed her through various stores, Melissa thrust hanger after hanger in my face with what appeared to be limp shreds of colored cloth but which were actually expensive articles of female apparel. She kept peppering me with questions like, "Do you like this?" or "Isn't this pretty?" or "How much do you think this costs?" or "Who would ever wear this?" for two fucking hours!

Tip to girls: The only articles of female apparel dangling from a hanger a guy has any clue what it will look like on is a bra or a thong.

#

*Runaway Jury*, the movie Melissa picked (when finally we made it to the movies), stars John Cusack and Rachel Weisz, the one woman in the world with whom Napster, Crusty, Giddy, and I would like to have sex. However, I neglected to mention this. Before couch time, I was not about to bring up anything that contradicted my stated preference for small-breasted girls or implied an appreciation of any female other than Melissa. It's true, I do like small breasts but I'm not crazy.

Melissa liked *Runaway Jury*. She liked John Cusack's and Rachel Weisz's relationship. I was hung up on all the plot holes.

"If you like sound plots," Melissa said, "you're going to have a hard time with *The Nutcracker*."

"*The Nutcracker* is a ballet. It's a fantasy. *Runaway Jury* pretends to be reality."

Melissa was about to reply when her cell phone rang. It was Katie.

I guess we didn't need to double since they could talk to each other almost as much by phone.

"No........Really........How was the symphony?.........The movie was awesome........John Cusack was his usual cute self........He didn't like it........... Plot holes..........Yeah. The writer thing..........What did Stephen say........ Really........Oh, my God, really........What are you wearing?......."

At the mention of Napster's name and what Katie was wearing, my ears perked up. Was Katie already in pajamas with nothing on underneath? Except just as the conversation got good, Melissa's voice sank to a level I could hear, but no longer distinguish the words. Like speed texting and shopping, it's a skill girls develop early—to talk at a level only the person you are addressing can understand yet not whisper. Whispering would obviously be hiding something. So I can't report what she said, although at the end of the call, Melissa stuck her phone back in her purse and confided, "Symphony's over. Band Camp's about to begin."

We headed to Melissa's apartment. We had our own Camp to attend.

#

The next day, when I straggled downstairs, I was alone. My family was at the Kruger's who have two daughters around Sarah's age who are more of a pain than Sarah is.

Because the Patriot's were playing a Monday night game, I had nothing to do, so I surfed channels and caught *The Sure Thing* on TCM. Another John Cusack movie. He was trucking to California with Daphne Zuniga, a great-looking, small-breasted, Hollywood actress. The movie's a combination road journey and desperate-guy-trying-to-get-laid flick. In this case, a corny, Hollywood quest with a sweet, PG ending you can see all the way from Cleveland. It was fun, even though when it ended, I found myself staring at the screen vacant-eyed with a fading cathode ray tube smile (still no plasma or LCD TV in our house), wondering, do they get married and live happily ever after, or do they break up and languish through life alone?

Before I could get too depressed, I dialed Napster. "Whose room did Katie sleep in? Yours or Salome's?"

Napster laughed a rueful laugh.

"OK," I said. "She slept in Salome's. But something must've happened."

"We watched the symphony. Katie and Salome were into it. Giddy liked it, too, but you know how p-whipped he is."

"Yeah. His mother's dragged him to museums since he was born. He told me, she's even taken him to flower shows."

"Mothers can really mess you up."

"My dad says, 'The hand that rocks the cradle rules the world.'"

"I don't know what that means," Napster said, "but after the symphony, Giddy was rocking Salome pretty good."

"Napster, that's gross. She's your sister."

"Yeah. The slut. She and Giddy claimed the couch. Katie and I dug in under the Ping-Pong table—no pillows, no blankets, just thin basement rug."

"You should've been better prepared. Didn't cub scouts teach you anything besides stealing doughnuts?"

"I didn't want to risk my mother doing a pre-symphony sweep."

"You could've beaten Salome to the couch."

"Sal arranged the sleepover, so she got the couch—the price of doing business."

"I don't know what that means."

"I don't either, but my uncle says it a lot."

"How'd it go?"

"Just when things were heating up, my mother yelled for us to come up for snacks. We had to charge upstairs and eat cake. Talk about a pain."

"In the balls. Yeah."

"After snacks, Giddy left and my mother whooshed Salome and Katie off to bed. I kept hoping Katie was going to sneak into my room, but she never did."

"Next time."

"Nah," Napster said. "After Katie left this morning, my mother did her *LA Law* routine. She kept clinking the ice in her scotch and firing questions. I think my mother's suspicious because Katie is much better looking than Salome's usual dog friends. So there's a hold on sleepovers. You and Crusty can stay over because my mother knows Salome has absolutely no interest in either of you."

"Thanks, I guess."

"Salome can have Betsy Schneider and Alison Tully over."

"Because she knows they're both too ugly for you to put the make on."

"My mother's explanation was because Salome has known them since they were like six. Shauna Redmond slips in, too, because she's Salome's best friend, even though she's kind of cute but not really busty."

"Maybe I should tell your mother it's safe for Salome to have any friends over that have an A cup size or less."

"I'd love to see my mother's face when you tell her that," Napster said. "I'll give you ten bucks."

"Ten bucks isn't enough."

"How much?"

I paused. "Maybe a thousand?"

"Do you take checks?"

"Not until you're president of the screw factory."

"Forget it."

"Well, you've still got Darlene and Katie," I consoled. "Nothing's changed that."

"True."

I asked Napster, "How long do you think you can play this game?"

"Never plan ahead, Stoner. That's your trouble. With women, you think too much."

#

The last day before Thanksgiving, I stayed late after school because Mr. Moorland wanted to talk about *The Looking Glass*. One of my jobs is proofing the mag before it goes to the printer. The job is not difficult because I run everything through a spellchecker, but mistakes still appear. I correct punctuation and stuff like "two" and "to" and "their" and "they're" the software often misses. Mr. Moorland hates mistakes since it gives an excuse to the kids who think they're English geniuses to run up and tell him they found an error on page 19—a quotation mark was missing. Brilliant. Let's see them write a good story.

At least, fall sports were over. I didn't have to run cross-country and freeze my ass off. It was the gym and intramural basketball until March. No pressure. And one harried teacher, Mr. Small, a science teacher who didn't give a damn what happened as long as we showed up, didn't kill anybody and didn't break anything expensive.

Basketball ended quickly because Mr. Small didn't want to stick around any longer than we did. We chose up teams, played a couple of short, half-court games, and hit the shower.

As I had to proof the copy before I left school, I trudged across campus to *The Looking Glass* office. When I got out of the elevator, who should I find leaning against the door like a dame in the Raymond Chandler novel I'd just read—Cyndi Swansey.

As I neared, Cyndi said, "Got two new poems for the winter issue."

"Cool." One of the benefits of Cyndi's post Halloween celebrity was that Karen Wechsler, who didn't like her first poem, asked her to submit more.

I unlocked the door to the office with the key Wechsler had lent me. (Only full editors have their own keys, which is annoying, especially to Napster, as you can imagine. Next year.)

Cyndi and I sat in the office's two comfy, leather, swing chairs while I glanced at her poems. They were in the haiku vein. Cyndi has Mrs. Kornhauser for English, and Kornhauser is a huge haiku fan. Cyndi's poems went:

1.

My mood is as dark as my menstrual blood.—
A boy passes me in the hall and smiles.
I want to rip his throat out with my nails.

2.

Maybe life isn't so bad.
You can jump on grass
And it still grows.

(reprinted with permission of *The Looking Glass*)

After I read her first poem, I thought of telling Cyndi about the History of Menstruation website but chickened out. Instead, I said, "I like 'em. The second is even upbeat."

"I wrote that the day my mother bought a pair of Manolo Blahniks."

"Manolo Whatniks?"

"Blahniks. Shoes. My mother spent the entire afternoon trying them with different outfits and left me alone."

"A cause for celebration?"

"I wrote the poem."

I shook my head. Cyndi's unique. "I'm going over the fall copy one more time and emailing it to Wechsler. It'll be out around exams. You'll be even more famous."

"Third-rate bank clerks want to be famous," Cyndi said. "I just want my poems to be read."

"Isn't that kind of the same thing? If no one's heard of you, who's going to read your poems?"

"I don't care how many drones have heard of me. I don't care what drones say."

"Who's a drone?"

"People without taste or ideas."

"I think kids here are pretty smart."

"Oh, if getting good marks on tests means you're smart, they're smart. But all the kids here care about is getting into a good school and making lots of money."

I felt myself flush. That sounded a lot like me. "Am I a drone?"

"On the surface, you're kind of drone-like, but unlike most kids, you've got ideas. You've got taste."

I smiled. It's always flattering when someone thinks you've got something. But then this was Cyndi. I asked, "Who decides all this? You?"

Cyndi shook her head. "It's self-evident."

"And I'm in. Well, welcome me to your world."

"It's not that exclusive."

"I think it is. How many people do you even talk to?"

"Numbers," Cyndi cried, holding her hands over her ears as if in pain. "No numbers. Too much like grades."

"You mean too much like the truth."

Swinging back and forth in our armchairs, we glared at each other, although neither one of us was really angry. We like giving each other a hard time. And now that I was looking at Cindi more closely, I could see that under her super black hair and whitish make-up, her features were pretty, and I had this thought—maybe it was my intuition working again—beneath her baggy black pants and black cotton shirt she wore tight black lace panties and a lacy black bra. I guess whenever I talk to Cyndi, I hope she'll give up the Goth disguise. Maybe Cyndi hopes I'll start wearing leather and chains.

"That ballerina, Melissa," Cyndi said, eyeing me appraisingly. "The one who won a prize. Is she your girlfriend?"

"You know Melissa?" I marveled.

Cyndi nodded. "She was on my field hockey team."

"Doesn't play field hockey. Just does ballet."

"I know. But the beginning of the year, her dance classes hadn't started, so she was on my team."

"Really?"

"Yeah."

I tried imagining Melissa in a field hockey outfit, passing the ball (or whatever they call it) to Cyndi. Another negative to cross-country is that the course doesn't go anywhere near the girls' athletic fields, so I don't see a lot of the girls in their uniforms. Those short field hockey skirts are sexy. I don't think I've ever seen Cyndi in a skirt, though I'd like to. An accidental flash might reveal the truth re: those black lace panties. —But what I was really thinking was that if Cyndi and Melissa were on the same field hockey team even for a day, Cyndi and Melissa would've changed in the girl's locker room. Cyndi might have seen Melissa naked. I mean, I've never seen Melissa naked. I've never come close to seeing Melissa naked. Suddenly, it was strange, realizing Cyndi might've seen Melissa naked and that Melissa might've seen Cyndi naked—without Cyndi's whitish face powder and black eyeliner. I bet if I asked Cyndi what Melissa's body looked like, she'd tell me. She was that kind of person. The problem was, I hated to admit to Cyndi I hadn't seen Melissa naked. Casually, I replied, "We've gone to the movies a couple of times."

"You two walk to lunch practically every day."

I wondered, "Do you think Melissa's a drone?"

"Melissa's not a drone. She's too tough."

"Tough?"

"If a girl's cute and giggles, guys can't see beyond that. I'm tough, but Melissa's tougher." I knew Cyndi wasn't talking about strength, even though Melissa was in good shape. The only sense I could make of her remark was that Cyndi was referring to how focused on ballet Melissa was.

"What about Napster?"

"Who?"

"Steve Belknap. I hang with him a lot."

Cyndi looked confused for a moment. "Oh. That short, preppy kid with brown hair?"

I nodded.

"What about him?"

"Is he a drone?"

Cyndi looked bored discussing Napster. "He's a drone. A fancy drone. If drones came in models like cars, he'd be a Mercedes 500."

Impressive. That was his father's car.

#

Thanksgiving!!!!

Thursday: —Turkey.

Friday: ---Winnipesaukee.

It was Darlene's turn, and Napster needed cover. However, as finals were immediately after Thanksgiving, in order to get away I had to promise my parents Salome would help me with my math. My parents would never have believed Napster and I would do any work. But Salome is responsible. My parents know if Salome says she will help, she will, which was the price I had to pay to get out of my house. And it was worth it. My Aunt Rebecca and Uncle Howard were visiting. My uncle is OK, but Aunt Rebecca is the loud, cheek-pinching type. She is my father's older sister and loves asking embarrassing questions. Once she heard about Melissa from my mother, she would make my life miserable. Anything was worth avoiding that, even studying algebra or taking the bus to Concord, which was how I got there.

"Darlene and Jesse are meeting us at the movies at eight," Napster announced while I unpacked in his room. "Darlene and I have an appointment for the beauty parlor at ten-fifteen. We can squeeze you and Jesse in if you want."

"Pass."

"Why?"

"I guess because Jesse and I hit it off so well."

"She's seeing you again."

"Because Darlene begged her."

"Why think negative?"

"Look," I said. "I'm happy to see the movie with Jesse. I'm happy to take her to the Barn. We don't have to make out. I like Melissa. I can wait until *The Nutcracker*."

"Why do you like waiting so much?"

"I need to feel some attraction."

"Bro, you're not a magnet."

"Give me a break. What movie's playing?"

"*The Matrix*."

"Everyone says it makes more sense the second time."

"Remember," Napster said. "Salome doesn't hear a whisper about us meeting Darlene and Jesse."

"Ahh, the web is tangling. Katie and Salome are now buds. I thought competition's a good thing."

"It is. But no need to rub it in."

#

Salome is not a procrastinator. I know it sounds crazy but she finishes papers days ahead of time. Thus as soon as I emerged from Napster's room, she grabbed me. A mere hour after unpacking, I found myself in the basement morosely staring at my math book. "Algebra's still arithmetic," Salome explained. "You're still multiplying, dividing, adding, and subtracting. Just don't get thrown by the vocabulary. Exponents and coefficients are simple if you remember what they are."

Then in the midst of spouting her math pabulum, Salome sneak attacked.

"Tell me," she asked. "What time are you and Nappy seeing Darlene and her townie friend tonight?"

Maybe it was the surprise, maybe it was looking at Salome over a math book, but suddenly she bore a strange resemblance to Mr. Ward. Her teeth seemed longer and sharper and her brown eyes, which had shut into slits, took on a reddish hue.

"No. No way," I stammered, but my denial was so feeble, I didn't even believe myself.

"You are," Salome cried. "I knew it."

More vehemently, I objected, "You said it, not me." But it was as if an F-16 had flown in, dropped a 500-pound bomb, and roared off. Salome returned to babbling on about math as if nothing had occurred. However, along with Napster's secret, my concentration was destroyed. After another ten minutes of Salome sounding like a TV left on in a room with no one in it, she acknowledged the reality. "OK. OK. Enough math for today. I'm sorry. I just needed to confirm. I won't tell Ka—uh—anyone."

"Nothing to tell," I said, sticking to the party line.

Salome nodded, trying to suppress a grin. "Tomorrow, we'll just do the lesson. I won't ask what you and Nappy did to—uh—I mean, did *with* Darlene and Jesse."

"Very funny," I remarked. "Just remember. You brought up all this. I revealed nothing."

"Right, right, right," Salome readily agreed, allowing me some measure of dignity. I departed and faced the unpleasant prospect of returning to Napster's room, —a task made more unpleasant since Napster was in it.

Napster knew at a glance. "Salome got it out of you, didn't she?"

"I didn't say anything," I protested. But in my eyes guilt lurked.

"Don't worry, dude; not your fault," Napster said. "Salome's like my mother that way. Sending you into her room was like placing a lamb in front of a raptor. You can't expect the lamb not to get eaten."

While I resented the analogy, I had no response. I had given up his secret faster than the raptor could gobble the lamb.

"Katie already knows about Darlene," Napster said, not overly disturbed. "If Salome squeals, it's just going to make Katie more jealous. I worry more about Darlene finding out about Katie."

"Darlene isn't going to grill me, is she?"

"Nah."

#

In the lobby of the theater, Darlene and Jesse wore their usual low-cut jeans and jerseys barely covering their ribs. But where Darlene's perfect, flat belly made my eyes glide down and down as her skin got softer and sexier until it was almost embarrassing to look (although I managed), Jesse's flesh bulged over her hips like a roll of dough. I don't know what over-weight girls think when they put on clothes like that. I guess maybe she wanted to dress like her friend. But she would have looked better, covering more rather than less.

I think it was the second time everyone had seen *The Matrix*, except Jesse, and she pretty much got it. At least, she didn't keep asking questions at the tensest times. Well, she did ask a couple of times but I could understand a couple. The first time I saw *The Matrix*, it took a while to figure out what was going on.

After the movie, along with practically everyone else, we shifted to the Barn.

We had to wait for a booth. Three groups were ahead of us, and Napster took our standing around as an excuse to forego the post movie snack and head straight for the main meal. "Do you guys want to come with us for a walk," he asked, looking straight at me, "or do you want to wait for a table?"

Of course, I'd already told Napster I didn't want to go to the beauty parlor, but Napster loves making me feel uncomfortable, so now—as he knew it would—I couldn't just say, no. If I said no without even glancing Jesse's way, it'd be like an insult, like I was announcing to the world I didn't find her attractive enough to make out with. So I let my eyes skip over to Jesse's to hold out, at least, the possibility of joining Napster and Darlene. But as our gaze met, Jesse's body kind of shrank, confirming our lack of attraction was mutual. So I was free to say, "We'll stay. Meet you here later."

I could see the amusement gleaming in Napster's eyes, but he didn't persist and Darlene stayed mum. With a wave, they took off. The way Darlene looked in those jeans, I couldn't blame Napster. It reminded me of how hot Melissa looked in her warrior princess costume. At the memory, I smiled fondly. "What's so funny?" Jesse asked.

"Just wondering if Napster and Darlene ever actually go for a walk?

Jesse shook her head. "It's straight for The *Loooove* Parlor."

#

Was it leaving the Barn early—or were they just worn out: —it sure as hell wasn't that they were becoming responsible—but Darlene and Napster shocked Jesse and me by returning a remarkable forty-five minutes before the Barn closed!

As Napster and Darlene slid into our booth, Darlene put her hand on Napster's, —and left it there. She didn't give his hand a squeeze and let it go as I'd seen her do before. Her hand stuck like Crazy Glue. A pretty serious maneuver. Darlene wasn't just saying she liked Napster. It was more as if she was claiming him. But Napster seemed unfazed. No part of him quivered nor did he move his hand away.

"I'm hungry," Napster pronounced. "Who wants pizza?" Napster turned to Darlene.

"I'll take a slice,"

Like a regular, I replied, "After ten, they don't sell slices. You have to buy a whole pie."

Napster gave a disbelieving stare.

I retorted, "I've spent a lot of time here lately."

"So let's buy a whole pie," Napster said.

"We had ice cream when you left."

"More for me," Napster said.

I don't know what it is, but some people just live right. Whatever they do, even if it's wrong, it comes out right. Napster is one of these people. At this juncture, the door opened, and two of the most beautiful girls I've ever seen sauntered in. If I had to guess, I would've said they came straight from heaven. Or maybe straight from hell. They were too hot to come from Southridge.

They were somewhere in their twenties. One girl was blonde, but that says nothing about her hair. It was like every cliché you've ever heard—long, satany, and soft, and it floated around her face as if she were ready for her close-up. Her lips were full and shaped like a secret, and when she glanced our way, her cobalt blue eyes transported me to a world of hot summer days, cloudless skies, and pure unadulterated sex. She wore a short, shiny maroon leather coat and shiny maroon leather boots that couldn't possibly protect against the weather. Their only purpose was to look good, which they did. When she unbuttoned her coat, I saw she had on a black skirt, which covered only what it absolutely had to. A tight gray jersey clung to her chest, revealing the shape of two lovely breasts that were as perfect as nature could make them. They jiggled slightly as she walked, explaining more than a billion words why guys worship tits.

Her buddy was Asian, but she moved and dressed with a swagger that said she was born in New York. Her tight jeans were cut even lower than Darlene's, if that were possible. She wasn't wearing a jacket, just a light orange tank top, and although she flaunted much smaller knockers than her friend, I don't think Napster minded as she wasn't wearing a bra and her nipples protruded as if the tank top were wet. She had large, dark, almond-shaped eyes, high cheekbones, a small nose, and a bright, quirky smile like a poem that didn't rhyme but you didn't want it to. Her hair was long and straight and jet black.

Everyone in the Barn stared at the girls. The guys stared with mouths agape. The women stared with sharp eyes, checking out the girls and checking out the guys checking out the girls. But our new arrivals seemed oblivious.

They swung over to the counter. The counter guy greeted them instantly. Like everyone else in the restaurant (since we were all listening), I heard the blonde say, "Two slices of pizza, please."

The counter guy—it was the same guy as before—mechanically uttered the party line. "No slices after ten. You have to order a whole pizza."

The blonde took the setback in stride, as if she didn't believe in setbacks, particularly from guys. She sighed, "Ohh, we only want two slices." I couldn't see if she pouted or batted her eyes, but whatever her expression, it was enough. While Danielle had done nothing for the guy, the rigid lines in his face now melted like a frozen river in spring. But to his credit, he still managed to talk as if he owned the place. "Oh, what the hell, I'll stick in another pie."

Like royalty, the blonde bestowed a "Thank you."

Napster, who was listening like all of us, was suddenly struck by a bolt of cool. He got up, marched right next to the girls, and said to the counter guy, "If you're putting in a pizza, I'll take the other slices."

It just took a nanosecond for the girls to register Napster was, like, fifteen but in the magnanimity of their beauty, they both graced Napster with a grin. From the silly look on Napster's face, the upward turn of their lips did indeed pack something powerful. Appearing much too happy for someone who had just ordered pizza, Napster didn't exactly stagger but kind of swayed back to our booth.

Darlene was annoyed but placed her hand back on his. "Did you get their numbers?"

"Just ordered slices."

Darlene bent forward and whispered to Jesse, although loudly enough for Napster and me to hear. "Actresses or hookers?"

Jesse whispered back, "Maybe they're models."

"They're not tall enough to be models. I think they're hookers."

"They can't be hookers." Napster said, "They're not with anybody. Do you think they came to Southridge to pick up guys?"

Darlene insisted, "Maybe they're with some guys and this is their break."

Napster sniggered, "Yeah, like they belong to the hookers union and get pizza breaks."

Darlene reddened. "Even hookers have to eat."

Jesse asked Napster, "What do you think they're doing here?"

"I don't know, but I'll ask."

Darlene and Jesse gasped. "You're going back?"

Napster loved it. "Sure." Still under the spell of those girls' smiles, he swung toward the counter. However, once there, Napster's boldness faded. The girls were talking rapidly to each other, not even glancing his way. Napster looked as out of place as if he'd wandered into the Beauty and Beyond Salon on a Saturday when it was full of middle-aged women in curlers. But as always, Napster was saved. "Pizza," the counter guy hollered.

The girls' attention returned to food. At the bubbling hot pizza's arrival, they "ooohed" and "aaahed," providing an opening for the counter guy and Napster. A hushed conversation broke out. The conversation lasted a few minutes and even produced laughter. We were stunned. Even Darlene was more impressed than annoyed. I mean, the girls were extraordinary.

When Napster returned to our table, he carried four slices of pizza and two paper plates. He sat down, slipped Darlene her slice, kept three slices for himself, and casually lifted one up. I grabbed his arm. He looked at me in feigned bewilderment. "What?"

"Spill it."

"What?"

"No games. Tell us what you and those girls talked about."

"You mean Nan and Jean."

"Yeah. Nan and Jean."

"Well," he said. "They're dancers." He shot me a knowing look. "They do belly dancing for a bunch of rock bands. They flew in from LA and are on their way to join the group in Burlington. They tour Canada and end in Boston for one night."

I gulped. "Boston?"

"Yeah. They said we should catch the show and say, 'Hi.'"

Darlene rolled her eyes, "It would've been cooler if they were hookers."

#

Brookline!

School!!

Finals!!!!

**Retttccchhhhhhh!!!!!!!!**

Every time I think of exams, I mentally vomit.

Noyce is not like public school where you can count on dumb kids lowering the curve. Except for a few flakes and fuck-ups, all the kids are smart and study hard.

Sometimes, I wonder, why can't everyone get together and say, "Look. Nobody study a lot this semester. The curve'll go down and we'll pretty much get the same grades we would've but it'll be a lot easier and we can watch TV and play video games as much as we want." Unfortunately, at a place like Noyce, it'll never work. All the lousy grade grubbers, study grinds, and brownnosers will agree because they'll be afraid not to. Then they'll go home and study hard because they like to. They get off on it. They're the kind of kids who bring three different colored pens to school for underlining, ask teachers for extra credit work, and whine about their grade point averages when they get an A-minus.

I hate those kind of kids, and Noyce reeks with them, especially the ones who lie about how they do on tests. They're the worst. When I finish a hard math or Spanish test and leave shaken and depressed, moaning how terrible I did, they buoy my spirit by saying they did lousy, too. So I think, wow, if a brain like Samantha or Jason or Ashley or whoever did badly, maybe everyone did and the teacher'll grade easier. Except when the test comes back, with a great deal of luck, I get a B- (without luck a C or C+), but the brainy Samanthas, Jasons, or Ashleys have a big, gaudy red A twinkling on their exams.

I don't mind them getting an A. In my good subjects, I get A's. What I hate is the assholes pretending they did lousy when in fact they aced the exam. I mean, no one gets an A without knowing it. OK, maybe you can get an A-minus or even a B-plus, but you know when you know. So, I say to the lying assholes, don't piss on my jeans, don't shit on my shoes. If you break a test's balls, say so.

#

Dec. 1st
8:56 p.m.
FROM: Balanchinebabe
TO: DownInDenver
Michael—Carmen is reaaally after Yuri. Remember him? The dancer from Russia. She came to class today and she's taken in the top of her leotards so you can see her boobs—whatever boobs she's got. Every time Yuri is around, she runs up to him, asking dumb questions and flaunting herself shamelessly. She thinks she's got a figure like Lindsey. I know you remember Lindsey, the girl who reaaaally has boobs. She's such a little slut. (Carmen not Lindsey.)

Last night I got first performance jitters bad. I mean, like, I always get jitters before the curtain, but first performance jitters are the worst. Way worse than finals. Waiting to go on, my heart beat so fast I thought it was going to jump out of my chest and hop like a rabbit into the orchestra. But when I got on stage, I calmed down. Sarah Lamb was the Snow Queen. You should see her. She's soooo beautiful. Bet you ace English and History. Math Wednesday. Don't worry.

You'll do fine. xoxoxo
Love,
M


Dec. 4th
3:45 p.m.
FROM: Balanchinebabe
TO: DownInDenver

Michael—Don't be down about math. Everyone thought it was hard. I heard Mr. Ward (the slime on the asshole of a toad) isn't that tough a grader because he likes to make the school think he's a great teacher. Anyway, it's over. Only French left for me. C'est bon. Don't you agree agrez-vous? If only Mrs. Levesque tested on ballet vocab I would get an A easy. Releve. Entrechat. Arabesque. Plie.

Good luck in Spanish!

Which reminds me. Carmen (the snot on the nose of a weasel) actually took my bar spot this afternoon. I think Carmen is trying to jinx me. We've been in this class for, like, three months, and everyone knows my spot. As if I am not stressed enough. This may not mean much to you (well, I know it doesn't), but it's like if Dory took your seat in math. Math is a bad example because we have assigned seats, but let's just say it was a regular class and that was your regular seat, you know what I mean. It doesn't have your name on it but everyone (particularly Mr. Ward) knows you sit right behind me. Except in ballet class it's tons more annoying. (Who is Dory anyway? He's soooo creepy.) I don't dance tonight. It's French, French, French. Sevlement le francais afte nuit.

Looking forward to classes, so we can meet before lunch. Next week, mon cheri.

xoxoxo
Love,
M


Dec. 5th
10:45 p.m.
FROM: Balanchinebabe

TO: DownInDenver

Michael— Sooooo tired!!! Just got home from another *Nutcracker*. Wish I had more energy, I'd tell you ALL about the performance. It was good. Everyone is settling in. I've been working on Mrs. Sullivan to get me a Friday or Saturday night. I soooo want you, Katie, and Steve to see me dance. Am I vain? Am I spoiled? Do I crave attention? Yes! Yes! Yes! Oh, well, I love the ballet so, I can't help it. We can party after. Do some kissin' and cuddlin'. That will be awesome. Carmen is still chasing Yuri and Yuri is still ignoring her. It's so much fun to watch.

Love,

xoxoxo

M

Dec. 6th

9:32 p.m.

FROM: Balanchinebabe

TO: DownInDenver

Michael—Friday! Exams are finis!!!!! I thought they were NEVER going to end. Back to classes. Can't wait to see you. Congrats on the B- in math!!!! You really showed Mr. Ward. [*Only because the first semester is easy. I flipped ahead in the book. Next semester, I don't think I have the chance of a weasel on a dragon's ass.] Read your story in the *Looking Glass*. The math teacher whose students are flies and, when they don't know the answer, he pulls off their wings. AWESOME. Then the bell rings and he squishes a student and eats him. I laughed so hard. How'd you think of that? I wonder if Ward read it. Can't wait to see his face Monday. Perhaps, you should have published next year. I do not think Mr. Ward has a sense of humor. Watch out. Guard your wings, mon amour.

xoxoxo

M

#

Darlene called.

Yes, Darlene called me. It was eight-thirty and I was in my room reading

*The Great Gatsby.* I was in the part describing those big parties Gatsby throws, and I was musing—what would happen if Melissa was a ballerina and I was a writer and we met at one of Gatsby's parties? —when the phone rang. I dismissed it because I knew it wouldn't be Melissa. These days she's too busy to call, and it wouldn't be any of my friends as they know they're not supposed to call between eight and ten, which are my "study hours." (No cell phones, no TV, no video games.) But sounding aggravated, my mother shouted, "It's a girl, Michael. Make it quick." My heart pounded. It must be Melissa. Could something have gone wrong with our *Nutcracker* plans? It was only a couple of days away. Then I remembered, when Melissa calls, my mother always yells, "It's Melissa for you." She knows it's Melissa because Melissa tells my mother her name. But if it wasn't Melissa, who could it be? Katie? Cyndi? Some other girl from school?

I grabbed the cordless in the hall but didn't answer until I was back in my room.

"Hello?" I said, a big question mark in my voice.

Darlene picked up on that. "It's me. Darlene."

"Darlene, how are you?" I said, really meaning, why the hell are you calling me?

Again Darlene answered my thoughts rather than my words. "You must be wondering why I'm calling. You don't mind, do you?"

"Why should I mind?"

"I don't know. How's Melissa?"

"Fine. We're going to…" I was about to say "see her in *The Nutcracker*," when I realized Napster was going with Katie. I had nearly stuck my foot in my mouth big time, so I kind of stammered, "to-to-to see *Blue Man Group*."

"Awesome." Thankfully, Darlene did not have Salome's mutant ability to detect lies—at least, not over the phone. "I saw it last year."

"Napster and I saw it last year, too, through school, but Melissa wasn't at Noyce, so we're going after she finishes with *The Nutcracker*." Whew. Now I have to take Melissa to *Blue Man Group*. I pushed on, "Whazzup? What are you doing for Christmas?"

"That's kinda why I'm calling. Have any ideas what I should get Nappy-pie?"

"Nappy-pie?"

"Don't you think Nappy-pie is funner to say than Nappy? I sort of adapted it from Salome. Just added my own twist." Darlene sounded proud she knew Napster's sister.

"Pie's your twist?"

'Uh-huh. What do you think?"

"Adorable."

"You guys. 'Nappy-pie' is cute. What should I get him?"

"For Christmas?"

"Uhhh. *Yuhhh.*"

"OK. OK. Let me think." As I pondered, I wondered what Darlene would call "Nappy-pie" if she knew he was taking Katie to *The Nutcracker.* Then I wondered what Melissa would call me, if I didn't get her a Christmas present. Then I realized I didn't even know Melissa's birthday. I needed to find that out. This girlfriend thing got more complicated every day.

"How about a video game?" I suggested. "Napster has a Play Station."

Darlene groaned, "No way. I'm not giving him anything that lets him spend more time in front of a TV." Hmmm. It seems Napster was playing video games when he should have been on the phone with Darlene. Or was he just using video games as an excuse while he was talking to Katie?

"Napster likes the Red Hot Chilli Peppers," I said. "How about a CD?" They could both listen to the CD.

Darlene was not impressed, "He can download any songs he wants. I want to give him something special. How 'bout a sweater?"

A sweater. Ugh. No guy wants a sweater. But from her rejection of my two good suggestions, I realized, even though she was asking my opinion, it wasn't really wanted. So I said. "Sure. Napster wears sweaters."

Darlene didn't hide her irritation. "I know he wears sweaters. Do you think he'd like one for Christmas?"

"He'd love a sweater."

"A store in Northridge sells beautiful Irish knit sweaters. Imported. Handmade. They're super thick and warm. Great for skiing."

"Napster skis."

"I know."

However, having asked as much as she felt she needed about Napster's "gift," Darlene veered the conversation toward her real concern.

"Speaking of skiing, are you coming up with Nappy-pie for Christmas?"

I got very cautious. "I suppose. We haven't made any plans. Sometimes the Belknaps are pretty busy during Christmas."

"I was hoping you'd have heard. Napster hasn't told me anything." Maybe a lot of my problem with secrets is that Napster has so many. "Don't you know?" Darlene's question was simple, but desperation clung to each word.

I felt bad, but I was glad I could say honestly, "I really don't." And I didn't. I mean, I know the Belknaps go to New Hampshire for Christmas, but exactly when and for how long I hadn't a clue. Well, OK, they usually go a couple of days before Christmas and stay until a couple of days before New Year's. However, as no one had said anything, I could remain vague with a clear conscience. "I guess he'll be going up. Why don't you ask him?"

"I sent two emails and he hasn't answered." Darlene's voice throbbed and I heard a snuffle.

"We just finished exams and a new semester's started. Everyone's going straight out."

Darlene's breath became hiccupy. For a second, it sounded as if she were going to lose it, but she made an effort and got herself under control. "I suppose."

"I am totally sure he'll email you," I said, and my voice rang with conviction. I knew Napster would keep both Darlene and Katie on his string as long as he could. Except Darlene, who previously was the sole object of Napster's affection, if you want to call it that, now had to share. Yet Darlene seemed consoled by my positivity. She took a deep breath. "Please don't tell Nappy I called. I-I don't want him to know I asked you about... about his present."

Great. Another secret. "Don't worry. I won't." And I promised myself I wouldn't. I'd wipe the entire call from my mind. No male code dictated I tell Napster about this. It was best for everyone, including me, if it were as if it never occurred.

But Darlene wasn't through. Suddenly, her voice cracked again, "Nappy and I...he...Oh, I know it's not fair to burden you with this. I'm sorry...but it's so hard when he doesn't call. I've...I've given him so much."

Wow. Did she mean what I thought she meant? "Darlene, I know he wants to keep on seeing you. Napster will call." It was another statement I could say with complete assurance. Why wouldn't he? He loves free sex. But out loud I joked, "Napster's a lazy bum. He might not even know what's happening yet with Christmas. I know he's really busy doing some work for his uncle." (After Thanksgiving, the screw company collects toys to give to the poor, and Saturday afternoons Napster helps out.)

Darlene forced a laugh, "I didn't think Napster ever worked."

"You got that right. Occasionally, his uncle makes him do something."

"Well, thanks for talking," Darlene sighed. "Remember, don't tell Nappy we spoke."

"Worry not. He'll definitely be in touch, and I'm sure he'll like the sweater."

As we hung up, Darlene's phrase, "I've given him so much," swept back and forth in my mind like a searchlight at a movie premiere. Did Napster get laid and not tell me? How could Napster keep *that* from me?! Only, I couldn't call him on it. I'd promised Darlene silence, and I wasn't about to deal her a worse hand than she already had.

#

One plus of my mother's excitement re: Melissa: —it was easy getting her to buy *Nutcracker* tickets. I didn't even have to mention Sarah. But as you might have guessed, Sarah wheedled her way in. Before the relentless pressure of a determined eleven year old, my mother cracked like Microsoft's Firewall under a hack attack. However, the deal is, as soon as the ballet ends and Sarah meets Melissa, my mom swoops Sarah up in the car and deposits her home. Salome's and Giddy's attendance was, of course, unavoidable, but I am fine with that. This way Mr. and Mrs. Belknap couldn't possibly object to Katie coming along with Napster. I mean, with the six of us, it's almost like a school event. Naturally, Melissa didn't care if the whole school went.

On the morning of the show, Sarah tried to worm her way along for the entire evening, but my mother nixed it.

Sarah (whining): Why can't I, Mom? It'll be fun.

Mom (firmly): Because you can't.

Sarah (whining): Why not?

Mom (firmly): Because your brother's going with his friends and he doesn't want you along.

Sarah (whining): Why not?

Mom (firmly): Your brother doesn't tag along when you're with your friends.

Sarah (whining): He doesn't want to.

Mom (firmly): Exactly. And he doesn't want you bothering him when he's with his friends. Just be happy you're going to *The Nutcracker*.

Sarah (whining): "But…"

Mom (firmly): Sarah, no "buts." That's it. Over. End of discussion.

Despite her morning spent whining, when everyone assembled at my house at six dressed and ready for the ballet, Sarah was excited and happy. She likes Salome a lot, and Napster is like a brother. Whenever she and Napster meet, they do these long, intricate handshakes. Sarah keeps up with Napster pretty well and comes up with moves of her own. They do finger wiggles and hand slides and elbow, shoulder, and hip bumps and then turn around and end with butt rubs. That Sarah was in one of her fancy party dresses didn't deter her. She laughed hysterically, particularly when she and Napster rubbed their butts in front of my friends.

The odd thing was after Sarah finished the butt rubbing and stopped shrieking in laughter, she got shy meeting Katie, who was the only one she didn't know. Even though Katie's a girl, she could barely look at her.

We piled in my mom's car, Napster and me in front, Sarah, Salome, Giddy, and Katie in back. Sarah squeezed in on Salome's lap and tried acting very adult, saying stuff like, "I love your dress," and "Your earrings are so pretty. Where'd you get them?" Sarah is amusing when she isn't being a brat.

#

The tourist guide says the Wang Center is designed after the Palace of Versailles, (Don't laugh. Wang is what the place is called after this Chinese guy who donated the money to restore the original theater.) The lobby is large and ornate. White and tan marble tiles stretch across the floor, and on either side of the lobby, three huge white, gold, and tan marble columns soar upward, supporting two levels of balconies. Intricate gilt vines curl and twist up the walls, and overarching the whole is a frescoed ceiling painted sky blue with harp playing cherubs perched on puffy white clouds. Three large chandeliers hang from the ceiling, dripping hundreds of glass crystals sparkling like raindrops in the moonlight. Amidst all this opulence, audience members sip champagne and nibble expensive sweets, waiting for the ballet to begin. The general effect is like a scene out of a Russian novel. One of those thousand-page jobs by Tolstoy or Dostoevsky. Actually, I haven't read any Russian novels yet, but I have seen the movies. The noblemen always wait till the second or third act to see their favorite dancer perform. Since in this case, my favorite dancer was my girlfriend, I thought, how prince-like can you get? It was almost like I had a mistress, except for the sleeping together part.

Sometimes, when you're plodding along, living with your parents, going to school, riding on buses and streetcars, you feel like a jerk, and that you're always going to be a jerk. Other times when you're with your friends, doing something cool life glitters like a movie set, and it's as if anything you imagine can happen. This was one of those times.

From the lobby, we filed into the theater and found our seats. Although the theater was much bigger than the lobby, it was decorated just as ornately. More gilt vines adorned the walls and the ceiling was painted the same sky blue, only instead of the harp-playing cherubs, renaissance figures floated around, playing a variety of ancient instruments—dulcimers, lutes, and recorders. Katie, however, didn't care about the murals. She dragged us down to the front to check out the real orchestra. She wanted to see if she knew any of the flute players. But no musicians were in the pit— just rows of chairs, music stands, kettle drums, cymbals, bells, a harp, a bunch of cellos, and lots of bass fiddles. Katie stood next to Sarah, doing the big sister bit, explaining the workings of the orchestra. Her voice was very authoritative, and a lot of adults nearby with kids started listening. Katie realized this, and ever eager to promote classical music, talked louder.

Gradually, musicians filed in. When two flute players entered, Katie waved. She knew one—a guy named Erickson from the New England Conservatory where Katie takes lessons. He spotted Katie and came over. Katie introduced Sarah and the rest of us. The guy talked to Katie for a couple of minutes until a bell rang, signaling the show was about to begin. Since the six of us are used to obeying bells, we hustled back to our seats

The plot of *The Nutcracker* is not complex. A mysterious guy named Drosselmeyer entertains at a Christmas party. He gives a nutcracker in the shape of a toy soldier to a girl named Clara. When the party ends, Clara falls asleep on a couch, which doesn't look very comfortable and is kind of strange because she must have her own bedroom upstairs. However, as it's a ballet, we won't go into plot holes. At midnight, Drosselmeyer sneaks back into the house, and all sorts of magic happens—the Christmas tree grows about twenty feet (although Melissa tells me, it's actually supposed to be that Clara shrinks), a battle breaks out between these big mice and a bunch of toy soldiers, and the nutcracker turns into a handsome prince in tights (what else?).

During intermission, the lobby was crowded, but what with everyone all dressed and polished, it didn't much matter. Some guys wore tuxes, and a lot of girls were in strapless dresses showing tons of smooth, bare skin. Katie and Salome fell into this category. Giddy, Napster, and I had been coerced into ties and jackets. We gathered into a group, talking. Since it was *The Nutcracker*, many in the audience were Sarah's age or younger, but Sarah didn't see anyone she knew, even though she snooped around. Happily for me, Sarah decided she was hungry and joined the pretzel line, which was a good place to keep her out of trouble as it was long and looped in its own pretzel-like curves through the lobby.

I turned to the group. "Well?"

"Love it," Katie announced.

"I like it, too," Salome said.

Napster turned to his sister. "Hey, Katie said she loves it. You just said you like it."

"I would have loved it," Salome said, "if we saw more of the prince. He didn't show up in those cute tights until the very end."

Napster stuck a finger in his mouth, accompanied by a loud gagging sound.

Salome ignored her brother and turned to Katie. "A totally great butt."

Katie agreed enthusiastically. "Totally."

"You should get in this orchestra," Salome suggested.

"When you're in the pit, your back is to the stage," Katie sighed. "You have to look at the conductor."

With a flip of her hand, Salome waved away that objection. "During rehearsals, you can check out their butts."

"True. Still…." Katie put her arm around Napster, hugging him closer and giving him a kiss on the cheek. "He's my bitch."

Napster pushed Katie away as everyone laughed. It was another of Alyson Hannigan's lines—this time from *American Pie II*.

"You don't mind that he can't crush beer cans with his ass cheeks?" Giddy said.

"No. I like him the way he is."

I wondered if that included dating Darlene on the side, but of course I kept that to myself. A hand tugged on the back of my jacket, and I looked down. Sarah held a large, salted pretzel up to my mouth. The pretzel already had a bite taken out of it, and Sarah's mouth was full.

"It's warm," she mumbled, wiggling the pretzel in front of me.

"Thanks," I said and took a bite, more to appease her than because I was hungry.

Giddy gazed down at Sarah and asked, "How'd you like the ballet?"

Sarah swallowed and said, "Great. But I want to see Melissa."

"We all want to see Melissa," Katie agreed. "She's supposed to come out right at the beginning of the second act."

#

The bell rang and we hustled back to our seats. Not long after, the conductor raised his baton and the first strands of the "Sugar Plum Fairy" wafted over us like mist from a lake. The curtain lifted, and the Sugar Plum Fairy herself pranced out on her toes. She was blonde and pretty and all in pink, and as she darted across the stage, you couldn't help but admire the fluid yet precise movement of her legs and feet. Gradually, the tempo of the music increased, but she had no trouble keeping up, her toe shoes flashing like arrows in the floodlights.

Then, lo and behold, in a gush of tinkling silvery bells, Melissa, Lindsey, Ariel, Tasha, Heather, and Carmen spun onto the stage. None of the girls looked nervous, I guess because they'd been performing this number for weeks. Still, the huge theater was packed—I couldn't see an empty seat.

The girls were wearing cream-colored tutus, the top of which looked like Wonder Woman's outfit but, except for Lindsey, not filled out as much. Around the waist, the design transformed into this little ruffled cream-colored skirt, which stuck straight out and which Wonder Woman never would've been caught dead in but which looked like what you'd imagine ballet dancers wearing, if ever in your life you've imagined ballet dancers. The girls were willowy, graceful, and sensual all at the same time, and I loved watching Melissa spinning and gliding as light and incandescent as a fairy. (Yes, a sylph, only without wings.)

The sole downer was that Yuri guy. He appeared a few tunes later in his Russian number. He was with two other guys doing some impressive leaps. But thankfully not in tights. The three wore these baggy red Cossack pants, and judging by the audience's long and loud response, the crowd liked the froglike Yuri and his buddies.

What with the dancers, the costumes, the sets, and the music, not to mention Melissa, the performance went over big. Even Napster enjoyed it. For the curtain call, we got to see Melissa again, although way in the back. At her appearance, the six of us clapped and yelled, and Katie did her two fingers-in-the-mouth, ear-piercing whistle. We couldn't tell if Melissa heard, but she looked flushed and happy. She was in between Lindsey and Carmen in a line of mostly girls all holding hands as they stepped forward and back, doing this special ballerina-curtain-call bow. I don't know why, but I really liked this bow. I mean, basically all the girls did was place their right toe behind their left foot and bend a little. Yet as simple as the movement was, somehow in the pretty cream-colored toe shoes the girls wore with the pinky cream-colored ribbons wrapped around their slender ankles, the step was so charming and feminine, I got all buzzy again. (Yeah. It doesn't take much.)

The curtain, which had risen and fallen and risen and fallen and risen and fallen to the audience's loud applause, finally descended and stayed down, and the lights in the theater brightened. As I gazed down our row, the only person looking annoyed was Sarah. She had to go home, although that made the rest of us, or at least me, happy. As we walked out, Sarah said, "Do we have to call Mom? Why don't we get something to eat first?"

"Sarah, you know the drill. Mom's picking you up. Before she gets here, Melissa will be out and you can meet her and leave. No changes. No games. No whining."

"I'm not whining," Sarah whined but shut up.

On the street, we waited near a large metal stage door with a group of parents who had kids in the ballet. Once in a while the door sprang open, releasing a musician or a couple of kids or one or two of the professional dancers. After about fifteen minutes, Melissa emerged, bursting out of the building with a great deal of energy. You would have thought she'd be tired, but she strode quickly onto the sidewalk, followed by Carmen and Yuri. As soon as Melissa glanced around, she saw us. I was pleased Yuri was in regular clothes. In a winter jacket, he looked almost normal, except he was short and overly handsome in this Abercrombie & Fitch greasy male model kind of way.

Melissa uttered a few words to Carmen and Yuri, then hurried toward us. Carmen and Yuri waved as she left—partly to her and partly to us—

but they continued on. I was glad they didn't stop. Introductions between a lot of people who don't know each other are a pain. I was also glad that in his regular clothes and winter coat, Yuri's retreating form did not cause any open-mouthed drooling from Katie and Salome.

As Melissa approached, Salome and Katie ran over, each in turn hugging Melissa in one of those girlie-girlie hugs where they touch shoulders and give each other cheek kisses that are more noise than actual contact. Katie and Salome were excited and frothy, complimenting Melissa on her dancing. In a pause the two girls took to catch their breaths, Giddy and Napster joined in, giving Melissa high fives, punching her shoulder, and tossing in a barrage of "awesomes," "excellents," and "radicals."

When everyone's excitement wound down, Melissa stepped back and spotted my sister standing quietly with me. Melissa walked over and said, "Hey. You must be Sarah."

Shyly, Sarah nodded. "I loved your dancing."

Melissa laughed. "All two minutes of it."

"You were wonderful," Sarah enthused.

"Thank you," Melissa said, genuinely flattered. "I'm glad you liked it."

"I did. It was beautiful."

I'm sure my friends were sincere in their praise, but they talked so loudly and so rapidly all at the same time, it somehow lacked the purity of Sarah's words, which came straight from her eleven-year-old heart. In the midst of the congratulations, a horn beeped. It was my mother in her white Ford Escort.

Sarah and Melissa glanced at each other. Sarah's face was again annoyed; Melissa's was anxious. She was about to meet my mother. I think it made her more nervous than dancing in front of three thousand people.

She said to Sarah, "I'll walk you to the car."

"Neat," Sarah said. Melissa grabbed Sarah's hand, I think more for courage than to help my sister.

When we reached the car, I opened the passenger-side door. Sarah jumped in and Melissa leaned over and waved to my mother, "Hi, Mrs. Steinman."

My mother flashed a huge smile and said, "Hi, Melissa. It's nice to finally meet you. Congratulations on your performance."

"Thanks," Melissa said.

Although their conversation was brief and very mundane, somehow I sensed all this chick stuff passing between them. My mom was checking out Melissa, and Melissa was conveying the message, *I'm a nice girl and I like your son.* It was as if Melissa were shopping in a store my mother owned and they were discussing a very special item—me.

Before my mother could say anything stupid or embarrassing, I shut the car door. Sarah rolled down the window and stuck her head out like a puppy dog. She gushed to Melissa, "I really like you."

Melissa squeezed Sarah's hand. "I like you, too."

I just wanted Sarah and my mom to go. "C'mon, Sarah, Mom's double-parked."

Melissa retreated onto the sidewalk and waved goodbye. For a second, Sarah stuck her head further out the window and whispered to me, "She's so pretty." Fortunately, at that moment, a couple of cars moved up behind the Escort and a cop whistled at my mother to go. My mom got flustered and leaned toward us and yelled a parting, "Don't stay out too late." She pulled Sarah down into her seat, waited for Sarah to snap on her seat belt, and eased the Escort back into traffic.

#

Food!!!!

It seems dancing in a ballet or watching one creates an appetite. The restaurant we decided upon was Fridays, mainly because it was close—just across the Commons. Fridays was crowded, but it helped that we were a party of six, so when a big table emptied, we got seated right away. The people waiting gave us dirty looks. They were thinking, "Hey, what's the story. We've been here longer. They're nothing but a bunch of high school kids." OK. It would have been cooler if they thought we were in college, but we are what we are. I did feel a pang of guilt since Friday's is Sarah's favorite restaurant. She likes to go to Fridays on her birthday. The waiters bring a big cake and sing the Fridays birthday song, which Sarah loves. I couldn't wait to tell her where we went just to see the furious expression on her face and watch her stomp off. I guess I didn't feel that guilty.

While we stuffed our faces, the main discussion, naturally, was ballet. Katie and Salome wanted to know about the guy who played the Nutcracker prince. Melissa said, "He's dreamy to look at, but he's got a boyfriend."

This statement elicited groans of dismay from Katie and Salome and crows of delight from Napster, Giddy, and me.

Never one to let an opportunity go by, Napster exclaimed, "I guess he's got his own uses for that beautiful butt of his."

"Eeewww," shrieked Katie and Salome. Giddy and I snickered. Forsaking the prince, the girls asked Melissa about the costumes.

Even more than Sarah, Melissa loves being the center of attention. Her face gets very animated and she uses her hands. Being a dancer with years of training, Melissa is particularly graceful when she talks with her hands, a fact, I am sure, she is not unaware of. In math, I love sitting behind her watching her play with her hair, but it is more fun facing her as she weaves her fingers like a magician. I suppose the others didn't find her hands as entrancing, but what she said was interesting, anyway.

"Underneath the ballet studio," she explained, "is a large costume department where we're fitted."

"How many costumes do you have?" Salome asked.

"One," Melissa replied. "The costumes are so expensive, they don't make a lot of extras. In fact," Melissa added, sensing an opportunity to amuse and astonish, "The whole two months *The Nutcracker* runs, they don't take a chance on damaging them, so they're not washed."

This fact elicited the expected "oh my Gods" from Katie and Salome and more snickers and snorts from Napster, Giddy, and me.

"But it's like your costume, isn't it?" Katie asked. "They fit it just for you?"

"Sort of. I wear it, and when I'm off, another girl my size wears it."

"You share the same sweaty costume with another girl?" Salome exclaimed. "That is so gross."

Melissa giggled. "The costumes go on over your tights. They don't touch your skin. The wardrobe people spray 'm down to sort of clean them."

"Oh my God. I couldn't stand that," Katie said. "In the YPO, I sit right behind this viola player who sweats like a pig, and that's pretty bad."

"For some people, you know, sweat's a turn on," Napster said.

Salome eyed her brother. "Anything's a turn on for you."

Katie stared at Napster. "Sweat. You like sweat. Should I not buy deodorant?" She said it humorously, but in her voice was a hint of—if that's really what you want, I'll go along. Napster caught the hint and smiled. His ego was getting bigger every day. He said, "I didn't say I like sweat. I said, 'Some people.' You guys know about Napoleon and Josephine?"

"What about 'em?" Melissa asked.

"Is this a joke?" Salome asked. "Are you setting us up for a joke?"

"I think it's a riddle," Giddy tossed in.

"Cut it out," Napster said. "This is good."

"We'll be the judge of that," Salome replied.

Katie asked, "Who's Josephine?"

Napster shook his head, "She's Napoleon's mistress, duh."

"No duh," Katie said. "I'm sure I never studied Josephine at Four Acres."

"I never heard of her, either," Salome added.

Giddy backed up Salome. "Hey, Naps, I was in your World Civilizations' class and we didn't study anything about Josephine."

Napster shrugged. "I saw it on a PBS special."

Salome's eyes widened. "You watched a PBS special. All I ever see you watch are *Baywatch* reruns."

"There's nothing wrong with *Baywatch* reruns."

"I know. It's such a classy show," Salome said.

"Hey, when Carmen Electra runs across the beach, it's like a ballet."

"Yeah," Salome said. "A boob ballet."

My eyes met Melissa's and we shared a grin.

Katie brought the subject back to sweat. She still wanted to know if she had to give up deodorants to keep her man happy. "What did the PBS special say, Nappy?"

"I'm glad someone has the intellectual curiosity to ask. You can learn a lot from PBS specials."

I shook my head. "I knew he didn't read it in a book."

"You guys. Listen," Napster said. "When Napoleon was off fighting, he wrote Josephine these long love letters. On the show, they read excerpts. One went—'I'll be home in a week. Don't wash.'"

Loud jeers and groans greeted this line.

Melissa said, "We just wear the same costume. We don't have sex." She eyed Napster. "Why does everything with boys have to be about sex?"

"Everything with girls is about sex."

"No, it's not," Melissa retorted.

Napster said, "Like girls wear pants down to their crotch and thongs for the comfort."

Giddy and I laughed, but none of the girls did. Katie said, "That's fashion." Even though she had never worn anything fashionable until three weeks ago, she was talking as if she had a lifetime subscription to *Vogue*. Clearly, Melissa had a new disciple.

"Fashion's fun," Salome agreed.

"It's fashion because girls buy the stuff," Napster said. "And why do girls buy it? Sex."

"There's nothing wrong with looking a little sexy," Salome said.

"Hey, I like sexy," Napster said. "But girls wear practically nothing. Then they accuse guys of staring."

I thought this was a telling remark and expected some sort of concession but of course I was wrong.

Very pointedly, Katie asked Napster, "Who have you been staring at?"

Very quickly, Napster replied, "I haven't been staring at anyone."

"Maybe I should wear lower cut jeans," Katie said. "Then you'll stare more at me."

"Don't encourage my brother," Salome said. "He's horny enough as it is."

As the subject had turned to fashion (at least as far as Melissa was concerned), she mentioned to Katie and Salome, "I always hit the malls for the after Christmas sales. Do you guys want to come?"

"Which mall?"

"Any. I don't care. Copley or Chestnut."

Salome said, "The Copley's got more stores."

"More is better," Melissa agreed, "Let's do Copley." All three girls started talking about clothes.

#

At Melissa's building, the six of us squeezed into the elevator. The elevator creaked when it took off, injecting an amusement park thrill into an otherwise refined elegance.

"I hear that noise every time," Katie worried. "It's not going to break?"

I teased, "We could be stuck here all night."

"Oh, no," Katie said. "I have to pee."

"It won't break," Melissa promised. "My mom says it's like tennis players grunting when they make a shot. It makes sounds like that to help it lift."

Napster said, "I bet those ballet guys wish they could grunt when they lift ballerinas."

"Except ballet isn't tennis," Salome snapped.

"Ahhh, who's going to mind a little grunting with all the noise those shoes make when they run back and forth?"

Melissa turned and stared directly at Napster. I thought she was mad, but she said, "Stephen, you heard that sound?

As everyone looked at Napster, he actually blushed. "Well, come on. Who didn't? What are those shoes made of? Wood?"

"I didn't notice," Giddy said.

"I did a couple of times," I said.

"Pointe shoes have to be hard," Melissa explained. "Everybody reinforces theirs with glue. Most of the girls don't like the sound, but I love it." Melissa turned to me and gave me one of her winks. "It's OK, Stephen. I'm proud of you. You must've been paying very close attention. You must reaaally like ballet."

"Yeah, yeah. I bet those guys would like ballet better if they could grunt."

"The guys are super strong," Melisssa said. "They don't need to grunt." Then she said to Katie, "Next year the building's getting a new elevator, but this one's fine. It's tested regularly."

Katie wasn't reassured, especially when the elevator halted at Melissa's floor and dropped six inches. She emitted a yelp, which made the rest of us laugh. Melissa unlocked the door as if she were used to it. "Step up, everyone. Dessert to the left. Bathroom to the right."

"Awesome," Salome said. "It goes straight into your house."

Signaling for us to follow, Melissa led us down the hall to the kitchen. (At Friday's, Melissa had warned five pints of Ben and Jerry's, plus assorted toppings, awaited in her fridge.) For the girls, it was an opportunity to play house, only they'd grown from toy tea sets and dolls into a real kitchen with real boyfriends. They asked what kind of sundaes we wanted and like Carol Brady clones bustled about making them. It was cute, because, while they acted like Carol Brady, they looked like Marcia Brady, although Melissa was the only blonde.

We ate the sundaes on bar stools at the island in the middle of the kitchen. Melissa seemed satisfied. Everyone liked her house and the ice cream. After dessert, we guys went into the living room and the girls continued doing their Carol Brady thing, cleaning up. A few minutes later, Melissa stuck her head out of the kitchen and announced, "Ice-cream enough for one more round. Customers?"

The three of us glanced up but didn't say anything.

"Going once…Going twice…"

We still looked blank, maybe because we were so full.

Like Birdsong, Melissa eye-checked us one by one. "Sure?"

At this point, Giddy caved. He is compulsively polite, and I guess he didn't eat as much as Napster and I did at Friday's. "I'll have one," he volunteered.

Melissa smiled. "Great. What do you want?"

"Vanilla."

"Good. A solid American choice. What on it?"

"Hot fudge and whip cream."

"Sticking to the traditional. I like that in a man," Melissa said, glancing over at Napster and me as if we were weaklings for not having seconds.

Melissa ducked into the kitchen.

After a short pause, her head reappeared. "Whoops. Sorry. Wasn't quick enough. The last of the fudge and whipped cream got tossed. Strawberries?"

As I said, Giddy is compulsively polite. "OK. Strawberries."

"Great."

Melissa disappeared only a second later to return, her hostess smile slightly wilted like unsold flowers at the supermarket.

"Damn. The strawberries are gone, too." An idea occurred to her. "Why don't you try blueberries? My mom buys this great blueberry jam. All natural."

Giddy didn't make a face and managed to sound somewhat enthusiastic. "Uh. I like blueberries." Melissa smiled an encouraging smile.

"Super. One blueberry sundae coming up. Anybody else?"

"Nahhhh," Napster and I said.

"Only Giddy is brave enough to try blueberries."

"Not just blueberries," Napster said. "ALL NATURAL blueberries."

Melissa crinkled her nose. "Go ahead. Scoff. It'll taste great." She vanished into the kitchen and appeared a minute later, holding a bottle with a red-and-gold crest and the words Napster had poked fun of, *All Natural* printed in a large, florid script. Wordlessly, she handed the bottle to me. It was new and the lid was sealed. Even though I had refused seconds, my job was to be the manly man and open it. Dutifully, I cracked the lid and handed the bottle back to Melissa.

We all stood in front of the living room window, which was about eight feet wide and reached almost from the floor to the ceiling, staring out at the Charles River. Waves shimmered darkly across its surface like the glittering scales of a snake, reflecting the red, blue, green, and silver lights from the city.

"Can you see the fireworks from here?" Giddy asked.

Every summer, the City of Boston puts on a Fourth of July concert followed by a spectacular fireworks display, which originates from a barge in the middle of the river.

"For sure," Melissa said. "The view is spectacular. My parents always have a party. When the fireworks go off, the windows shake. You know those big, blossomy fireworks that look like dandelions when they explode?"

Everyone nodded.

"They shoot so close, it's like they zoom right into the living room."

I mentioned before that when Melissa gets excited she starts talking with her hands. Now, for emphasis, she illustrated the way the fireworks burst, except Melissa forgot I had cracked the lid, and as her hands swooped upward mimicking an expanding arc, the blueberries did not need any further encouragement. In obedience to Newton's First Law of Motion (I liked science in the seventh grade when it didn't include math), the lid flew off, followed closely by globs of organic blueberries. In case you've never eaten *all natural blueberry preserve*, it's not like ordinary jam. Ordinary jam is thick, smooth, and heavy. *All natural preserve* is loose, syrupy and full of whole, sun-ripened, genetically unmodified, organic blueberries. I know because as the lumpy, liquidy concoction spurted into the air, each gooey, blue glob spread out like real fireworks into perfect little solar systems of spinning, sparkling blueberries and juice before descending one after the other on the plush, new, one-hundred-percent, all-natural, gold wool rug. SPLAT. SPLAT. SPLAT. SPLATT. SPLATTT. SPPLLLAAAATTTTTTT.

At the sight, Melissa's expressive fingers froze. In fact, all of Melissa froze. She stared down at the formerly immaculate rug dotted with small blue puddles and gasped. Her face could not have displayed more horror if she were gazing at a corpse sprawled in a pool of blood. "*Oh My God*!!!" she moaned, each word packing such despair and dread just the tone popped Salome and Katie out of the kitchen like toast.

"What?" Salome asked.

Melissa extended a flawless finger. Salome and Katie's eyes followed.

At the sight of the stains, the two girls emitted the same gasping, groaning noises, albeit with not quite the same intensity. Ordinarily, I would have enjoyed hearing all these female moans, if only the situation weren't so terrible.

Melissa turned to me, "I can't believe I forgot you opened the bottle."

I was glad she remembered she had asked me to open it.

Like a sick cow, Katie bleated, "What should we do?"

"No one do anything," Salome ordered. "Let's think. If we do the wrong thing, we'll just make it worse."

While we thought, everyone gazed at Melissa. It was her house. Her rug. Her mother.

Melissa drew herself up. She could maintain calm about a little stain. She was a dancer. She knew what pressure was. Assuming a pre-performance pose (hands clasped at her waist, back straight, stomach in, and only trembling slightly), she suggested, "Let's get spoons and scoop up the puddles before more soaks in." Everyone nodded. This plan made sense. Melissa bent, and with her thumb and finger, picked up the lid. "At least, the top landed on its back," she tittered nervously.

Melissa screwed the lid firmly on the offending bottle, and the three girls vanished into the kitchen. A few seconds later, they emerged, holding spoons, extra-strength paper towels, and a bowl. Like three washerwomen, they fell to their knees, carefully scraping up the blueberries and juice.

Phase One of the operation proceeded smoothly. We guys looked on silently but supportively. Even Napster realized the gravity of the situation and refrained from wise remarks.

Every once in a while, Melissa muttered as she spooned, "My mother's going to kill me for this."

Katie and Salome murmured sympathetically, "It was an accident. It could've happened to anyone."

Melissa continued muttering, "When the rug arrived, my mother was so thrilled. It's only a month old. She ordered the color special."

The blueberries and juice were soon scooped into the bowl and the girls stood to examine their work. In some ways, the rug looked better; in others, worse. I mean, it was true the clumps of blueberries as well as the pools of juice were gone, but the stains that remained scowled up at us like angry Smurfs—big, bold and blue.

"Let's dump this stuff in the kitchen," Katie said. The girls withdrew with the bowls and towels and reappeared a few seconds later.

"I think lemon juice is supposed to work," Katie suggested.

Salome advised, "My mother uses mineral water and Murphy soap."

Glumly, Melissa stared at the rug. I felt really bad for her. I said, "I think there's a CVS on Boylston that's open. I could run over and get some rug cleaner."

At my words, Melissa's jaw dropped lower than the mouth on my Halloween cat mask, and the stars on her cheeks turned as red as if she'd just walked out on the Wang stage without a costume. "Oh my GOD! After the rug was put in, my dad stuck this bottle of special carpet cleaner right in my face. It was soooo humiliating the way he made such a big deal of it."

Like a line of corps dancers, our eyes swiveled in unison toward Melissa.

"OK. OK. He was right. He did need to make a big deal of it." Melissa ran for the closet and returned, her long-fingered hands like a model's displaying the pint sized bottle of clear liquid. "You dab it on, wait a few minutes, and dab it off."

"Awesome," Katie said. "Let's get more towels."

The girls retreated into the kitchen and returned, each clutching a new roll of Bounty. They again dropped to their knees, passing the cleaning fluid to each other and pressing gently at the stains.

It worked.

After a few minutes the stains lost their intense blueish hue and turned sort of dark amber. Hope reigned. A few smiles appeared. We guys watched with more interest as the girls dabbed and waited, dabbed and waited, and dabbed some more. The dark amber stains gained a slightly melancholy grayish-gold tinge as if they were making an earnest effort to display the color of the rug but were not quite up to it—kind of like me in math.

Another pall fell over the group. Giddy looked at his watch, "It's eleven-thirty."

Melissa muttered. "You guys better go."

"I'll stay," Katie offered.

"No," Melissa said. "There's no sense. I can work on the rug. It's not hard. It's getting better."

"I hate to leave you….."

"I'll stay," I said. "We can get rid of what's left of the stains."

The truth was, I wasn't sure, but I didn't want to abandon Melissa.

Napster encouraged, "Stoner can clean. I can vouch for all the times we've gotten away with spilling stuff."

"Yeah. Napster did the spilling and I did the cleaning."

"Guys," Salome scolded. "Melissa needs help, not jokes."

"I'm helping," I said.

Melissa agreed, "Mikey can help."

"Yeah," Napster said, "Mikey can do it."

No one wanted to leave Melissa, but it didn't take six to clean. Mr. Belknap was supposed to pick everyone up at the Chestnut Hill T-Stop at twelve and drive them home. Napster could tell his dad I stuck around longer and was going to catch the last train. Mr. Belknap liked to be one of the boys. He would understand, and it was easy for me to walk home from the T.

When they put on their coats, Katie and Salome gave Melissa supportive hugs. The girls dug up their best happy faces and raved some more over Melissa's ballet performance. But it didn't lift the gloom.

After the elevator door closed, Melissa and I walked back into the living room. Miraculously, as if in our absence Melissa's fairy godmother had waved her magic wand, it actually took a few seconds to locate the stains. It seemed the drier they got, the more they blended in. A heartening turn of events.

Melissa said, "That's not bad. Let's let them dry a few more minutes."

"Yeah," I said, thinking, we could stretch out on the vast unstained portion of the carpet and make out. However, Melissa was not in a kissing mood, which I understood. However, she did snuggle in my arms for reassurance. I told her everyone enjoyed the party, and her spilling the jam did not ruin it.

After ten minutes, the alarm clock that always seemed to tick in her brain rang. Her head lifted and she peered passed my shoulder at the stains. "Not bad," she said, leaning over and tentatively touching one. "It's almost dry. Let's try again."

We worked the stains some more, and they continued fading. After half an hour, they were so faint, even wet they were hard to see. I suggested adjusting the furniture. Because the stains were near the picture window, by judiciously moving the chair on the right side of the window about four inches, we covered the biggest stain, and the smaller stains were close enough to fall in the shadows of the legs, which made them almost invisible. But it was now a quarter past twelve. I had to hustle to catch the last train. Melissa urged, "You'd better go. I think we've done as much as we can."

"I'll call in the morning. You can always blame me. You can say I spilled the jam."

"Don't be silly. I don't want my parents blaming you. Besides what are they really going to do? They won't kill me."

"No. Just torture you mentally for the next ten years."

"Yeah. They'll yell and groan and grumble and sigh and act all martyred and stuff. The worst part is, every time I want to do something my mom doesn't want me to, she'll bring it up along with every other stupid thing I've done since I was, like, three. But she won't kill me."

I stared at the stains. "You know, I think you're going to be OK. I know where the stains are, and I can barely see them. Moving the furniture really helped."

Melissa nodded. "That was a great idea. I'm doing one more round and going to bed."

We walked into the hall, and while I didn't get a kiss on the rug, I did get a long, long, long kiss by the door.

#

Dec. 14th
11:18 a.m.
FROM: Balanchinebabe
TO: DownInDenver
Parents sat by window in dining room digesting big Sunday breakfast like lizards in the sun. Watched scullers on Charles for like an hour. Didn't notice a thing. Thank God, old age and the stress of raising a teenage daughter has ruined their eyesight. Keep your fingers crossed. So far, chock one up for the kids!!!!
    M

#

Around 4 p.m., Melissa called.
"Guess what?"
"What?"
"My mom and I had a little after-ballet-party talk. She actually sat in the chair in the living room. You know, the one we moved—the green one

with the leg on the stain."

"Know it. How'd it go?" I asked, although from her gleeful tone, I could tell it went well.

"Unbelievable. Mom chatted me up on everything, and I, like, sat on that terrible ugly green couch right across from her."

"Know it."

"You can't believe how nervous I was. My stomach was totally butter-flies and bees. Seriously worse than first performance jitters. I mean, her left foot was right next to one of the stains, and I kept on wanting to check how close it was but I couldn't. I didn't want her to see me look down, and I couldn't look her in the eye. I was afraid I might burst out laughing. I had to, like, spot on a point right above her head and stare at it as hard as I could, sort of like doing a turn. I am sooo lucky I am a dancer. I couldn't have done it without my training. I mean she quizzed me for, like, a half hour about the party and the whole time her foot was right there beside the stain, and I sooo wanted to laugh, like, I thought I was going to die. At the end I started to giggle."

"You giggled."

"Yes."

"About nothing?"

"Sort of. My mom asked like, 'How did the boys enjoy the ballet?' And I started to giggle. Luckily, I giggle a lot, and I think my mother thought I was giggling because maybe you guys had a hard time with the ballet. But when I couldn't stop giggling, she asked, 'Are you all right?' I said, 'Yuh-huh,' but she got all squiggly-eyed and suspicious. It was cool in a way. She didn't have a clue. Finally, she said I must be having performance stress since it's near the end of the run, and I've been dancing, like, twice a week, and I'm only fifteen. My mother always has to throw in my age."

"Yeah."

"So, I said, I have been dancing in *The Nutcracker* for, like, eight years and I do not have performance stress. I like performing. I'm just in a silly mood."

"And she bought it."

"Sort of. She got up and said, 'Maybe. But I want you to go to bed early tonight and get lot's of rest.' So I went totally solemn and sincere and prom-ised, 'I will, Mom.' And that was it."

"Wow. That's a whole lot better than ten years of nagging."

"I know. And the best part's, New Year's is in a couple of weeks. My parents throw a big formal party every year. If they see the stains after that, they'll think it was someone at the party. I am soooo fully getting away with this."

#

On Monday, waiting for the lunch doors to open, Napster, Giddy, Salome, and Katie crowded around Melissa and me. Melissa was glowing. She got to tell her story again. High fives flew all around. The other kids in line wondered what the celebration was about but we didn't say a thing. It was more fun letting them think we were having secret doings and wild weekends rather than spending Saturday night on our knees cleaning blueberry stains.

At the end of Melissa's story, Napster suggested, "You don't have to wait till New Year's. Put a Christmas tree in the living room. It'll hide everything."

Melissa shook her head. "My mother only allows us to get those dumb silver plastic trees. And we put it in the den."

Katie and Salome clucked sympathetically.

Melissa continued, "Plastic trees are sooo gross. We haven't had a real tree since we lived in a house. My mom said, 'Real trees are pretty, but the needles will ruin the rug."

We all laughed hysterically at that.

Not giving up, Napster said, "Well, even a plastic tree in the den will help. It'll keep people out of the living room."

Ever supportive of Napster, Katie added, "That's true, Meliss, don't you think?"

"Whatever."

#

The Noyce Christmas dance is on the last Friday before vacation. It was a dance I'd miss because Melissa had another *Nutcracker* performance. However, I didn't mind. Melissa didn't have many performances left. Naturally, Napster urged me to go. Loyalty to girls was not a major factor in his life. Even Melissa and Katie said I should go. Still, I resisted. I didn't want to go by myself, and I didn't want to go as a third wheel with Napster and Katie. Neither option offered much fun. If I danced with a lot of girls and looked as if I was enjoying myself, Katie would report that to Melissa, and I'd have a lot of explaining to do. If I didn't dance much and mooned around, Katie was going to report that, too, and I'd look like a jerk. Saturday, Melissa was getting her final *Nutcracker* performance schedule, and we were supposed to do something the first evening she had free. That was good enough for me. That and Christmas vacation. I mean, no math for a month.

I admit as we got closer to the dance and everyone was talking about who was going with whom and all that crap, it was kind of a downer. But I wasn't interested in going to the dance just to be seen, and I'm not interested in being popular, so it didn't bother me much. The kids I hang out with know about Melissa, and the kids I don't, I was just as happy they didn't know.

Sometimes, it's true I fantasize about being popular but popularity isn't necessarily what it's cut out to be. Like last week, I was playing intramural basketball, and everyone was bored and not very into the game. I had the ball in the back court, so I decided to take a three pointer, which nine times out of ten I'd miss, which is why I play intramural basketball. But by some miracle, it went in. Swish. Chip McConnel, who is a senior on the varsity and whose nickname is Chip McCool (the name says it all), saw the ball whisper through and went, "Nice shot, Stoner."

I was stunned. Not only had Chip McCool talked to me, he knew my name. But Chip McCool is known for being a good guy. When I left the gym, he was skipping practice early, and we were walking practically side-by-side. Chip said, "You goin' to the dance, Stoner?"

It would've been great to say buddy-to-buddy, "Yeah," then have Chip ask, "Who you goin' with?" and reply casually, "Melissa Worth." And, OK, he wouldn't have a clue who Melissa Worth was, but that wouldn't matter. She was a girl—a chick—and we could've continued our buddy-like conversation, and the next time he strolled by and I was with Napster or Giddy or Crusty, I could've said, "Hey," and he'd've said, "Hey," and they'd've been really impressed.

Instead to his question I had to say, "Nah." OK, maybe I could've launched into a long explanation about how Melissa, my girlfriend, was in the *Nutcracker*, and couldn't make it Friday, but it would've been really involved, and Chip would've been long gone before I finished. However, to my, "Nah," Chip was sympathetic. He said, "Tough being a sophomore."

"Yeah."

Then Chip surprised me and said, "Girls are bitches. I just got dumped by Jenna Lawson. Right before the fuckin' dance."

I knew Chip had gotten dumped by Jenna Lawson. Everyone in school had heard. Chip McCool was a six-two guard on the basketball team—too cool to be a forward and freaky tall—and Jenna Lawson was a cheerleader. Now, cheerleaders at Noyce are not as important as they are at other schools: A,—as stated, we don't have football, so the girls cheer mostly in the winter for the basketball team; and B,—lots of girls who would look good in a cheerleading outfit like Kristen St. Clair or Melissa or Katie or Salome think cheerleading is sexist or stupid or demeaning or they just don't have the time. But Jenna Lawson is blonde and very fine, and no matter how much you make fun of the cheerleaders, a few of them, with Jenna Lawson at the top of the pyramid, are definitely wet-dream worthy. But why was Chip telling me that Jenna Lawson had dumped him. Was I—a sophomore—supposed to offer sympathy? Was he not going to the dance? Was he looking for a buddy to hang out with on Friday?

Luckily, I was too stunned to say anything and didn't make a total ass of myself because Chip continued, "I'm going with Shannon Flynn."

"Wow!" I almost exclaimed but managed to keep my mouth shut. A lot of guys (including me) consider Shannon Flynn hotter than Jenna Lawson. It's true Shannon Flynn is not blonde. She is one of those black-haired, fair-skinned Irish girls. I mean, her skin is so soft and smooth, you'd throw away all of your porn downloads just for the chance of holding her hand, and when she looks your way, her blue eyes are, like, permanently on high beam. And I haven't even mentioned her figure. Tall, curvy and lithe describes it—not in a showy way—in an understated, elegant way. Napster is, of course, a Jenna Lawson fan. Jenna Lawson fills out a sweater in a way Shannon Flynn never will. But while I wouldn't throw Jenna Lawson out of bed, if votes are to be cast and rallies held, put me down firmly in the Shannon Flynn camp.

Chip continued, "For all I care, Jenna can go fuck herself. Do you know what she said when she dumped me?"

I'd been trying to keep my attitude casual but respectful. Now I had to say something. I responded as simply as I could, "No."

It was all Chip needed. He replied, "She told me it was time to move on. What she really meant was, —time to move up. I hear she met some sophomore on the Harvard hockey team."

Again, I almost said, "Wow," but refrained. Silence once more was the right thing.

"Fuck the bitch," Chip said. "Hey, whatta you think of Shannon Flynn?"

With absolute sincerity, I said, "She's pretty. She reminds me of Jennifer Connelly."

Chip was interested. "Who's Jennifer Connelly? Does she go here?"

I didn't laugh. Another good move. Breaking into nerdish guffaws at the ignorance of the star of the basketball team when he's being nice was not smart.

"Jennifer Connelly is an actress. She's the girl in *The Rocketeer.*"

"Oh." Comparing Shannon to an actress pleased him. He said, "Is that the one about the guy who flies around with the rocket on his back."

"Yeah."

"I liked that movie. Jennifer Connelly, huh? Didn't she have big tits?"

Chip's puzzled tone required an explanation. "I was thinking of her face."

"Ahhhh," Chip said, enlightened. "Shannon does kinda look like her with the black hair and all."

"Yeah."

Inwardly, I groaned. He doesn't even appreciate Shannon. He doesn't have a clue how beautiful she is.

We reached the parking lot. Chip had a car. "Need a ride?"

Wow once more. A ride with Chip McConnel. I'd love for Napster or Crusty to see me leaving the parking lot, riding shotgun with Mr. McCool. Unfortunately, my mother was picking me up. I had my semi-annual dentist appointment. Perfect timing. The story of my life. At least I had the presence of mind to avoid mentioning it was with my mother. "Nah. No thanks." I said. "Gotta ride."

Chip nodded, "Later."

As Chip pulled out of the parking lot in his green Jeep Cherokee, momentarily I imagined, what if Melissa and I did go to the dance. What if I went up to Chip and said, "Hey," with Melissa on my arm. I mean, he'd definitely say, "Hey," back. I mean, the four of us could talk. Melissa, me, Chip and Shannon. How bad would that be? Then I remembered Chip's immediate and intense interest in whom Jennifer Connelly was. Despite going to the dance with Shannon, he was clearly a wolf on the prowl. Suddenly, I shuddered at the thought of introducing Melissa to Chip. Even if she did have smaller breasts than Shannon, she was a target. Fresh sophomore meat. The fewer seniors who knew Melissa the better. Especially popular basketball playing seniors who've just broken up with their girlfriends.

#

Napster tried one last time to get me to go to the dance. Napster wanted someone to occupy Katie while he went off with Brian Anthony and Mitt Snelling, two complete goof-offs with whom Napster occasionally chases trouble. Brian and Mitt's idea of a kick is to sneak in a bottle of their fathers's scotch, duck into an empty room, and chug liquor until they get drunk and puke. Sometimes, when they get drunk, they find the courage to ask a girl to dance and make fools of themselves by tripping over her, or even better, puking on her.

At the Halloween dance, Mitt Snelling puked on Susie Parker, who could've gotten him into serious trouble if she'd made a big deal of it—but she was nice and just went to the ladies room and cleaned the puke off. It helped that she was wearing a costume, not an expensive dress. Crusty told me about this. I didn't see it myself. I was, of course, groping Melissa in Mr. Moorland's garage.

While I don't see the fun in sneaking around the dance, drinking, Napster does. I mean, he's not stupid enough to get wasted at a dance and puke on a girl, and he's too lucky to ever get caught near a bottle on school property. But like I say, he does occasionally hang with Brian and Mitt. It's the call of his dark side.

When Napster finished drinking with his buddies, he wanted me to guard the most convenient closet, bathroom, or equipment room while he and Katie made out for, like, an hour. What a pain. I had no interest doing sentry duty at the dance. After I expressed these sentiments, Napster actually had the balls to say, "Katie's looking forward to dancing with you, dude. She thinks you're good. You can bring a book for the hall."

"Yeah. Right. I always bring books to a dance." I mean, babysitting my sister is more fun than babysitting Napster.

"Man, you're really letting me down," Napster said.

"Sometimes, that's what best friends are for."

#

Friday night, I stayed home with Sarah. She'd gone with my mom to rent some DVDs. Sarah being Sarah rented *Freaky Friday* and *The Parent Trap*. When she showed them, she said she rented them for me. What a liar. No wonder she likes Napster. But staying home while everyone else was at the dance put me in a sort of sensitive mood. Even though I could've gone to the dance, I felt lonely and a little down. It was actually distracting having my sister around. Instead of shouting, "You twerp I'm not watching Lindsay Nobrain," I sighed and said, "Which one do you want to watch first?"

*Parent Trap.*

*Freaky Friday.*

Halfway through *Freaky Friday*, Napster called. I took the call in the kitchen. He said, "Bro, you are not missing a thing. The dance is prodigiously dull. All Katie wants to do is dance. Brian and Mitt brought a bottle, but Katie won't go near it. Her dad is picking us up and she says if he smells alcohol on her breath, she'll be grounded until she's, like, fifty and if he smells alcohol on me he'll never let me near her again."

"Katie doesn't realize what a good thing that might be."

Napster ignored me. "It's all your fault. If you'd showed up, I could be drinking with Brian and Mitt, and you could be dancing with Katie."

"What fun."

"Better than watching chicklet movies with your sister."

"We're bonding. We're watching Lindsay Lohan before she became such a loser."

"You mean before she had breasts.… What a waste. As my mom says— you know she's the philosopher of the family—'Every minute is a test to live fully,' and you're still sharpening your number 2 pencil. Dude, what time is it, anyway?"

"Quarter past ten."

"Great. At ten-thirty Katie promised we can stop dancing and slip off somewhere. She said that'll gives us forty-five minutes to make out."

"At least, she's organized."

"She's got a metronome up her ass."

"Melissa has a fucking clock up her ass, too."

Sarah shouted from the den, "Mikey, get off the phone and stop swearing or I'll tell Mom. I want to watch the rest of the movie."

"What's stopping you?"

"I paused it."

"Well, fucking unpause it."

"I'm telling Mom."

"Hey, guttermouth, you're worse than I am."

"I am not, fuckface," Sarah yelled.

Napster said, "I can't believe you're spending Friday night with your sister, calling each other names."

"Like I'd rather hide in the supply closet drinking with Brian and Mitt."

"Whatever gets you off," Napster said. "Katie's just emerged from the ladies room. Gotta go."

"Grab those minutes by the balls."

"Katie's gonna do that."

"Mikeeey!" Sarah yelled.

To get back at me for the interruption, Sarah reversed *Freaky Friday* three whole scenes before the spot we left off.

#

At eleven-thirty, Sarah was struggling to stay awake. Usually, she goes to bed around nine, and she couldn't resist sleep anymore. She lay on the couch curled under a quilt in her lavender, floral, *American Girl* pjs with Gumby, her stuffed giraffe, tucked under her right arm and the remote held in a death grip in her left. But mentally, she was a zombie. Dull-eyed, she stared at the tube, and no matter how hard she tried to keep her eyelids open, slowly they slid shut, her head slumped forward, and the remote almost fell. Perhaps it was nearly losing the remote that roused her, but at this point, she started up, opened her eyes wide, and gripped the remote more firmly only after another few minutes to fade. This cycle repeated three or four times until at last, Sarah nodded off and stayed off. But I have to give her credit. She never lost her grip on the remote, and I didn't dare dislodge it for fear of waking her. Instead, I went to my room and turned on my computer. It was late enough for Melissa to have returned from the ballet.

Dec. 18th
   10:57 p.m.
   FROM: Balanchinebabe

236

TO: DownInDenver

Hey. —Another performance finis. I love ballet, but with school and homework…Whew!!! Thank God, it's Christmas. (Is that a pun? Am too tired to know.) I wonder how the dance went. The school dance, that is. Haven't heard from Katie. Have you heard from Napster? Or are they still locked in some closet? Let's see a movie or something Monday. No homework! I love vacations. Call me tomorrow.
TTYL

#

The next day, it took two phone calls, three emails, and thirty-five minutes of IMing to arrive at our final, final, final decision, which was to do what our original plan was—a movie at the Copley and back to Melissa's. With half the effort, we could've planned a bank robbery or, at least, started a new school club. As Melissa's father was in Chicago, we had to come back to her house early. Melissa's mom gets nervous with her dad away. That didn't bother me since, the earlier we returned, the more couch time we'd have. It'd been too long since our bodies were meshed together. I was also curious to check out THE STAIN. Melissa said she barely noticed it now. The farther it got from the day of the deed, the more she lost track of exactly where it was.

Since we were seeing each other Monday and Christmas was Friday, I figured I'd better buy Melissa a present. She'd already informed me she was visiting relatives over Christmas, but I still needed to give her a present. It was also pretty obvious her gift should relate to ballet. I looked up *ballet* in the old Internet—the Yellow Pages—was referred to *dance*, and under *dance* saw a bunch of stores. As I glanced down the list, the Dance Emporium caught my eye. It was in Newton Centre, one T-stop west of Chestnut Hill.

#

Walking into the store, I immediately felt out of place. I mean, the Boston Ballet building is big, and plenty of guys work and visit there. The Dance Emporium is small and intensely chicky. The estrogen count is almost as high as Victoria's Secrets. —OK. I've never actually been in a Victoria's Secret, but it felt like when I'm in the mall, walking by and furtively glance in the window, except here I was *actually* inside. Buying something. What? Everywhere I looked were leotards, tiaras, little speckled tank tops, ballet shoes, and frilly skirts. Then I spotted a counter filled with something I could sort of relate to—jerseys. Cautiously, I approached. On the top shelf was this pile of long sleeve navy blue jerseys with a small silver dancer near the shoulder. Perfect. However, as soon as the clerk approached—this good-looking, ash-blonde college girl—I realized she was going to ask me what size Melissa wore, and I suspected breast size would become involved in some mutually understood but unmentionable way, and I was going to have to say stuff like, she's not as big as you, or you don't have the same proportions, or you're built differently, or whatever and I did not feel up to this kind of exchange, particularly with this good-looking girl. And I guess I am both intuitive and prescient because as soon as the girl took the jersey out of the display, she said, "These are very popular. Do you know your girlfriend's size?"

Even though I tried not to blush, my cheeks turned slightly red. I tried thinking of neck and arm measurements but the only size I could think of was, "Small, but a nice handful." However, I didn't say anything. I was momentarily tongue-tied.

The sales girl looked at me quizzically. Finally, I stammered, "I-I don't know."

Helpfully, the sales girl held the jersey up to her neck. "Is she my size?"

God, this was going as badly as I feared. Melissa was definitely not the sales girl's size. Melissa was much smaller than the sales girl. Could I really say that? Does everything with girls have to be about breasts? I stood, staring as the girl held the jersey in front of her. At last, I managed to shake my head, no.

Talya—she was wearing a nametag that said her name was Talya—must've realized my predicament and thought it was sweet. She thought the whole idea that I was buying a present for my ballet-dancing girlfriend was sweet. She didn't interpret my numb stare as perverted.

To my relief, she lowered the jersey and put it back. She didn't say another word about chest or bust size or any other euphemism for breasts. She took the discrete way out and said, "Maybe we should look at some accessories."

I nodded. "Accessories sounds good."

As we walked over to the accessories section, we talked. Talya was a dancer from Ohio. She took classes at the Boston Ballet, but she didn't seem as serious as Melissa, or maybe she wasn't as good, or perhaps she was another casualty of the-well-developed-chest syndrome, which was why she was a sophomore at BC.

As I stood gawking at the dance bags, scarves, ribbons, tape, and rosin, Talya said, "What price range were you thinking?"

This question was almost as embarrassing as Melissa's jersey size. It was like, how much is your girlfriend worth? I paused, wondering if the price I had in mind would strike her as too low. In any case, I was stuck with it. All the cash I had in my pocket was two twenties, and I couldn't spend the whole amount on Melissa. They had good ice-cream stores in Newton Centre. As I hesitated, Talya made her own calculation on the depth of our relationship. "How about something in the twenty-to-thirty dollar range?"

I hoped that price meant she thought our relationship was deep. Once more I said, "Sounds good."

"How about a pair of leg warmers?" She motioned to where dozens of colorful leg warmers hung from Plexiglas hooks.

"These go from seventeen ninety-five to..." She examined a price tag. "...Thirty-nine ninety-five."

I recalled the girls outside of Melissa's class. A lot of them had on leg warmers. Leg warmers struck me as pretty, yet practical, the price range was right, and my head was spinning from being in the store.

"What color do you think she'd like?" Talya asked.

She held up a dark purple pair of leg warmers. "These are very nice."

Other than a stated preference for black for Halloween, I didn't have a clue what colors Melissa liked, but I didn't remember ever seeing her in dark purple. "How about another color?"

Talya smiled. Another color. She had plenty of colors. This was a shop for girls. "How about pink?" she suggested. "All girls like pink." She held up another pair in pink.

"How much are those?"

Talya turned over the price tag. "Twenty-four ninety-five."

"I'll take them."

"Good." Talya grinned. "You made the right choice."

Talya wrapped the leg warmers in that thin, crinkly tissue paper they have in clothes stores, placed the leg warmers in a navy blue box with the silver logo in the corner, and dropped the box in a navy blue bag with the same logo. She held the bag out to me. "Your girlfriend is going to love these. She's lucky to have a thoughtful guy like you."

I blushed again. God, am I a candy.

#

Monday night, riding up the elevator to Melissa's, I felt good. I had the present, and our movie plans would return us quickly to her condo (and the couch). I hoped Melissa was going to like the present. Despite Talya's enthusiasm, I remembered only a few days before at the mall Melissa dangling all those clothes in front of my face. She might as well have dangled a tampon for all the advice I could give her. But I needn't have worried. When Melissa opened the elevator door, her eyes locked on the Dance Emporium bag, and her cheeks burst into stars. "The Dance Emporium," she exclaimed. "You've been to the Dance Emporium. What were you doing there?"

"As if you don't know."

"A present!"

"Uh-huh."

"For me?"

"Uh-huh."

"For Christmas."

"Yep."

"That's so nice."

"That's me. Mr. Nice Guy."

"I love the Emporium. I buy stuff there all the time."

I shrugged like a nice guy who was also a man of the world.

"What is it?" Melissa bubbled in her best gift-receiving manner.

"Open it and see. Merry Christmas." I handed her the bag.

She took the bag and peeked inside. "Their boxes are sooo pretty." She extracted the package from the bag slowly, drawing out her pleasure. Lifting the box up to me as if I'd never seen it before, she said. "Don't you love the silver dancer?"

"Yeah."

Melissa jiggled the box, trying to guess its contents.

"It's clothes," she prattled, more to herself than to me, but I could tell she was thinking, what kind of ballet clothes could I—a guy who knew less about ballet than the blood in the blister on the tip of her little toe— buy her? But it was from the Emporium. Hope reigned. Carefully, she slid

240

the ribbon off, preserving the bow and raising the cover. Nestled in the tissue paper lay the pink leg warmers. She emitted a pleased squeal. "Leg warmers. Oh, I love them. They're perfect. Really." Judging from the stars on her cheeks, which remained out, I think she did like them. She hugged and kissed me but not on my lips, mostly on my cheek. I think she got me near my ear. Then she rushed down the hall and returned, holding a small box wrapped in gold paper.

"For you. Open it." She had a very confident look as if she knew it was something I would like.

She was right. It was three black-and-white DVDs: —*The Postman Always Rings Twice, The Blue Angel,* and *Double Indemnity.* As I looked them over, I couldn't help adding the cost. They must've been, like, $9.95 each. Ka-ching, Ka-ching, Ka-ching. Thirty bucks. Uh-oh. Melissa had spent five dollars more than me. Did I value our relationship less? Was Melissa mentally comparing the prices? Was I in trouble? Still, five bucks. What did it matter? I mean, I bought the leg warmers myself.

"Thanks," I said and kissed her on the lips, but she broke the kiss off right away.

"Michael, my mother's still up."

"Just a thank you."

"Tell that to my mom. Do you like the DVDs?"

"They look great," I said, but I'd never heard of any of them. I shoved them in my jacket pocket.

"My mom says they're classics."

#

Since it was Christmas, we decided to see *Bad Santa. Bad Santa* was rated R for pervasive language, strong sexual content, and occasional violence. Oh boy.

Movie ratings are so lame. As if we never heard four letter words—they're practically the only words kids use—and if we wanted strong sexual content, we couldn't go on the Internet and see things a billion times worse. But the Copley isn't Southridge where the ticket sellers and ticket buyers are friends.

As we stood in the lobby, staring at the movie times, I figured, lots of people think I'm older. "Let's just go for it. I'll get the tickets."

"Katie and I were carded here once," Melissa said. "It was soooo embarrassing. I mean, most people think Katie is, like, in college." That was girl-speak for saying Katie is built like a brick shithouse. "They made me feel like I was twelve. I'm not doing that again."

"OK. Let's buy tickets for another movie and sneak into *Bad Santa.*"

Melissa nixed that, too. "They guard this place like Tiffany's. Let's ask someone to buy us tickets."

Melissa didn't mind suggesting this course of action since she knew who would do the asking. Me. It was the same old, same old. When things get dirty and unpleasant, the guy does it.

"I'd rather sneak in," I said, delaying the inevitable.

"What if we get caught? It's so much easier to ask."

Real easy. For her.

Surveying the ticket line for suckers, I saw a lot of couples. They were preoccupied talking to each other, and I didn't want to break in on some guy trying to be cool in front of his girl. Maybe the guy would buy the ticket to show off what a good sport he was, or maybe he would growl, "Get lost." I didn't like the odds. Then three college girls sidled up to the line. Perfect. Melissa came to the same conclusion. "Ask them. They'll do it."

I took a deep breath and approached the last of the three. The girl was wearing a light-gray down jacket that hung to her knees, so I had no idea of her body. But she had a pleasant face, just on the pretty side of plain, and she was smiling in a sweet, I'm-easy-to-talk-to manner, although the small silver ring on her left eyebrow indicated she was striving for an edgier flavor. But since the ring was small and way in the corner, the overall impression remained of friendliness. "Excuse me," I said. "We want to see *Bad Santa,*" I pointed to Melissa. I figured, as a girl, she'd like to help the romance along. "We're not seventeen. If I give you the money, will you buy us tickets?"

She inspected Melissa. Then me. Then laughed. (Why are girls always laughing at me?) "Sure." She was chewing gum, which she stuck between her back teeth and her cheek. "Two tickets. *Bad Santa.*" I handed her our money and watched as she rejoined the line. A minute or two later, she reached the window and slid our cash toward the cashier. The girl in the ticket booth didn't even look up.

It was easy.

#

*Bad Santa* is an OK movie, but it's no *School of Rock*. Melissa and I shared a couple of laughs, but that was it. Of course, sharing a couple of laughs with a girl you like adds two stars to any movie. I hate to sound mushy, but getting involved with a girl is mushy. Like when we left Melissa's house, she put on this long red-and-white woolen stocking cap with a bright red tassel. Adjusting the cap in the mirror, Melissa carefully evened the cap and then, once it was straight, gave it a slight tilt, casually flipping the tassel over one shoulder before glancing up. I couldn't believe how adorable she looked. My heart squished around like a kid at Water World. I was lost in mushland and enjoying it.

After the movie, we walked directly to Melissa's apartment. No Marche. No window shopping. Melissa was in a hurry. I was in complete agreement. When the elevator brought us to Melissa's floor, her mother was nowhere in sight. I cherished the silence.

As soon as we hung up our coats, Melissa took me into the living room. I stared hard next to the chair because that's where the stains were, but I couldn't see anything. I shrugged my shoulders in a questioning look.

Melissa walked a few feet, pointed a dainty, highly-trained toe, and patted the spots one by one. The movement couldn't have been more enchanting if she'd done it on stage.

"I guess you're safe," I said. "I can barely see them. They really blend in."

Melissa agreed. "Your idea of adjusting the chair did it. Otherwise my mother might've noticed."

I didn't deny the claim.

"Would you like anything?" Melissa asked. "Anything except a blueberry sundae."

We laughed.

"Nope."

I didn't want that kind of reward.

"Let's go into the den," Melissa said. "We've got to talk."

The den was exactly where I wanted to go. It was fun walking behind Melissa. She was slim, but she had that delicious dancer's ass.

We got to the den and sat down on the couch. I settled back, wanting to put my arm around her, but Melissa did not lean near me. She looked serious. Too serious. She sat with her back straight and her hands fixed on her knees. Like a broken appendage, my arm hung useless by my side.

Melissa gazed into my eyes with a look of great tenderness, but she didn't smile. Her hands remained on her knees as quietly she pronounced, "I don't know how to say this, Michael. Really, I don't. But I know I have to say it right away. You're wonderful. Really wonderful. The nicest person I've ever met. Being with you has been great. Really it has. We've had some super times. But…" She inhaled deeply and jumbled her next words all in a rush. "Something's happened, I didn't expect to happen. Really, I didn't, but it did. So…so even though it isn't easy. I have to tell you right away… I'm sorry…but I…I don't love you anymore."

Strange as it may seem, at her words my first thought was, *Wow, she loved me*. Even with those damn emails, I never believed it. She continued gazing at me with great tenderness, but it was a tenderness I now dimly understood masked a not-so-kind intent. Her look was full of pity and curiosity, like a scientist who's grown fond of a lab dog but still has to kill it. As if she felt she had to make sure the news penetrated, she went on, "I don't think we should go out anymore."

Got it.

Melissa was Danielling me. This was the raspberry. The kiss-off. The deep six. The smelly scram. The grassy knoll. The Jersey jilt. She didn't want to see me anymore, except in math class where I'd be the creepy ex sitting behind her.

My mind spun into this kind of numb zone.

I could think, but I was disconnected—from myself, from the room, from Melissa—as if I were somewhere distant looking down. It was like when you cut your hand, —a deep cut right to the bone. You know it's going to bleed and hurt a lot, but for a moment there's no blood or pain. The instant is vivid and surreal, almost as if time has stopped, and if you tried, you could take the second back and make the cut disappear. But just when you have that thought, time advances one tiny, irreversible tick, and dark red blood appears, oozing out, rolling down your hand, trickling to the floor. Way deep down your stomach churns, but it's still more from the idea than the pain. You feel woozy and vulnerable and terribly, terribly mortal and alone, but there's still no pain. You know the pain will come, but for that suspended, disembodied moment, all that exists is the thick red blood, dripping to the floor until inevitably time ticks once more, and a throbbing ache begins. At first, it's like a small, narrow pulse. Then it swells and pounds, blazing down your arm, and your entire body sweats and burns.

As I stared at Melissa, I felt the same woozy nausea, the same sweating and burning, the same gut-loosening loneliness, weakness, and despair. Yet the more I confronted the reality, the more my brain screamed, No, it can't be! What was the reason? The cause? The crime? Why did this rejection occur? It was so completely out of the blue. Yet the evidence was clear: —the knife, the blood, the strange pitying look, the unyielding dismissal in her tone. At last, I managed to stammer, "Wh-what have I done? What happened?"

"Nothing happened."

"Nothing?"

"OK. Something."

"What?"

"It's hard to explain."

"I don't care....Explain."

"I know. I'm sorry but—but I just feel differently. I...I just don't feel the same about...about us anymore."

"Why?"

Melissa thought hard as if struggling to explain it to herself as well as to me. "You haven't done anything. Really, it's just..."

"I don't get it. One minute you love me, and the next you don't."

"It wasn't one minute. It happened over the last couple of weeks."

"We've barely seen each other."

"That's one of the reasons."

"You wanted it that way. You were too busy."

"I know, Michael. It's not your fault. It's mine."

When Melissa said, "It's not your fault. It's mine," this weird, stupid memory of this *Seinfeld* episode popped into my head where George's girlfriend breaks up with him and says, "It's not you. It's me," and George screams, "You can't say, 'It's not you. It's me,' that's my line. I invented that line." I mean, here I was having the first girl I ever cared for tell me she didn't love me anymore, and all I could think of was a *Seinfeld* episode. A TV show. Not even a serious movie. A sitcom, and I wasn't even thinking of a scene Seinfeld was in, but that jerk George who I never liked. What was wrong with me? It was crazy, stupid, and depressing all at the same time. Yet as sick and miserable as Melissa's words made me feel, at the absurdity of my thoughts, I almost laughed. The craziness of my reaction must have shown in my eyes because Melissa's expression went from tenderness to alarm. She must've thought I was losing it, and maybe for a moment I was. —Then, I remembered, in that *Seinfeld* episode, George said "It's not you, it's me," always meant someone else. Did Melissa love someone else? But who? Someone at school? For the rest of the year, was I going to sit in math, salivating over her beautiful hair, knowing some shithead junior or senior was touching it, running his fingers through it?

"You weren't around and I needed someone." Melissa continued.

"I can't believe you're saying this. You wouldn't *let* me be around."

"I know. That's why it's not your fault. I needed someone who could."

"Who?"

"Someone."

"You're telling me you love someone else."

Melissa nodded. She wasn't even embarrassed to say it.

This bitter trail of black bile snaked upward from my stomach, coiling in the back of my throat like the rancid remains of something foul—all while the thought hammered, *Who? Damn her. Who?* She barely spent any time at school.

Then, even before she could pronounce the name, it hit. "Yuri?"

"Yes."

"I thought Carmen was after Yuri."

Melissa smiled. She dared smile. She was so full of her victory, she smiled right in my face. "She was. But he likes me."

I wanted in some way to destroy that proud simper, but all I could do was sneer, "Congratulations."

Her eyes lowered. "It was an accident."

"Sure."

"It's true. I didn't do anything. During *Nutcracker*, we were together all the time. I couldn't help it. Like I said, you weren't around."

"How could I be?"

"I know. I'm sorry. That's why it's better this way. Yuri and I are involved in so many of the same things." I couldn't believe how casually she said, "Yuri and I," like they were some long-established couple.

"All these weeks, you've been sending me these lovey-dovey emails."

"It didn't get serious until recently."

Serious! Did serious mean she kissed him? All while we were emailing, all while we were walking together to lunch, all while we were on our date, behind my back she's making out with Yuri. Or was I naïve? Did "serious" mean she was doing a lot more? Yuri was eighteen. From Europe. From Russia. Imagining it was like an x-rated horror movie in my brain.

I could barely breathe.

I couldn't even accuse her of what I wanted. I couldn't utter the words. I could only manage, "You kissed him?"

Melissa looked down and didn't say anything.

"How could you cheat on me like this?"

"Didn't cheat," Melissa snapped, "You don't own me. I couldn't talk to you about it over the phone or in an email or math. I couldn't tell you like that. I'm sorry. I—I just don't love you anymore." And it was true. When she raised her eyes, no love shone. Everything we once had—gone.

How could I not have known? How could I not have had a clue? How could I have thought by this time we'd be horizontal on the couch?

And the way Melissa held herself—so composed, so self-satisfied, so smug. My body trembled with an almost uncontrollable anger. I could no longer sit docilely beside her, getting blasted down to my soul. I leapt to my feet and roared, "You weren't waiting to see me! You were just waiting to be sure!"

At the ferocity in my voice, Melissa recoiled.

"Shhhh, Michael. Please. You don't have to shout. You're going to wake my mother."

Ah, yes, *mother*. It was low of her, hiding behind her mother. That must've been a fun mother/daughter chat. Michael was out. Yuri was in. The big Russian star. What a coup. "I see. You do whatever you want, but I need to be quiet?"

"That's not it. I know you're upset. But you don't have to shout and be nasty."

"I'm nasty. What about you? Sneaking behind my back."

Melissa bit her lip. "I wasn't sneaking. I could've gone out with lots of guys at school, but I didn't because I liked you."

"Am I supposed to be grateful?"

"Be whatever you want. Yuri's different. We have so much in common. We talk about it all the time."

"All the time. You really are a bitch."

Melissa's eyes locked. "Enough. It's late. There's no use discussing this now."

Even as my fury grew, I realized it was just like with Danielle. My anger only made my exit easier for Melissa. She didn't have to explain anymore, pity anymore, understand anymore. Like Dory's fly, I was left to crawl away on my belly in my new existence without wings.

Terminated.

Exterminated.

Thump.

Thwap.

Squish.

"You'd better go. I'll see you in school. Thank you for the present. I really like it."

"Great. School doesn't start for three weeks."

Melissa sighed and her voice softened. "Michael, it wasn't anyone's fault. Really. I still want to be friends. You're such a special person. Funny and smart and sweet. Can't we still be friends?"

Damn her to hell. Friends. —Danielle, I wanted to be friends with. Maybe someday I could weasel my way into Danielle's pants. And Danielle lived in Stowe. Out of sight. I never had to see her or her boyfriend—. What was his name? I'd already forgotten. —Jameel. —Jaimie—Oh, yeah. Jared. The wonderful, lucky Jared.

But Melissa? How could we kid and pal around? How could I talk to her every day, wondering how much Yuri was getting? How much Melissa was giving? I liked Melissa too much and I hated Melissa too much all at the same time. In comedies, people joke about this sort of break-up stuff. But this wasn't a comedy. This was real. This was my life.

"Well?" Melissa said, giving me a cheery smile. "Friends?"

I didn't reply.

Still trying to be encouraging, she said, "I understand. Think about it. I know it's hard."

And that was it.

I burst, "Go fuck your-self!"

At last, Melissa had made me a bad boy.

Melissa rose to her feet. "OK. Go. Now."

I didn't object.

I turned and headed down the hall. Without a word, Melissa followed.

At the elevator, I thought of the last time we'd stood in that spot, we'd kissed. While the elevator rose, we'd kissed. And when the elevator stopped at her floor, we'd kissed. We kissed until we couldn't kiss anymore.

Now, we glared, resentful, angry, and wary, our physical beings as foreign, incompatible, and repellent as aliens. I stabbed the button for the elevator. We both heard the familiar creak as it made its reluctant, arduous journey to Melissa's floor. Neither of us stirred. For a moment, she looked as if she wanted to say something, as if she might want to reach out and, at least, touch my hand, but I didn't move and neither did she. When the elevator arrived, I yanked open the door. Melissa whispered, "Bye."

I stepped into the elevator. The door clanged shut. I pushed the lobby button. The elevator groaned as it descended. Faintly, I heard Melissa press against the door and call, "Michael...."

But I was already gone.

#

I felt like I was in a coffin—as if I were trapped in a tiny, stuffy box. Down, down, down, I descended—to hell, or was I already in hell? Except with another lurch, the elevator landed and the door opened and I stepped into the large, plush lobby, but the dead, trapped feeling remained. One minute, my life had been happy. On solid ground. The next, Melissa had said she didn't love me anymore and I was a wraithe, a phantom, a specter, wandering through an illusory, shadowy world. The color had even gone out of the paintings. They looked dull, gloomy, washed out. If anyone had seen me, they would have thought I was crazy, sick, or drunk. My body staggered toward the lobby door, and I stumbled into the fresh night air. It didn't help. A black hole inside me had sucked all the joy out.

A few hours before, Melissa and I had been so close. She'd been part of me. I'd been part of her. We were a match. A team. Partners. We'd just exchanged Christmas presents. God, what a farce that was. What a fool I was, going to that ballet store, fretting over her present. I imagined the expression on Talya's face if she ever found out Melissa wasn't even in love with me when I bought the damn thing. And Melissa shopped at that store. Maybe Talya would find out. I tried recalling if I'd mentioned Melissa's name. I didn't think I had. Talya wouldn't remember anyway.

It was so pathetic.

My mom and dad and sister were going to wonder why Melissa never called or why I never called her.

And Napster. I was going to have to tell him. He has two girl friends and I can't keep one. Then I remembered Katie, and it struck me—had she known? She must've. Girls always talk about stuff like that. Did Katie tell Napster? Did he know and not tell me? I couldn't believe it. I mean, we were best friends. Napster wouldn't keep the confidence of a girl over me. Not Napster. But really, what difference would it've made? It wouldn't have changed anything. Melissa would still have dumped me, and I'd still feel dead and empty inside. The only thing that would have changed is I wouldn't have bought the damn present.

I reached the subway and got on. Six people were in the car. None of them looked happy. But they were happier than me.

I thought of Chip McCool. He'd been dumped. If someone as cool as Chip McCool had been dumped, why should I feel bad?

I guess because I didn't have a backup as pretty as Shannon Flynn. I didn't have anyone. Worse, I still liked Melissa. The bitch. I still liked her hair and her eyes and her lips and that special flirty, crooked smile—which once, a long, long time ago, had seemed meant only for me—except now it was boxed, wrapped, ribboned, and regifted. For Yuri. I gritted my teeth. Yes. Yuri. I didn't want to think about him, but in my mind's eye, I couldn't erase the picture of Melissa drooling over his ass. Damn her. Damn his ass. At least I wouldn't have to deal with Melissa and Yuri at school, holding hands in the hall or making out in class before the teacher came in or rolling in the woods while I ran by during cross-country.

Although one tragic irony did occur to me. —It was now even more important to study math. I mean, it was bad enough looking like a fool when Melissa liked me. Since she'd dumped me, I couldn't give her the satisfaction she'd not only jettisoned a guy whose flat ass didn't make girls salivate.—She'd ditched a guy who was smaller brained than my sister's stuffed giraffe. As incredible as it seemed, I was going to have to study math harder without Melissa than with her.

I had three weeks to get myself together. Three weeks until I had to walk into math and say, "Hey," coolly enough, so that I wouldn't get a "Hey" back accompanied by that "be-kind-to-the-spaz-because-I-know-it's-hard" look. If she gave me that look, I'd what? Never speak to her again? Not much revenge. What would she care? Luckily, barely anyone at school knew about us. Another benefit of anonymity. No glory. No shame. And I didn't have to worry about Chip McCool stealing Melissa. She was already gone.

Suddenly, I understood Darlene. I understood her anxiety and her pain. Melissa's dumping me gave me a lot more sympathy. Not that my sympathy would persuade me to tell Napster to be careful of Darlene's feelings. To tell Napster to try not to break Darlene's heart. Even though for the first time I understood what those words meant. I thought of how often Marianne and Elinore had spoken them in Jane Austen and how silly, trite, and old-fashioned they had seemed. But when Melissa had said she didn't love me anymore, it had ripped something growing within. Something I didn't know was growing until I felt the tear. Shreds of her smile, her voice, her laugh, her glance were scattered all over my insides like roots that when you pulled them out never came out clean. The torn ends clung to the earth. How long would those ends twist deeper and deeper before they died? — Yes, now I understood Marianne and Elinor. Now I understood Darlene. It was funny. The only people I didn't understand were Napster and Melissa. And they were the closest to me.

#

The next morning when I awoke, I felt OK.

For about two seconds.

Then I remembered.

Then I got depressed.

I tried to distract myself, but every time I became lost in something before too long, the thought snuck in like a stray mongrel creeping home— maybe it'd be fun to call Melissa—except I couldn't call Melissa. I couldn't ever call Melissa.

My mom knew right away something was wrong and wanted to know what, but I said, "Nothing." Even my sister remarked I looked "bummed." But she figured a teacher had assigned a big paper or something over Christmas. "Is it really long?" she asked.

When I didn't answer, her face got a stunned look, "Oh my God, how long? Ten pages?"

A long paper on a boring subject is one of the worst things Sarah can imagine, particularly as in high school she knows you can't put in pictures.

"No, brat," I said. "Go. You're bothering me." And I shooed her away like Dory shooing a fly. But I let Sarah keep her wings.

Around four, Napster called.

"Wazzup?" he said.

I told him.

He sounded surprised. "What a ho!"

"You didn't know?"

"How would I?"

"Katie."

"Oh, yeah. She didn't say a word. Girls are such bitches."

"It's not Katie's fault. Don't get mad at her."

"Nah. Are you OK?"

"I guess so."

"You'll get over it. Next time, find a girl who's cute and has tits."

"I don't know."

"You sound really down. I agree she's hot and she's got those great legs and ass, but there's lots of girls hotter than she is. Do you want to come up? We're here till New Year's. Darlene said her cousin from Boston's visiting."

"More cousins!" I exclaimed.

"Darlene's Italian."

"From the hair removal branch of the family?"

"Yeah. She's sixteen."

"Is she cute? Does she have tits?"

Napster laughed. "Darlene said she's cute. And I bet she has a great ass and tits. I think big tits run in the family. And she's got her license already. You always do well with older women."

"My great record with Danielle. One kiss."

"She was a senior, dude. That was way cool."

"What about your parents?"

"They won't care. They like you. They always talk about how serious you are. They think you're a good influence. They don't know you're just serious about getting laid."

#

Meanwhile, my somber appearance, plus my not vanishing into my room every couple of hours to use the phone, plus no calls from a certain fifteen-year-old female who began every call —"Hi, Mrs. Steinman, this is

Melissa. Is Michael there?", —plus my staying in my room every evening finally clued my mother onto the reason for my mental deterioration. When I made it down for food around noon on Thursday, my mother asked, "Did you and Melissa have a fight?"

"Not exactly a fight."

"Oh." My mother paused for a while. I think she was trying to figure out a tactful way to ask if Melissa had dumped me. "Are the two of you OK?"

"I'm really not interested in discussing the subject," I said.

"Oh." I could tell by the mixture of sadness and concern in her tone, she knew. "That's too bad. We're here if you want to talk about it."

"OK." Like, I really wanted to talk about my breakup with my parents. What was she thinking?

"Well," my mother said, talking about it anyway, "teenage girls are very difficult. The younger they are, the worse it is. When I was in high school, I didn't date until I was a junior."

I did not care what my mother did in high school. I had to deal with what kids do in high school today. As silence seemed the safest response, I did not say anything. I just hoped my mother would leave me alone. And she did, especially since I grabbed the plate of sandwiches and ate in the den, moodily watching TV.

After that conversation, however, I was surprised. My parents were astonishingly tactful. They didn't ask why we broke up or suggest I call Melissa and make up or grill me for details. Even my sister, who must've been warned not to say anything, kept her mouth shut. I think it's the most decent thing she's ever done. I mean, she could have had a field day. She could have given me a hard time in a gazillion ways. But she didn't. As far as the family went, it was as if Melissa never existed, which was fine by me.

Like a crumb of undigested cheese, Melissa's name only came up once when my Aunt Rebecca, during a holiday dinner, turned to me and said in this incredibly loud voice so every single person, I mean, like all twenty of them, at the table could hear. "Michael, your mother told me last week you have a little girlfriend. She says she danced in *The Nutcracker*."

Everyone's eyes riveted on me, especially my cousins, —Tiffany and Todd. Tiffany is a snob and a sophomore at Wellesley. Todd is sort of OK and a senior at Newton High. Todd is the latest math genius in the family and has gotten accepted early decision at Brandeis. He's my father's brother's son, but he seems to have inherited my father's math genes. Anyway, I must've turned bright red because I felt my cheeks get hot. But I wasn't about to tell my aunt and half my family, including Todd and Tiffany, that my "little dancer girlfriend" had slipped on her pointe shoes and relevéd and sautéd (OK, I looked them up.) on my soul. So I said, "Yes, she did," which was true, and my red face didn't give anything away. It could've meant I was too embarrassed to talk about my girlfriend, so no one suspected anything.

As she was close enough—only one seat away—my aunt pinched my cheek and continued to everyone in general, "I can't believe Michael is old enough to have a girlfriend. Before you know it, Sarah will be bringing boys home. Isn't that right, Sarah?" It was Sarah's turn to blush. Her big round cheeks flamed crimson and she sat, staring down at her plate, while my aunt got in one more dig. "Sarah's so cute she's going to break all the boys' hearts like they're Hershey bars."

Luckily for Sarah, she was too far away for my aunt to pinch. Even I must admit her cheeks are pretty pinchable. But she was down at the end of the table with Richie and Elizabeth, who are my mother's sister's kids, and who are eight and five, too young for Aunt Rebecca's teasing.

At this point, my mother, who had caused the problem in the first place, stepped in. She diverted Aunt Rebecca's attention by asking if she wanted another slice of turkey and more stuffing. Even more than teasing, Aunt Rebecca loves to eat, so I was saved. Aunt Rebecca took a big helping of both and quieted down like a cow lost in the charm of chewing.

After dinner, I was somewhat worried Todd and Tiffany might quiz me about my girlfriend, but they were happy enough talking about themselves.

#

What else could I do?

I took Napster up on Winnipesaukee. I had no delusions about starting any sort of serious relationship with Darlene's cousin, but in my more optimistic moments, I hoped she would be—please!—just a little pretty and maybe, just maybe, —only interested in hooking up. This way if we had lots of wild beauty-parlor sex, I could forget Melissa. I had thought falling in love is what I wanted, but as much fun as falling in love was, it made getting dumped hurt a lot worse. Of course, just as I'd never met a fourteen-year-old girl at a party who liked giving blow jobs in closets, I'd never met a girl who just wanted to hook up.

My life reminded me of this exhibit I saw once at the Museum of Science. It's this one inch square of dirt magnified a couple of hundred times, so you get to see these incredibly little bugs. These bugs are so tiny they live their whole lives and never run into fellow tiny bugs that are an inch above, below, or beside them. That's how my life felt. No matter how tantalizingly close some girl might be who just wanted to have sex, I know our paths will never cross. Even if I know a girl who supposedly pops in and out of guys' beds, when I talk to that girl, she discovers morals.

As I unpacked in Napster's room, Napster said encouragingly, "Don't worry, dude. Darlene's cousin's fine."

I stared at him skeptically.

"Really, man, I'm not shitting you. Darlene showed me a picture."

"What about her body?"

"I thought you don't care about bodies."

"I don't care about mega breasts. I care if she's fat."

"The photo only showed her face, but you can be sure she's not as skinny as Melissa." Just hearing Melissa's name made me wince. I think Napster caught that and hurried on. "I told Darlene the kind of girls you like. She said you'll like her cousin. Darlene said to tell you she looks like Natalie Wood, whoever that is."

#

Amazingly, Darlene's cousin, Katrina Petrucci, does look like Natalie Wood (she's a movie star). At least, the way Natalie Wood looks in *West Side Story*. Katrina has dark brown hair, kind of a chestnutty complexion, big, doe-like eyes, and full lips. Her figure is good, too. I mean, I know Natalie Wood is much more beautiful than Katrina. But Katrina is close enough, so appearance-wise I had no complaints.

We met at the Barn. We ate something and talked OK, and because no one wanted to see the movie *In America*, which was playing, we walked around town for like thirty minutes before arriving at the river. All lit up, the falls are pretty, but Niagara it isn't.

I wasn't surprised when Napster turned to the three of us and said, "I can get the same effect in my shower. Let's go somewhere warm." I don't know if Katrina thought Napster meant we were heading back to the Barn, but she didn't say anything, and Darlene didn't say anything, and I kept my mouth shut as well.

More quickly than Melissa's march to the mall, our path brought us to the Beauty and Beyond Hair Salon. Once inside, Napster and Darlene unzipped their jackets, removed their hats and gloves, and disappeared into the office. Katrina and I settled on the couch in the reception area. It is a long, thinly-cushioned, navy blue couch without arms at the ends. Katrina sat as far away from me as she could without falling off. Napster and Darlene's disappearance did not put her in a romantic mood. But even though Katrina sat at the farthest end of the couch and the stench of the beauty parlor chemicals filled my nostrils, I didn't mind. I was near enough to enjoy the V of Katrina's plum colored sweater and her push up bra that blessed me with the sight of two beautiful mounds of flesh. I say "blessed" because in between her breasts dangled a silver cross. The reverence I felt wasn't exactly religious, but I did think about Christ and how, if I could magically shrink myself down and hang on that cross, crucified or not, life might not be so bad. Katrina was not as stacked as Katie or Darlene, but Melissa so blessed would've considered herself cursed.

Katrina was a sophomore at St. Bonaventure's in Somerville, which is an all girls' school, and I guess the nuns or whoever had gotten into her head because, besides sitting as far away from me as she could, after what must've been an hour, Katie started glancing at the office door and muttering comments like, "Darlene could stay in there all night," or "Darlene is clueless about anybody but herself," or "Darlene'd better be out by eleven. We've got to get up early to help with a family lunch." (It was déjà vu with Jesse all over again, only Katrina had a much better body.) As more minutes limped by, the scope of Katrina's muttering widened. "I wonder if Napster really likes Darlene? Darlene says he does, but I think he just likes to fool around." As Katrina made this accusation her eyes flitted on the back room and then on me.

What was I supposed to say? I had to defend Napster. "Napster likes Darlene."

Katrina wasn't convinced, and I could see from the way she gazed at me I was up to my neck in her pool of guilt by association. Finally, I'd found a girl who thought I was a bad boy, —only she didn't like bad boys.

"In case you haven't noticed," Katrina said, folding her arms in front of her. "Darlene's not that responsible. She's gotten me into lots of trouble before."

Another window into Darlene's past.

"Like what?"

"Like last summer, my father brought up our motorboat and moored it on the lake. We weren't supposed to go near it, but one night Darlene persuaded me to swim out. All she said we were gonna do was sit in the boat and, you know, talk. But as soon as we climbed in, Darlene found the key, and next thing we're cruising across the lake to some guy's house. "'Cept our cruise didn't last long. We ran out of gas practically in the middle of the lake. Course, we didn't have our cells 'cause we swam out. We floated around in that stupid boat, like, for hours, and I was about ready to kill Darlene when some kids who were out drinking cruised by and towed us back. And who's waiting on shore when we get in?—My dad. Mad as hell. We were grounded, like, for the rest of the summer."

Katrina told the story with a great deal of heat. I could tell the memory still rankled. Was this the time to show life had burdened us with similar companions?

"Napster's like that, too," I said.

Except Katrina wasn't interested in bonding.

Despite her problems with Darlene, Katie only seemed interested in dirt to make Napster look bad. "What's Napster like in school? Is he popular?"

To let her know I understood her game, I answered, "You mean with girls?"

Katrina's cheeks flushed. As her skin was dark, the color was hard to see, but it was there. It lent a softer, gentler look to her face, which was strange as she was being anything but. Nonetheless, the color made her pretty face even prettier, and I found myself edging closer. She matched my movement by pivoting her body slightly further away. "Not just with girls," Katrina replied. "With everyone."

"It's a small school. Napster and I just try to get by."

Katrina persisted. "Does your school have many dances?"

"We have small dances off and on when kids get it together, and maybe three big dances."

"Do you both go?"

"I went to the Halloween dance but not the Christmas dance."

"Why not?"

I wasn't about to mention Melissa. "I didn't feel like it. I mean, I know all the sophomore girls. There's only about forty. I don't have to get dressed up and pay ten bucks to meet them," which was true. But mentally, I was scrambling because I knew Katrina's next questions would be stuff like, "Did Napster go?" and "Who did Napster go with?" and since I was going to have to lie, and it's well established I don't lie well (if I were a spy, I'd get shot the first day). I checked my watch, and fortunately it was close enough to Katrina's eleven p.m. deadline to throw her off script. "Well, look at that," I said. "Ten-forty. Shouldn't you start working on getting Darlene out?"

Katrina glared at the back room and nodded.

I asked, "What are you going to do?"

"I am pounding on that door."

"Cool. Go for it."

As far as I was concerned, the problem was strictly between Katrina and Darlene. My response, however, did not please Katrina.

"Maybe you could," she said, for the first time flashing a warm, glossy, cherry-lipped smile. Bad boy or not, she expected me to do the gentleman-ly thing and volunteer. It's amazing how girls can turn on a dime. Katrina might've been cold all night, but she knew how to be a woman when she wanted.

"Me?"

"Napster's your friend."

"Darlene's your cousin. I don't have to wake up early. I don't give a damn when they emerge."

"Please," Katrina implored. "We've got to be back on time. Please. You do it."

Like most girls, Katrina didn't care about groveling as long as she got her way, and since I'm not the bad boy she thought, and I didn't want any more questions about Napster, I was stuck once more. But I resolved not to do her bidding exactly. Instead of pounding on the door, I yelled, "Hey, in there! Almost eleven. Katrina needs to get home."

Silence.

I yelled louder, "Katrina needs to go!"

More silence.

I yelled again, "Katrina...."

"We hear you."

At the sound of Napster's muffled voice, Katrina relaxed like a content-ed cat. She stretched her arms and wriggled back into the couch.

Ten minutes later, Napster and Darlene appeared, a little more dishev-eled than usual, but otherwise intact.

Smoothing her hair, Darlene said to Katrina, "Happy?"

"Uh-huh."

"Well, if we gotta go. Let's go." Darlene placed her hand on Napster's shoulder. "Katrina's dad's real strict. Stricter than my mom."

"Is that possible?" Napster said.

Darlene nodded. "He went to seminarian school for two years before he left and married Katrina's mom."

Suddenly, that cross dangling between Katrina's breasts took on a whole new meaning.

We walked out the door and said good-bye in front of the Beauty and Beyond Hair Salon.

Because the entire time we were in the beauty parlor Katrina had acted as if she had an even bigger cross up her ass, I was resigned to a nod and a brief clasp of the hand. Instead, I was stunned when Katrina stepped forward and boldly thrust her face toward me, open mouthed. Our kiss wasn't a light peck, either. She put her hands around my neck, pulled me toward her, and kissed hard with tongue. Just before she eased away, she whispered, "Thanks," and retreated beside Darlene. As the two headed off, they both waved.

Wow, I wondered, was Katrina's performance for my benefit or Darlene's?

#

On the way home, Napster said, "You've got to admit, Katrina's pretty choice. What happened in the waiting room? When you said goodbye, I thought she was going to swallow you."

"Nothing happened. All she did was sit as far away as possible and quiz me about you."

"What'd she want to know?"

"If you really cared about Darlene and if you fooled around with other girls."

Napster stared at me intently. "What'd you say?"

I looked as innocent as I was. "Didn't say a thing."

"You're sure?"

"Positive."

"Good. So do you like her? Katrina clearly likes you."

"You say that about everyone."

"C'mon. She grabbed you like a giant squid," Napster said. "I think Katrina's perfect. She's sort of like you. Prissy but horny."

"I'm not prissy."

Napster grinned. "Go after her. She'll complain less about me."

"What about her dad and the seminary?"

"He left the seminary to marry her mom. He was probably beating off more than you. Too bad we can't see'em tomorrow. I bet Katrina's big into rules. One kiss on the first date. A little titty on the second. On the third date, she could go wild."

"What number date is this for you and Darlene?"

"You know I don't date."

"Why can't we see'em tomorrow?"

"So you do want to see Katrina."

"Just thinking about you."

"You're just thinking about those knockers. In that purple sweater with that cross swingin' in between, they looked like the answer to every young man's prayers."

"You noticed the cross, too."

"How could I help but?" Napster said. "It's Christmas. That's the problem. The big family do-ha. Give Katrina a call when we get back. I'll get her number from Darlene. You and Katrina fit. You need a girl with tits."

#

When I awoke the next day, it was late, even for me. Napster wasn't around. I washed, dressed, made my bed, and headed to the kitchen. Neither Napster nor Salome was there. Just Mrs. Belknap. As I entered, she picked up a bowl of her usual great pancake batter and poured some into a pan.

"Where is everybody?" I asked.

"Stephen ate an hour ago," she said.

"He should have woken me."

"I sent him to the grocery store. I used all the eggs and milk for breakfast. For supper, I'm baking a cake. You still like chocolate cake, don't you?"

I nodded.

"At Stephen's birthday parties when you were little, your mouth was always covered in chocolate."

Crap. Why do parents say things like this? As Mrs. Belknap wasn't my mother, I couldn't groan and walk out of the room. I sat there, pretending I thought the image of my mouth covered in chocolate was adorable. However, as quickly as I could, I tried bringing Mrs. Belknap back to the issue at hand—where Napster was. "Is Stephen walking?"

"He can't drive. He'd better be walking."

"I thought he might've gone with Mr. Belknap."

"Mr. Belknap's skiing."

"Mr. Belknap really likes the outdoors."

Mrs. Belknap nodded. "That's why we're here." As Mrs. Belknap slid a couple of thick, fluffy brown pancakes on my plate, she added, "Stephen seems to be seeing a lot of this Katie girl."

It's official. I'm the go-to source on Napster's sex life. But the last person I would willingly reveal any information to was his mom.

"They're just friends."

Mrs. Belknap looked skeptical. "I suppose we'll find out just how good friends in February."

I couldn't help it. I snorted and nearly did my own version of a spit take. February 8th, of course, is Napster's birthday when he and Salome finally get to date.

Mrs. Belknap leaned against the kitchen counter, facing me. She picked up the drink that was never far from her hand and said, "I wish you kids weren't in such a rush. Stephen and Salome just won't listen. We know they're sneaking around behind our backs."

Mrs. Belknap scrutinized my face for a reaction. I kept my expression as blank as possible. Maybe I succeeded. Maybe I didn't. Mrs. Belknap didn't let on. After a pause, she continued, "Love is a drug, you know, worse than alcohol." She jiggled the ice in her glass. "One sip and anything can happen. It's like taking a drink without knowing what's in it. Sadness. Fun. Pain. Jealousy. Excitement. It's all possible. That's why kids get messed up. All they want is the good stuff. The fun. The excitement. Love means a lot more. Relationships take work like anything else. Graduating Noyce and getting into a good college takes a lot of effort and commitment. You know that. Love takes the same—only it's lifelong. When you're a teenager, you don't understand. You want what's easy. Kids just go by their feelings. One day, they're in love. The next, they're not. All very dramatic. For a kid, being fifteen is drama enough. Salome is the worst. With all the hormones pumping in her, most days she can barely think straight. How can you expect to fall in love when every morning you're a different person than the night before? Salome is very bright, but she's like a windmill. The slightest breeze blows from school or her friends and she starts spinning......"

Wow, I thought, for a girl, Salome seemed pretty stable.

"And Stephen," Mrs. Belknap continued, "He thinks he has to be so cool and distant, but he's really very sensitive."

Napster sensitive? She's got to be kidding. Napster is about as sensitive as a rhinoceros' horn.

Mrs. Belknap went on, "Teenage girls can really be cruel with boys. So much for them is about status and competition."

Right on there, Mrs. Belknap.

"I'd just as soon Stephen went out with lots of girls."

Well, you have your wish.

"Mr. Belknap and I were friends first. We had similar interests. Similar goals. We didn't even meet till I was twenty-four and he was twenty-nine. By then, we'd both reached a point where we were serious about making a commitment. You're a teenager for such a short time. I know there's lots of pressure to have a girlfriend, but what's more important is to make the right preparations for life." I was trying to look both earnest and interested. I guess I wasn't succeeding because Mrs. Belknap glanced at me and caught herself. Meditatively, she stared at her drink, took another sip, and poured the contents into the sink, even though plenty of drink was still left. "Enough lecturing," she said. "Stephen and Salome hate it when I do. They call me the 'philosopher mom.' Another pancake?" She smiled a lopsided smile. For a second, it reminded me of Melissa. It was freaky. I mean, Mrs. Belknap is forty or something and Napster's mom. But something about the shape of her lips and the way one side of her mouth kind of slanted down gave me shivers.

To her question of pancakes, I quickly assented. "Sure."

Mrs. Belknap picked up the batter and went about frying more. She stopped talking about love.

I kept thinking about Melissa.

Over and over, I heard her last soft, "Michael." Over and over, I saw myself holding and kissing her. Over and over, I felt the sweet, liquid, smoothness of her lips. I wanted to grab onto the memories and think them so hard they became real. But they floated in my mind, evanescent, out of reach, faint phosphorescent flickers. I was in the Matrix, only I couldn't make what I wanted happen.

To distract myself, I thought of Katrina. I thought of her breasts half-submerged in her plum sweater. I thought, probably Napster was right. Having broken the ice and kissed, on our second date we probably could do more. The frustrating thing was, no matter how much more we did, Katrina would never be Melissa. Katrina's body was fantastic, that was for sure, but she wasn't really that easy or fun to talk to. We sort of got along, at least for part of the night, but Katrina didn't make me laugh. Katrina didn't make my heart feel like magic. Most of the time with Katrina, I felt more alone than when I was by myself.

Sure, I could use Katrina to make people think I had a girlfriend, that I was over Melissa, that she didn't matter anymore. But while I could fool Salome, Giddy, Crusty, Katie, my parents, Napster, and maybe even Melissa, I couldn't fool myself. I felt like a puzzle only one piece fit. Every other girl seemed too tall, too short, too dark, too heavy, too loud, too quiet, too dumb, too strange, too normal, too everything, except Melissa.

Which meant searching—classrooms, malls, parties, beaches, dances, restaurants, parks, bookstores—until I found the next special, wonderful, perfect, ideal someone until that wonderful, perfect, ideal, special someone discovered I wasn't the person she thought I was or the person she desired me to be or the person her friends thought I should be or her mother expected me to be or maybe just until she found a cooler, cuter, hotter, older, richer, smarter, dreamier special someone, and I would be dumped again.

Love.

It was one big unending delusion.

Yet everyone thought love was the answer.

Why?

Maybe because life was so much worse alone.

Maybe Mrs. Belknap was right. Maybe love was just a drug, an opiate everyone—even not knowing it—got hooked on. I had all the symptoms. Like Mrs. Kopechne taught in Chemical Dependency class—all I could think about was how much I wanted it and how—no matter what—I was going to get it because love, —that incredible high of a mind-fuck, —was what I needed to escape on, climb on, soar on forever and ever like an eagle in the sky, because like every other drug, love was its own ecstasy and its own despair; its own courage and its own fear; its own craving and its own cure; and I wanted to suck it, snort it, shoot it, eat it, absorb it through whatever organ or orifice I could so that, at least for a few blinding, frenzied, exalted moments, I would lose the pain and madness its absence drove me to. Because I hurt so bad. Because without it, I was useless, ugly, sick, and afraid. Love was the only way I could feel decent again, human again, normal again, well again, sane again, safe again, right again, and most of all, immune again from the pain of never holding Melissa, never caressing Melissa, never kissing Melissa, and yet, every day sitting behind her in math with her hair falling loose over my desk like some kind of damn glorious golden dawn. If I loved someone else and someone else loved me, it wouldn't matter what Melissa did. But the trouble was like any drug. —Where to find it? Where to score? On what street corner? In what alley? On what website? In what pharmacy? Love had no prescription. No distributer. No marketer. No peddler. No pusher. No mob. No lab. No factory. No store. Love couldn't be bought, bribed, swindled or stolen. You couldn't force, control, or fake it. Like some damn miracle, love had to happen on its own.

Naturally.

Napster and Willoughby stole it. All Napster and Willoughby wanted was what they could score. And if I went out with Katrina—and in the end, I figured I would—I wouldn't be any different. —I would say or do whatever I had to. I would lie, deceive, trick, cheat. Myself as well as her. Even while it was obvious whatever gratification I obtained wouldn't make me whole, wouldn't make me touch, smell, hear, taste, see, feel, know, experience the miracle. The antidote. The remedy. The cure. But what choice did I have? I needed a girl so bad.

How could I prevent myself from calling?

How could I not try to get as much as I could?

Even when all I wanted was for Katrina to be Melissa.

I wondered why Mrs. Belknap had brought the subject up in the first place. Had Napster told her Melissa and I had split? I didn't think Napster would. It'd just give his mother another argument for waiting. Maybe my mother had told Mrs. Belknap. They talked. How embarrassing would that be? Not that I would ever accuse my mother of it. I would never mention the subject.

At least Mrs. Belknap had made me think Melissa's leaving was less my fault; that it was due to some crazed part of Melissa's teen, female brain, and if she ever grew out of it, maybe she'd come back. Only after being pawed over by Yuri, would I want her back?

I told myself again, don't think about Yuri, don't think about Melissa, and don't ever think about Melissa and Yuri—except I couldn't get them out of my mind.

The way Mrs. Belknap went on and on about love made me wonder if she'd once had her heart broken. I suppose it's true. Doesn't everyone? Aren't hearts made to be broken? Isn't that part of love's game? Yet it was difficult to imagine. I mean, Mrs. Belknap is Napster's mom. She had just cooked this delicious pancake breakfast on her six burner, Thermador, stainless steel stove. How strange. How bizarre. How weird if chaos and despair once raged inside her, and weirder—still did. Yet that drink was always in her hand.

I remembered some of the photos I'd seen of the Belknaps. The separate pictures of Mr. and Mrs. Belknap in high school and college. They always seemed so self-contained. So in control. So cool. Always with friends. Always smiling. Always in perfect, happy, faultless worlds. My parents have the same perfect, happy, faultless pictures. Straight up. In the moment. Satisfied. Content. Centered. Never the instant before or after. Never the second between the seconds. Never the point above, below, or beside. Never the lost look. Never the averted eyes. Never the fearful soul. Could anyone's life actually be like that? Could anyone's parents?

Or was it all fake and make-believe? All pretense and show? All fog and illusion? Like my cross-country picture. Was the most real part not in the photos? Were we all posers like Cyndi, only with different masks? Me. Melissa. Katie. Darlene. Napster. Salome. Giddy. Certainly Crusty. Even Chip McCool. I mean, how crazy is it to be cool? In its own way, it has to be as strange and surreal as being Dory. Chip was just kinder to sophomores and flies.

Was the truest part left over like a dead man's closet full of clothes? Unseen. Hidden. Outside the edges. Beyond the screen.

Except for a few brief moments, Melissa and I had walked together in the sky. For a few brief seconds, we had flown.

That was true. That was real.

And maybe taking an accurate, honest account of myself, I'd fly again. As depressed as I was, I knew I wasn't hopeless. My heart still beat. I could mend. I was only fifteen. I had too much strength left. Too much spirit left. Too much love left. Too much *me* left.

More than one past exists. More than one future. I could get up. I could once more sprout wings.

When you read a book, every once in a while you glance at how many pages are left to see what the chances are of certain expected or unexpected events to occur. Will Melissa and I get back together? Will Napster, Darlene, and Katie keep on? Will I get into Harvard? Will Melissa become a ballerina? Will I go to LA and write movies?

I don't know.

The only thing I know is that none of it is as it should be, none of it is as it is taught, none of it is as it's drawn, none of it is as it's written on the blackboard. It's all four lanes with no signs, no lights, no tollbooths, no speed limits, no stops, no guard rails and no directions. And if I ever get to wherever it is, —will I be better or worse? Will I hurt her, or she hurt me?

OK.

I still have Harvard and Hollywood and all my other grand intentions and inventions that seem so firm and solid until they melt and vanish like wishes in the air.

In two-and-a-half years, I'll be out of high school.

In five years, I'll be twenty.

Imagine all the words and sounds and scenes.

Imagine all the maybes and the seems.

True, they look a long way away. True, getting over Melissa is going to be harder and take longer than I thought.

But I have time.

Life is time.

Ever since I started writing, I wondered when I would know the purpose. The design. The goal. The aim. The dream.

When the story was done. Over. Finished. Closed. Concluded. Wrapped. Ceased.

The end.
The beginning.

Now I know.

## ABOUT THE AUTHOR

David Ira Rottenberg is a graduate of Columbia University. He has published two novels and co-authored three business books. He has written for publications such as Boston Magazine and the Boston Globe. His poems have appeared in poetry magazines throughout the United States and he has written a collection of poems about the ballet, *Soldiers of Beauty*. *Gwendolyn, the Graceful Pig* is his popular children's book; *Gwendolyn Goes Hollywood* is his equally popular sequel. A third children's book, *Margarita's Star*, has recently been published.